# A CHANGE OF TIDE

# A Change of Tide

## D. C. Contor

The Legend of the Salt of the Earth
BOOK ONE

For information contact:
D.C. Contor: dccontor@gmail.com

Cover design by D. C. Contor
Formatting by D. C. Contor
ISBN: 979-8-9899051-2-6
First Edition: May 2024
10 9 8 7 6 5 4 3 2

*For my husband,*
*who was there when this series was*
*no more than scribbled notes on a*
*scratch piece of paper,*
*who was there through the late*
*night plot sessions,*
*who cheered me on when I decided*
*to publish myself,*
*and who has always been there*
*every step of the way.*

*I couldn't have done this without*
*you. I heart Y circle horse-shoe.*

*And for my four little monkeys.*
*You're everything mysterious and*
*magickal in my story.*

*Piping down the valleys wild*
*Piping songs of pleasant glee*
*On a cloud I saw a child.*
*And he laughing said to me.*

*Pipe a song about a Lamb;*
*So I piped with merry chear,*
*Piper pipe that song again—*
*So I piped, he wept to hear.*

*Drop thy pipe thy happy pipe*
*Sing thy songs of happy chear,*
*So I sung the same again*
*While he wept with joy to hear*

*Piper sit thee down and write*
*In a book that all may read—*
*So he vanish'd from my sight.*
*And I pluck'd a hollow reed.*

*And I made a rural pen,*
*And I stain'd the water clear,*
*And I wrote my happy songs*
*Every child may joy to hear*

—William Blake's "Introduction"
from *Songs of Innocence*

# Prologue

Time transforms all truth into stories and stories into legend. My time is no exception. I have recounted this tale many times, but I have never written it. And now, time chews away at my memories. So as the millennial anniversary of our story approaches, I thought it only fitting to record it now. I've spent the last few hundred years tracking down and compiling journal entries, scraps of notes, and as many of the letters as I could find. The words we pen to each other often tell our stories better than we can, but I'm getting ahead of myself.

These stories I record now are known as the Legend of the Salt of the Earth. Though in my time, we simply called them life. The beginning seems the most natural place to start, but as you'll see, there are so very many beginnings. We could start with the Sylphids and the origin of Magick, but that feels a bit too far back. We could start with the birth of each of our girls, but even that feels too far. Perhaps, yes, the best place to start is with the vision that wasn't a vision.

Our story really starts with three girls and a prophecy, except our psychic-medium didn't know was a prophecy when she had it. She just thought it was a normal, albeit terrifying, vision. Before we go too much further, I would like to introduce you to each of the girls.

Meet Neldyn "Nelly" Hansen:

Dec. 2, 08

I'm so freaking sick of Whitney. All she does is talk trash about me, but when push comes to shove, she surfs like a noob. Not that she'll ever admit it. It's all just stupid excuses—'The wave was too fast,' 'The sun was in my eyes,' 'A seal bumped my board,' Waah, Waah, Waaaaah. I wish she'd actually get better and pose real competition or just shut up. Preferably both.

Wyatt and I spent like 8 hours out today. I got a mean tube. He got barbecued. I told him to put sunblock on, but he was too macho for that. Now he's a lobster.

Dad keeps harping on me about my grades because 'It's senior year and it's time to think about college.' I don't need college. I don't even need high school. It's all ridiculous. After this next comp, I'm going to get a legit big time sponsor and go fully pro. Career made. I mean, freaking Rip Curl called and said they want ME! This next comp seals the deal, and I definitely won't be using chemistry or algebra when I win.

Of course, Dad says that if nothing else, I should graduate so I have a backup plan in case I can't surf anymore. Yeah, like that will happen.


I know she comes across rather abrasively. She was always a bit like the ocean: intimidating if you don't quite know how to read her. You see, life gave Nelly a lesson young. She misunderstood strong for unfeeling, so she's been shoving every feeling down ever since. But she does feel, though she rarely admits it, even to herself.

Next up, I'd like you to meet Nikki Rodrigues:


December 2, 2008

Only three more days, and I'll be an official, legal adult! I seriously can't wait to graduate and move far, FAR away. Mom hassled me again today about making friends. This is the fourth new station in the last two years (we're in civilian housing this time). Dad is deployed to a war-torn country, Kam is waaay over-stressing the trombone and will probably end up with an ulcer by the time he turns 11, but sure, Mom, let's worry about me making friends that will last for a whole six months before I leave for college anyway.

She DOES NOT get it. It's not that I don't want friends. It's just if I'm going to bother going through all the trouble to make some, I might as well wait until college. I'll be there for four years. In a row. 1-2-3-4. All in the same place. Of course, I could be there now since I have more than enough credits to graduate, but Mom can't fathom me missing my senior year. It's supposed to be the peak of my whole life.

That better not be true. How completely lame would that be?

Anyway, I'm debating playing hooky on my birthday and finishing the last of my college applications. I'm looking at universities on the east coast. It's not that I don't like California (Dad is probably going to be stationed here at least another year). It's just if I stay here, Mom will definitely try to control the rest of my life.

Though Nikki's upbringing gave her a dandelion lifestyle—floating from place to place and never relying on her roots—her soul has always been a shepherd's tree, digging deep to pull strength from the earth and reaching up to find warmth from the sun. Her journey pruned her painfully, though purposefully, but I'm jumping ahead of myself again.

Let's meet our final in this trio of wonderful girls, Emma Hugos, our seer of visions and prophecies:

2 December 2008

I keep meditating like Grandma instructed, but the vision won't come on demand. They never have before, so I'm not sure why Grandma suddenly expects them to now. Maybe she thinks that I've had this vision the longest, so my connection with it should be the strongest? Maybe my subconscious just doesn't want to go through that again. My conscious sure doesn't. A girl can only be expected to experience her own death so many times.

Our dear Emma, so young yet so full of responsibility. She's stronger than anyone thinks is even possible—including herself. She is like the glass on an aquarium, willingly transparent but under such pressure only few understand. She, too, is mid-senior year when our story starts, which will be soon, I promise.

There are many more wonderful people for you to meet (like Kam, Nikki's younger boy-genius brother; Tom, Nelly's chill widower dad; and Ethel, Emma's mysterious grandmother), but we'll get there when we get there. For now, I have one final item of business. You see, I felt this story was important to record before time completely erases it from my memory. I knew all these people quite intimately once upon a time.

Time. What an odd friend.

To my final item, the thing you absolutely must remember is this: not everything will be revealed at once. I warn you of the turns, the twists, the hidden figures, the unanswered questions, and I offer you my assurance. If you are patient and studious, all will be revealed. I will not leave you, though the path grows dark.

I will be with you every step of the way.

# Chapter One

## Wednesday, December 5th



Dec. 5, 08

The Christmas Eve Invitational is in 18 days. I'm feeling pretty good about it, but I don't want to jinx myself. I just keep going over it in my head: Rip Curl called. They want me. Me! They're coming all the way to dinky little Otter Sands, CA specifically to watch the invitational, specifically to watch me. Wyatt says it's a crazy big deal.

He's not wrong. I mean, this could be it. It's so close I can almost taste it.

Nelly checked her white water-proof Roxy watch. It was not quite 5 AM.

"Jo!" Nelly yelled from her room. "Get your butt moving! No one cares what bikini you've got on!" There was no reason to worry about waking up Tom, Jo and Nelly's dad. A weekday morning meant a morning run for him, so he was already gone.

"Five minutes!" came the yell from down the hall.

"Fine, but I'm leaving in five with or without you!" Nelly yelled back as she closed her journal. She grabbed her duffle, walked through the house, and out the front door, not stopping until she reached her 1999 red Toyota Tacoma. She threw her bag in the truck and checked their boards again. Both surf boards were laying flat in the truck's bed: Nelly's favorite board—a green and blue 5'6" Takayama Humu Fish—was nestled safely between towels. Resting atop the fish was Jo's preferred board, a hot pink and neon yellow 6' Scorpion (also by Takayama) with an old towel over the nose to protect it from bumping the tailgate.

We'll leave Nelly flipping through radio stations and yelling some more at Jo (who was struggling to choose between her pink top with yellow bottoms or her yellow top with pink bottoms), and I'll tell you more about our girl. Nelly was a force. She had navy blue eyes, which narrowed anytime she accepted a challenge. She was short, only an inch over five feet but powerfully built. Her years of carving waves translated into one muscle-packed little body. She had never dyed her hair, though people often thought she did because her roots were quite dark even though the rest of her hair was more caramel blonde; this was an effect of Nelly's spending more time in the ocean than out. Surfing was life. Sure, she did other things, like going out with cute guys, many cute guys, but she dumped most of them because they got whiny about the amount of time she spent at the beach. Wyatt Fletcher was really the only guy who was consistently in her life, but as they'd known each other since they were in diapers, he never registered as a guy to her; he was her best friend, and as such, he would never ask her to give up surfing. He knew her blood was salt water, and her heart beat with the tide. There was no separating that girl from the ocean.

Jo finally picked—yellow with pink bottoms.

The sisters argued all the way to the beach. It was the same argument they had a million mornings before:

"If you'd just pick out the suit the night before," Nelly said as she drove down the hill through the misty morning.

"I know, I know," Jo said, crossing her arms. "Sunrise isn't for another two hours. It's called *dawn* patrol, Nels. You know, dawn, as in 'when the sun comes up.'"

Nelly rolled her eyes, holding the wheel with her knee as she put her shoulder-length hair up in a tight ponytail. "You know you don't have to come."

"Like I'm catching the bus to school," Jo scoffed.

"Whatever," Nelly said. "Just please, can you be on time tomorrow?" She clicked on her blinker.

"I will," Jo said.

"I don't care about being a little late to school, but you know how Dad gets, so if we don't leave on time and we can't be late to school, every minute we lose is—"

"A lost minute surfing. I know. I know!" Jo said, batting away Nelly's familiar complaint. "Oh, look!" Jo pointed to a car as Nelly pulled into the dirt lot next to the beach and parked. "Grace and her dad are here!" Jo opened her door.

"Cool," Nelly said absently as she rummaged through the back of the truck. "Jo, you put my wetsuit back in here, didn't you?"

Jo stood on the doorframe, using the height of the truck to scan the ocean for her best friend; the wind snatched Nelly's question before Jo heard it. She hopped down and began getting dressed for the freezing water.

"Jo," Nelly said louder, elongating the vowel.

"What?"

"You borrowed my suit yesterday and said you'd put it back. Where is it?"

Jo gasped as she wiggled into her own wetsuit. "I forgot! I washed it for you, though. It's hanging in Dad's shower." Jo squinted and apologized. "Do you want mine?" She gestured to the suit, already pulled halfway up to her middle.

"No," Nelly grunted. She grabbed a white long sleeve rash guard, murmuring to herself about how unfair it was that Jo fit all her things, but she somehow didn't fit any of Jo's.

The girls locked up, grabbed their boards, and ran down the cold sand into the even colder water. Jo took off towards her best friend, Grace, while Nelly paddled to the lineup, scanning to see if Wyatt was there yet. There were only two surfers in the lineup, both hunched on longboards as they waited for waves: the first was Frank, the owner a local surf shop on Main, and the other was Lenny, an old and retired PE teacher who loved to tell anyone who would listen about how he'd surfed with the Duke once on a trip to Hawai'i.

No Wyatt.

Nelly sat up briefly on her board, to spin around and face the shore, before laying down again. As a shortboarder, most of her body was already in the water, and being in the water was slightly warmer than being in the wind. Her thin rash guard offered little protection against the cold.

The swell came in. Three perfect waves. Nelly waited for Frank and Lenny to line up and take their waves. Finally, the third wave was hers. She paddled for it, the rush warming her body. She caught it easily and popped up. Carving her way up the wave, Nelly snapped back sending a spray of water above her. She floated over the whitewater, pumping to catch more speed. Nelly dug deep into a front-side bottom turn and kissed the lip of the wave before flying off the board and cannonballing into the water. A short ride, but a fun one.

Nelly popped up and whooped.

"Nice one!" Jo called from several yards away.

Nelly pumped her arm and hopped back on her board. She duck dived under the incoming wave before paddling back out to the lineup.

She caught perfect wave after perfect wave after perfect wave for hours. It was unlike anything she had ever experienced. Now, the sun was up and shining brightly. As she sat in the lineup waiting for her next wave, her watch beeped, warning her that it was already 7:45. She had time for one more wave, and then she and Jo needed to get back to the truck and get to school. Sighing, Nelly pushed the button on her watch to stop it beeping and scanned the horizon for Jo. The next set was coming in. Lenny caught the first wave in the set. Nelly stretched up to peek at the incoming waves, holding on her rails for balance. As she moved her arms down, her right elbow hit her leg and scratched something.

"Ow," Nelly said, grabbing her elbow. The fabric around her elbow was shredded. She looked down at her leg. At first, she thought she'd caught some debris, a bit of a branch or something like that, but when she looked at her leg, she saw it: the patch on her skin that was shiny and iridescent black. Nelly touched the patch. It was rough, like shark's skin, like fish scales.

Pulling her hand back quickly, Nelly said, "What the—"

An unseen wave pummeled her from behind, sending her through the washing machine. Instincts kicked in, and Nelly covered her head and neck with her arms, curling her body up into a ball to wait out the wave before popping up again. As she came up, she saw Jo, only feet from her and ready to paddle back out.

"We have to go," Nelly said, pale and eyes wide.

"Is everything okay?" Jo asked when she saw Nelly.

"Come on." Nelly hopped back on her board and paddled back to shore as fast as she could. Her brain was already pushing back at the panic, shoving it down and explaining it away. As soon as she was on the sand again, she looked at her leg. The scaly patch was gone. "I'm fine, I'm fine, I'm fine," Nelly murmured to herself as she fiddled with her leash. She had no idea her life was about to change in a way she couldn't have begun to imagine.

"Hey!" Jo hopped off her board, popping it under her arm before running over to Nelly. "Are you okay? You look super green."

"What?" Nelly touched her face and glanced at her hand, as though expecting her skin to have turned key lime green.

"Green—like you're going to puke," Jo said, exasperated.

"Oh, right." Nelly shook her head, ignoring the knot forming in her stomach. "No, I'm fine. Let's go or we'll be late, and Dad'll have a fit." Nelly popped her board under her arm and ran back to the truck.

We're going to leave Nelly to head to school. We'll meet back up with her later. For now, you need to see what Nikki is up to.





Groaning, Nikki closed her journal and turned up the radio, losing herself in the lyrics to "Rhiannon." She leaned back in her seat and closed her eyes. This was probably her favorite Stevie Nicks' song, though "Landslide" was a close second. Before we get too much further into this story, you need to know a few things about Nikki Margret Rodrigues. The first thing you should know is she would be mortified I told you her middle name.

The second thing you should probably know is she doesn't look in the mirror very often. If she had, she would have noticed her green eyes looked remarkably different: a golden ring had shown up around her pupil the moment she turned 18. Instead, Nikki had brushed her teeth, quickly French braided her mouse-brown hair (a color she hated), and run out the door like she did every morning. As for the rest of her appearance, Nikki was tall, around 5-foot-8, and despite her mother's olive complexion, Nikki was quite pale and much to her chagrin, unable to tan. She discovered this when they first moved to California a few months ago. She had spent much of her first month covered in aloe vera. There is one last thing you need to know about Nikki before we move on: she had a one sibling, a brother, Kam (short for Kameron), who was also her best friend, despite his being a solid seven years younger. A life of bouncing from assignment to assignment had left the two very close. This particular morning, he had before-school band practice, and she had dropped him off at the middle school, which was just across the street from Otter Sands High School.

This brings us back to Nikki, who was still sulking in her parked car at the high school. She stared absently at the white-washed cinder block outer walls of OSHS as Stevie Nicks sang about Rhiannon having more magic than love. Nikki pulled her hair out of its usual braid, a nervous irritable energy running under her skin. She bounced her leg as Stevie held out Rhiannon's name just before the DJ started talking.

"Good morning, Otter Sands! DJ Mark here for another sunny California morning," said the deep voice over the radio. "Some sad news has the police asking for help. Around four this morning, a local woman was put into a coma after a devastating hit and run on Third and Main. If you know anything about this, please call OSPD immediately."

A pit the size of a golf ball formed in Nikki's stomach. She groaned again, this time feeling guilty for complaining over something as simple has having to attend school on her birthday when somewhere else, someone was fighting for her life. She sighed and shoved her journal and keys into her backpack. The hem of her light green summer dress danced around her knees as Nikki dragged herself up to the stairs which led to glass double doors marked "DOORS REMAIN LOCKED DURING SCHOOL HOURS." Her hair, now free of its braid, blew wildly in her face; this small act of defiance felt powerful, as though despite showing up at school according to her mother's wishes and despite the middle name in her mother's image, Nikki Margret Rodrigues was still her own person—a person who was late to French, again.

As Nikki walked through the hall, empty save for a few fellow stragglers, she saw Madame Fleur, her French teacher, had left the second door, the one nearer to the back of the classroom, cracked open. Nikki carefully opened the door just enough for her to slip through.

In her usual white blouse and black A-lined skirt, Madame was writing the day's assignment on the whiteboard with her customary green marker—she believed in inserting as much color as she could into the world, evidenced by her magenta shawl and matching beaded heels.

Tip-toeing, Nikki made her way to an open desk at the back of the classroom. She had almost made it when—

"Mademoiselle Rodrigues," Madame Fleur said, still facing the board.

Nikki stopped mid-stride as Madame turned to look at her. "Oui, Madame?" Nikki said, warmth rising to her cheeks.

The entire class turned to look at Nikki. She stood up straight, so she looked less like a Bigfoot sighting.

"Bienvenue en classe. Assieds-toi, s'il te plaît." Madame Fleur raised her eyebrows in a look of clear disapproval. Though, there seemed to be the ghost of a smirk on her perfectly lined lips, also magenta.

"Oui, Madame. Merci," Nikki said, following her teacher's instructions and sliding into her seat. Being late to class was an automatic detention in Madame Fleur's class—the few times Nikki had served detention were a direct result of being late to French. Nikki had no way of knowing that Madame's sudden show of mercy was simply because, as a teacher, Madame knew today was her birthday.

As it was, Nikki settled into her desk and pulled out her books. She flipped through her notebook and found an empty page. She dated it and then opened up her French book, turning to page 156 as her stomach grumbled. In her rush to get out the door this morning, she had completely forgotten breakfast. As she flipped pages, her mind wandered to the little donut shop her maternal grandparents had taken her to in New Orleans.

When the Rodrigues family had moved from Arkansas to California this past summer, they had met up with Grandma and Grandpa, who were road-tripping to all their favorite cities. New Orleans held many favorite eats, but Grandpa's favorite was a donut shop that made donuts as big as plate. Nikki had been overwhelmed with the many options, so she had chosen a classic: chocolate with rainbow sprinkles. It was easily the most delicious donut she had ever had.

Alas, her French class had no such shop, so she picked up her pen and glanced up at the board to see what Madame had written so she could copy it in her notebook. Except, when Nikki looked back down to her notebook, there was a large donut sticking to the page: chocolate with rainbow sprinkles. Her heart caught in her chest. Her brain raced, trying to make sense of the donut's sudden appearance. Goosebumps enveloped her as her panic rose like bile.

Somewhere in the back of her brain, her military kid training kicked in—a whole life filled with packing go-bags and family-run fire and emergency drills meant she was good in an emergency, usually.

Nikki could almost hear her dad's voice telling her to close her eyes, take a deep breath, and then, clear-headed, make a choice. She did as her dad's voice instructed. When she opened her eyes, the donut was still resting on her notebook, so as carefully and slowly as she could, she moved the notebook under her desk and set it on her lap. For the rest of her French class, she picked away at the donut with her left hand (no point in wasting a perfectly good breakfast) and scribbled her French notes on a scratch piece of paper.

By the time class was over, despite her efforts, Nikki's pointer finger and thumb were sticky and discolored from the creamy chocolate frosting. She packed away her things and darted into the bathroom to wash her hands. She found herself alone, which would turn out to be quite the blessing, for as she dried her hands, Nikki looked up in the mirror. A single thought floated across her mind: 'I wonder what my hair would look like black.'

That's it.

One thought.

Then, a blink later, it was.

Her hair was black as thunder.

A piercing scream filled the bathroom, and it took Nikki a moment to realize it was coming from her. Slapping her hands over her mouth, she backed up into one of the bathroom stalls, locking it immediately. Nikki swallowed, trying to force the frenzy building in her chest to quiet. She braced herself on the stall door and closed her eyes.

"Feel your feet, feel your feet," she whispered as she focused on the feeling of her feet in her shoes. She had worn her favorite red converse. Nikki pushed her toes down, trying to feel each individual pad pressing down, trying to feel the texture of her sock being compressed between her foot and shoe. Rand, her dad, had taught her the simple trick when she was about 10; he had told her it was what he did anytime he felt overwhelmed.

Several deep breaths later, Nikki opened her eyes. The rush in her chest had subsided, though her mind still raced.

"I can do this," she whispered. Wiggling her toes one last time, she blew out a breath, and opened her eyes and the stall door. She peeked through the door to ensure she was alone before she opened it fully and walked over to the mirror. With her new darker hair, Nikki's green eyes shined; they no longer faded into her face. She finally noticed the golden ring around her pupils. She touched her cheek. "What happened?"

Somewhere in her brain, floated in the thought, 'Well, at least it isn't bubblegum pink. Mom would freak if…' but before the thought finished, Nikki's hair had (you guessed it) turned bright pink. Nikki white-knuckled the sink and inhaled sharply. 'Black as night, black as night, black as night!' her brain screamed.

She blinked.

Her hair was raven black once again.

"Okay," Nikki said. "Home, now." She grabbed her bag and charged to the exit, dodging through the masses of students all headed to their next classes.

We're going to leave Nikki heading home (don't worry, she gets home safely), and jump back to Nelly. I promise we'll see Emma soon, but Nelly is about to get some life changing information.

(Later)

This morning, Jo and I hit the surf like we do everyday before school. The ocean must know it's my birthday or something because it was perfect waves all morning.

But before I could catch my last wave, something weird happened. Something I don't even, I mean, if I hadn't seen it, if I hadn't FELT IT, I wouldn't even believe it.

I found a patch of scales on my skin, but not like they came from a fish and were just on my leg, but like GROWING on my leg. Like instead of skin: SCALES!

I ate a wave, and by the time I made it to shore, no scales. Jo could see I was freaked out but I didn't tell her. I mean, I thought about it, but I know her. She'd say I'm crazy. I'm not crazy.

I am not crazy.

Am I?

Wishing she had grabbed a sweatshirt, Nelly wiggled in her white t-shirt, now wet from her still damp bright blue bikini top. Goosebumps raced over Nelly's arms and up her back; she blamed the air-conditioned chemistry classroom. Mrs. Hammond stood at the front of the class in her usual fish-printed mumu (today's was purple) and drew molecules on the board. Nelly's mind was not on chemistry; rather, it was racing with the morning's events. This was the third time she'd been invited to compete in the Christmas Eve invitational. She'd missed the first year because they'd been in North Idaho for a funeral. Last year, she had to decline again because she'd had an impossibly bad stomach flu, and her dad, Tom, forced her to stay home—something about how blowing chunks while surfing was basically chumming. Nelly thought it was a load of crap, but her dad's number one rule was safety first. The invitational wasn't, on its own, a big time event, but as its name suggested, it was invitation-only. If she turned them down for a third year in a row, there was no guarantee they'd invite her back.

Nelly absently flipped through the pages of her open chemistry book. She couldn't risk declining the invitation again, especially not with Rip Curl coming. The thought of Rip Curl made her stomach flip and not in the happy-excited way it used to. Nelly gritted her teeth and took a long slow breath through her nose. The fact was she couldn't compete under such high scrutiny and risk having scales show up all over her legs. No brand would want a girl with a weird fishy skin condition showing off their high-brand bikinis and rash guards, least of all Rip Curl.

Rubbing her face with her hands, Nelly's fingers brushed the scar that ran parallel to her eyebrow almost down to the outer corner of her eye. She acquired the scar wiping out on surf that was way too big for her; she had paddled back out after her board had clocked her in the face and caught her first ever tube with blood streaming down her face. She had smiled the entire time the doctor stitched her up.

Nelly was pulled from her thoughts by her lab partner elbowing her in the side. Nelly gaped at the girl and mouthed "What?"

"Di-hydrogen monoxide," the girl whispered.

"What?" Nelly whispered back.

The girl widened her eyes and nodded toward the front of the class. Nelly turned and saw Mrs. Hammond heading towards her, holding a giant model of molecules.

"Miss Hansen," Mrs. Hammond said, her eyes narrowing. "What molecule am I holding?"

Nelly's mouth hung open, her brain blank; at least it was, until her lab partner elbowed her again. "Di-hydrogen monoxide," Nelly spouted.

"And its more common name, Miss Hansen?"

Brain racing, Nelly flipped through her book, but before she found the page, her brain caught up. "Water," she said, looking up at her teacher.

Mrs. Hammond's stern look softened. "Very good. Pay attention, please." She went back up to her mass of molecules, rearranging them in preparation for the next unsuspecting student.

"Thanks," Nelly whispered to her lab partner.

"No problem," the girl said, glancing up; her bright blue eyes stared at Nelly through purple, sparkly horn-rimmed glasses for a moment before returning to her doodle. "I'm Emma by the way." (I told you we'd see her soon.)

"Oh, right," Nelly said. "I'm Nel—"

"Neldyn, but you go by Nelly. I know. We've been in every science class together since seventh grade," Emma said, not looking up from her paper; she had drawn an intricate bunch of rue flowers and was now tracing each with her yellow highlighter.

"Right," Nelly said again. Her stomach flopped unpleasantly.

Emma wore a mustard yellow blouse, flowing and tied at the neck with a white ribbon. Most of her hair was down though several small braids peeked through the loose strands: some braids had beads on them, others were braided with yarn. The burgundy, emerald, and plum stood in stark contrast to Emma's blonde beachy waves. Hanging from her neck was a simple chain carrying a silver wedding band, and a large, almost clear, stone. The wedding band had belonged to the her late mother, but of course, Nelly would not learn this until much later.

"I'm not great with names," Nelly said.

"It's okay, but you ought to pay attention before Mrs. Hammond gives you detention," Emma whispered, still focused on her drawing.

"But—"

"Miss Hansen, I already warned you once." Mrs. Hammond walked up to Nelly's side of the worktable and put down a pink slip.

"Sorry, Mrs. Hammond," Nelly mumbled. The bell rang, signaling the end of the class, though unfortunately for Nelly, not the end of the day.

I did promise we'd return to Nikki, and so we will.


December 5, 2008 (later)

Today started like any other day. I was late to French class (again), and I was starving. I was thinking about donuts, and all of the sudden I had one. The fact that's not even the weirdest thing that happened is a testament to HOW weird things got.

My hair changed color—and not like a little but drastically,... THREE TIMES! All on its own! I 100% skipped the rest of school today. NO WAY I was staying at school and risking it changing a fourth time IN FRONT of someone else!

So I got home and decided to take a shower, trying to relax. Except a freaking octopus attacked me in the shower. AN OCTOPUS!! I wasn't even thinking about an octopus! I mean, the pony I was thinking about—not in the shower but later. The poor little guy.

He seemed as startled as I was, and I will admit to thinking about the lion, but only for like for one second! He was as confused as the pony, until he realized he could eat me. He wasn't so confused after that. I managed to think about him going home before he could get me—obviously. I'm not writing from the "beyond."

I just don't understand what's going on. Where did this come from? I didn't pull any sword from a stone. I didn't get an owl or magic dragon ring. No long lost family member showed up to tell me to fulfill my destiny.

WHAT IS HAPPENING?!

I just wish my mom was home so I could

Like a mudslide, nausea washed over Nikki. She groaned and ran to the bathroom, managing to open the toilet lid just in time. She flushed and rinsed her mouth out once she had finished. Sweating, she splashed her face with some cool water and looked at herself in the mirror.

"Mom is going to freak," she said to her reflection. Given the day she'd had, Nikki half expected it to respond. It didn't.

Nikki went back to her room and crawled under her covers, closing her eyes and breathing deeply. The honest truth was—despite the panic attacks, the almost lion attack, and the just sudden-out-of-the-blue-ness of the whole situation—this was actually Nikki's dream.

I suppose there is one last thing I should have mentioned about Nikki: she was an avid reader, and her favorite genre was fantasy, specifically stories where seemingly normal, average people suddenly found themselves gifted with mysterious powers. She had devoured the Harry Potter Series. A deep longing followed her as she finished each book. The Gemma Doyle Trilogy had left her hollow and aching for her missing piece. So now, as she curled under her sheets, the realization of magick soaked into her like rain into the Kalahari, filling her broken spaces with possibility.

Several hours later, Nikki's panic had passed into delicate excitement. More than anything, she was curious as to the origins of her apparent powers. Nikki was pacing in the kitchen when the front door opened.

"Mom!" Nikki squeaked, running to the hallway and almost bumping into her mom.

"Happy birthday, dear!" Margret's muffled voice came from behind brown paper grocery sacks. "Go get the other bags from the car, please." She made her way into the kitchen and set the bags on the island.

"Mom, we need to talk." Nikki followed close behind her.

With a manicured hand, Margret pushed her sunglasses atop her golden-blonde bob, her darker roots barely showing. "In a minute," she said, rifling through the bags. "Look what I found!" She pulled out Styrofoam wrapped in plastic and flipped it around to show Nikki a whole fish. "I thought we could have fish tacos for dinner." Looking at Nikki for the first time since she got home, Margret held the fish with her palms while she did spirit fingers.

"Uh," Nikki said. All thoughts of magic were pushed from her mind by the watery eye of the fish labeled "golden pompano" staring at her below the sticker stating he was $3.65 per pound.

"Your hair!" Margret's voice fell as her hands closed over the fish. She sighed. "Couldn't you have at least cut it? A bob would be so cute on you."

Nikki rolled her eyes. "I like my hair long, and," she added, eyeing the fish, "I don't really like fish."

"Right. Well, I'll eat the fish, and you and Kam can have regular tacos. I think I bought beef," Margret said, digging through the bag.

"I have magic powers," Nikki blurted out. Her hands jumped immediately to her mouth.

"Excuse me?" Margret said in the same tone she used that one time she heard Nikki swear.

At that moment, the door opened again, and Kam came in, dragging his trombone case behind him. "What the heck, you guys?!" He pushed his mop of dirty blond hair from his face.

"Did you walk home?" Margret asked, gasping and dropping the fish. She ran to Kam as though he may have been wounded.

"No," Kam said. "Jody's mom gave me a ride, but I still had to lug this thing up the front steps," he added, plopping his massive trombone case down in the hallway.

"Nikki, today was your day to pick up your brother. How could you forget him?" Margret's green eyes flashed. All five feet and three and a half inches of her tensed, ready to pounce.

"I had kind of a lot going on," Nikki said with what she hoped was a meaningful look.

"That is no excuse!" Margret snapped. "Is this some lame attempt to prove you can do what you want now that you're eighteen?"

"I—what?" Nikki scoffed. "No, I forgot today was my day because I had a lot going on." She enunciated the last four words.

"I can't believe you forgot your brother," Margret said, tousling Kam's hair, hugging him to her, and glaring at Nikki.

"Mom," Kam said, gesticulating. "It's not like she said, 'Gee, who's Kam?' when you asked. Besides, you've forgotten to pick me up loads—" Kam glanced up, caught the look in his mother's eyes, wiggled his way out of her grasp, and said quickly, "Well, I better get to practicing. I've got that tricky solo." He pushed his trombone to his room as fast as he could, screeching down the hall before he shut his door.

Margret huffed and began unpacking the grocery bags she had brought in with unnecessary roughness. "Bring in the rest of the groceries."

Nikki searched Margret's face for any softness. "But, Mom—"

"Now," Margret said, finality dripping from the single word. She turned her back on Nikki.

Eyes glistening, Nikki clenched her jaw as her lip quivered. Margret stood stiff and still in front of her. Nikki found herself being pulled between two basic desires: following her own path which held new and unexplored magic, and following the path set for her by a loving, albeit overbearing, mother. She opened her mouth and clenched her fists; she was going to tell Margret about everything, about what really happened with her hair and about the pony and the lion and the octopus. As Nikki stood there, her frenzied heart beating in her throat, she seemed to collapse in on herself, her shoulders slumped, her head dropped, and her hands hung, deflated at her sides. Wiping her eyes, Nikki shuffled outside to unload her own birthday cake.

(later)
    In detention, again. Dad is going to be pissed. It's my third one this week. In my defense, this one I got for being polite— not that I think Dad is going to buy that.

Nelly let her pen fall from her hand into the gutter of her journal and rested her face on her hand.

Today's detention supervisor was Mr. Tuffin, a squat man with large black glasses that made him look like a bug. He sat at the front of the cafeteria, where detention was always served. Occasionally, he glanced up from his copy of *Frankenstein* just long enough to tell off some kid for talking.

At one of the long tables, Nelly stared into her emerald green backpack, debating whether she should use her hour of detention time to do her English or her chemistry homework. Neither felt particularly tempting.

Wyatt ran up; his usually tanned skin was pink and peeling, his curly brown hair frizzled out from his post-PE shower. "Detention?" he asked.

"Scored it in chem. You, too?" Nelly asked; spending detention with her best friend would at least make it less miserable.

"Not today," Wyatt said. "Actually, I meant to ask you earlier and totally spaced. You up for a night surf?"

"Totally," Nelly answered automatically.

"Good," Wyatt said, his eyes brightening. "Night surfs on your birthday are always the best. You know the ocean respects birthdays."

"Right." Nelly chuckled.

"I gotta run. My mom gave me the car today, so I have to pick the kids up," Wyatt said, referencing his younger siblings. "Point Arena, like 7?" He checked his watch and started walking. "I gotta go."

"That's kind of a drive," Nelly called after him.

Wyatt called back, "Bring a tanker. I'll bring glow sticks." He waved behind him and ran off.

Nelly closed her eyes and took a slow deep breath.

The table rocked—not a lot, but enough that Nelly opened her eyes. A hunky teenage boy with dark locs sat in front of her. He flashed a smile at Nelly.

"Andy," Nelly said, trying to keep her voice steady. To say she was not pleased to see her most recent of ex-boyfriends would be a perfect example of understatement. "What are you doing here?"

"Detention." Andy waggled his brows.

Nelly looked at him. "I mean here." She put her pointer finger on the table. "There's like a million tables to sit at. Go pick one."

"I know, babe, but you're at this one," Andy said.

Nelly felt his foot touch hers under the table. She pulled her feet under her. "Don't," she said, warning in her voice.

"Come on, baby," Andy cooed. "You know I—"

"Stop," Nelly said, putting a hand up. "I am not, and never was your 'baby,' and I don't want to hear more lies. We're done."

"Come on," Andy said, leaning towards her.

Nelly recoiled as he neared. "You're drunk," she said under her breath. She didn't want anything to do with him, but she wasn't a snitch either. "Sober up." Nelly picked up her books and bag and moved to a table closer to Mr. Tuffin.

We're going to leave Nelly to serve her detention and speak to her father about said detention (believe me, if you've ever been at a friends house when your friend was getting in trouble, you know exactly what Nelly is in for). Let's finally see what Emma is up to.

5 December 2008

I saw Nikki for a minute this morning. She was sitting in her car, but I haven't seen her since. Although, if it started, I wouldn't be surprised if she raced home. I've heard it can be quite terrifying. I also saw Nelly today. She's definitely changed. I can sense it in her; it's faint but there.

The project Mr. Miranda is going to give us tomorrow will help them get a better grasp on what's happening, and the faster they accept it, the faster we can start working together. If we can do that, we might live through this.

Emma closed her journal and looked around the high school library; it was small and had three main sections—fiction, non-fiction, and resource materials—each divided into a few slightly more specific genres after that. The white-washed cinder block peeked through the bookcases and various posters encouraging students to read. She sat at a wooden table in the non-fiction section, nestled between autobiographies and histories.

Packing her things, Emma felt a wash of cold flood her body. She leaned forward, bracing herself on the table as her eyesight blurred.

*A boy was walking through the hall; he was tall and ragged with a freckled face—probably a sophomore. His pants were suddenly wet, and the students around him burst into laughter, taunting him. A red-headed girl walked away from him, a crushed and empty water bottle in her hand.*

As the vision subsided, Emma's eyesight returned to normal. She grabbed her things and made her way to the hallway. Almost immediately, she saw him, freckled face and all. Head down, but keeping her eyes on the boy, Emma strode towards him. It didn't take much, just a small bump, and an "Oh, sorry!" The boy barely even registered what had happened. The disgruntled redhead, water bottle still full, frowned and shrugged, before heading back to her gaggle of friends.

Meanwhile, Emma exited the building and sighed as she breathed in the warm humidity of the afternoon air. The perfect weather felt like a birthday present just for her, warming her skin, even if it didn't completely soothe her troubled heart. She was forever plagued by one question: why couldn't people just be kind to each other? Emma knew better than most that life was not guaranteed; time was a fair-weather friend. Of course, dealing with the dead as a psychic-medium provided Emma much more empathy than the average 18-year old.

# Chapter Two

## Thursday, December 6th

Dec. 6, 08

How would Dad deal with this? Get back on the horse. That's what Dad would say.

~~But for the first time in my life, I'm scar~~ I just need to figure out how to get over this. It's just another hurdle. I've gotten over hurdles before. I can do it again. Probably. I probably can. I stayed out again today. I told Jo I pulled something yesterday and I want to make sure it heals before the invitational.

I definitely can't stay out of the water forever, but can I risk getting back in?

Nelly had moved through her day as if in autopilot. Her brain felt coated in an iridescent black fog so thick she hadn't even noticed Wyatt's absence. It was now lunch, and she sat alone in the cafeteria. The tightening knot in her stomach left no room for much of an appetite. Staring at the variety of yellow-orange foods on her plate without really seeing them, Nelly pushed her steamed carrots into her mac and cheese, completely unaware that a group of girls had stopped at her table, until their ringleader cleared her throat.

Half Filipino, half Samoan, Whitney towered over Nelly. It wasn't much of a feat, though, because Whitney was a full foot taller. She flipped her smooth black curls behind her. "Missed you on the lineup, Hansen."

"I'm surprised you showed up at all," Nelly said, not bothering to look up from the slice of canned peach she was pushing into her carrot and noodle pile.

Whitney pursed her lips and then leaned on the table. "Why don't you just give me the sponsors and save yourself the embarrassment of losing?"

Nelly chuckled. "The sponsors wouldn't want you if you were the last surfer alive."

"Then why did Roxy call my dad?" Whitney stood tall, crossing her arms. She smiled at her friends, who seemed genuinely impressed.

"Probably because your dad left a message for them to call him back, and the Roxy reps are polite," Nelly said, shrugging.

Whitney scowled. "We'll see who's laughing at the invitational."

"Everyone knows you only got invited because your dad is on the committee this year," Nelly said, finally looking at Whitney.

Whitney gasped. "Well—"

"Well what?" Nelly asked, dropping her fork on her plate, rolling her eyes, and standing.

Whitney scoffed and said, "Well, at least I know how to keep my boyfriend happy."

Nelly barked out a laugh and sat back down. "Congratulations. Do you want a trophy for that? You're not going to win one any other way." She smirked and added, "Unless you're voted 'Most Irritating.'"

"Whatever, loser," Whitney spat, turning on her heel. Her friends followed close behind.

Nelly picked up her fork, sighed, and dropped it back onto her plate, pushing the whole thing away and laying her head on her arms. Gritting her teeth, she tried to take deep breaths.

Whitney and Nelly had been friends when Whitney first moved to Otter Sands ten years ago. In their sixth grade year, Whitney's dad got a new job making many figures; her ego grew with every extra zero on her dad's paycheck. By high school, Whitney had blacklisted Nelly because of the one thing Daddy could not buy her: surf trophies.

For a while, Whitney was merely annoying but bearable. That was until a competition two years ago in which Whitney placed second while Nelly barely scraped into third. This single second place trophy fed Whitney's wild delusions of talent—did it matter to her that Nelly had competed while dealing with a fever of 103? Of course not.

Between Nelly's deep breaths, Whitney's face kept floating into her mind. If she didn't compete in the invitational, Whitney would become completely impossible. Nelly gave up on trying to calm herself; instead, she headed to her next class, throwing out her uneaten food as she left the cafe.


December 6, 2008

No magic today so far...if you don't count the fact I hit every light right as it went green on the way to school this morning...and I'm not. It is kind of weird that yesterday things were popping in and out of existence all day, and now today, nothing. Although, maybe I should be grateful?

Anyway, Mom is pretending I don't exist at all, which is, of course, super fun for me. Kam noticed this and mentioned it. I told him I must have done something, but I didn't know what, which isn't technically a lie. I mean, I'm pretty sure it's because I said I have magic, but who knows? It's my turn to pick up Kam again. Mom has back to back showings on a house tonight, and the last couple doesn't get off until late. She's usually in a cheerful mood after showing a house, so maybe I'll exist again?


Nikki chewed on her cheek as she traded her journal for her history notebook. Class wouldn't start for another minute or two, so she flipped slowly through the filled pages until she came to an empty one. She doodled the date on the top of the page as she waited.

At the front of the classroom, the history teacher was flipping through papers of his own, sorting them into piles on his desk before stapling each into a packet. Now, Mr. Miranda is really only briefly in this story, but as he's one of my favorite people, I want to tell you a bit about him. For starters, his first name was Stephen, not Steve. He was a rail of man who could go from zero to one hundred in less than six seconds. He taught purely because he loved teaching high school history.

You see, Mr. Miranda had won a jackpot several years ago (several hundreds of thousands which certainly made his teacher pay stretch further), but the only evidence of his increase of wealth was the renewing of his relaxed nature. Mr.

Miranda would have gone on teaching until his dying day; however, the year he turned 60, his daughter, and only child, married a man from Spain and moved there with him. So Mr. and Mrs. Miranda packed up their things, waved so long to the US of A, and lived their remaining years chasing grandchildren and learning as much Spanish (and Spanish history) as they could. He was the sort of man who deserved every bit of good luck that came his way.

Back in 2008, dressed in his usual Kirkland pants and Old Navy button-up, Mr. Miranda finished arranging his packets of paper and stood at the front of the classroom just as the bell rang and Nelly skidded into the room.

"Cutting it close, aren't we, Miss Hansen?" Mr. Miranda said, smirking.

"Sorry, sir," Nelly said.

"Don't bother sitting." He rifled through the packets. "Today," he said to the class. "We will be starting our group projects for winter break. You may now groan collectively."

The class did.

"Beautifully done," Mr. Miranda said as he successfully found what he was looking for. "Now that's out of the way, I'll announce groups."

Nikki grinned. Mr. Miranda was easily her favorite teacher.

"Once you've got your project packets, please move your desks together. Let's start with you, Miss Hansen." Mr. Miranda handed her the papers. "You will be with Nikki Rodrigues and Emma Hugos."

Nikki waved Nelly over as Emma scooted her desk closer.

"Hey," Nelly said, sitting as Mr. Miranda announced the next group (Whitney Johnson, John Davies, and Wyatt Fletcher). "So what are we doing exactly?"

Nikki shrugged at the same time Emma said, "You've still got the packets."

"Oh, right," Nelly said, handing a packet of stapled paper each to Nikki and Emma.

Emma pulled out her purple horn-rimmed glasses and read, "'Family History Winter Project'—"

"Creative title," Nelly murmured.

Emma grinned and continued, "'Due January fourth, two-thousand and nine.'"

"Isn't that like the day we come back to school?" Nelly asked.

"I think so," Nikki said.

Emma looked at the two of them over her glasses, looking remarkably like every single librarian ever.

Nikki mimed zipping her lip while Nelly mouthed 'sorry.'

Clearing her throat, Emma read some more: "'Our families' stories shape us, and understanding their stories can help us make better choices as we write our own. Each group has three people in it, so three family members should be researched and reported on in class via oral presentation. Your project has been broken up into a series of tasks.' Well, this doesn't sound too hard."

"Look," Nikki said, turning a page. There were four pages total. "'Task one: each group member will go home today, find a name within their family to research (preferably someone who has already passed on), and bring the name to class tomorrow. To ensure due diligence, each group member will be researching the family member of another group member and not his/her own.'" Her voice fell as she read the last line.

"Wait," Nelly said. "So I bring a name, but one of you does the research?"

"Seems like it," Nikki said, glancing over the rest of the papers. Under task one were four others, and on the back of that paper were several more paragraphs. The last few pages outlined criteria for the project and included the rubric by which it would be graded.

"This is going to be the most boring project," Nelly complained. "I mean, who wants to research a bunch of old people who spent all day playing canasta with their cats?"

"Can you *play* canasta with cats?" Nikki asked. "Isn't it a card game? Now, I could see shuffleboard…"

Nelly gave Nikki a sideways glance.

Nikki pursed her lips, suppressing a grin.

"I think we probably have more interesting people in our families than canasta players, even if they did manage to teach their cats to play," Emma said as she pulled out her notebook.

"I can look through my dad's files when I get home," Nikki said. "I mean, I don't know what I'll find, but…" She shrugged. The thought of classmates digging through her family history, especially given all the strange things that had happened in the last 24 hours, sat like a lump in her throat. She had no way of knowing Nelly was feeling exactly the same.

The three sat in silence as Mr. Miranda announced the names of the last group members (Andy Wilson, Bud Rogers, and Michelle Nakayama). Mr. Miranda saved the girls from the awkwardness, albeit momentarily, as he called the class's attention.

"I want you all to take the next nine minutes and ask each other the questions I've written up on the board." Mr. Miranda gestured to the board behind him as he continued speaking, "These questions are designed to get you thinking, get those memories churning around! Get to work!"

"Okay," Emma said, leaning slightly forward in her desk to see the board. "Question one says 'does your family have any tall tales or myths?'"

"That's kind of a weird question," Nikki said. She glanced at Nelly. "What?"

Nelly sat, lips pursed, and eyes wide.

"What is it?" Emma asked.

"We actually do," Nelly almost whispered. "I mean, my family does."

"Does what?" Nikki asked.

"Have a myth in our family—I mean, it's not a myth exactly, more like a mystery, I guess." She sighed. "My mom told me the story when I was a kid, but my dad reckons it's not true or that it's been massively exaggerated," Nelly explained.

"Well, now you have to tell us," Nikki said.

"It's probably not even true," Nelly insisted.

"Who cares?" Emma said, scooting closer.

"Fine," Nelly said, crossing her arms. "So my mom told me about this lady—I think it was supposed to be her great-great-grandmother or something. Anyway, so this great-grandma got married in Denmark, but the happy couple wanted to come to the states—new life, new opportunities, all that. So he comes first, gets a job, and then like a year later is able to pay for a ticket for her to come. Apparently, her ship sunk on the way. Everyone else gave the people on the boat up for dead. I think it was winter so the chances of surviving in the water were basically zero," Nelly added. "Well, Great-Grandpa didn't give up. He just kept walking the shoreline near where he lived. Everyone called him crazy, but then—"

"No way." Nikki leaned forward.

"I told you it's probably not true." Nelly smirked. "So one day, he's walking the shoreline like always, and there she is. Cold but alive. No one else survived the shipwreck. Just her." Nelly sat back in her seat. "Like I said, it's impossible. It *can't* be true."

"I don't care if it's impossible. You should pick her," Nikki said.

"Agreed," Emma said.

Nelly shrugged. "What about either of you? Any impossible myths in your families?"

"I have someone in mind," Emma said.

"Who?" Nelly asked.

Right then, Mr. Miranda spoke, "Attention, class! Now I want to go over a few more things about this project before the bell rings, so eyes up here."


6 December 2008

Nelly brought up Jess today in class, not by name, but she knows her story, so that's good. The information I have from Jess will be very enlightening, but I need a reason to give it to Nelly. Otherwise, I might scare her off. Jess told me about a journal that belonged to her daughter. Apparently only one of their kind can open it. I haven't been able find it, but Jess told me it's out there. I'll keep it all to myself until the right time, though. Poor Nelly. The transformation she's undergoing must be terrifying enough; she certainly doesn't need the weird girl from science making it worse.

Nikki on the other hand, well, I'm not sure about her. I can sense her magick in her, and her hair is darker than it was Tuesday, which could be magick but not necessarily.

Emma's chest felt full and fluttery; her body flooded with warmth as her eyesight blurred.

*Nikki sat at a computer and typed 'witch' into her search bar. She deleted it and ran her fingers through her black hair. Nikki straightened up, rolling her shoulders back; she retyped 'witch,' and pressed enter.*

I think it might be okay. Curiosity may have killed the cat, but that cat didn't have the prowess these girls do.

Emma left her journal open and dipped the nib of her quill in a small cup of water, swishing it around until the dark blue ink had dispersed, leaving the nib clean. She had a love for the nearly lost way of writing. Closing her inkwell, Emma turned the events of the last few days over in her mind. She knew for sure now that Nikki and Nelly were the two from her vision; the question was whether she could convince them to help her and get them trained in time—of course, training meant finding mentors, which could be a problem.

"Miss Emma!" called Rachelle, Emma's aunt and legal guardian. "Come see what I've got!"

Getting up, Emma smiled as she went to investigate her aunt's latest hobby; last month had been ceramics, and the month before that, Rachelle had taken up water colors. It seemed the only hobby that hung around was knitting; Rachelle had knitted for longer than Emma could remember, much longer than the two had lived together.

Halfway through the door, Rachelle was bent over pushing her newest hobby (a package wrapped in brown paper) into the house. She threw her pink knitted handbag onto the hallway floor. Her glossy graying hair tumbled out of its messy bun.

Stifling a laugh, Emma found her disheveled aunt with the package half resting on the floor and half resting on her shoes as she quickly reinstated her bun. "Need a hand?"

"Please," Rachelle said, bending down again.

The two were able to heave the package to the kitchen table with a loud thunk.

"Jeez," Emma said, collapsing into a chair. "You need to get lighter hobbies. We're not as young as we once were."

"Oh pish," Rachelle said, waving a hand at Emma.

"Eventually your back is going to give out on us, and then where will we be?"

"On the floor, probably." Rachelle giggled. Her hazel eyes flashed in her olive face. Rachelle was the human embodiment of a spring day: soft, bright, and full of hope. "Okay, so!" she said, clapping her hands together. "Any guesses?"

"Well, it's heavy," Emma said, poking the paper like a cat pokes a downed fly.

Rachelle gently swatted at Emma's hand. "Now, now. You have to guess like those mere mortals you go to school with."

Emma grinned. It was marble. She could feel it—and not just in her back—but she could also feel her aunt's excitement. "Koa?" she guessed.

"Ooo," Rachelle said, eyes bright. "Excellent guess, but no."

"I sense woodworking in our future," Emma mock-murmured.

"Ha. Ha." Rachelle squinted at Emma. "Guess again."

"Concrete."

"Nope." Rachelle put her hands on her hips.

"I give up."

"One more guess."

Emma sighed, staring up at the ceiling like she was trying to figure out her last guess. Finally she said, "Oak."

"Nope!" Rachelle said. She tore off the paper, revealing a white, sparkling slab. "It's marble!"

"For what?" Emma asked.

"Carving, like Michelangelo and Bernini!" Rachelle said, hand on her own shoulder, posing like the David statue.

"Didn't Michelangelo use a lot, like *a lot* a lot, of marble?" Emma asked as she ran her fingers over the cool marble slab.

"Well," Rachelle said, dropping her hand and shrugging, "I figured I ought to start small and work my way up."

Emma nodded. "It looks like the beginnings of a fun adventure."

"I hope you don't mind eating dinner on the island for a bit," Rachelle said.

Emma laughed.

After a dinner of eggplant lasagna, complete with toasted slices of Rachelle's homemade sourdough, Emma walked down the street to the local library. As she stepped from the cool humid California evening into the dry chill of the library, Emma relaxed into the familiar comfort found in stacks of books. She waved to her favorite librarian, a woman who always wore bright reds and oranges, which complimented her deep brown skin.

"Any news, Gabby?" Emma asked.

"The computer lab might be worth a peek," Gabby said, pointing with her elbow as she tied her maroon-colored micro braids behind her. "Oh, wait!" Gabby added, ducking under the circulation desk. She reappeared with a giant, hole-riddled book that smelled heavily of mothballs. She cleared her throat and said, "This came in today, donation from the Woodsworth family."

Emma's eyes widened. "I heard she had passed." She gingerly lifted the book from Gabby's hands. "I assume this one stays in the library."

Gabby nodded.

"Thanks so much," Emma said, smiling. She carried the giant book to the back of the library, making sure to pass the computer lab as she did. Emma recognized Nikki's back through the window of the lab door. Nikki was sitting at a computer closest to the door; Emma stopped to watch her.

Nikki typed "witch" into her internet browser but quickly deleted it. She ran her fingers through her hair, rolled her shoulders, retyped "witch," and pushed the search button. Nikki turned around, looking at the lab door, but Emma was already walking away. Neither girl knew the true magnitude of the storm that was to come, though both sensed the rain.

# Chapter Three

## Friday, December 7th

December 7, 2008

Emailed Dad. I went digging through his files, and I found a photocopy of a drawing. It's a sketch of 5 women standing in front of a barn. The back was labeled "Aisling O'Crean" in Dad's handwriting. I asked Mom about it, but she just got mad at me for going through Dad's stuff. I told her it was for school; she told me to pick someone from her family. She said I didn't need to learn about some black sheep in dad's family. The thing is one lady in the drawing looks a lot like me: same eyes, same chin, she even does her hair in one long braid like I do. I picked her. Of course, since Dad's deployed, he'll take at least a week to respond.

This was not, by any means, the first deployment Nikki had dealt with—Rand, Nikki's dad, had spent a few months here and a few months there on various trainings and missions throughout her entire life; he'd served for a year in Bosnia in '97; only three years ago, he'd gone to Korea for a year. So this year-long deployment was not a new experience for the Rodrigues family, but Nikki knew it felt different; she understood what war meant this time. Of course, she really needn't have worried. By now, Nikki should have at least suspected her dad had more protection than the simple Kevlar and ceramic-plated body armor his fellow soldiers wore, yet she had not made the connection, though I'm sure you have.

"Miss Rodrigues, put it away please," Mr. Miranda said.

"Sorry, sir," Nikki said, shoving her journal in her bag.

"For the last fifteen minutes of class," Mr. Miranda continued, "I want you to get into your groups, and trade names." He picked up a pile of papers and started passing them out as students moved into their groups. "Use these worksheets as a guide while doing your research on each other's families. Come prepared with research on Monday. For today, share whatever you do know about your family name with your group members." Mr. Miranda waved today's book (*The Anatomy of Peace*) in the air, a gesture the class knew meant 'get to work.'

"Well," Nelly said, handing her name to Emma. "You've heard my story."

Emma looked at the name in her hand: Jess Pedersen. "Oh you picked her! Yay!"

"Here," Nikki said, handing her name to Nelly.

"Who is Aisling O'Crean?" Nelly asked, sounding the name out slowly.

"I don't know," Nikki admitted. "I found this," she added, digging through her bag and pulling out the photocopy. "I think this one might be her." Nikki handed the paper to Nelly and pointed to a woman.

"Holy cow," Emma said, peeking over Nelly's shoulder. "You're almost identical."

"She even does her hair the same," Nelly said, glancing at Nikki's braid which hung over her shoulder.

"I know," Nikki said, pushing her braid to her back. "That's kind of why I picked her. I don't really know anything about her." Nikki shrugged. "I mean, other than she was apparently a black sheep in my dad's family. That is according to my mom, so grain of salt and all that."

"Fair enough," Nelly said. "But still, a black sheep is something interesting, right?" She flipped the photocopy over and saw Aisling O'Crean's name scrawled on the back. "Hey, did you see this?"

"What?" Nikki leaned closer.

"Look, under her name." Nelly pointed.

"I missed that," Nikki said, taking the paper from Nelly's hand. In small print, almost obscured by the tail of the 'g' in Aisling's name, was written 4 numbers and two letters: 1692, MA.

"Any idea what that means?" Nelly asked.

"Perhaps the year?" Emma suggested.

Nikki shrugged. "Probably."

"I guess I'll find out since I'm the one doing the research," Nelly said. "At least I've got a starting point."

Emma nodded, saying, "Right, here's mine." She handed a paper to Nikki.

"Madam Ethel Ortega."

"That's my grandmother," Emma said before Nikki could ask.

"When did she die?" Nelly asked.

"Oh, she's alive," Emma said. "She lives here in Otter Sands. I thought she would be fun to use for the project. She used to work for the circus and tell people's fortunes."

"She sounds way cool," Nikki said.

"Would you like to meet her?" Emma asked. "We can go over to her house after school today."

Nikki and Nelly briefly glanced and each other, and then both said, "Sure."

"Oh," Nikki groaned, shoulders falling as she slapped her hand to her face. "My mom has her knitting circle today."

"Oh! Does she go to the one at the Purr-ling Kitten on Main?" Emma asked.

"Uh, I think so," Nikki said.

"My aunt goes to the same one," Emma said brightly.

"What does knitting have to do with meeting Emma's grandma?" Nelly's brow furrowed.

"Well, it means I have to wait for my brother after school, and the middle school gets out like half an hour after us. Do you guys mind waiting?"

"Gotchya," Nelly said. "That's fine. I can wait."

"Me, too. We'll meet you out front," Emma said.


Dec. 7, 08

It's been two days. Still haven't surfed. My whole body feels tight.

Surfing has ALWAYS been the plan. I don't—I'm not sure who I am if I don't surf.


Sitting outside on the stairs leading up to the school, Nelly shoved her journal in her bag. She gritted her teeth, trying to breath through the growing knot in her stomach. If she could just loosen it a little, she might be able to figure this thing out, or maybe figuring this out was how she loosened it? Before she could stew anymore on this conundrum, Emma walked up.

"Hey," Emma said, sitting next to Nelly. "Are you okay?"

"Fine," Nelly lied. "Just hungry."

"Oh, well, my grandma has a tendency to feed people whether they're hungry or not, so you're in luck." Emma grinned.

Nelly cracked a smile. "So, what's your grandma like?"

"Think *Golden Girls* meets Esmeralda from *The Hunchback of Notre Dame*," Emma said.

"She sounds awesome." Nelly thought of the only grandparent she had ever known: her late paternal grandmother, a frumpy old woman who lived in a house that perpetually smelled of foot cream and old cabbage.

"She is, but I should probably warn you—"

"Can we please just go home?" said the voice of a ten-year-old boy.

Nelly and Emma stood up and saw Nikki coming around the corner with her younger brother, who carried a giant black case.

"Over here," Emma called to Nikki. She waved and ran down the steps.

"Right," Nikki said, steering Kam over to the stairs. "Emma, Nelly, this is my brother Kameron. Kam, this is Emma and Nelly."

Nelly gave a small wave from the top of the stairs, but Emma (who was at the bottom of the stairs) stuck out her hand and shook Kam's. As his small hand clasped hers, Emma was flooded with cold.

*Kam was running, screaming. Suddenly, he was floating in the air like a balloon; something held his feet—no, was tied to his feet.*

"Ouch!" Kam squeaked.

"Oh." Emma blinked rapidly, jerking her hand back. "Sorry," she added, as her eyesight finally cleared. "Sometimes I don't know my own strength. Are you alright?"

Kam nodded, rubbing his hand.

"Um." Emma's brain raced with what she had seen; what had been mere desire to get to her grandma's house swelled uncomfortably into urgency. "I usually walk to my grandma's, but—"

"If you guys don't mind riding in the back with some boards, I can drive," Nelly said as she came down the steps.

"That works," Nikki said, eyeing Kam, who had set his case down. "Give me a minute to stick his stuff in my car, and we'll be back." Nikki picked Kam's case up and led him towards the car. "Are you okay?" she whispered.

"What?" Kam asked.

"Your hand," Nikki said, gesturing with her free hand.

"Oh, yeah," Kam said. "That's fine, but do we have to go wherever we're going?"

"Emma's grandma's house, and yes, it's for a group project," Nikki said as she unlocked the trunk.

"But I want to go home. I'm hungry." Kam helped heave his trombone case into the trunk. He took off his backpack and threw it in after.

"If Emma's grandma doesn't feed you, we can grab food on the way home," Nikki said, closing the trunk.

"What if I want a whole pack of cookies?" Kam put his hands on his hips. "Completely mine?"

Nikki grinned. "Absolutely."

"Fine." Kam stuck his hand out to seal the deal. "Double-stuff."

Nikki laughed as she shook his hand and then tousled his hair. "Come on. They're waiting for us."

As they all loaded into Nelly's truck, Kam watching Emma climb into the truck bed, Nikki walked over to the driver's side, where Nelly was sitting, putting on her sunglasses.

"Hey, can Kam ride in here with you? My mom won't care too much if I fall out the back of a truck, but she'd kill me if anything happened to Kam." Nikki glanced at her brother.

"Totally," Nelly said. "My dad is the same way with me and my sister." She cleared off the seat.

"Hey, bud," Nikki said, before Kam could get into the truck bed, "you're up front with Nelly."

"Nikki," Kam said, emphasizing the second syllable of her name. "I'm big enough to ride in the back."

"Mom would kill me," Nikki said, raising her eyebrows.

"Mom doesn't have to know," Kam said, mirroring her tone and brows.

"Cookies," Nikki said, leaning towards him.

Kam rolled his eyes and headed to the passenger side door. After he had buckled his seatbelt, Kam glanced at Nelly, who was waiting for Nikki and Emma to get settled before backing up out of her parking spot.

"So, uh," Nelly said, watching Nikki give a thumbs-up. "How old are you?"

"Ten," Kam said. "But I'll be eleven in July," he added.

Nelly cracked the little window that opened to the back. "Emma," she called. "Where am I going?"

"Do you know where Crescent Street is?" Emma asked.

"Yeah," Nelly said.

"1377 Crescent," Emma said.

Nelly nodded, closed the window, and backed up.

"This is kind of a small truck, no offense," Kam said to Nelly, as they drove off.

Nelly laughed. "None taken," she said. "My dad said if I was dragging more than teenagers and surf boards around, I'd need a bigger rig, but as it is…" Nelly shrugged. "So you're kind of young to be in middle school, no offense," she added with a smile.

"I'm kind of super smart." Kam shrugged this time and added, "But Nikki says I'm not supposed to say that a lot."

"Well, Mr. Genius, want to pick the radio station?" Nelly gestured to the radio as she flicked her blinker.

"Sure," Kam said, lighting up as he started twisting the tuning knob.

Nelly smiled. There was something about this kid that reminded her of herself at that age. She grinned as she listened to him find an oldies station and sing along to a Beatles song. After a few Beach Boys, and Bon Jovi songs, Nelly pulled up to 1377 Crescent Street.

"I should warn you," Emma said as they all piled out. "Grandma never really left her circus days behind her."

"Circus?" Kam asked.

Just then, a very short older woman came out of the house. She had a long gray braid tucked up and around her head. Her green eyes flashed out from her olive skin, which was weathered and soft. A cascade of silvery bangles danced and jingled on her naked wrists; she wore a white billowy top with sleeves that flowed to her elbows. The bottom of her blouse was tucked into the top of a maroon-almost-brown skirt which whirled around her ankles, blown by a wind that wasn't there. Madam Ethel Ortega was simultaneously homey and otherworldly.

"Emma," Ethel said, kissing both of Emma's cheeks. "These must be your friends." She hugged Nelly, and then Nikki. Upon seeing Kam, Ethel's eyes darkened, and her smile faltered. "You did not tell me you were bringing the boy."

Kam's eyes widened and flickered to Nikki.

Ethel touched his shoulders gently with the tips of her middle fingers. She pulled her hands back, touching her fingertips to her thumbs. "Turn," she told him. Kam slowly turned around. When he faced her again, Ethel nodded and said, "Welcome to my home, Kameron."

7 December 2008

Grandma fed us, no surprise there. Now she's setting out her materials and a large pillar candle, which suggests she's doing readings today. That would be a surprise, but also a good way to offer guidance about the girls' challenges without seeming to know too much. There aren't many laws of magick, but the ones that are there tend to be important. (At least, that's what Grandma and Rachelle keep telling me.)

Closing her journal, Emma glanced around the living room. Nelly had disappeared into the bathroom, leaving the other three to lounge on the various couches. The three sat happily digesting their meal of chicken salad sandwiches on croissants complete with a variety of vegetables cut into sticks, perfect for dipping in the salad dressing of their choice (Ethel was an avid dressing maker).

The room itself was warm and eclectic. Light came through the many windows, though the windows were not the only source of light. A variety of lamps were scattered around the room, some with stain-glass lamp shades and others with cloth, some even looked homemade. The walls were covered with pictures of differing shapes and sizes. Some of the pictures were black and white and clearly older photographs; a few featured a younger Ethel with a man, and then the two with a baby girl (baby Rachelle), and then the two with two young girls. At a certain point, the man no longer appeared in the photos but the young girls, Rachelle and Amy (Emma's mother), grew into women. Young Emma appeared in pictures, and then quite suddenly, Amy disappeared leaving behind Ethel, Rachelle, and Emma. The bits of wall not covered in the family's history were painted clary sage. A large dark cabinet took over most of the back wall. It was from this cabinet Ethel removed a variety of decanters and set them on the table in the dining room.

Kam watched as Ethel made several trips (she had already turned down all offers of help). He peeked over the couch into the dining room, watching as Ethel now set her collection of jars on the table in front of the decanters.

"What's she doing?" Kam whispered to Nikki.

Nikki shrugged and glanced at Emma, who sat on the loveseat between the couches.

"I suspect we'll find out soon," Emma whispered to Kam.

Just as Nelly came out of the bathroom, Ethel came into the living room. "If you would all join me around the table please," Ethel said with her hands clasped at her chest. "Emma, dear, will you grab the tea cups?"

Emma nodded and went into the kitchen as the others followed Ethel into the dining room. This room was much smaller than the living room and could only be described as bright and a bit beachy: sawn oak floors (like the rest of the house), cream-colored walls, and two windows, the largest of which was framed by sky blue curtains. Natural light filled the space, reflecting and sparkling off all the jars and decanters on the long walnut table. If that table could tell stories, well, I suppose you wouldn't need me. This table would become the center of many adventures, and on this, their first adventure, it kept its most interesting secret covered with a wide jute table runner.

On one side of the table sat Nikki and Kam, their backs to the kitchen. Nelly sat across from them. Ethel sat at the end of the table, closest to the door.

"Are you going to read our tea leaves or something?" Nelly asked Ethel as Emma set down a tray of tea cups on the table and took a seat next to Kam.

"Oh, no, dear," Ethel said. "I don't waste time with such parlor tricks."

Nelly gestured to the tea cups. "But—"

"This is a *reading*," Ethel explained, which of course meant nothing to anyone who actually needed an explanation. "Why don't we start with you, dear," she said, gesturing to Nikki.

"Me? Uh, sure." Nikki stood. "What do I do?"

"Take a cup, and choose a liquid from any of the decanters, and then add however much of whichever ingredients from the jars you like," Ethel said, moving the large pale pillar candle closer to her.

"Just whatever?" Nikki said, as she grabbed one of the tea cups.

"Whatever feels like it speaks to you."

Nikki nodded, feeling this spoke crazy to her, but reaching for a long sleek decanter all the same. She poured its white liquid into her cup; a sharp tang met her nose. Nikki was sure it was buttermilk but didn't want to ask. Instead, she moved on to choosing ingredients. There were dozens of jars varying in size from baby-food-sized to quart-sized. Each was filled with something different: salt, pepper, sand, various dried herbs, various fresh ones, bits of petals, raw sugar, and many things Nikki couldn't identify (I could tell you everything, but really it would sound less like a story and more like a shopping list. Rest assured, I'll let you know what you need to know, but for now, let your imagination run wild).

Glancing into her tea cup of probably buttermilk, Nikki closed her eyes for a second and tried to "feel" the jars "speak" to her as Ethel had said. She pinched some raw sugar and sprinkled it in. Then, as if the jars suddenly became backlit, Nikki knew exactly which jars to use. Now, even though Nikki couldn't identify everything she put in the cup, I will tell you her specific ingredients because I know you're curious: fresh thyme, fir needles, and daisy petals, dried fern, a tuft of dandelion, and a small sprig of rosemary. The concoction looked, well, frankly like something a child would create in the backyard and hand to his mother as 'tea' (which she would have praised him for and then dumped into the grass while his back was turned).

"Are you finished?" Ethel asked.

"I think so," Nikki said.

"Very well, I'll take that," Ethel said, standing and reaching out for Nikki's cup, which Nikki willingly gave.

"Bring your chair here, dear," Ethel said, gesturing in front of her as she sat. As Nikki moved the chair carefully—sitting almost knee to knee with Ethel, perpendicular to the table—Ethel held the tea cup in her hands, one palm under the cup while the other covered the top. She closed her fingers over the cup and muttered something no one could understand. It seemed to satisfy her because Ethel set the cup down on the table. "We're going to let that meld for a moment. Have you ever had your palms read?"

Nikki shook her head.

"Your hand," Ethel said, extending her own, palm up, towards Nikki, who put her hand, palm up, in Ethel's hand; the old woman traced the lines on Nikki's palm. "You are of great power," she continued, as she looked at Nikki's hand. "Your heart is pure and understanding. You must learn more about who you are and connect with the earth. You must understand your destiny." Ethel released Nikki's hand.

"Destiny?" Nikki said, studying her palm, hoping to see whatever it was Ethel saw.

"Yes," Ethel said. "Your heart is of the earth. You must connect to it if you wish to harness your potential." She turned her attention back to the cup, which she picked up and held between both hands as she rested her arms on her legs.

"How did that happen?" Nikki asked as she saw the inside of the cup, for the contents had changed significantly from the white and muddled mess to an almost translucent emerald green. The tea cup seemed to contain its own current; glittery shapes formed on the surface in various shades of green, some brighter, and some much darker than base liquid.

"Magick," Ethel said, with a sparkle in her eye.

Nikki was unable to tell if Ethel was joking—she wasn't.

"Watch." Ethel nodded down to the cup. As the images unfolded in front of the two, Ethel spoke quietly. "You have divine power in you." The image shifted. "Ah, you are adding imagination to a relationship; you are gentle and unhurried. You are cautious, but peaceful and content."

Between Ethel's translations of the shapes and their constant shifting, Nikki found it difficult to follow along, let alone think of questions to ask. The image shifted again, this time into something any of us would easily recognized: a series of small stars.

"You're about to embark on an adventure," Ethel continued, "the stars imply growth and imagination; they represent time itself."

The stars morphed into three lines and then four before combining into one spiral.

"Earth and the water," Ethel mumbled almost to herself. To Nikki, she said quite clearly, "Your ambitions are to join the three parts of mind and four elements. You seek growth."

Nikki nodded, wishing she could take notes as the image swirled again.

"You have achieved purification of your desires; you've already tuned in your will," Ethel said before the shapes changed again. "You have much strength. You bring balance to the opposites. This is important, very important."

Once again, an image you or I could actually recognize as a real shape rather than a mere blob appeared: a sword.

"You dream of finding your true path. You are up for a challenge, ready to prove you can overcome any obstacle," Ethel explained. The images began shifting between shapes faster. Ethel rattled off meanings, almost desperate to keep up. "Your perception of self is encouraging—you have strength and power." Shift. "Your desire cosmic consciousness: you want control over yourself and your environment." Shift. "You seek a new earth, a new mind and body." Shift. "You seek balance."

The tea cup made one last shape: the moon.

"A warning," Ethel said solemnly. "You need to see that you will grow gradually, not all at once. You have both a wild and tame nature to your abilities. This is of the utmost importance: do not dwell on your losses. Do not linger on your mistakes. Learn to move ahead," Ethel said. "You risk losing even more if you cannot learn to move forward."

The surface of the magickal tea shuttered and was still. The green faded until the liquid looked like nothing more interesting than water; no evidence of the ingredients remained.

Once again, Nikki found herself asking "How did that—"

"Would you be a dear and put your cup in the sink?" Ethel said, handing her the tea cup. "I'm afraid the *how* is rather long and complicated just now."

"Uh, sure," Nikki said. She stood and moved into the kitchen. Had she had her wits about her, she might have pressed Ethel, but as it was, between the clear and obvious magick that had taken place and the massive amount of mystifying information dumped into her brain, Nikki was overwhelmed. The odd thing, at least for Nikki, was despite the overwhelm, she also felt genuinely grateful. One day she would understand these answers, though she did not right now.

"Emma?" Ethel said.

Emma sat up straighter. "Yes?"

"You're next."

"But I—"

"Make an old woman happy," Ethel insisted.

Emma picked up a tea cup and stood. She glanced at her grandmother once before beginning to create her concoction. Emma moved more quickly than Nikki had (now sitting at the table once again). From a short decanter, she poured a light yellow liquid (Rachelle's homemade dandelion oil) into her tea cup, following it with just a splash of olive oil from a square decanter.

Nikki shifted in her seat while Nelly, jaw clenched, kept her expression stony. The two sat, not knowing they were opposite ends of the pendulum: one filled with wonder at the present while the other slowly filled with fear of the future.

Meanwhile, Kam sat, completely fascinated by everything that was happening; he watched as Ethel lit the candle and moved her hands over the flame, as though trying to catch the smoke: her bottom hand moved toward her, palm facing her, while her top hand moved away, palm out, and then they switched places. She repeated this gesture several times.

Emma had moved on to the jars and had just added her last ingredient: dried cactus. She handed the cup to Ethel before taking a seat. As Emma positioned herself in the chair, knee to knee with her grandmother, Ethel performed the same bit of magick over the tea cup as she had with Nikki's, palms and fingers encasing the cup. The concoction of oils, bits of flowers, and herbs melted together. Ethel placed the cup on the table.

Ethel took Emma by the hands; her aged and weathered hands clasped Emma's soft, ringless fingers. She looked into her granddaughter's eyes and smiled, nodding encouragingly. "Go ahead and take the cup," she said, releasing Emma.

Emma placed the cup in Ethel's hands, and the two watched as the now opaque golden liquid exposed its secrets upon its surface.

"There will be a binding of forces, using powers to guard against repression. Yes. Now the union of opposite but complementary parts." Ethel glanced at the girls.

Nikki and Nelly looked at each other, but Emma's eyes were locked on the cup.

"Grandma." A new shape was forming.

"What do you see?" Ethel asked.

"A—a cat?" Emma guessed. She had studied some of this but not nearly enough to be sure of anything she saw.

"A suggestion of clairvoyant powers," Ethel said. "What else?"

"I'm not sure." The golden shapes were muddled.

"The lion," Ethel said. "Divine power."

Emma nodded.

"And now?"

"A mountain range, maybe?"

"The three peaks, and they represent attainment on the three planes of consciousness," Ethel said slowly.

Emma shook her head slightly, as if she didn't believe what Ethel was telling her. As I'm sure you've gathered, Emma was quite familiar with her psychic-medium powers, but this was news (even to her), for attaining all three planes was essentially unheard of. Most psychics attained one level, but almost no one attained all three. A mounting pressure crept up Emma's spine. She took a steadying breath.

The shapes shifted again.

"You see the others in this relationship as being able to bring balance, for the ultimate goal is balance." Ethel studied the golden liquid. The shape morphed into something unmistakable: a skull and scythe.

Emma nodded and said calmly, "Change. Of course, that's natural. Is there another meaning?"

"Eternal life," Ethel said. The skull and scythe swirled into the shape of a goblet. "Fulfilled hopes and wishes. You are the awakening. To those who are ignorant, you bring fear; to those who understand, you bring freedom."

Emma sat a bit taller. She took a deep breath and nodded as though accepting a calling. "I understand."

"My dear," Ethel said, patting Emma's hand as the goblet swirled away. "You too receive a warning, a warning of ignorance. You and the others must turn to your inner powers, your inner light. There is hope as there is always hope. Strength is found in creativity and inspiration; seek to follow your inner light, and the way will show itself to you."

Emma nodded as the liquid faded from its opaque gold to clear and water-like.

Ethel set the cup on the table, and the two hugged.

"Thank you, Grandma," Emma whispered.

When their embrace ended, Ethel held Emma's face between her hands—she didn't say anything; she simply raised her eyebrows, kissed Emma's forehead, and released her.

Emma took her cup to the kitchen.

Ethel began her cleansing ritual with the candle, briefly meeting Nelly's nervous eyes. Ethel nodded. "My dear."

Nelly fidgeted in her seat. "I mean, I'm—" She sighed. "Okay." She shook her head slightly as she moved, holding her cup. She, too, moved quickly. Nelly found a decanter filled with what appeared to be (and was in fact) water. She sprinkled in some chunky sea salt, a bit of nori, fresh thyme, dried magnolia, and hyacinth petals. Without looking at the old woman, Nelly handed Ethel the cup and took her seat.

After Ethel had performed her bit of muttering magick and set Nelly's now churning mixture on the table, Ethel put her hand out to Nelly. "Your hand, dear."

Nelly chewed on her cheek but gave Ethel her hand.

Examining the lines on Nelly's hand, Ethel said, "Your heart is of water."

"I am a surfer," Nelly said.

"Yes," Ethel said. "Your power comes from water. You are connected but not enough for what is to come." Ethel ran her index finger down the center of

Nelly's palm. "You will need to access your greater power. You are ignorant."

"Ignorant? What power?" Nelly pulled her hand away from Ethel as if she had burned it.

Ethel looked at Emma. "They don't know." It wasn't a question.

Emma shook her head, adding, "Not yet."

Satisfied with this answer, Ethel took Nelly's cup and held it so they could both watch the now shimmering dark blue translucent liquid. As the shapes began forming, their colors changed from dark green to purple to black. Ethel spoke, "Your past is hidden in shadow, yet all will be revealed soon."

Nelly nodded, but the color of the unidentifiable shapes was eerily familiar. Her palms sweat. Maybe this wasn't such a good idea. Nelly's stomach felt like someone was tap dancing all over it.

"You are surrounded by unconditional love," Ethel continued. "Be mindful of this love, for it is through love our greatest powers are often made accessible." Nelly's shapes moved much slower than either Emma's or Nikki's. "Your happiness will be fulfilled; you will find achievement, love, and compassion."

"Sounds pretty good," Nelly said, breathing easier.

"An upside down triangle is the ancient symbol for water," Ethel said, pointing into the cup. "Water was the first mirror. The reflection in water is almost always upside down, so you must look beneath the surface—beyond appearance—to find deeper truth."

Nelly grunted, unsure exactly how to respond.

The shapes shifted again. "Power is offered, but it must be nurtured."

"Power?"

Ethel didn't address Nelly's question, for the image had swirled. "Ships," she said. "A safe voyage. A sign of subconscious reflection." Ethel looked at Nelly, as though willing her to understand the gravity of this reading. "You have great power at your fingertips," Ethel said. "It has followed you your entire life. Though once dormant, it is available to you now, but you must reach for it. Look inside yourself."

"I don't know what—"

"I know, dear," Ethel said softly. "Look." She gestured into the cup.

"A rook? Like in chess?" Nelly recognized this shape—Tom, her dad, was a big chess player.

Ethel smiled. "The tower," she said. "It represents an awakening. Do you fear knowledge?"

"I—I don't think so?" Nelly's palms were beginning to sweat again.

"Be open to your awakening," Ethel said gently. The tower disappeared in a swirl. "All secrets are available to you if you know how to fish for them. This here," she said pointing into the cup at a little squiggle, "represents meditation and revelation. Seek your answers with the knowledge they will come if you are patient." Slowly, the squiggle and accompanying shapes morphed into a single black star. Ethel smiled. "Good fortune." Ethel believed the reading to be over, but the concoction in the cup had one last message.

"What's happening?" Nelly asked. The tea cup had started to vibrate.

"I don't—" Ethel couldn't finish her sentence. Her breath caught in her chest. The images at the top of Nelly's cup seemed to be fighting, black and green figures swirled. It would stop for a moment on the black star and then shift madly to an acid green face with horns coming from the head.

Even Nelly knew this was not a good omen. "What's happening?" she asked again.

The cup shook violently and crashed onto the floor. The liquid sizzled for a moment; the acid green face shone brightly and then swirled; the black star shimmered for barely a second before the liquid become nothing more than water.

Ethel swallowed. "A final warning: the image of the devil."

"What's it mean?" Nikki asked.

Nelly stared at the floor, the remnants of ceramic and water swimming in her vision.

"It represents a failure to use discrimination," Ethel said in a low voice. Her eyes were also glued to the water on her floor. "It is what happens when we do not seek the truth beneath the surface. It is ignorance, lack of light, black magick." Ethel looked at Nelly. "If you choose to accept your power, to seek the truth beneath appearances, your outcome will be a celebration; however, if you do not accept your power, if you accept appearances, if you choose to remain in ignorance, your outcome will be a dark one indeed."

"I—I," Nelly stuttered. Her stomach churned. If she opened her mouth again, she was sure more than simple words would come out. She gulped, pinching her lips together and shaking her head. "I'll be in the truck," she managed to mumble before she disappeared out the front door.

"Emma, be a dear and get me something to mop this up," Ethel said, leaning over to pick up the shattered tea cup.

"Of course," Emma said, disappearing in to the kitchen.

"Here," Kam said. He quickly took now empty tray and brought it over to Ethel.

"Clever boy," Ethel said, carefully setting bits of broken ceramic on tray. "Thank you, dear. Be careful not to cut yourself," she added as Kam helped pick up the larger pieces.

"Here," Emma said. She handed Ethel a paper bag and a handful of paper towels.

When the mess was cleaned up, the four sat back down.

"Kameron," Ethel said. "May I read your palm?"

"Um," Kam said. "Sure." After he had sat across from Ethel, he put his hand out. His mouth sat in a determined dash across his face.

Ethel gently took his hand and studied the lines. "My dear, you are destined for great things. You will make your father proud." She patted him on the hand.

Kam looked at Nikki and Emma and relaxed into a smile.

A shadow passed over Ethel's heart, though the smile did not leave her eyes. She saw a darkness coming for the boy. She thought she understood it and believed by hiding it from him, she might spare him from it. For she had frequently seen darkness come to those who sought to avoid it, but even the great Madam Ethel Ortega could not see all. Perhaps if she had, she might have chosen to warn him after all.


It was a quiet ride back to the school. Nelly and Kam sat in the silent cab while Nikki rode alone in the back. Emma had stayed at her grandmother's house. Though separate, the girls were subconsciously united, for each mulled over the masses of information she had received.

When the three finally arrived back to the school, Kam shot off towards the Suzuki, now the only other car in the parking lot. Nikki went over to the driver's side of the truck, where Nelly still sat.

"Thanks for the ride," Nikki said a bit lamely.

Nelly nodded.

"So," Nikki said. "Should we trade phone numbers? I mean, we'll probably need to get in contact outside of school eventually."

"Sure" Nelly said.

Nikki pulled out her phone and punched in number as Nelly rattled it off. "I got Emma's before we left. Do you want hers, too?"

Nelly nodded as she dug through her bag; when she found her phone missing, she pulled out a sharpie. Sighing, Nelly popped the cap off. "Okay, shoot."

Nikki gave her number and then Emma's while Nelly wrote both on the inside of her palm, putting the name of each girl next to her number. "I'll grab emails later."

# Chapter Four

## Saturday. December 8th

December 8, 2008

    Good gravy, yesterday was nuts. I went to Emma's grandma's house (cool place, Victorian meets major hippy) and so much happened. I wanted to write last night but Mom—well, it doesn't really matter. Here's everything I remember. Madam Ortega (that's Emma's grandma) read my palm and had me make this weird mix in a tea cup, and she read that, too. It was literally a bunch of leaves in a cup of sour milk that magically changed into this gorgeous green liquid with all these shapes on top that meant different stuff. It was WILD.

    Other things I remember: Madam Ortega is apparently a medium. That means she talks to dead people! Anyway, so I interviewed Madam O for the project, and she told me this amazing story about the first time she saw (and helped) a dead person. Madam O was only like seven, and this girl, Heidi, needed her help. The short version is Madam O was able to help her, and she's been helping dead people ever since.

    Madam O told me all about mediums and about how she can see people's auras. But the weird doesn't stop there. Apparently Rupert (that's Madam O's late husband) had a great grandma who was an ELF! Being a medium skips a generation, so that means neither Rachelle

(Emma's aunt) or Amy (Emma's late mom) were mediums, BUT Emma IS!! She told me Emma is also psychic (something to do with seeing the future). I mean, on the one hand, how is any of this even possible? On the other, I'm 87% sure I'm a witch, so I guess it's very possible.

Speaking of witch (haha), here's my big struggle: while Madam O was doing my reading, she mentioned "potential" and "powers" several times. So does she know I'm a witch? Or is she talking about the "power" we each have over our lives? Like hippy dippy stuff? I haven't actually told anyone, well, Mom, but I don't think that counts. This isn't the kind of thing you just go around saying out loud. They used to burn you at the stake for that.

So do I tell Madam O or Emma? They might be able to help, but also, maybe not. What if Madam O's stories are just that? Stories. She was in the circus. Maybe she spent so many years telling stories for her act that she started to believe them?

But some of the things she told me...

While Nikki had always been a bit of a wild spirit (it drove Margret insane), this was a bit too wild even for her, a bit too unknown. Luckily, her magick was on her side. So when Nikki dropped her pen and muttered, "I wish I knew what to do," her magick responded.

The pen rose as though held by an invisible hand—Nikki jumped off her bed and backed into the corner of the room, keeping her eyes on the pen, which wrote two words and dropped. Nikki stood in that corner for a few minutes, but it felt like hours. Finally, she inched towards the bed, ready to spring back to the corner if anything happened. She read the two scribbled words:

Tell her.

You and I know her magick was offering her help, but she merely believed, at least for this immediate moment, that her pen was possessed. A strange mixture of fear and relief filled her. Possessed or not, at least something offered her an answer.

"How is that even possible?" Nikki whispered. She poked the pen and jerked back. Nothing happened. She tried this exercise once more, and when again, nothing happened, she picked up her pen.

Okay, THAT was weird. That handwriting isn't mine. My pen wrote it all by itself. Or maybe, but no that's impossible, but what's really impossible? I mean, what if my magic did that? Maybe my magic thinks I should tell Emma. Thinks? Can magic think??

Curiosity and fear wrestled within her as the question echoed in her mind: Can magic think? Nikki licked her lips and wrung her hands, willing them to stop shaking so much. Then Ethel's words from yesterday's reading floated through Nikki's mind, as if Ethel was in the room, whispering in her ears: "You have both a wild and tame nature to your abilities."

"Magic is wild," Nikki whispered to herself. The thought should have been scary; it should have sent fear rushing through her; it should have sent her flying under her covers, hiding from the world. However, it did none of these things; instead, Nikki found peace.

Nikki's door flew open. Margret stood in the doorframe, flushed and frantic. "Why are you still in your pjs? You're going to be late. I know I said I'd take Kam, but I have a meeting in twenty minutes. If I stop to drop him off, I'll be late. Mr. Okoro will not be kept waiting!" After saying all of this in a single breath, Margret hurried over to Kam's room, knocked once, and opened the door.

"Mom," Kam groaned, burrowing into his blankets.

"Get up." Margret threw off his covers. When she saw his threadbare X-wing pjs, she sighed. "Kameron, I thought I told you to throw those out."

"They're warm," he insisted, hopping out of his bed and running to the bathroom.

Margret grumbled as she yanked the covers up on Kam's bed, promptly smoothing them before tucking in the edges. "They're practically see-through. They can't possibly be warm."

"Mom," Nikki said, leaning on Kam's doorframe. "What's the big deal?"

"He can't hold onto things just because your father gave them to him. He'll be home soon and can give Kam some new pajamas then." Margret wiped a tear away before it could mess with her mascara. "Oh, these allergies."

Nikki hugged her mom. "Dad'll be home in four months. Four months."

"I know," Margret said, patting Nikki's back. She pulled back from the hug and fiddled with Nikki's hair. "I know you like it dark, but couldn't you at least cut it?"

"What about Mr. Okoro?"

Margret's eyes widened. "Oh my goodness, you're right!" She glanced at her make-up in the hallway mirror, blew kisses, and said, "I love you both! Make good choices!" A jingle of car keys and slam of the door later, she was gone.

"Can we make bad choices? Just once?" Kam's head popped out of the bathroom, toothpaste foam dripping from his mouth.

"Finish brushing your teeth, and we'll talk," Nikki said. She went into the kitchen to put the kettle on and plug her phone in to charge.

"What's for breakfast?" Kam asked, sliding into the kitchen.

"How about chocolate chip pancakes?" Nikki pulled a bowl from a cupboard.

"Do we have peanut butter?"

"You check, and I'll start on the batter." Nikki said.

They chatted as Nikki cooked and Kam ate. After finishing his fourth helping of pancakes slathered in peanut butter and syrup, Kam put his fork and sticky plate in the sink. He washed his hands and asked, "Do you think Dad will actually come home this time?"

"What do you mean?" Nikki sipped on her orange juice.

"Well, he was supposed to be home by now, but then he got the extension, so he'll be home in April, but will he actually come home, or will he get another extension?" Kam said.

Nikki sighed, knowing what she was going to say next was not what he wanted to hear. "Bud, I don't know. I hope he'll come home. I hope he won't get another extension, but I really don't know."

Kam's shoulders slumped, and he blew his breath through his lips.

"Hey," Nikki said, throwing an arm over his ten-year-old shoulders that carried more worry than they should. "Why don't you go watch TV in Mom and Dad's room? I don't think Mom would mind as long as you wash your sticky face before you get in her bed."

Kam touched his mouth and felt syrup remnants. He grinned, washed his face in the sink, and ran to their parents' room.

As she listened to Kam sing along with the SpongeBob theme song, Nikki smiled to herself and pulled her phone off the charging cable. She had a text message from Emma.

**Emma:** Hey, I wanted to see if Kam is okay. Grandma can be kind of intense. Did she scare him at all?

**Nikki:** Nah, he's a tough kid. Thanks for checking though.

**Emma:** Absolutely.

**Nikki:** Hey, can I ask you a question?

**Emma:** Sure.

**Nikki:** Are you really psychic? Your grandma said you were but I wasn't sure if she was for real or if it was part of a circus act.

**Emma:** I'm a psychic-medium. Basically I have visions of the future, and I help spirits finish their unfinished business.

**Nikki:** That's wicked cool. So how do your visions work?

As Nikki waited for Emma to respond back, she rinsed dishes and put them in the dishwasher, all the while wondering if she was overstepping by asking how visions worked. If someone had asked Nikki how being a witch worked, she wouldn't have an answer. She grabbed her phone and tapped out another message.

**Nikki:** I mean, if it's too hard to explain, don't worry about it. I didn't mean to pry.

**Emma:** Oh, it's okay. I was trying to find a way to explain it in a way that won't freak you out. Most people tend to freak out.

**Nikki:** It takes a lot to freak me out these days.

**Emma:** So basically, I see a vision; it literally takes over my physical sight, and I see glimpses of the future. It's not set in stone though, so it might happen, but it also might not.

**Nikki:** That sounds confusing.

**Emma:** It can be.

**Nikki:** Can I tell you something?

**Emma:** Sure.

We have the advantage of hindsight; therefore, we know Nikki's magick had told her to tell Emma. Nikki had no such advantage as she lived through this moment, and while she mentally reasoned it was a good thing to do, her stomach still felt like she had swallowed a school of goldfish as she typed her message. She took a deep breath and hit the 'send' button.

```
Nikki: First a question. Do you believe in
magic?
Emma: Depends. Do you mean magic or magick?
Nikki: What's the difference?
Emma: Magic is pretend. It's fairy stories and
Barbie princess movies. Magick is real. It
exists in our world.
Nikki: Magick then.
Emma: Yes.
Nikki: I have magick. I think I might be a
witch or something.
Emma: I'm so pleased you found out!! And it's
not "or something." You ARE a witch!
```

Nikki had to reread Emma's response several times before it sunk in. She fought the temptation to throw her phone; instead, she opted to stand and pace around the kitchen, fuming, and muttering to herself: "She could have told me; she should have told me. I mean, okay, I might not have believed her, or I might have thought she was crazy." The more she muttered, the more she realized Emma had been right to wait, though this logic did nothing for the tightness in her chest. Gritting her teeth, she tapped out another message.

```
Nikki: How long have you known?
Emma: A while.
Nikki: Meaning?
Emma: I considered telling you, but after talking
with Rachelle, we both thought it would be better
to let you find out on your own and discover you
could trust me. If I was wrong, I'd be exposing
magick, and that's never a good idea.
```

        **Nikki**: Makes sense, I guess. So what now? How
        did this even happen?
        **Emma**: Now you learn to control your powers. It
        happened because of who your parents are. It's
        in your blood.
        **Nikki**: Why didn't anyone tell me this would
        happen?
        **Emma**: I'm not sure. For now, practice controlling
        your powers. I've got to run, but I'll see
        you Monday. Nelly will have some interesting
        information on Aisling O'Crean for you.

One word stuck out in that last message: "powers." Plural. Nikki wondered what other powers she had. As far as she knew, she had one power (making stuff appear). Nikki caught sight of her empty glass, closed her eyes, and thought, 'I want more orange juice.' There was a small pop. Nikki cracked open one eye. The glass was still empty. She opened her eyes fully. A steady dripping sound came from the refrigerator. Tentatively, Nikki walked toward the fridge. She opened the door only to discover every single orange had burst, including the jug of orange juice. Sticky pulp and juice trickled down every surface in the refrigerator.

Nikki sighed. "This will probably be safer to clean sans magick."


Dec. 8, 08
    Still haven't been in the water. Is it weird I almost think it would be easier to get in the water if I had been bitten by a shark? I mean, that happens to other people, you know? There are other surfers who keep surfing after their attacks, but I've never heard of anyone else sprouting scales. What if it's just the one spot? I might be able to cover it up. If it spreads to my whole body, it could be the end of my career.
    I have to know. Today. I have to know today. Right now.

Nelly was not made for standing still. She rushed around the room, tossing her journal in a duffle bag, along with a towel, and a pair of sweatpants. After shoving on her lucky black bikini, she threw her clothes back on and carried her duffle into the front of the house, chucking it onto the futon in the front room.

"Where're you headed, kid?" Tom, Nelly's tall and scruffy dad, stood behind the island in the kitchen. He wore an old rust-red Strong Current long sleeve and some khaki shorts. His salt and pepper hair and beard were growing more salt than pepper these days.

"Beach," Nelly said, grabbing a banana out of the fruit bowl on the island.

Tom pulled out the blender and rattled around in the fridge, pulling out various fruits, a bag of spinach, a quart of milk, and a carton of Greek yogurt.

While he rummages through the cupboard looking for his protein powder, I'll tell you more about the Hansen home and specifically, their kitchen, which might be one of my favorite places. Their house wasn't particularly large, though it was what Margret would have described as 'a three bed, one bath.' Because it was an open plan, the front room, dining room, and kitchen were really all the same room. Bamboo flooring covered the whole house. The kitchen? Well, I did tell you it's one of my favorites: butcher-block counter tops, fern colored cabinets, the island I've already mentioned, and all of it framed by bright yellow walls. (Melinda, Nelly's mom, had loved changing the color of the kitchen every few years. Yellow was the last color she had picked.) All in all, it was a gorgeous little kitchen all on its own, but what made it so wonderful, so special, was the way everyone lived together in the kitchen; it was the heart of the Hansen home—it saw all the happiness, pain, and growth of the family. It would one day wax heavy with history, become haunted even. But I'm getting ahead of myself again.

Back to Tom, who set the canister of protein powder on the island. "Not surfing?" he asked, glancing at Nelly as he threw a handful of strawberries, green and all, into the blender.

"No," Nelly said, not meeting his eyes; he knew. She knew he knew. "I just need to clear my head, you know?"

"Mmm." He dumped a scoop of vanilla protein powder on top of the strawberries.

"Like you know how you say that sometimes if you're having an off day, trying to go out and force it just puts more bad mojo out there? I don't need more bad mojo," Nelly said, hoping she sounded as casual as she meant to.

"Off day, huh? Sounds more like it's been an off week." Into the blender went a handful of spinach, which Tom packed down with a wooden spoon.

Nelly sighed. "What did Jo say?"

"Nothing," Tom said, eyeballing the milk as he poured. "I just noticed your board hasn't moved, and your rainbow of wax hasn't changed since Wednesday. Is there anything you want to talk about?"

"I just–" Nelly struggled for the words. "I'm not—it was—I mean…" She sighed, running her fingers through her short hair. "I'm hoping the Cove will help me sort it out."

"Well, take your time. Your mom always said not to push you girls too hard," he said and then started the blender. He had a way of avoiding further conversation after mentioning Melinda, which usually involved a loud kitchen appliance. "Have fun, be home by five. I'm grilling tonight," he yelled over the blender. He waved, keeping his eyes on his churning smoothie.

After waving half-heartedly, not bothering to say anything over the burring of the blender, Nelly hopped in her little truck and drove down the hill. She paused at the stop sign, debating between going right and taking the more direct but more populated road or going left and taking the less direct but also less busy road. She flipped on her right blinker, which clicked loudly in the quiet of the car. Following the road down to main, Nelly cleared her throat in an attempt to break through the suffocating silence. It didn't work. She turned on the radio, turning it back off almost immediately. The cheery sounds of DJ Mark were too much. Instead, she started talking to herself. She did this before any surf meet that she was particularly nervous about (though of course, she'd never admit to being nervous).

"It's going to be fine," she said quietly as she waited at the light before turning left onto Main.

The silence pushed back.

"It will be fine," she repeated, a bit louder, a bit more urgently. She had timed the lights perfectly. After rolling through two more greens, she pulled into the parking lot across the street from the Cove.

The Cove was a mysterious place, a secret place. To anyone walking by, the entrance was nothing more than a cliff side completely covered by bushy brambles and thorny weeds with an unreachable ocean far below. Even the path to the Cove was a family secret, one that Nelly had shared only with Wyatt.

She sat in the car for a second, looking around to make sure she was alone. Once she was positive no one else was around, Nelly crossed the street and passed through the brambles, ducking down as she disappeared down the path. When she reached the fifty-seventh step, she turned a sharp left and walked, seeming to go away from the beach. She hiked for a bit before finally, coming down the slope leading her straight to the little cove. It had been years since she had laid eyes on the place.

"I forgot how beautiful this place is," she thought aloud.

The Cove was comprised of a sheltered bay of crystal clear water that broke on soft white sand. Great sheer walls of bedrock and greenstone protected the Cove. Nelly looked out to the ocean and started taking off her extra layer.

"You're probably overreacting," she said to herself. "I mean, it wouldn't be the first time we blew something out of proportion. It's probably nothing. Maybe it was a trick of the sun, or something weird like that." Her brain agreed with this logic; her gut did not.

Nelly turned to face the ocean again. The wind blew her sun-kissed hair from her face. The sun was shining deliciously, warming Nelly's tanned skin. "It's now or never," she said and ran to the break, diving into the frigid waters.

First the freezing pain of the 55-degree water hit Nelly; then, a new and more intense pain overwhelmed her senses. At first she thought she was being stabbed, repeatedly stabbed all over her body, but the sensation changed, and a small corner of Nelly's mind wondered if somehow she had been set on fire. Every nerve in her body ignited. Pain screamed in her bones; she could feel them cracking and shifting, twisting and melding. Each stab, each crack, each twist sent colors flying before her eyes: vivid reds, deep oranges, blinding yellows, and just as she thought she was going to reach white, going to reach the end of her ability to withstand whatever was happening to her, everything went blue.

The pain retreated and a calm, soothing coolness washed over her. Her mind felt squishy and intangible, almost separated from her. Nelly reached out to touch the blue, only half-conscious it was not a color in her mind but the ocean water surrounding her. She tried to touch it, move her hand through it, but her hand wouldn't move. A hand Nelly had never seen before moved through the water in front of her. This hand was strange; the back of it was iridescent and tinted tea green with a delicate webbing between the fingers. The skin looked more like the sharp-toothed scales of a shark than the smooth skin of a human. Nelly wanted a closer look at this strange hand and found it was moving closer to her, as though responding to her thoughts. The fingers opened and closed; the webbing contracted and expanded. Nelly was curious what the palm of the hand looked like, and the hand again, responding to her thoughts, moved so she could see. As the hand opened, there on the palm, in her own handwriting, were the names and numbers of Nikki and Emma.

Then, she realized what I'm sure you've already figured out: The greenish, webbed hand was hers.

The fuzzy, floaty feeling in her brain dissipated immediately. Nelly became aware of how long she had been underwater, yet her lungs did not scream for air. She looked down, trying to gain her bearings, and that was when she saw it. Where her legs should have been was a long, black tail, complete with a gray-black fluke.

"What the—" Nelly slapped her hands over her mouth. She had spoken underwater. This was too much. She clawed her way to the surface, avoiding movement in her legs as much as she could. As the top of her head breached the line between water and air, a thought struck her: She could clearly breathe underwater, but could she still breathe above it? She sunk down. Nelly took a deep breath underwater and blew it out, preparing herself before shoving her head above the water. She held her breath for a second. Then, slowly, she sipped the air, waiting to see if she choked. She could still breathe air; though, it tasted differently. It felt colder and crisp; it reminded her of Christmases spent in northern Idaho with her dad's older brother, Roger, before he passed.

With that hurdle successfully navigated, Nelly turned her attention to getting out of the water as fast as possible. She dragged her lower body out of the water and onto the sand. Nelly felt her body changing again; strangely, this time, there was no searing pain. She chanced a glance at her lower half and was relieved to discover she had legs and toes again. Noticing her bikini bottoms were nowhere to be seen, Nelly found herself incredibly grateful that she was alone. It was not the first time she had lost part of her bathing suit to the ocean. She scrambled up to her bag and wrenched on the sweatpants she had thrown in there earlier.

Nelly collapsed onto the sand. The brief taste of relief dissipated as the magnitude of what had just happened hit her. If someone had come up to Nelly an hour before this moment and carved out her entire chest with a white hot scoop, she would have felt more whole and more alive than she did now. She stared out into the waves. There had only ever been one place where Nelly could be completely herself, no need to be stronger than she was, no need to hide the broken pieces that she had shaped into a recognizable person, no need to pretend, but now…

"I can never go in the ocean again."


8 December 2008

We have twenty-four days to prepare, provided they even want to help. I mean, just because I've seen them help doesn't mean they will, but I hope they do. It's all up to them, really.

The idea of having to face whatever was coming alone made Emma feel sick. So she did what she always did when she felt overwhelmed by helplessness and began making a plan. The gears in her head turned: The laws around magick were clear, but perhaps if there was a way to at least figure out who Nikki and Nelly's mentors would be; then, she could—there was a loud crash in the kitchen followed by a shout. Emma jumped up from her desk and bolted into the kitchen. She found Rachelle laughing hysterically on the floor, covered in what appeared to be sawdust.

"What happened?" Emma said, reaching to help her aunt up off the floor.

"I was testing an electric chisel for my sculpting project, and I had the genius idea of attaching a bag to the tool—it says that you can do that, but of course I didn't have the right kind of bag and foolishly assumed any bag would work. I tested the chisel out on some wood, and wouldn't you know it? It exploded," Rachelle explained quickly. Standing up, she laughed again. "I even thought 'this might explode' as I hooked it up." Rachelle sighed. "Ah, all's well that ends well, I guess."

"I guess so," Emma said, brushing sawdust off her aunt's shoulders.

"How's your Saturday going?" Rachelle asked, opening the kitchen window. "You've been locked away in your room all day."

"Sorry," Emma said, pulling the broom off its hook by the refrigerator. "But there is some good news."

"Oh?"

"Nikki messaged me. She's definitely found out about her powers; I was actually wondering if I could find out who her mentor is, I might be able to—"

"Emma," Rachelle said in her motherly tone.

"I wouldn't interfere…exactly." Emma leaned on the broom. "I just thought if I could at least have a vision and maybe see—"

Rachelle put her hands on Emma's shoulders. "Now I know you're worried, and you're just trying to help, but you have to remember the laws we have for magick are there for a reason."

"And they have to find their mentors on their own." Emma groaned.

"That is the way it works," Rachelle said.

"But why?" Emma asked.

"Oh, dear," Rachelle said. "I think Grandma might be able to answer that better than I can."

Emma raised an eyebrow and frowned.

"Oh, fine," Rachelle said, brushing bits of sawdust off the two stools at the island. She sat on one and patted the other.

Emma leaned the broom against the island and sat.

"You know how Grandma talks about how magick can be used, but it's also wild?"

Emma nodded.

"Well," Rachelle said as she brushed sawdust from the island top. "Each magickal being must build his or her own relationship with magick and part of that is the seeking of a mentor. If a mentor, for good or ill, is pushed onto a magickal being not ready to be taught, or unwilling to be taught, the wild nature of magick can turn…" She paused, looking for the right word, "rebellious."

"So, they have to find their own mentors because they have to be receptive to being taught?"

Rachelle nodded and added, "Otherwise their relationship with magick will be as useful as that of a harsh master with a wild horse. Everyone will just ended up bloodied and covered in mud."

Emma groaned.

"I know its hard," Rachelle said, hugging her niece.

Emma sighed, breathing in the smell of her aunt: sawdust from the bag explosion, and geranium oil for her eczema.

"Now, how is Nelly doing?"

"I'm not sure," Emma said, pulling back from the hug. "She's very private. I mean, we've been in the same science class for the past six years, but she just barely noticed me in chem class the other day, and I sit right next to her." Emma sighed again. This was not the first time she had gone unnoticed, unremembered. In fact, most of her life had been this way.

"Maybe she needs a friend," Rachelle said.

"She's only had one friend for as long as I've known her."

"True as that may be," Rachelle said. "Given what she's going through, I'm sure she needs a friend."

# Chapter Five

## Sunday, December 9th

Dec. 9, 08

Alone and sitting on her bed, Nelly stared at her blank journal page with the date hovering expectantly in the left-hand corner. I wish I could say somewhere in the last 24 hours, she had accepted her change and was now thrilled with being a mermaid, but that would be a lie. The truth was she hadn't really ever learned to process feelings; she usually sweated through them, outwardly working as she inwardly shoved any unwanted feelings into her darkest parts where no one would find them.

But this could not be sweated through. This could not be shoved down. This demanded to be seen, and Nelly was lost, spinning in uncertainty and heartache. The closest she had come to acknowledging what was happening was looking 'mermaid' up on the internet; her search had produced a bunch of artistic renderings of women that were half fish and had long flowing locks, several ads for mermaid-themed television shows, and a wiki-page which told her all about the mythical creatures. Nelly hadn't bothered with the page; clearly whatever information they had compiled on mythical mermaids would be pointless since she was very real.

"Hey." Jo stood at Nelly's open door. "Writing about your boyfriend? What's the current one's name?" Jo waggled her eyebrows. Though only two years apart, the sisters could not have been more different. Where Nelly was at most a mere inch over five feet tall and rather square and strong, Jo was a mere inch shy of six feet, lean and mostly leg. She had bright eyes and dark hair, which she always sprayed with UV protectant because, while Jo liked surfing and the sun, she didn't like how brassy it made her hair. Nelly could not have cared less.

Nelly sighed. "It *was* Andy Wilson. Current status: single."

"Ooo, he's the gorgeous one, isn't he?"

"He's pretty alright." Nelly scoffed and added, murmuring, "Pretty like a devil." She breathed deeply. "After Andy cheated, I swore off guys for a bit. They're all liars anyway."

"Ugh," Jo said, making a face. "What a jerk. Well, you can do better. I know there's someone amazing out there for you."

Nelly gave a half-hearted smile. "Thanks."

"Sure." Jo pulled at her skirt, which was just long enough to cover the subject matter.

"What is it?" Nelly recognized the nervousness in her younger sister.

"So…you should call Wyatt." Jo tried to play it cool, but her poker face was notoriously bad. She groaned and rolled her eyes. "At least pick up when he calls you. He's been a real pest."

Nelly narrowed her eyes. That wasn't making Jo nervous. Wyatt pestered her all the time; he was practically Jo's older brother. "And?" Nelly pushed.

"And…" Jo pulled at her skirt again. "Where have you been? Like you never miss dawn patrol, and you haven't been in the lineup since your birthday."

"I just—" It was Nelly's turn to fidget nervously. "I haven't felt good."

Jo scoffed. "Oh right, Miss I'll-surf-unless-I'm-dead gets the sniffles and takes a week off? Yeah, I don't think so." Jo stood akimbo.

"I don't know why it even matters," Nelly shot back defensively.

Jo was speechless for a moment. Finally, she managed to say, "Are you serious right now?" Her arms dropped to her sides.

Nelly rubbed her eyes.

"You don't want to talk to me, fine," Jo said, putting up a hand. "But Wyatt isn't the only one who's noticed."

Nelly looked at Jo. "What's that supposed to mean?"

Jo fidgeted with the hem of her skirt and spat out, "Whitney is telling everyone that you chickened out of the Christmas Eve Invitational because you're scared she's going to beat you, so you're pretending you're sick again, like last year."

There it was. Nelly was sure Jo expected an explosion from her, because in the past, that's exactly what would have followed, but yesterday's discovery had changed more about Nelly than her legs. That deep hollowness carved its way through Nelly's chest. She swallowed the lump building in her throat and asked, "Does anyone believe her?"

"Not really," Jo admitted. "At least, not right now, but the longer you're missing from the lineup…" Jo shrugged.

Nelly nodded silently.

"Dad's noticed," Jo added. "I mean, he didn't say anything exactly. He just asked if I knew what was up with you."

Nelly nodded again.

"Well," Jo said, popping a knuckle in her hand. "You should talk to Wyatt at least." She watched Nelly for a second before leaving the room.

Nelly could hear Tom ask Jo if things were okay.

"She's always talked to you more than me," Jo said, her voice echoing through the hallway. There was the familiar crunch of gravel as a car pulled up in the driveway and a short honk. "That's Grace. We're going to the movies."

"Have fun," Tom said. This was unusual behavior; Tom typically asked which movie, which theater, how long the movie was, when she'd be back, who all was going, who was driving, did they need a ride, and may have even mentioned the skirt—but today, he just let Jo go.

As she sat in her room, Nelly considered telling him. Maybe Tom could help. Maybe he would know someone who could—and maybe he wouldn't. Maybe he'd think she was a freak. Tom's track record wasn't on his side. When Nelly had gotten her first period—well, she had been sure he was going to pass out. Practically every girl went through menstruation, but how many became mermaids? She'd have to tell him eventually, though. Nelly terrible at keeping secrets.

The phone rang a few times and then went to the machine. Nelly walked out into the living room.

"Hey Tom, this is Frank. Just calling officially from Surf, Wear, and Tear," said a man to the machine. "Jo's board is all cleaned up and ready to go. You can come by and pick it up any time you want. Oh, and tell that prodigy surfer of yours to make her way back to the lineup. She's missed. Okay, well, call me when you want to pick up the board. Later, Tom."

Nelly walked around the back rooms. "Dad?"

No answer.

"Dad?" she called a little louder, poking her head through a kitchen window, which looked out to the garage.

Still no answer.

Taped to the front door was a note. Nelly ripped it off and read, "Gone surfing. Will be back around 5. Dad."


December 9, 2008

I don't know what to do. Emma told me to practice—oh yeah, I told her. Anyway, my attempts have all ended in messes, some worse than others. No one has died. Yet.

I wish I knew someone who could help. I mean, I know I know Emma, but someone like me. I want someone who understands my magic—or magick I guess. I need help from another witch.


Nikki heard someone knock on the door; she listened for a moment, and when she heard Margret answer the door and start talking with whomever it was, Nikki kept writing.

I wonder if there's a cousin somewhere who knows something. If I could just find someone

"Nikki," Margret called from the kitchen.

"Coming," Nikki called back. Sighing, she closed her journal and walked into the kitchen.

Magret was standing there, arms crossed, and lips pursed. Next to Margret was an older woman. The older woman was in her late seventies. Her clothes made her look like she was on fire: bright reds, rich yellows, and shimmering golds, all of it long and flowing. Her blonde-gray hair sat in a loose bun at the top of her head. This woman was well-traveled with the wisdom of life etched on her face.

"Uh," Nikki said. "Hi." The woman's bright blue eyes seemed familiar to Nikki for some reason (a reason which I'm sure you've already figured out, so let's see how long it takes Nikki).

"Merry meet, dear," the older woman said to Nikki. "I'm—"

"Care to explain this?" Margret spoke to Nikki, while simultaneously putting her hand up to the woman.

"What—wait—I don't—" Nikki fumbled.

"Don't be silly, Mags. She doesn't know who I am. How can she explain anything?" said the older woman.

"Don't call me that." Margret bristled, crossing her arms.

"Nikki," the woman said. "You summoned me."

"Summoned?" Nikki repeated.

"That's impossible," Margret said.

"Who is—I'm sorry." Nikki turned from Margret to the woman. "Who are you?"

"Why would you call her if you don't know who she is?" Margret asked.

"But I didn't—"

"Of course you didn't *call* me, dear," the old woman explained. "You *summoned* me. Don't you want help with your powers?"

"I—Yes," Nikki said, stunned. "But how did you—"

"She doesn't have powers," Margret cut in, whispering the last word.

"Yes I do," Nikki said. "I told you."

"Nonsense." Margret dismissed Nikki with a wave of her hand. "She can't. It's impossible; Rand stripped them after she was born." Margret crossed her arms again as she said this to the woman.

"Wait, you knew?" Nikki rounded on her mom. "You knew the whole time? I told you, and you didn't say anything! Why didn't you tell me I'm magickal?"

"Keep your voice down," Margret hissed through clenched teeth. "I didn't tell you because it's immaterial as you are most certainly not magical."

"I am," Nikki almost shouted. Seeing Margret's glare, Nikki dropped her voice. "I told you! You never listen. Mom, I summoned a whole pony for crying out loud!"

"Alive?" the woman asked.

Nikki nodded.

"You've got a lot of power, kiddo," the woman said, clapping and laughing.

"You did this to her," Margret spat at the woman.

"Enough," the woman said to Margret in what could only be described as a mom voice.

Immediately, Nikki knew exactly why this woman was so familiar. "You're my dad's mom, aren't you?" Nikki asked. The intonation of that 'enough' was one Nikki had heard from her father her whole life—usually when she hadn't been listening to her mom and her dad had to step in.

"Yes, dear," the woman said. "My name is Kaitlyn McKenzie. Most of my friends call me Kait; you can, too, if you like."

Nikki's brows furrowed. "But shouldn't you be Rodrigues?"

"Oh no," Kait said. "We keep our maiden names." Her eyes twinkled.


9 December 2008

Christmas is in sixteen days. New Year's is in twenty-three. It all feels so close.

I haven't had any visions lately. It's strange. Usually I have at least one a day. I'm trying to distract myself with figuring out Christmas presents for Rachelle and Grandma.

Speaking of Grandma, I'm still worried she pushed Nelly too much. Grandma's used to the days when you told people what you knew. Of course, life was different in the circus. She could tell people they'd be eaten by a lion and not only would they thank her for the "entertainment," they'd pay her for it, too.


Emma chuckled to herself, leaving her journal open to dry as she cleaned her quill's nib. For now, she could do nothing more, except wait. She looked around her room. It wasn't a particularly large room, but it was beautifully Emma: eclectic, bold jewel tones, beads, and fluffy pillows. Three of her walls had been painted a deliciously dark teal. The fourth wall, the one behind her bed, was golden rod and covered with a hanging mixture of fairy lights and clear beads. Emma had several pictures hanging in her room. All of the pictures had frames, and each frame (a treasure found while thrifting) had been painted in varying shades of purple and blue.

Most of the images featured Emma's mother, Amy, a woman with wild curly blonde hair, the same eyes as Emma, and the same mouth as Ethel. Amy was the only constant in the pictures; Emma's age and the setting varied wildly: Amy and Emma (age 2) in Maine with a lighthouse and another little girl in the background, Amy and Emma (age 3) laying in a wildflower field in Vermont, Amy and Emma (age 5) playing at a lake in Michigan, Amy and Emma (age 6) at the White Cliffs of Dover in England, Amy and Emma (age 9) at the Eiffel Tower in France, Amy and Emma (age 10) in front of a cabin in Montana. There were a few pictures of Amy alone and only one photo of her pregnant with

Emma. The rest of the pictures were a combination of snapshots (from favorite trips Emma had gone on with her aunt and grandmother) and artwork, some Emma's, some she had bought on her travels.

Nearly every piece of furniture in Emma's room had been thrifted by Rachelle. Aside from the desk and bed, Emma only had two other pieces of furniture in her room, a small nightstand, and a vintage dresser, which stood next to the door. Above the dresser was a gold-framed photo of Amy and Emma from Emma's 11th birthday. It was the last picture they took together. Amy died seven months later.

Sighing, Emma pulled out her sticker-covered laptop and logged into her email. She had six emails, most were junk, but there was one that looked particularly interesting from Nikki.

"'Sorry to dump all this on you,'" Emma muttered, reading aloud. "'I literally have no one else I can ask, other than my mom, but as she's currently pretending I don't even exist, I doubt I'd get much from her….except maybe a swift kick. Kidding. Mostly.'" Emma chuckled at Nikki's ability to crack a joke amid a freak out. Emma finished reading Nikki's email (which recounted the meeting of Kait), scanned it a second time to make sure she hadn't misunderstood, and then shouted, "YES!"

"What is it?" Rachelle called from the kitchen.

Emma hopped up and ran over to Rachelle. "Nikki! She found her mentor by her own free will and choice!"

"Wonderful!" Rachelle clapped. "So when do we invite them for dinner?"

"Good question," Emma said, returning to her open laptop. She quickly scrolled over the email again before saying, "Nikki said her Grandma Kait didn't give her any contact information or tell her anything really except that they'd need a space for practicing. As far as I can tell," she added, still scrolling, "Nikki has no way of contacting her."

"Wait, Kait?" Rachelle scratched her ear and muttered to herself, "It couldn't—she couldn't be—well, actually, I suppose—"

"What are you talking about?"

"Do you know—is Nikki talking about Kait McKenzie?"

"I don't know," Emma admitted. "She didn't give me a last name. Why? What do you know?"

"Of course," Rachelle said, palming her forehead. "I don't know why I didn't make the connection before. I always forget witches keep their maiden names. It makes tracking family lines almost impossible—which actually, I think is the point."

"So who is Kait McKenzie?" Emma pressed.

"Right," Rachelle said and snapped her fingers. "Kait is a witch from one of the oldest magickal families this side of the equator. Their magickal line goes back ages, thousands of years. Very respectable. Do you know if—did Nikki say where Kait was going?"

"No, she did mention that Kait has a friend in the ar—oh!" Emma said as it dawned on her.

If the Kait Rachelle was talking about was, in fact, the same Kait Nikki was talking about, and if Rachelle knew this Kait, then that meant…

Rachelle smiled and said, "I know exactly where to find her."

# Chapter Six

## Monday, December 10th

December 10, 2008

    This morning's run did nothing for my restlessness. I still feel ready to jump out of my skin. It's like I have a swarm of bees following me around.

    In other news, watching Kam meet Grandma yesterday was so cute. He asked her a million questions (mostly about what Dad was like when he was a kid). Grandma was super clever answering him but not saying a word about magick the whole time.

    Mom, on the other hand, is blowing this whole Grandma thing out of proportion. She changed both the landline number and her cell number. Not that she bothered telling me this. I found out when I tried calling both (I need to know if I'm picking Kam up today), and neither could be "completed as dialed." Now, I don't know my home phone number, or if I'm supposed to pick up Kam or not. I told him I'd stop by anyway.

    French is starting.

Nikki shoved her journal in her backpack and pulled out her textbook, wishing they were like normal schools with normal students who got to use lockers. But who was she kidding? Normal students? She and Emma, and she suspected Nelly, were as far from normal as normal got.

"Bonjour classe! Avez-vous eu du plaisir avec vos devoirs?" Madame Fleur came into the class, her red scarf flying behind her.

"Oui," the class said in unison.

"Voyons en pratique nos verbes. Maintenant, répétez après moi," Madame Fleur said. They conjugated verbs for the next half hour. Madame Fleur then paired them up and had them practice saying their favorite fruits and vegetables and why they liked them.

All the while, Nikki felt the buzzing, the restlessness that hovered right under her skin. Eventually, she'd realize this feeling was her magick trying to communicate to her, but for right now, she had no idea that something was very wrong.

Dec. 10, 08

Okay, so obviously I have to keep this thing a secret. I can't tell anyone about it ever. They'd either think 1-I'm lying to get attention, 2-I can't handle the pressure of going pro, or 3-I've gone totally nuts, and I'll get locked up in the happy farm.

I've waited my whole life for two things: going pro and becoming an adult. Now both of those are totally shot. This is the worst.

"Class," Mrs. Hammond said, eyeballing Nelly. "Please turn your books to page 203."

Nelly looked at her chemistry book, flipping through the pages until she found 203. They were looking at formulas of some kind, but it might as well have been Egyptian hieroglyphs for how much she understood.

A small piece of paper poked her left elbow; Nelly turned and saw Emma pushing the folded paper over to her. Nelly glanced at Mrs. Hammond, who was writing on the board and then carefully, unfolded the paper.

Hey, are you okay? You seem stressed out.

Nelly let out a dry laugh. She grimaced at Emma and slid the paper back without writing anything. A moment later, it came back. When Nelly looked at Emma, Emma smiled encouragingly before returning her attention to Mrs. Hammond at the board. Nelly looked at the paper.

I found some cool information on Jess Pedersen. I think it might help you sort out what's going on.

How is information on some dead person supposed to help me? How did you even find anything?

All I can say for now is history repeats itself.

Nelly glanced at Emma, who smiled and continued with her chemistry notes. Nelly gritted her teeth. Her heart felt the icy fingers of fear encircling it as she wondered if Emma knew she was a mermaid. Her brain told her, logically, it was impossible; she had only found out two days ago, so how could Emma know?

For the rest of class, Nelly kept her eyes focused on either the board or her book, and though Mrs. Hammond thought Nelly was the epitome of attentiveness, Nelly's thoughts were far from chemistry. She was wrestling with this secret, this secret that burned inside of her, this secret that demanded attention. The more she thought about it, the more she knew it was not the type of thing to share with every Tom, Dick, and Harry; although there was one Tom she was going to have to tell sooner or later.


10 December 2008

Nelly seemed pretty nervous in chem today. I wish I could tell her everything I know right now, but I have to time it and frame it correctly. Jess Pedersen was a fascinating woman. She didn't have any unfinished business, so I had to get a hold of her the old fashioned way. Turns out Nelly is one mermaid in a long generation of them—but they've kept their secret so well only her line knows about it. They never even told their spouses unless they were one hundred percent positive the kids got it too, and sometimes not even then.


Emma looked up from her journal and saw Nikki walking towards her. "Oh hi." She closed her journal as Nikki sat down in the desk next to hers. They had a few minutes until history started. "How was your weekend?"

Nikki widened her eyes and cocked her head with a crooked smile.

Emma smiled. "That bad?"

"My mom is pretending I don't exist," Nikki said, putting her bag down and adjusting her black yoga pants. "My long lost grandma left me no contact information, and I have no idea if I'm supposed to pick Kam up today because my mom changed all the phone numbers."

"Well," Emma said. "I can't help with your mom or Kam, but I do know where your grandma is."

"You do?" Nikki leaned closer.

Emma grinned and waggled her eyebrows. "Apparently, your grandma and my grandma go way back."

Nikki audibly sighed. "Duh. I should have known. I mean how many—" She glanced around and lowered her voice to a whisper. "How many magickal little old ladies are there around here?"

"More than you'd think." Emma whispered back.

Before Nikki could ask Emma exactly what she meant, the bell rang, and the last stragglers filed in, including Nelly, who came in and sat next to Wyatt on the other side of the classroom. He leaned over and started whispering to her, but she waved him off as Mr. Miranda started class.

"All right, class, today is information exchange day. Here's what I want you to do." Mr. Miranda walked around the class passing out worksheets. "Move into your groups, and answer these questions." He handed Emma three worksheets before moving on to the next student.

Students shuffled around the classroom, some grumbling, some chatting. Chairs scraped across the floor as desks were moved into groups, and finally our three girls were seated together. Emma passed the papers out to Nikki and Nelly and then pulled out her purple horn-rimmed glasses. The girls read over the questions.

1. What is this person's story?
2. What can we learn from this story?
3. What is one interesting thing about this person that you've discovered?
4. Do you see any similarities between this person and his/her relation in your group?

"Well, these don't look too hard to answer," Emma said to Nikki and Nelly. "Who wants to go first?"

"I can. So question one," Nikki said. "Madam Ortega told me about how she was born into the circus—her mom was an acrobat and her dad was an accountant. Apparently, her great-grandfather won the circus in a card game."

"Is that true?" Nelly asked.

"Yes," Emma said, grinning. "I guess it was a pretty serious game of go-fish."

Nikki chuckled. "Anyway, so when she was like seven, she saw this girl who looked different. Madam Ortega described her as 'slightly transparent,'" Nikki said, reading from her notes. "The girl needed help sending a message to her family. Madam Ortega found the family that night and gave them the message, and the girl was able to pass on. So, question two—"

"Stop. Rewind," Nelly said, putting a hand up. "Pass on? Pass on where?"

"I don't know. Whatever comes after death, I guess," Nikki said.

Nelly looked at Emma. "Your grandma can see dead people? Like creepy actually dead people?"

"Yes," Emma said. "And no."

Nelly raised her eyebrows.

"Yes, she can see the actually dead. No, they're not creepy. They usually look just like they did in life, except they're a sort of transparent and glow a bit," Emma explained.

"Uh, okay." Nelly squished her face together as she composed herself. "Which part of 'transparent' and 'glowing' isn't creepy? I mean—"

"I think she means they're not gruesome," Nikki cut in. "Besides, from the way Madam Ortega told the story, the girl wasn't creepy, just sad."

"Fair," Nelly conceded, rubbing her arm. She was beginning to experience the sensing of other magicks, but of course, she didn't realize this; Nelly simply blamed the sensation on general unease and her increased irritability due to severe lack of surfing.

"Anyway, question two," Nikki said. "Well, I think we can learn to help. I mean, Madam Ortega didn't know the girl at all, but she still helped her. Question three? I think it's super interesting that she can see auras."

"What are those?" Nelly asked.

"Right, so…" Nikki said, scratching her head. "They're people's energy, I think." She glanced at her notes again. "Madam Ortega told me the parents had gray auras because they were overwhelmed with grief, but their kids had a mix of gray and gold because there was some grief but also some excitement because they were at the circus."

Nelly nodded and pursed her lips.

"So," Nikki said. "Last question," she briefly looked at Emma, who nodded. Nikki leaned closer to Nelly and said, "Emma is a medium, too."

Nelly leaned back and looked at Emma with an expression that suggested Nelly had been informed Emma could spontaneously explode. "Are you serious?" Nelly whispered.

Emma nodded, looking more serious and less whimsical than usual.

Nelly leaned forward. "Wait, like you for reals see dead people?"

Emma nodded again. She leaned towards Nelly and added, "It's not an all the time thing. Just as I'm needed. It's kind of like being a volunteer firefighter."

"That's heavy stuff," Nelly said, her jaw relaxing a little.

"Wait," Nikki said, also leaning in. "We're not really putting that on the paper, though, are we?"

"Let's not," Emma said. "Put down that I'm into weird stuff, too."

"So who wants to go next?" Nikki asked, as she scribbled in their edited answers.

"I'll go," Nelly said quickly. She was very much a rip off the Band-Aid type girl, and at this precise moment, she was hoping to get her part over with as fast as possible and ditch the rest of the class; she was definitely queasy enough to go to the nurse's office. "So, Aisling O'Crean lived a super long time ago. Like the late sixteen-hundreds. She and her family lived in Salem, Massachusetts—hence '1692, MA' on the photo. MA. Massachusetts."

"Makes sense," Nikki said. "I don't know why I didn't see that."

Nelly nodded. "So, I found out she was tried and found guilty of witchcraft. I found a book that had a little more information. I guess after she was, uh…" Nelly looked up at Nikki before she continued, "burned at the stake. Her family—her husband, two daughters, and a son—all moved to Ireland. They had originally come from there for a better life, but after the trials, they just went back home." She shrugged, as though it might take away the sting of this news.

"I guess we know why she was the black sheep of the family," Nikki said, understanding more than ever what Aisling must have gone through. "Did it say whether her family knew she was a witch?"

"No." Nelly frowned slightly. "Some local girl saw Aisling milking the family cow and heard her whispering weird words. The girl said that all the other cows had run dry, but the O'Crean's cow still made milk. Pretty nuts, huh?"

"No kidding," Emma said.

"So question two—we can learn, um," Nelly said. "Not to milk our cows in public?"

"That works for me," Emma said.

"Or that if you're going to do magick, you better make sure you don't have an audience," Nikki suggested.

"Uh, yeah. That works, too." Nelly shifted in her seat. "Question three…I think it was interesting, but mostly sad, how her family moved all the way from Ireland to have a better life, but ended up having a worse one and having to go back. I mean I'm sure Ireland is awesome, but it just blows that Aisling died, and they ended up at square one anyway."

"Last question," Emma said, pointing to number four.

"Um, unless you're a witch, too, I think the thing that is most common with you guys is the way you look," Nelly said to Nikki. "Right down to the braid."

Nikki took a deep breath, ready to tell Nelly everything.

"Okay, my turn," Emma cut in, giving Nikki a look that said 'Not yet.' "I found out Jess Pedersen's story goes a little beyond what your mom told you, Nelly. Apparently she had a baby nine months after she came ashore. There was nothing odd about it. Like you said, Jess and her husband had been married before he left Denmark, so it's natural to assume that when he found her they, uh, *celebrated* their reunion sometime within a few weeks of her coming back."

"Yeah, is that it?" Nelly grunted. She hadn't noticed Nikki's breath or Emma's odd behavior. She was too consumed with the kaleidoscope of butterflies growing in her stomach.

"No, actually," Emma said. "Once she had the baby, her husband passed away. Apparently he caught pneumonia, or something like it. He only got to hold the baby long enough for the two of them to pick a name for her: Rán. Her father picked it. According to my research, he said that she just looked like she belonged in the water, and Jess agreed."

"How do you know this?" Nelly asked, white-knuckling the edges of her chair. Her sudden suspicion of Emma's methods did little to calm her queasiness. Emma *had* just admitted to talking to dead people.

"The priest at the little girl's christening kept accounts of all the children he blessed and any story he heard the parents tell. Apparently the father was on his deathbed, so they christened the child in the house instead of in the church. It sounds like the priest overheard Jess and her husband talking about the baby's name," Emma said.

"Did the priest say anything else?" Nikki asked.

"Just that Rán seemed like an odd name for a little girl."

"It kind of is weird," Nikki said.

"I thought so too, so I did a little research into it. Both Jess and her husband were Danish, right? They must have grown up hearing about Norse mythology, kind of like we grow up hearing about Greek mythology—you know, Apollo, Hercules, Zeus, Aphrodite, and Athena?" Emma said.

"Make sure you're answering all the questions," said Mr. Miranda as he peeked over *What Hath God Wrought*.

Emma peered down at the sheet.

"You're still telling her story," Nikki prompted. "So you were doing research, what'd you find?"

Nelly grimaced and nodded. The butterflies had turned into a swarm of bees, vibrating and pinching. He leg bounced madly.

"Rán is a Norse sea goddess," Emma said.

"My ancestor was a goddess?" Nelly grunted.

"No, she was named after a goddess." Emma scratched question one out. "What we can learn from her story—which there is more of, but I'll tell you later—is that names carry a lot of meaning. No mother names her daughter after a goddess without good reason, especially a goddess whose name translates to 'theft and robbery,'" Emma said matter-of-factly.

"What's something interesting you learned about her?" Nikki asked.

"Well, rumor has it that Jess' daughter, Rán, was not completely human," Emma said, lowering her voice. "I followed the lineage right down to you, Nelly, and all along the way there are rumors." Emma glanced around. "The families themselves were always guarded and secretive, but the neighbors talked."

"What did they say? The neighbors, the rumors?" Nikki asked.

Emma spoke quietly, but quickly, having noticed the greenish tinge to Nelly's pained expression. "The rumors spoke mostly of the children, children that seem to be more at home in the water than on land, children that weren't entirely human, children that were mermaids."

Nelly swallowed, and then said, "Well, they're just rumors. Mermaids don't even exist." She smashed her notebook back in her bag, got up, and ran out.


December 10, 2008 (later)

I feel like the tee up to a bad joke. Emma basically told Nelly that her ancestor was a mermaid—Nelly freaked. Who can blame her? Meanwhile I'm over here wondering how a psychic-medium, a witch, and a mermaid all got put in a group project together.

I'm waiting for Emma. We're going to head over to her grandma's place and see my grandma.

Nikki's phone buzzed. She looked at it: Kam's School. "Hello."

"Hey, Nikki," Kam squeaked out from the other side of the phone. "It's me. So we start our long practices today. I won't be done until six."

"Wow," Nikki said. "Do you want me to bring you something to eat?"

"No, that's okay. Mr. Melkin doesn't like us to eat because it gets our instruments gross. Will you pick me up at six, oh and can Jody get a ride home, too?"

"Sure," Nikki said, mentally making a note to take them both to grab a bite after practice. She couldn't understand why Kam sounded so excited. She had sat in on those practices; that band teacher yelled, a lot. "See you then."

"Okay, bye," Kam said and hung up.

Nikki set an alarm on her phone as Emma walked up to the car and hopped in the passenger seat.

"Are we waiting for Kam?" Emma asked, buckling her seatbelt.

"No," Nikki said. "He's got band practice until six."

Emma grimaced.

"That's what I said." Nikki laughed, shrugging. "He sounded excited about it, but I always knew he was a weird kid. I wonder if he suspects how weird I am."

"Well," Emma said. "There's a good chance he's your kind of weird, too."

"So question about that," Nikki said, backing out of the school parking lot. "My mom said something about my dad getting rid of my powers, but like obviously my dad didn't get rid of them since I have them, but why did I never know?"

"Your dad couldn't actually get rid of your powers, so he likely bound them— meaning you couldn't use them. He probably bound them when you were pretty young, so odds are you were too little to retain any memories of magick."

"So why do I have magick now?" Nikki waited at the stop sign.

"When you became eighteen, the bind was lifted to give you the opportunity to choose your fate. It is in your hands now."

"Hypothetically, if I didn't want my powers, could my dad bind them again?" Nikki asked not meeting Emma's eye.

"Nope," Emma said simply. "You would have to relinquish them. That's why the bind exists—that way one day, when the witch is ready, she can face her powers. To relinquish your powers is to give them up completely. You'd have no way of ever getting them back," Emma said. "It's not a decision to take lightly."

"I can see that," Nikki said. "Based on my mom's reaction, I'm guessing she didn't want to tell me and told Dad not to tell me."

The rest of the drive, they talked about the very real possibility of Nelly being a mermaid, pulling up to Ethel's house just as Emma started explaining some of the differences between fictional and non-fictional mermaids. Upon opening the door, the girls were greeted by Kait, who was dressed in soft yellows and oranges.

"Merry meet, little witch!" Kait hugged Nikki.

"Hi," Nikki said. "This is Emma, Grandma. Emma this is—"

"We've met." Kait pulled Emma in for a hug as she let go of Nikki.

"Wait, what?" Nikki said.

"Ethel had Rachelle and Emma over for dinner yesterday, and I got to meet this lovely lady," Kait said, keeping an arm over Emma, who looked as comfortable with Kait as she did with her own grandma. "They also filled me in on a few things, and we need to talk. Your need to train is much more important than I first thought."

"What do you mean?" Nikki said looked from Kait to Emma and then back again.

Kait turned to Emma. "What all have you told her?"

"Not much," Emma admitted.

Kait nodded and then looked beyond Nikki at the door, as though expecting someone else to come in after her. "Where's the third?"

"She hasn't fully accepted her powers," Emma said.

"Well," Kait said, giving Emma's shoulder a little squeeze before letting go. "We'll have to make do with what we've got. Hopefully she comes around soon."

"What are you talking about?" Nikki asked.

"Take a seat," Kait said, gesturing to the dining room table before she disappeared into the kitchen.

Ethel came in almost as soon as Kait left; she carried a tray, which held four teacups, a pot of tea, and containers of honey, and cream. The girls sat, and Ethel poured the tea. "Hello, girls," she said. "Emma, why don't you fill Nikki in while I help Kait with the sandwiches."

Emma nodded and took a small breath, which she blew out of her mouth quickly. "Okay, so you know how I'm psychic?"

"Yeah," Nikki said. "That's the part that sees the future, right?"

"Yes, and technically, psychics can see the fabric of time: the past, the present, or the future. Most of us see just one, and I see the future, but I only have visions that I will actually be there to witness. Anyway, eleven years ago, I had a vision. It was kind of fuzzy, which made it harder to decipher, but there were a few things I saw very clearly."

"Which were?" Nikki pressed.

"Two teenage girls standing with me, streamers, and fire. I also heard laughter."

"And I'm one of the two girls?" Nikki asked.

"Yes. I was seven when I had the vision, so I didn't actually know you at the time, but I've had it several times since then. It's always exactly the same. I had it again in October, and I recognized you."

"So that's why you and Rachelle were talking about telling me," Nikki said, connecting conversations.

Emma nodded, adding, "I realized Nelly was one of the girls our freshman year of high school."

"So she is *definitely* a mermaid?" Nikki asked.

"Yup."

"This is wild," Nikki said, shaking her head. "I just—give me a second." She stood and started gesticulating and pacing around the space in front of the door and table. "You, me, and Nelly?" She paced. "A psychic-medium, a witch, and a mermaid?" She paced. "Something with standing, streamers, laughter, and fire?" Nikki paused her pacing. "So, what now?"

"In my vision, there were also the fuzzy bits, parts that weren't clear, but over the years, I've been able to piece things together. I think we're meant to stop…" Emma paused, looking for the right word. She shook her head and continued, "I don't know, something. I heard one other thing very clearly: screaming. Lots of screaming. Part of it feels like I'm watching everything happen through thick fog, but then parts of it sound like I'm underwater. I only get brief flashes of clarity. It feels dark. It feels like—" Emma swallowed. "I mean, I remember when I first had it, I thought I died."

"Died?" Nikki squeaked.

"It fades to black, and it's dark, but it's not actually dark it just…I don't know. I was only seven the first time. It was terrifying."

"No kidding." Nikki pushed her braid to her back and started pacing again. "So when does this happen?"

"Good question," Emma said. "My best guess is around Christmas or maybe New Year's. Streamers could indicate a celebration of some kind."

"But it could be any time?" Nikki said, leaning on the table with both hands. "I mean, it could be someone's birthday party? All you really know is that the three of us will be there, and there's streamers and fire, right?"

Emma sighed. "Yes and no. The thing about my visions is that they're fluid. Sometimes they happen exactly as I see them, but sometimes they don't happen like I saw them at all. Sometimes I'm supposed to help it happen or stop it from happening all together, but other times I'm not supposed to do anything. I just act as a witness and watch."

"Sheesh," Nikki said. "How do you know the difference?"

"Skill," said Ethel coming into the dining room and carrying two plates, each holding a large bacon, lettuce, and tomato sandwich, sliced cucumber, chopped carrots, and a generous serving of hummus; she set one plate in front of Emma, and the other in front of Nikki's empty seat. Kait followed shortly after, carrying two more plates.

"Well," Emma said, blushing slightly. "It's more like a feeling that comes with the visions. I've learned to trust myself and my instincts."

Nikki covered her face with her hands and rubbed her eyes. "You know this is insane, right?"

"Yup," Emma said, dipping a cucumber in her hummus.

Nikki smeared her hands over her face, clapped them together, and said, "So how do we train for this so we don't die?"


(later)

Can she know? I mean, she said my ancestor's daughter was a suspected mermaid and that she traced the line all the way down to me, but does that mean Emma thinks I'm a mermaid? Or does she know?

This isn't fair. This isn't how it was supposed to go. I had a plan and turning into a fish was NEVER part of the plan.


"Ugh!" Nelly chucked her journal at the wall, where it hit with a solid thud.

There was a soft knock on her door. "Hey, Nels?" Tom opened her bedroom door, tentatively. "Dinner is ready."

She groaned, and mumbled, "Okay."

"Anything you want to talk about?" Tom asked.

"Not yet. I'll be out in a sec." As Tom left, Nelly took a deep breath, shoving the cold and steely fear down. It mixed with the hot anger bubbling in her stomach. Nelly gritted her teeth and took another deep breath, holding it for a moment before blowing it out her nose. Someday she would learn to use her breath to process these feelings, not to simply push them away for later, but for today, she popped her neck and headed out to the dining room.

"Nelly!" Carrying a handful of plates and cutlery, Jo ran over to Nelly and whispered, "I don't know where you were this morning, but you missed some awesome rides. Also Whitney is telling everyone you're 100% dropping out of the next competition."

Nelly rolled her eyes as she sat down at the table.

As she finished setting the table, Jo added, "I can't keep defending you. The best defense is a good offense, so you probably ought to get out there and show her what you've got."

"Please." Nelly scoffed. "I surf better on my worst day than she does on her best."

"So you're coming tomorrow?" Jo asked as she sat down. She raised her brows.

"Hot plate coming through." Tom held a sizzling cast-iron pan filled with caramelized onions, and green and red bell peppers, sliced and deliciously blackened. He set the pan on a hot pad, which was already on the table.

"I didn't know we were having Christmas Fajitas already," Nelly said, pouring herself some juice.

"Well, I wanted to try a new seasoning on the chicken before Christmas." Tom smiled and went back for the chicken.

"So when are you telling Dad you're not surfing anymore?" Jo whispered once their dad was back in the kitchen.

"I didn't say that," Nelly shot back.

"You didn't deny it," Jo said, cocking her head to the side—an attitude move that made its sole appearance when Jo was confident in her argument.

"Why are you pestering me about this?" Nelly rearranged the bowls of diced tomatoes, sour cream, and sliced avocado on the table simply to give her hands something to do.

"Because you're being weird. Usually if you're sick enough to not surf, you have to miss school. And we still have to basically duct tape you to your bed to keep out of the ocean. So—" Jo brought up her hand and began counting with her fingers. "You miss surfing, but don't miss school, plus you seem to be doing all of it voluntarily." Jo held up three fingers. "Weird, weird, weird. Doesn't take a rocket scientist, Nels."

"Hot plate," Tom said, carrying another sizzling cast iron pan, this time filled with browned chicken that smelled heavily of cumin and chili.

"I'm starving," Nelly said.

Throughout the entire meal, Nelly successfully managed to steer the conversation away from surfing, despite Jo's many attempts to talk shop. As they were clearing up after the meal, Jo washing dishes, and Nelly putting leftovers in recycled yogurt and cool-whip containers, Tom stood at the island, wiping his cast iron pans with a paper towel and a bit of bacon grease from yesterday's breakfast. He glanced at Nelly as she determined which container would be the proper size for the leftover chicken.

Tom cleared his throat and said, "So are you thinking of getting back in the water?"

Nelly looked up, eyes wide as a kid caught in Mom's secret stash of chocolate. "Uh—well—uh, I mean…" she mumbled.

Tom smiled. He looked a little sad, but mostly affectionate. "You're not surfing anymore, are you?"

Nelly closed her eyes and shook her head, shoulders slumping.

Tom sighed and set his pan down.

"Are you mad?" Nelly asked.

Tom chuckled softly. "No, of course not," he said, moving around the island. He pulled Nelly into a hug that she gratefully accepted. "I'm disappointed. Not *in* you, but *for* you. I know how much you loved it, and you've got such talent. You've worked so hard at surfing, and I know not going pro like you planned has got to be pretty gut-wrenching." Tom released Nelly from the hug and put his hands on her shoulders so he could look at her eye to eye. "So you're really done?"

Nelly nodded again. "I mean, maybe not forever, but I definitely can't compete ever again."

Tom clicked his tongue and then said, "Your mom warned me this day would come; I'll be the first to admit I didn't believe her, but she was right. Again. Sit down a sec. I need to grab something for you." He went to his room.

Jo looked at Nelly and mouthed "What?!"

Nelly shrugged. She was just as bewildered as Jo.

Tom came back a few seconds later with a small package. "Your mom said to give this to you the day you told me you couldn't surf anymore." He handed it to Nelly.

I'm sure you've already figured out what this package is, but of course Nelly had not. To her, it simply appeared to be book-shaped; mostly, she noticed the crinkled brown paper covering the package, the long thin strip of green fishnet which was tied around it, and the shells that hung from the knot on its front.

Nelly set it on the table and hugged Tom. "Thanks for not totally freaking out," she said.

Tom chuckled again. "Well, I hope that whatever it is that keeps you from surfing doesn't stop you from following your soul, kid. Your path is there. It might not turn out the way you planned, but it'll be better than you could imagine."

"Would you have done it again?" Jo asked. She had quietly watched everything unfold from her spot in the kitchen.

"What do you mean?" Tom asked.

"Knowing now what you know, would you have still married Mom knowing you were going to lose her and have to raise us alone?" Jo asked, her voice cracking. "Is your life better than you imagined?" Tears welled in her eyes, but she fought to keep them back.

Tom stuck his arm out to her and beckoned her with his hand.

Jo came over and joined the hug.

"I would do it again in a heartbeat," Tom said. "Losing your mom was probably the hardest thing I've ever done, but she didn't leave me empty-handed." He gave each girl a squeeze. "We've had our ups and downs, but Mom is here with us, and I wouldn't trade our family for anything."

"Not even all the money in the world?" Jo said.

"Not even all the money in the world," Tom said. He kissed the top of each of his girls' heads.

Later that night, alone in her room, Nelly opened the package. It was a book, as she had suspected, but it was also the strangest book she had ever seen: it had a turquoise cover with a yellowish circle in the center. Nelly touched the circle; it was hard and carved in the middle. She would discover later it was turtle shell. She tried opening the book, but the pages seemed sealed to each other. The book would not open. Nelly suddenly remembered what Emma had said about her ancestors being secretive and knew instinctively what to do next. Nelly took the book to the bathroom and filled the tub with an inch of water. She knelt over the edge and placed the book in, partially sure it would work, partially wondering if she'd need ocean water. As soon as she submerged the book, the pages loosened, and the book popped open.

*My darling little girl,*

*If you're reading this, you've discovered our secret. It's passed down from generation to generation. I could never tell your father; there was never the right moment. Do not make the same mistakes I did. Confide in him and your sister. They are your family. They deserve to know and to be a part of your life.*

Nelly traced the words with her fingers. "Mom?"

# Chapter Seven

## Tuesday, December 11th

11 December 2008

Hallelujah! Things are moving along well: Nikki knows about her powers, has a mentor, and will begin training very soon. We are still waiting on Nelly, but I have a feeling she'll come around. But there is one giant way in which things are not well at all. I haven't had a vision since I shook Kam's hand on Friday. Grandma seems to think it's a result of not meditating as often as I should, but I feel blocked. I feel blind, and even though I can't explain why, it feels intentional.

Emma shook her head and sighed. "I'm being silly," she mumbled to herself as she put her journal away. Since Kam had Christmas concert rehearsals for the next two weeks, the girls had decided to continue going to Ethel's after school. Emma waited by Nikki's car trying to talk herself out of her seemingly irrational gut instinct, which is something one must never do, but as Emma was still only 18 years old, she had not learned this important lesson yet.

"Hey," Nikki said, coming up to the car. "Sorry I'm late."

"It's alright," Emma said. "So," she added as Nikki unlocked the car. "Um, I have something to tell you." She sat down in the passenger seat.

"More?" Nikki said, fastening her seatbelt.

"Technically," Emma said, "less."

As she backed out of her parking spot, Nikki glanced at Emma quizzically. "What do you mean?"

"I mean I haven't seen anything in days," Emma said. "Which I know doesn't seem like a big deal. It's just—I don't know…"

"Is it possible that this is a 'no news is good news' thing?" Nikki asked.

Emma barked out a hollow laugh. "I wish, but I've never experienced anything like this. I mean, I know it might sound dramatic, but I feel literally blind."

"How many visions do you usually have a day?"

"At minimum? One. On average? Three to five," Emma said.

"Holy cow. That's like thirty visions a week," Nikki said, gaping.

"They're not long or super impressive," Emma admitted. "I see mostly small things."

"Small things like how most of what we see is normal, average day-to-day stuff and not massive historical events every day?"

"Exactly."

Nikki pulled into Ethel's driveway and parked. The girls went into the house without knocking; Ethel had told Nikki she was as welcome as Emma to come in any time.

Kait and Ethel were deep in discussion seated next to each other on the closest of the couches. The older women looked up when the girls walked through the open door.

"Merry Meet, girls," Kait said, standing up.

"Are you hungry? Do you need anything before we get started?" Ethel asked as she, too, stood.

"No," Emma said, hugging her grandmother. The two started towards the kitchen but stopped abruptly.

Hugging Kait, Nikki said, "Let's get to work." She and Kait looked at Ethel and Emma, who both had their eyes fixed on the wall.

"What is it?" Kait asked.

Emma extended her hand behind her as she took a slow step backwards. Nikki reached out, taking Emma's hand. As their fingers made contact, the semi-transparent shape of a woman appeared in front of Ethel and Emma, exactly in the spot they were staring. Kait took a sharp breath in—because Kait still had an arm around Nikki, she, too, could now see the apparition.

The woman was average looking, average height and weight, with short brown hair that looked as though it had been buzzed in places. Her bright green eyes shone with wild haste. Her image seemed to flicker between complete transparency and opaqueness.

"I don't have time," the woman said.

"What's your name?" Emma asked gently.

"No. I—I—" Her image quivered. "I'm not dead, but I think I might be soon."

"Do you need us to save you?" Emma asked. Years of practice had bestowed Emma with a steadiness to her voice despite the tremor she felt inside.

"No," the woman said, her eyes softening, a small smile playing on her lips briefly. "I am beyond your abilities, but my son." The haste grew in her eyes again. "In this in-between place, I can see. Time moves—" As she looked around, her form dimmed. "I don't have time." She put a hand to her forehead. "Listen," she said, taking a step forward. "My death is coming soon. He will discover his powers, but he's going to burn the world, he's going to drown it in water." Her appearance waned.

"What's his name?" Emma asked, her urgency now audible.

The woman's face contorted. "Oh." She vanished.

After a moment, Nikki said, "What th—"

"My son." The woman's appearance waxed strong.

Nikki jumped.

"Please," the woman said, looking at Emma. "I've seen it. You two and the third." Flickering like a bad light bulb, she glanced at Nikki. "The four elements, you're the only ones…of time…He's going to…You must save him—" Her form dimmed. "Stop him. Save the earth, you are the salt…the earth can stop... You can't let him—" and her image quivered and then disappeared. This time she did not return.

"What was that?" Nikki asked.

"A coma," Ethel said wisely.

The color drained from Emma's face as she turned to her grandmother. "That's why she said her death was coming. She was…" Emma swallowed.

"She was still alive," Ethel confirmed. "That's why she could not hold her image. Her body kept pulling her back."

"Is that what being a medium is like? You're going about your day and then—boom—you're talking to some half-alive person?" Nikki asked.

"The half-alive part isn't typical," Emma admitted. "Otherwise, yes."

"What do you think she meant by 'You must save him. Stop him'?" Nikki asked.

Ethel shook her head. "Perhaps if you stop her son, you can save him?"

"The fire," Emma said.

"Is that what you think she meant?" Nikki asked, eyes wide.

"She said he is going to burn the world," Emma said, wearing her fear like a coat, thick and uncomfortably hot.

Silence swallowed the room as they all wondered how a small fire could translate into the burning of the world.

Emma was the first to break the spell of stillness. "I'll be in the library. I need to write everything down before I forget it." She grabbed her bag and disappeared to the back of the house.

"So," Nikki said after a few moments. "What do *I* do?"

"Read," Kait and Ethel said together. Kait wagged her finger as she slipped into a back room.

"Wait. Are you serious?"

"All magick begins in books," Ethel said, beckoning Nikki to the dining room as she walked.

"Here you are," Kait said as she returned and laid a whole armful of books on the dining room table.

"There has to be over a dozen here." Nikki picked up a dingy yellow tome that smelled heavily of mothballs. It looked like it had been rebound since its original binding. The pages were no thicker than tissue paper but luckily sturdier.

"Yes, dear; better get cracking." Kait smiled, before adding, "Ethel, would you like me to put the kettle on?"

"Yes, please." Ethel began stacking the books. "Nikki, you'll need to read these first, and that one," she snatched the yellow mothball book out of Nikki's hands, "you don't need to worry about until later." She pushed a pile of six books towards Nikki.

"So, start on the top?" Nikki looked at the large leather-bound book on the top. The leather looked to be in good condition, which it was, having been recently waxed.

"Yes, and make sure you don't spill anything on these books." Ethel peered over the yellow book she was now flipping through. "Most of them are older than the pyramids." She raised her eyebrows as if to make a point before settling back down with the yellow book.

"But—" Nikki's face scrunched up as she shook her head. "Paper wasn't even invented until after the pyramids, wasn't it?"

"Just because the humans didn't have it doesn't mean we didn't," Ethel said from behind her book.

Considering this, Nikki grabbed the leather-bound book and opened it. *A Record of the Prophecies Made by the High Priestess the Second: Mella Vates* was written across the title page in a spidery handwriting. Nikki mouthed the name 'Mella Vates.' Sighing, she sat down and began reading through the second High Priestess' prophecies.

Dec. 11, 08

Nikki and Emma went back over to Emma's grandma's place today. They asked if I wanted to come, but I lied and said my dad needed me home. After the freaky things that happened the first time I went there and all the stuff that has happened since, I think I'm going to steer clear of that whole place. I'll do my part for the project, and then I'm done. I've got my whole life to figure out now that I can't surf because I'm

Nelly sighed. She was sitting in the middle of her unmade bed, staring at the wall without seeing it. The word 'mermaid' buzzed through her mind like the world's peskiest fly. Flopping back onto her pillows, Nelly sighed audibly as she wondered how she was supposed to rewrite her entire life. Rolling to her side, she flicked her journal closed. Nelly was now face to face with Rán's journal, which sat idly on her nightstand (of course, she only thought of it as her mother's book). Grumbling, she rolled over to her other side. Nelly had made up her mind to never turn into a mermaid ever again. It was bad enough that she couldn't surf; there was no way she could go through the painful process of turning every time she set foot in the ocean. As Nelly sat up, glancing at her mother's book again and debating whether she wanted to read more, her cell phone rang. She looked down at the caller ID: WYATT. She picked it up.

"Hey," she said.

"YOU'RE ALIVE!"

Nelly jerked the phone away from her face. "Dude," she shouted at it. "Not so loud."

"Sorry," Wyatt said.

Nelly moved the phone back to her ear.

"I'm just stoked to hear from you. I haven't seen you at the lineup, and you're not talking to me at school. What! Is! Up!"

Nelly sighed. "I haven't felt well."

"Bull! This is me. What's wrong?"

Nelly felt strange keeping a secret from Wyatt. They had never kept secrets from each other before. She had been there for him in first grade when his parents divorced, and he was there for her when her mom died the next year. There was nothing they didn't share, yet Nelly still couldn't bring herself to tell him that she turned into a—that she was part fish.

"Nothing," she lied. "I just need a break."

"Break? From what? Surfing?" Wyatt scoffed.

"All of it," Nelly said; she could hear the stress in her voice. "Do you really want me to talk to you about every girl problem I have?"

"You never had issues telling me about your period and all that other girl stuff before. I've heard it all, so what's your deal?" Wyatt shot back.

She had known it was a long shot. "Forget it, Wyatt. But just remember that you leave every other summer to hang with your dad in Nebraska. Do I complain about how you don't call me every second while you're there, or about how you don't tell me every little thing that's going on in your life?"

"Wow," he said, his voice low. "Seriously, Nels? That's how you want to play this?"

She might as well have punched him in the gut; she could hear the hurt in his voice. "Wyatt, I'm—"

"It's like I don't even know you anymore. You know what? Just forget it." He hung up.

"Ugh!" Nelly flopped onto her bed, rolling over and screaming into her pillow.

"What's going on in here?" Jo came into Nelly's room. "Were you—were you yelling at Wyatt?" She looked genuinely concerned.

"Yes," Nelly said, her voice muffled by her pillow.

"You know why he's pissed, right?"

Nelly sat up and looked at her sister. "Cause I missed dawn patrol for the last week, and I haven't called back in a while?" Nelly guessed.

"No." Jo scoffed. "He had this huge surprise party planned for your birthday, and you bailed on him. He looked like a total grom. He waited for like five hours after everyone else had called you a no-show." Jo sat next to Nelly on the bed.

"He did not! He would have made up some excuse or something—asked me if I wanted to hang out, or go bowling or—"

"Or night surfing?" Jo prompted.

Nelly groaned, sinking back into her pillow. "No wonder he's so pissed."

Jo shrugged. "You should cut the guy a little slack, you know?"

Nelly's phone buzzed again. She looked at it: ANDY. Nelly answered, "Stop calling me!" and hung up before he could say anything. "Ugh. When did everything get so complicated?"

Jo shrugged again. She got up, and as she walked out of the room, she said, "I know what always clears my head."

Nelly glanced at her mom's journal. She picked it up and threw on a hoodie before grabbing her keys, hopping in her truck, and heading to the Cove. The drive was silent and uneventful.

"I'm not getting in the water," she said aloud as she pulled into the parking lot. The hike down to the Cove was easier this time. The ocean was flat and glassy. Nelly sat at water line, letting it lap gently at her toes—nothing fishy happened. She set her mom's book down in the water, and it sprang open, back to the page with her mom's writing on it.

"Mom," Nelly said, touching the page gently. "What do I do? I don't want to be this. I just want my life back."

She didn't dare flip a page yet. She wasn't ready. Even though she had thought about it before, it was too possible right now, too real, to try. This was the place where everything she had known transformed, where everything she had dreamed died, where she had changed. Wyatt was right; he didn't know her anymore and neither did she.

11 December 2008

Nothing since the meeting with the woman. At least my medium powers seem to be in working order even if my psychic ones aren't. Rachelle said my lack of visions might be stress-related. I mean, I can see where she's coming from. I haven't been exactly religious in my meditation lately, but it feels

Emma chewed on her nail.

sinister. Maybe I'm being overly dramatic, but I feel purposely blinded, like it's not something I can control, but something is controlling me?

"I need sleep," Emma said to herself as she ran her hands through her hair. She closed her journal and flopped down onto her bed. Guilt crept through her body. She had just admitted to being less than disciplined in her meditation. Letting her body slide out of her bed and onto her floor, Emma grumbled. She grabbed a pillow from her bed and threw it on the floor. She sat on it, cross-legged, and rocked around a bit, hands on her knees, eyes closed. She continued to wiggle and readjust. There was a soft knock at the door.

"Come in," Emma called, her eyes still closed.

"It's me," Nikki said, glancing around the room until she found Emma seated on the floor. "What are you doing?"

Emma opened her eyes and looked at Nikki. "I'm trying to meditate, but I'm not having much luck." Emma clapped her hands on her thighs and stood up, stretching her back. "So, what did you need?"

"I thought you needed something," Nikki said. "I was told you called Ethel and told her you needed me at your house right away."

Emma furrowed her brows. "That's strange. I would've just called you." She put her hands on her hips.

"That's what I thought. So, you don't need anything?" Nikki asked.

Emma shrugged. "Not really. Sorry to drag you out here."

Nikki chuckled. "No worries. It was nice to get a break from my mom ignoring me." Nikki turned to go back through Emma's bedroom door.

Emma reached out to pat her friend's shoulder, and as soon as her hand touched Nikki's shoulder, Emma was pulled into a vision:

*"HOLD IT, NELLY!" someone screamed.*

*"I'M TRYING! It's too big; I can't control it—I'm not powerful enough," Nelly cried back.*

*A giant wall of water threatened to crush her; she was standing with her legs apart and arms up, palms out, as though she was literally using her body to hold the water back. Suddenly Nikki was at her side; she grabbed one of Nelly's outstretched hands and lifted her own.*

*"Get them out of here!" Nikki yelled. She began murmuring words—a different language? The wall of water crashed down on all of them.*

Emma sat up in her bed, coughing violently. Her lungs burned, her head swam, and her heart pounded madly in her chest. When she had finally caught her breath, she looked around her room. Where was Nikki? She grabbed her analog alarm clock; it was three in the morning.

It was just a dream. Everything had just been a dream.

Emma jumped out of bed and raced down the hallway, calling for Rachelle the whole way.

Rachelle opened her bedroom door. Although she was closer to sixty than forty, at this moment Rachelle looked reminiscent of 5-year-old Shirley Temple, her hair in curlers, while she rubbed the sleep from her eyes. "What? What is it? Are you okay?" Rachelle said, her voice as bleary as her eyesight.

"I had a vision, but it wasn't a vision vision. It was like a dream vision. Like I was sleeping, but I didn't know I was asleep, and I had a vision, so I thought it was a vision, but then I woke up, and it was actually a dream," Emma explained quickly.

"Slow down," Rachelle said, patting Emma's shoulder.

Emma explained what had happened, this time slowly, and in order of her experiences. When she had finished, Rachelle looked at Emma. "We need tea," Rachelle said, finally.

Emma followed Rachelle to the kitchen and sat down on a stool at the island. She picked at her fingernails as Rachelle prepared the two mugs of tea.

"So you touched Nikki and had the vision?" Rachelle asked, handing Emma a mug of chamomile.

"Yes," Emma said as she took the mug and set it on the counter.

"Perhaps you couldn't get the vision without the help from Nikki," Rachelle said, almost to herself. She sipped her tea.

"But it was a dream. She wasn't actually there to lend me her power," Emma insisted.

"No," Rachelle said slowly, "but you thought she was."

"So, you're saying the fact I haven't had visions is in my head? That I'm…" Emma paused, trying to find the right word. "What? Afraid? That I'm afraid of what I'll see?" Emma frowned, torn between being hurt by the notion that this may have been her fault after all and wanting to get answers, even if she was at fault.

"I don't know about that," Rachelle said. "But I do know two are often more powerful than one. I need to call Mom about this." She squeezed Emma's shoulder, encouraged her to drink her tea, and left to phone Ethel and fill her in.


December 11, 2008

Emma and I went over to her grandma's to learn how to train, and we got some weird message from an almost dead lady about stopping or saving (or both??) her son. After that, cue a million hours of reading. Grandma said my official training can begin tomorrow, provided I finish my reading. All million pages of it. I've read so many prophecies, I've got them bouncing around in my brain. I'm too tired to try and concentrate, especially since I have no idea what I'm even reading for.

"Hey," Kam said. "Grandma dropped this off for you." He handed Nikki a crumpled envelope.

She reached across her bed to take it. "Thanks." Nikki waited until he went back to his room before opening it:

My dearest little witch,
　　There is an emergency to which I must attend. I will be back as soon as I possibly can—I would not leave unless I thought it vitally important. Until I return, study meditation with Emma.
　　Blessed Be,
　　Grandma Kait

"Great," Nikki said under her breath. She checked the time on her phone. It was already half past eleven, definitely too late to call Emma. This would have to wait until morning. Nikki put her journal away. She turned her bedroom light off and her bedside light on, snuggling down to read more:

> While several magickal creatures, such as mermaids, witches, mediums, and raijū, already appear human and are thus able to easily hide their magick to avoid persecution, other magickal creatures, such as fairies, elves, phoenix, and dragons, have had to learn how to take on human form so as to blend seamlessly in with those around them. Although some claim—

Nikki would not discover what it was that some claimed until morning, for she had fallen fast asleep.

#  Chapter Eight

## Wednesday, December 12th

Dec. 12, 08

    Everything in me tells me to fight this, and I was thinking about my birthday and how Jo forgot to put my wetsuit in the truck, so I couldn't wear it that first time. So, maybe, just maybe, the wetsuit will keep me from turning into a fish. Maybe it will give me enough of a barrier. I have to at least try.

It didn't take Nelly very long to gather her necessary items: her wetsuit from the dry rack, a block of surf wax, a pair of sweatpants from her laundry basket, and her mother's journal from her nightstand. With these items gathered and shoved, rather unceremoniously, into her trusty duffle bag, Nelly headed out to the garage, tossing the duffle into the truck cab before deciding on which surfboard to bring. She looked at usual board, the same 5'6" green and blue Humu Fish she rode the last time she had surfed. Her eyes moved over to one of Tom's longboards, a bright blue 10-foot Randy Rarick noserider. She opted for the longboard and pulled it down from the rack, carefully loading it into her truck. She tied it down, double checked the straps, and hopped in the driver's seat.

"This has to work," Nelly whispered to herself as she backed out. This was not the first time she had skipped school to surf, but…

The end of that thought pulsed through her mind like a threat: it might be the last, it might be the last, it might be the last.

How she made it down to the Cove without hurting herself or dropping the 10-foot board, she never really knew, but somehow both safely arrived on the soft sand of the beach. Nelly unwrapped a new bar of Mr. Zog's surf wax, shoving the plastic in her pocket. Breathing in the familiar coconutty scent of the pink round, she waxed down her dad's board with a fresh coat. She shimmied out of her clothes. She had put on her favorite black bikini top and a pair of blue bottoms she was pretty sure were hers (they weren't—they were Jo's).

Nelly wiggled into her wetsuit and zipped up her back by pulling up the long strap tied to her zipper. She took a deep breath, rolled her shoulders, and took a moment to read the waves: windier than yesterday, incoming swell, little choppy, but doable on a longboard. Her mouth set a hard and determined line across her face as she picked up the board and carried it over to the water. The waves lapped at her toes, playful and cool. Nelly swallowed, taking one more deep breath before plopping the board in the water. As the bottom of the board met the surface of the water, Nelly kept her hands on the rails, gracefully slipping her knees underneath her, resting on the deck. Only her fingers and her toes got wet.

Nothing fishy happened.

"Okay," Nelly said, nodding. She settled on her knees and paddled, her arms going into the water up to her elbows.

Still nothing happened.

She paddled out beyond the break, turned her board around, and watched over her shoulder. The next set was coming. Laying down on her belly, Nelly paddled. It had been ages since she longboarded. She felt the wave pick up her board, and she popped up, bouncing a little to get back in the pocket. The white water tickled her toes.

A surge of happiness bloomed in her chest as hope landed like a bird on her shoulder. This could work. As she rode the next wave, her mind mapped out a plan in which she could gradually get more and more of her body in the water until she figured out what triggered the fishy curse. Then, she'd just pull back. Nelly successfully caught several more waves, riding a few of them all the way onto the shore. She lined up for another wave, paddled, caught it, and was just wondering how short of a board she could get on when it happened. Something bumped her from her board, and she went flying into the ocean with a huge splash.

The effect was immediate.

"NO!" Nelly screamed, clawing her way towards the surface, desperate to climb back on the board. It was too late. The bone-melting pain overwhelmed her body. This time she had the wherewithal to look down as it happened. Everything seemed to move in slow motion. Nelly expected to see her tail fighting to burst through the wetsuit, but there was no struggle. Her tail shredded the wetsuit like it was nothing more than wet paper.

She sank to the ocean floor. Even though sand was soft and warm, Nelly was consumed by the cold of her confirmed fears. She had changed. It was over. Everything was really over. She had thought she could fight it, thought she could surf despite it, thought she could still live her dream, but it was really over this time. She couldn't risk a wipe out in front of anyone, let alone an entire panel of detail-oriented surf judges. Her career was finished just as it had started to take off.

It was only then she allowed herself to cry. She hadn't lost herself to tears like this since the death of her mother.


12 December 2008

Nelly wasn't at school today. Wyatt was, though he had quite the black cloud hovering above him. Speaking of black ominous clouds, the visions of drowning in water felt more than a bit ominous after the woman's warning of her son drowning the earth in water.

In other news, Nikki told me in class today that Kait left last night. It seems like quite a few people are going, as Nikki put it, "AWOL," lately. She was left instructions to begin training and meditating with me. Now I wish I would have studied and practiced meditating more seriously. At least Nikki won't feel incompetent because we'll probably be at the same level.


"Hey," Nikki said, unbuckling her seatbelt. "We're here."

Emma looked up. "Sorry I'm not much for conversation today."

"Don't worry about it," Nikki said. "I have a lot on my mind, too."

No 'Merry Meet' greeted them as they entered the house this time. Instead, Ethel's voice called to them from the back of the house. "Emma, is that you?"

"Yes," Emma called back.

"We have a lot to cover. Meet me in the library."

"Where's that?" Nikki asked, dropping her bag on the couch.

"Come on," Emma said, leading the way through the kitchen to a room at the back of the house.

In place of a door hung a purple velvet curtain covered in intricate patterns which had been embroidered in golden thread. They pushed past the curtain, entering into what seemed to be another world. The room was much bigger on the inside. There were built-in bookcases all along the walls, each endlessly tall and disappearing into the vast darkness overhead. Every single shelf was filled. Books, every shape and size, every color and binding, were crammed onto the shelves. The spaces not filled with books held candles. A dim orange glow filled the space for the candles were the main light source. The library smelled of clove, citrus, and vanilla. Plush jewel-toned cushions were piled in a corner. It was all magick, of course (I don't recommend you try this at home as you're likely to set fire to something).

"Hello, dears," Ethel said, handing each girl a plush cushion. "Kait and I spoke and thought it was of utmost importance we begin your meditation training as soon as possible." Ethel turned to Emma. "Have you told Nikki?"

Emma shook her head, taking a emerald cushion. Ethel gestured to Nikki, who sat on her maroon cushion while Emma relayed the early morning's events.

"Wait a minute," Nikki said after Emma had finished. "You think I can help you have visions? Does magick even work that way?"

"Some magicks are fully transferable, and others can be shared," Emma said. "Like how you and Kait were able to see the woman in a coma through my medium magick. If our magicks weren't compatible, that wouldn't have worked."

"Fair point," Nikki conceded. "Did you know we were compatible before you tried it?"

"I had a hunch, but I didn't know for sure," Emma admitted.

Nikki nodded, and added, "That makes sense. Plus in your vision in the dream—or whatever—I helped Nelly by holding her hand, so we might make each other stronger."

"But I warn you, now," Ethel said, raising a finger. "Not all magicks traverse so easily. You two, and I suspect the mermaid when she comes around, have a special bond which allows your magicks to intermingle easily. Were another witch and psychic or medium to attempt the same things, they would not necessarily have the same results."

"Why not?" Nikki asked.

Ethel shrugged. "Magick has its own designs, if you will, its own plan.

We can wield the powers afforded to us through the elements, but no one truly grasps all that magick is and can do."

"Does meditation help us tune into magick then?" Nikki asked.

"Precisely," Ethel said. "Care to explain further?"

"Sure," Emma said. "Meditation is helpful for all magickal beings. It allows us to clear our minds and become more in tune with our spirits, thus more in tune with our magicks, like you said. Also," she added, "receiving visions can be mentally, physically, and emotionally rigorous and therefore, exhausting. Meditation is kind of a way to mentally and emotionally exercise so I'm able to focus and withstand the power of my visions."

"Let's get started," Ethel said. "First close your eyes and get comfortable on your cushions. It's nearly impossible to meditate properly if you are uncomfortable."

After a few moments of silence and wiggling on everyone's part, the three settled in.

"Next," Ethel said, keeping her eyes closed and speaking softly to the girls. "I want you to locate your heartbeat. Try to find its rhythm in your body. You might feel it strongest in your chest or perhaps your thumbs. Quiet your mind, and search your body for the beating sensation."

Ethel fell easily into her rhythm, and despite Emma's negligence, she, too, found her heartbeat and rhythm quickly. Nikki, on the other hand, tried to focus, but thoughts kept bouncing through her mind. She kept guiding her mind back to her heartbeat. Her hands had an almost uncontrollable desire to fiddle around, so she intertwined her fingers together and relaxed them on her lap. It was then she felt the beat of her heart pumping blood through her hands. Suddenly, as if someone had turned on a switch, she could feel it all over her body. Her fingers released, and her hands relaxed onto her knees. Thoughts still floated through her mind, but they seemed less distracting and more like soft clouds blowing in a breeze, just passing through with no intention of staying.

Ethel spoke softly, "Once you've found your heartbeat, breathe in through your nose and out through your mouth in one long breath." Ethel then made a noise that sounded somewhere between a whistle and the sound the wind makes when it blows through a leafless tree.

Nikki and Emma did it in turn.

"Good," Ethel said. "Focus on a question, something you don't know, something you want to understand. I want you to keep that question in your mind as you focus on your heartbeat and breathe in and out slowly through your nose." They sat in silence.

Nikki noted the lack of clocks in the room; no obnoxious ticking bothered her. She enjoyed the silence. Sitting quietly, focusing on her question—how to harness her powers—Nikki realized the first step was meditation. Meditation wasn't busy work. Kait hadn't meant it to keep Nikki simply occupied. Kait had left clear instructions: study meditation.


December 12, 2008

 I meditated for the first time in my life, and I TOTALLY get why Grandma said I need this as part of my training. I feel so much more in tune with my power. I was practicing making things appear after we meditated, and it was super easy—admittedly it was all small stuff: pens, pencils, ice cream cones—BUT the point is it WORKED! Every Dang TIME!!

 We're going to get back at it in a few minutes. We stopped to take a bathroom break, get a snack, and read. Luckily today is Mom's turn to pick up Kam so I can take extra time. I already told her I was going to a friend's house to work on a school project—technically it's not a total lie. I am at my friend's (grandma's) house, and I am working on a project related to school...if you count saving the school and possibly the whole world as a project. Who knows? Maybe the coma lady was looney tunes and nothing is coming...

 A girl can dream.


Nikki traded her journal for a book from her magickal homework pile. The girls had been instructed to do some more reading while they were taking a break from meditating. Nikki had already finished *A Record of Prophecies Made by the High Priestess the Second: Mella Vates, The Journey Through Another Realm, A Guide to Meditation, Creatures of Legend and Lore,* and *The Elemental Magicks.*

She had been allowed to take books home and had spent almost every spare minute she had, including breaks between classes, reading. The books were fascinating. Everything was so new but felt so old. It also felt strangely familiar, as though all this information was a thought she'd had long ago, and reading about it had simply rekindled the knowledge. She propped open *The Earth Children*. The dark green cover smelled of rich black soil. Nikki had always been the bookworm of her family, but this was different. Never had she felt so connected to books. Never had she run so fast towards the light they were bringing her. At the end of a book, she usually felt a little sad the adventure was over, like no one would ever understand that she had experienced everything along with the protagonist. These books were different. These left her with peace and excitement.

"Have you read these?" Nikki asked Emma.

"A long time ago, but yes. Do you like them?" Emma asked from behind her own studies.

"This stuff is amazing. I would have said *The Elemental Magicks* was my favorite, but I think *The Earth Children* might beat it. I mean listen to this: 'In the time before The Gathering, the children of the Earth walked freely, without fear. These witches, as they are now called, understood the Earth in a way that has faded beyond living memory. They lived and breathed with the Earth. They did more than simply read her lunar and star charts. They understood the moods of the moon; the sparkle of the stars spoke to them in a language long since lost. The Earth children felt sick when she was sick, and they took it upon themselves to cleanse and heal her. They mourned the death brought of winter and rejoiced in the birth of spring.' It's incredible," Nikki said.

"It's also heartbreaking," Emma said, closing her own book. "To lose an entire way of being." She shook her head and pursed her lips.

Nikki nodded, looking back at the book. After a moment, she said, "What gathering are they talking about?"

"I believe that's referencing the legend of *The* Gathering," Ethel said as she came in carrying a tray complete with a teapot, teacups on saucers, and a basket filled with freshly baked chocolate chip cookies. "The legend says that at the binding of time—"

"Binding?" Emma interrupted. "Don't you mean the *beginning* of time?"

"Ah, yes. Of course," Ethel said, smiling. "At the beginning of time, there was a gathering of thirteen members, each holding one of the thirteen elemental magicks—"

"But that's impossible," Emma said as she grabbed a cookie. "There are only ten elements."

"It is called a legend," Ethel said, emphasizing the last word.

"So, what did the legend say?" Nikki took a bite of her cookie.

"The Gathering was held at a time when there was complete peace between the elemental magicks—"

"Is there not peace now?" Nikki asked.

"Individually, more or less. Collectively, I'm afraid not. Old wounds run deep," Ethel explained with a sigh.

"So what did The Gathering do?" Nikki absently stirred her tea.

"They each combined a bit of their magick to cast the greatest of all the spells," Ethel said.

"Which was what?" Emma asked.

Ethel shrugged. "The legend never says, or if it does, I've failed to find a reference. Now," she said with a clap as she stood. "You two eat up quickly, and come back to the library. We still have work to do." Ethel left, taking her tea with her.

"Do you think The Gathering was real?" Nikki asked, grabbing another cookie.

"I doubt it." Emma took a long sip of her tea. "There could never be thirteen elements because they come in pairs, and anyway, there are only ten."

"What are the ten elements?" Nikki asked.

"Well," Emma explained, "there's earth and air—witches and fairies; fire and water—phoenix and mermaids—"

"Wait, a minute, so everyone has their own element?" Nikki asked, stirring her tea.

"More or less."

"And witches have earth?"

Emma nodded. "It's actually one of the most versatile of the elemental magicks. You can use it for creation; you can use it for travel, but that's pretty advanced—"

"What about time travel?" Nikki asked, thinking of the man in the blue box from her dad's favorite show. "Is that like a spell or would that be an element?"

Emma laughed. "It's definitely not an element. I don't know about any kind of spell, but I read once that raijū—"

"It's getting late," Ethel called.

The girls glanced at each other, guzzled the rest of their tea, crammed their cookies in their mouths, and darted back to the library.

"Sit across from each other," Ethel said, once they had all gotten comfortable. "First we're going to meditate for a little bit to get you two grounded. Once there, I'll tell you to raise your hands. You'll touch, palm to palm. Understand?"

"Um, what if Emma has a vision?" Nikki grimaced.

"That *is* the idea," Ethel said. "Though I see your point. Advice, Emma?"

"Don't fight the vision. Let it take you where it needs to," Emma said. "You might feel yourself doing or saying something; let it happen, and pay attention to it. Most of the time I just watch it."

Nikki nodded, regretting scarfing down those three cookies, which now swam uneasily in her stomach.

Closing their eyes, the girls took the time to align their spines and roll their shoulders. They found their heartbeats and breathed. A few moments later, the girls heard Ethel say, "Now bring your hands together."

They barely touched fingertips when the vision consumed them.

*Emma and Nikki walked into someone's backyard. Emma handed a blonde girl a bright pink flier. A small bonfire burned. Twinkle lights lined the back porch. There were kids from school there, chatting happily and roasting marshmallows. Emma waved to someone. But something was wrong. Everything blurred suddenly; time shifted. Without warning, the earth moved beneath them. A nearby telephone pole crashed into the bonfire sending flames and sparks everywhere. The grass burned—a pile of kindling caught; everything was in flames. People ran, screaming, and Nikki grabbed Emma's hand and started whispering words in a different language. Nikki abruptly shook Emma's hands. Nikki repeated the words slower, so Emma could follow along. The flames died down. All went dark.*

"Woah," Nikki said, opening her eyes.

Ethel quietly shushed her and glanced at the girls' hands, which she was holding together. Maintaining eye contact, Ethel removed her hand slowly and nodded towards Emma whose eyes were still closed.

A few seconds later, Emma opened her eyes and took a deep breath. Both girls lowered their hands.

"Are your visions always so intense?" Nikki asked, rubbing her head.

"No. Could you feel that heat?" Emma asked, rubbing her arms, sure she would find singed hairs.

"That fire was huge," Nikki agreed.

"Girls?" Ethel said. "What did you see?"

Emma and Nikki explained what had happened, taking turns in their recounting of events.

"And then it all went black," Nikki finished.

"You passed out," Emma said. "I stayed in the vision a little bit longer. I think controlling the fire is going to take a lot out of you."

"So, what happened after I passed out?" Nikki asked.

"Not much; someone called 911. Naturally the fire department, a police car, and an ambulance all showed up. One of the paramedics moved you. He said something about smoke inhalation. I ran with it," Emma said with a small smile. "At least we know what we're fighting."

"What about the wave?" Nikki asked.

"I think it might have been just part of the dream. I mean it was a dream, so maybe the dream was to tell me how to get more visions, but the vision in it wasn't a real vision." Emma shrugged. "That's my best guess."

"So Nelly doesn't help us then?"

"Maybe. Visions are one possible outcome. She might be there, and then if she's there, you might not get so drained."

"What do you think the bonfire is for?" Nikki asked. "Did you get to read that pink flyer?"

"No, I was hoping you did. A New Year's Eve celebration? Maybe?" Emma said.

"I guess it could be." Nikki sighed. "You weren't kidding when you said visions are a lot of guesswork."

# Chapter Nine

## Thursday, December 13th

December 13, 2008

    Remind me to take an aspirin the next time I help Emma. My head is still pounding, and it's not just from the vision itself. Emma wasn't kidding when she said being psychic is mostly guessing. I can't even wrap my head around it.

    Also, I'm in major hot water with Mom. SHE forgot it was her turn to pick Kam up. Kam couldn't even call her because SHE changed the number, and SHE didn't tell him the new number. But apparently, this is all MY fault. I had my phone off. If I had had my phone on, there wouldn't have been a problem, therefore my fault...

Nikki's saving grace was the fact Jody's mom had given Kam a ride; if Margret had had to go to the school to pick up a sad, lonely, hungry Kam, there would have been serious consequences. As it was, Nikki had received a lecture and been assigned the responsibility of picking up Kam for the rest of the school year. It was a solution that made life easier on everyone; no more remembering whose turn it was. Nikki had wondered vaguely why they hadn't always done it this way but luckily had the presence of mind not to ask.

Nikki pulled her lunch tray in front of her—it was pizza day.

Emma sat down next to Nikki, but before either girl could say anything, Nelly joined them and said, "Hey," which frankly surprised all three of them.

"Hi," Nikki said slowly.

"It's good to see you," Emma said.

"So," Nelly said a bit lamely. Then she was quiet.

Nikki glanced at Emma, who sat relaxed, eating her pizza.

After what seemed like the longest, most awkward silence in the history of teenagers, Nelly spoke again, "So."

The awkwardness did not abate.

"How have you been?" Nikki asked.

"Good," Nelly said, but even as the words left her mouth, sweat coated her palms. She wiped her hands on her red Bermuda shorts as her brain screamed at her: 'Why are you here? What were you thinking?' Something in her gut told her she could trust these girls, despite her many attempts to push that instinct away. Before she could stop herself, Nelly found herself saying, "Can I tell you something?"

This one question triggered a series of three actions.

First, Nikki began bouncing her leg, her nervous energy flooding the table.

Second, Emma responded, "Of course." She felt Nikki's nervousness and wished, not for the last time that her powers included telepathy. You see, Emma understood that Nelly was like a wounded animal: she had to be approached with patience and caution. If either of them spooked her, there was a good chance they'd lose her, but Nikki hadn't spent much time around wounded animals, which brings us back to the fact that telepathy is not in the wheelhouse of psychic-mediums.

And if only these two actions had been taken, everything might have been alright, but then the third and really unfortunate thing happened:

Nikki spoke, "If it helps, we know."

Emma closed her eyes and braced for impact.

Nelly looked like Nikki had just slapped her in the face. "You what?" she spat.

"I only meant…" Nikki looked at Emma for help, but Emma just shook her head.

"This was a mistake." Nelly put her hands on the table as she stood up.

Nikki grabbed Nelly's wrist. "Please," Nikki said. "You have to help us."

"Us?" Nelly said.

"Me and Emma; I'm a witch, and there's this bonfire. It's going to be super danger—"

"No." A horrified look flashed across Nelly's face as she wrenched her wrist out of Nikki's grasp. "I can't help. I'm never turning into a—that *thing* again." Nelly shook her head. "I never should have said anything." She strode away from the table as fast as she could.

Nikki stood, but Emma pulled her back down.

"Don't bother," Emma said. "She needs to help us willingly, and she's definitely not willing right now."

Nikki collapsed onto the bench just as a blonde girl came up to their table and said, "Hey, ladies!"

"Sarah, it's you!" Emma gasped. It was the girl from her vision.

Sarah pursed her lips. "Mhmm...anyway," she said slowly. "I'm having a little Christmas break celebration on the twentieth." She handed them each a bright pink flier. "Don't tell anyone, but it's also the eve of the Winter Solstice. I'm crazy into that stuff." She laughed and then added straight-faced, "But, seriously, don't tell anyone—I'm not actually sure why I told you." A dazed look passed across her face briefly; then, Sarah raised her eyebrows, smiled, said, "Hope you guys can make it," and skipped off.

"Emma, I don't think it happens on New Year's Eve," Nikki said, looking at the flier.

BYOM–Bring Your Own Mallows!!
Winter break bonfire.
December 20th!
Graham crackers and chocolate will be provided.
Bring a treat to share!
RSVP before December 17th

It listed an address and phone number Nikki assumed belonged to Sarah. "This is it," Nikki said, pointing at the flier. "This is where it happens. This is *when* it happens, and now we know what it is, too. Oh, why do I feel weird?" She shook her hands as if trying to physically shake off the energy buzzing under her skin.

"Because you're excited you finally know when this will all go down, but also super freaked because it means we have way less time than we did before?" Emma suggested.

Nikki nodded. "I guess Nelly won't be joining us after all."

"She might. You never know," Emma said, folding the flier.

Dec. 13, 08

Why did I think I could trust them? My gut has never led me wrong before, but—what if Nikki did a spell on me? Apparently she's a witch. I mean, I can't think of any other reason I would have told them I'm a—whatever. Sure, I didn't exactly tell them, but I was going to, but then Nikki said they already knew. This whole time they knew.

Now they want my help, but there's no way I can

Nelly groaned. The bell rang. She watched everyone else in the cafeteria start their mass migration to their various classes. She was supposed to join them, but instead she headed out to the parking lot, got in her truck, and drove home. When she got home, she curled up in bed and stayed there for the rest of the day, wondering who she could trust if she couldn't even trust her own judgment anymore.

# Chapter Ten

## Friday, December 14th



Just as Nikki came out of the bathroom, Emma put her journal away and said, "So, how is Kam sounding? On his trombone, I mean."

"Good," Nikki said, plopping down on the couch across from Emma. "Apparently all that yelling the band teacher does actually works. Kam sounds like he's playing real music, which is a nice change from the dying duck noises."

Emma laughed. "Dying duck. That's good."

Nikki chuckled and stood up, stretching her arms above her. "Where's your grandma?"

Emma shrugged.

Nikki walked over to the front door to peek out the window. An envelope sat on the table. "Hey, Em. This is addressed to you." Nikki handed it to Emma, who walked over.

Emma ripped open the envelope and pulled a letter out, scanning it. "Right," she said to herself.

"What's it say?" Nikki asked, trying (unsuccessfully) to peek over Emma's shoulder.

Emma folded the paper and stuck it in her pocket. "We need to prepare" is all she said before she went into the kitchen with Nikki following behind like an incredibly curious puppy.

"Prepare for what?" Nikki asked.

"Take these." Emma handed Nikki four fat pillar candles. "Put the white candle on East, the orange on South, the blue on West, and the brown on North. I'll be right back." She turned and ran up the stairs at the back of the kitchen.

"What the heck does that mean?" Nikki mumbled to herself. She carried the candles over to the table and carefully set them down. As she did, her hand brushed the jute table runner she had noticed during her very first visit to Ethel's home. Nikki spotted a mark carved into the dark walnut tabletop; the tiniest corner of the marking was barely poking out from under the jute. She glanced around briefly before moving the runner completely to the side.

Carved into the top of the table were four small circles connected together by a giant circle. "It's a compass," Nikki whispered, tracing her fingers over the word North, which was under the first of the smaller circles.

"Oh good," Emma said, coming into the dining room. "I knew you'd figure it out." She was carrying two small bags.

"So what are we doing?" Nikki asked as she placed the candles.

"A séance," Emma said, putting her hand into the larger of the two bags and pulling out a clear stone. "Moonstone to the East; it will help enhance any natural psychic abilities and will also help with our wishes of the future, particularly to communicate with whichever spirit we're contacting today." She placed the clear stone in the same circle as the white candle.

"Wait, like for real? Like real dead people? Isn't this dangerous? Are we really summoning the dead?" Nikki placed the last candle, the orange one, in the small circle carved above the word South.

"Yes," Emma said. "Yes, it can be, and technically no." She pulled a purple stone from the bag. "Amethyst to the West to aid in keeping our emotions at ease and as we contact the past, to keep peace, love, and happiness in the circle. Amethyst also increases psychic abilities." Emma smiled and put it in the same circle as the blue candle.

Nikki put a hand up to stop Emma. "Explain your 'yes, yes, it can be, no.'"

Emma smiled. "Yes, for real. Yes, real dead people. It can be dangerous depending on the spirits, but that's why we always take protective measures." She pulled a red stone from the bag. "Garnet goes to the South to support awareness of present energy."

"And no?"

"No, you don't summon the dead," Emma said. "Well, not technically. *Summoning* implies we have some kind of control over spirits, and we don't. What we do is more like inviting." She pulled the last stone from the bag, an opal. "We put this one on last. It's a natural amplifier."

"So who are we *inviting*?" Nikki asked.

Emma's whole face crinkled into a grin. "That's the surprise."

"You know, don't you?"

At that moment, Gabby came in, carrying two paper bags and said, "Merry Meet, girls! Can you put these in the kitchen, Nikki? And Emma, can you get some jars? Your grandma said you'd know where they are; she left the florist's right behind me."

"Of course!" Emma rushed off to the kitchen.

"Sure," Nikki said, taking the bags from Gabby.

As Nikki had not yet been formally introduced to Gabby, she got to wonder who this mysterious woman was as she helped unload the bunches of flowers. Gabby was taller than Nikki, had maroon-colored micro braids, and wore a crimson cloak over a white long-sleeve button-up blouse, which stood in a complimentary contrast to her deep brown skin. Her square glasses framed hazel eyes. She took off her cloak.

"I can finish, if you'll hang this up for me," Gabby said, holding the cloak out to Nikki.

"Sure," Nikki said again. As she hung up the cloak, a memory clicked into place. "You're the librarian at the public library," Nikki said as she walked back into the kitchen.

"Guilty," Gabby said, smiling and putting out her hand. "Gabby Oswin." She shook Nikki's hand. "Your grandmother gave me this to give to you," she added, handing Nikki an envelope.

As Nikki tore it open, Ethel came in carrying more flowers and began chatting with Emma and Gabby, but as they spoke of nothing consequential and I know you're curious as to what Kait wrote to Nikki, we'll ignore the conversation and focus our attention on the letter instead.

My dear little witch,

I send this letter with Gabby to let you know you can trust her. She's a witch, like you and me. She's been trained in all the elemental magicks and has a natural gift in the magick of fire. She will mentor you in my place until I can return. I'm sorry I had to leave you, but it was unavoidable, of this, be assured.

Blessed Be,
Grandma Kait

"So," Nikki said, folding the letter and looking at Gabby. "How do you know my grandmother?"

"Kait and my older sister, Simone, were friends back in Ireland," Gabby said.

"But you don't sound—" Nikki said. "*She* doesn't sound—"

Gabby smiled. "No, we don't sound Irish. I was born here in the states, but Kait and Simone came when they were kids. They got made fun of for their accents, so they learned to speak without them."

"Kids can be so mean," Emma said, putting the flowers in mason jars, one type of flower per jar.

Gabby nodded and touched each jar, magickally filling it with a few inches of water.

Nikki stood bug-eyed and mouth agape before she finally managed to say, "You've got to teach me that."

"Absolutely!" Gabby laughed. "But I think we'll focus on fire first."

"So what are the flowers for?"

Just then Rachelle came in through the front door. "I'm not late, am I?"

"Not yet," Ethel said.

"Oh perfect!" Rachelle put her purse and keys on the couch and joined everyone over at the table.

"Everyone pick a jar," Ethel said, grabbing one jar filled with red geranium and one with carnations. The rest of the jars were picked up, one per person. "Emma."

"Clover to the east for love, luck, and success." Emma placed her jar on the letters carved into the table spelling out the word 'East.'

"Carnation to the west for strength and energy." Ethel said, placing the jar on the first two letters of 'West.' "Rachelle, if you will?"

"Chrysanthemum to the west for protection and survival." Rachelle placed her jar next to the one Ethel had just set down.

"Red geranium to the south for guests and protection," Ethel said, placing her remaining jar over the word 'South.' "Now you two."

"Very well," Gabby said. She turned to Nikki. "You'll go after I do, okay?"

Nikki nodded.

"Buttercup to the north for divination and energy." Gabby placed her jar on the first two letters of 'North.' "Repeat after me: daisy to the north for protection."

Nikki did, placing her jar next to Gabby's.

"Emma," Ethel said. "Do you have the opal?"

"Yes, Grandma, right here."

"Good. Gabby, the lights, please," Ethel said.

Gabby waved her hand: the drapes closed, the electric lights turned off, and all of the candles lit except the brown one.

"That was awesome," Nikki said.

Gabby smiled. "I'll teach you that, too."

"Gabby and Nikki stand to the north; Emma to the south, I'll stand to the east, and Rachelle, the west. Everyone take hands," Ethel said, holding her hands out at waist height. Everyone held hands. They created an almost circle, which would be completed once Ethel and Emma joined hands. "Gabby and Emma, same time, please."

"Ready?" Gabby asked Emma.

Emma nodded, putting the opal in the same circle as the brown candle and taking Ethel's hand as soon as the opal was down. At the same exact moment, Gabby lit the candle with a small breath.

Nikki felt it. Something had changed. Later, Nikki would reflect back on this séance and recall it felt like a surge of energy had filled the room; in time, she would learn to recognize this feeling as magick.

"The spirit world is opened," Emma said, grinning at her friend. "The pressure you feel in your heart is normal," she added.

"It's like my whole body is suddenly awake after being asleep for hundreds of years. I can feel everything around me," Nikki said. The hair all over her body stood on end as every one of her nerves sparked gently.

Ethel smiled. "Now we need to call Aisling to us."

"Aisling?" Nikki repeated. "Like Aisling O'Crean?"

"The one and the same," Emma said. She glanced at her grandmother, who nodded. Emma continued, "Nikki, because she's your ancestor, it will be your call she will recognize the most. Repeat after me, and then we'll all say it together, okay?"

Nikki nodded.

Emma cleared her throat and closed her eyes. Her blonde hair hung around her face, and as she began to speak, an unearthly breeze blew her hair from her face. "Souls of the Earth, the Fire, the Water, the Air, we call you to send us your sister, Aisling O'Crean."

Rachelle squeezed Nikki's hand.

Nikki repeated.

Emma continued, "Souls of the future, the present, the past, and those of possibility, we call you to send us your sister, Aisling O'Crean."

Nikki echoed without prompting.

"Together, now," Emma said.

"Souls of the Earth, the Fire, the Water, the Air, we call you to send us your sister, Aisling O'Crean. Souls of the future, the present, the past, and those of possibility, we call you to send us your sister, Aisling O'Crean," they all repeated.

What had been a slight breeze picked up to a firm wind; the candles flickered, but since they had been magickally lit, they could not be blown out. Slivers of smoke trailed up from each candle. The five women continued to repeat their chant.

"I hear you," a voice said in barely a whisper.

"Aisling?" Nikki called.

The wind quieted.

"Yes, you wear my face," Aisling said in English thickly accented with Irish. She started as a voice coming from the smoke, but it grew more opaque, finally taking the shape of a woman. Slowly, she became denser, and her lines grew more defined.

Nikki blinked; looking at Aisling felt like looking in a mirror.

Aisling was dressed like a pilgrim that made it into the Technicolor era. Her skirt was a rich, pumpkin orange, her sleeves golden yellow. Her light brown leather bodice was tied with an almost black leather string. Her white underclothing peeked through her top and sleeves, maintaining her modesty.

"You're my ancestor," Nikki said, finally.

"You're of my blood? Do you share the gift?" Aisling spoke with melodic breathiness.

"I'm a witch, if that's what you mean," Nikki said.

"What is the year?" Aisling asked.

"2008," Nikki answered.

"Much time has passed." Aisling nodded. "I knew this day would come. I burned because I knew this day would come. I've got one message for you, lass. It was given to me ages ago." Aisling, who had been standing on the table, now sat, and looked Nikki eye to eye. "You will need to be brave, and trust in your powers. They will take you where you need to go. Trust the earth's love. He is strong. Time is not what you think. Follow the earth and learn how to listen. The first step is always listening." Aisling reached out and touched Nikki's cheek.

Nikki felt a coolness, like that from a hand which held a cold drink too long.

"I best be off, wee witch. I can move on now; my work is done."

"Wait, I have so many questions," Nikki said. It was too late though, Aisling had faded, and that feeling, that electric exposed feeling Nikki had had earlier, was gone.

December 14, 2008

I spoke to Aisling O'Crean today. We did a séance at Madam Ortega's house. It was bizarre in the most wonderful way. Anyways, Aisling didn't tell me anything I didn't already know. I mean I think the whole "Trust the earth" or whatever was a little woo-woo, but I'll take it. I don't really know what it means, but I'll gladly accept any advice I can get about being a witch. Gabby—unlike Grandma—gave me a phone number and an address, so I can contact her about starting my training in 'the magick of fire.'

I totally feel like I'm in one of those books about kids who get to wake up one day with magick powers! It's freaky and wonderful all at the same time.

Nikki had to go pick up Kam from band practice after the séance, and Emma had asked if she could get a ride. Rachelle would have given her a ride, but it was Knitting Circle night.

"Journaling down your experiences?" Emma asked as they sat in the car waiting for Kam.

"Yeah, I don't want to forget how I felt," Nikki said, closing her journal.

"Recording experiences can be vital," Emma said, smiling. Suddenly, she felt cold. "Give me your hand," she said, taking Nikki's hand before the witch could respond.

*There was the silhouette of a person, someone crying.*

"That's it?" Nikki asked.

"I think that's the shortest vision I've ever had," Emma said.

"No offense, but compared to the bonfire one, this one was kind of lame," Nikki said.

"True," Emma said, but she looked worried.

"What's wrong?"

"Well, sometimes the lame ones are the most important," Emma admitted; she couldn't shake the feeling she knew the person, that she *should* recognize the silhouette.

Kam tapped on the trunk. Nikki popped it and got out of the car to help him with his trombone.

December who knows, who cares.

Life is basically over. I can't think of one thing that would make it worse. So, I figured I might as well read Mom's book. It's not like she can give me worse news than the fish curse.

Nelly put her own journal away and pulled out her mom's. She went into the bathroom and filled up the bathtub with hot water. Hair up in a half-attempted bun, and bikini on, she sank in the steamy water. As the book loosened, she wondered why she only turned into a mermaid in the ocean, but the book opened in any water. Nelly turned the water off and reread her mom's entry once again, laying down in the tub. Then, for the first time, she flipped the page.

I know this discovery will be beyond heartbreaking for you. Josephine will be thrilled (yes, she's one, too), but her dreams of surfing stretched simply to enjoying the water. You wanted so much more. I am so sorry. I wish I knew how to tell you this is truly the greatest gift I could give you. My lille havfrue, I wish I could tell you there is a way to do both. There isn't, but I can promise if you're willing to make the trade, it will be a choice *you never regret.*

*Read this journal, and learn the secrets kept here since the first mermaid in our line. Four generations of mermaids have written in this journal. I hope you will begin as the fifth.*

*I love you, havfrue. I love you deeply.*

*Love, Mom*

Nelly had forgotten her mother's pet name for her, *havfrue*. She had never been told where it came from, or how she got it. She closed the journal, hugging it to her chest, and curling around it. She had spent a lot of time lately in the fetal position; maybe she did it as a subconscious cry for her mother, or maybe she did it because it felt protective somehow—like it might prevent any more change. All Nelly knew for sure was that life had changed, and of all the changes, this was the one that hurt the most.

#  Chapter Eleven

## Saturday, December 15th

December 16, 2008

    Not going to lie. I'm SO EXCITED! Today is my first official not-just-meditating training. Given our primary goal (to stop a raging bonfire), Gabby thought it would be best to focus on the magick of fire. While I'm excited to do this, I'll be the first to admit I don't really get why they can't handle the bonfire. Like why can't Gabby and Ethel do it? Maybe I'll ask Gabby about that today.

It was a valid question of course, perhaps the question we all ask when tasked with a responsibility for which we feel woefully inadequate. Nikki didn't have much time to dwell on her inadequacies though, because the purr of an engine told her someone had pulled into the driveway; she put her journal away, left her pre-written note for Margret on the counter, and darted out the door, locking it before she left.

"Hey," Nikki said, as she opened the passenger door.

"Come on in," Gabby said. "Does your mom know where you're going?"

"I left a note," Nikki said, buckling her seatbelt.

"Which says?" Gabby prodded.

"I went to the library with Emma to do homework?"

"And if your mom decided to stop by the library?"

"I'd be sunk," Nikki admitted, starting to undo her seatbelt; Gabby stopped her.

"I've got it." Gabby closed her eyes, raised a hand, and pointed to the house with her three middle fingers. "Now it says you're at my house, and lists my name, address, and phone number."

"Now I am sunk."

"Less than you'd be if you lied," Gabby said, backing out of the driveway.

"I guess."

"So," Gabby said as she drove. "Your dad bound your powers as a baby?"

"Yup," Nikki said. "Grandma tell you?"

"Yes," Gabby said, watching a red light, her blinker clicking rhythmically.

"Figured. Hey, question."

"Shoot." Gabby turned left down a winding road.

"So girls witches, boys…wizards? Warlocks? Also witches?" Nikki asked.

"Witches." Gabby glanced at Nikki and then explained, "Technically, there are wizards, sorcerers and sorceresses, but it's kind of how doctors can be general doctors, or they can be OBs, or podiatrists."

"So all sharks are fish but not all fish are sharks?" Nikki said.

Gabby laughed. "Yeah, I guess you could put it that way. We're all witches, but we go through different trainings after basic training."

"So I'm doing basic right now?"

Gabby nodded as she turned right onto her loop. "Yes, and after you've finished, you can always further your education and go more niche if you want."

"Like what? Can anyone be anything?"

"Yes and no. The various specializations are mostly non-gendered, meaning anyone can do it, but there are certain magicks that are gender specific. For example, certain magicks are entrusted only to women." Gabby said, pulling into her driveway.

"Like what?" Nikki asked.

"Hydromemorology." Gabby unbuckled. "We're here."

"Wait," Nikki said, hopping out of the passenger side and closing the door behind her. "You made that up. The hydro-morph-ology thing."

Gabby laughed as she opened the front door to the small green house and dropped her keys in a red ceramic bowl on a table in the hall. "Hydromemorology, and it does sound made up, doesn't it? But it's real. It's the study of the memories of water," Gabby said, taking her coat off. "So, what do you think?"

Nikki had expected an interior similar to Ethel's library: dark curtains, lots of candles, mystical and magickal. Instead, she was met with bright rooms and clean lines. Gabby's decor was a combination of old world and new world: African baskets hung on one wall, a Brigid Goddess set sat on the mantle over the fireplace, and a gold wire basket held some cozy throws next to a emerald green mid-century modern couch. Sprinkled all around were houseplants; each served a magickal purpose, but as Nikki had not started this study, she just thought them pretty and green.

"I like it. I thought it would be…" Nikki said.

"More witchy?" Gabby offered.

"Yeah, less normal," Nikki said.

"People think witches are all black cats, cloaks, and pumpkins, but we're just like humans. We have differences in taste, and mine are pretty normal," Gabby said as a black and white Maine Coon jumped into her arms. "Good boy, Phineas," she cooed, cuddling him for a moment before setting him down. He ran off.

Nikki watched as the cat disappeared down the hallway and said, "But you have powers, how can you be normal?"

"Rule one of normal: there's no such thing as normal. Everyone has something they're scared other people will think is weird or abnormal. Think about a pastry chef."

"A pastry chef?" Nikki asked.

"Yes. They can create these incredible desserts, and they have a ton of specialty tools they can use, but they don't leave them out everywhere all the time, right?" Gabby opened a drawer and removed a few candles. "Most chefs do things other than just make pastry. Their whole identity isn't crafted around choux." Gabby laughed. "Magick is obviously a lot bigger than pastry." Gabby placed the candles on the floor and walked around the room. She pointed next to the candles on the floor, and said, "Sit there a minute. I want to do a few precautionary spells before we get started."

"Okay," Nikki said, glad she had chosen yoga pants and a t-shirt instead of her usual summer dress.

"Protegat nos ab igne. Protegat nos de flamma. Protegat nos sic ut discamus Magica ignis in tuto," Gabby said. As she repeated herself, she walked around the living room, fingers spread, palms down, like she was feeling the air. She looked like a swimmer sculling. "All right, I think we're ready."

"What did you do?" Nikki asked. "What did you say?"

"I cast a protection spell. It'll basically keep us from burning my place down." Gabby sat on the floor across from Nikki.

"And by 'us,' you mean 'me,' right?" Nikki said with a slight frown.

"Well, yeah," Gabby said. "In all fairness, when I'm trying any new magick, I always cast protection spells first. I like my place; I don't want to rebuild every time I want to study something new."

"That makes me feel better," Nikki said.

"Let's get started. The first thing I want to teach you is how to move fire." Gabby blew on a candle, lighting it. "We'll start with the basics. Use your hand to move the fire, and we'll move on to the eloquence of breathing fire later on. Have you been taught to meditate?"

"Just once by Madam Ortega," Nikki said.

"We'll start there. Once your mind is quieted and focused, let me know," Gabby said. They both closed their eyes and sat in silence for a little while. The cat came in and rubbed himself on Gabby's arms and under her chin before curling up in front of her, leaning against her crossed ankles.

After a little while, Nikki said, "I'm ready."

"Do you remember where the candles are without opening your eyes?"

"Yes."

"Which one is lit?"

Nikki thought for a moment. "The one on my right."

"Now, using your hand move the flame from the right candle to the left in whatever hand motion that feels most natural to you," Gabby said.

"Okay." Nikki put up her right hand, palm up, fingers slightly spread, index finger pointing in the direction of the lit candle. As she tried focusing on the flame, she furrowed her brow.

"Open your eyes," Gabby said quickly.

Nikki did and saw that the flame had quadrupled in size. It wasn't an out-of-control fire, but the flame was unnaturally large for the pillar candles they were using. As she and Gabby watched it, it shrunk back down to its original size.

"Did I…" Nikki asked.

"What were you thinking about?"

"I was thinking it would be easier to feel the flame if it was larger," Nikki admitted.

"Kait wasn't kidding when she said you've got a lot of power," Gabby said, petting her cat. "Let's try again." They did the exercise three more times, and each time Nikki succeeded only in making the flame larger.

"I don't think I can do this," Nikki finally said.

"Of course you can; you're just overthinking it." Gabby smiled at her softly. As a recovering overthinker, she recognized the symptoms.

"So what? I'm just supposed to wave my hand and move the flame?" Nikki said, and as if to prove her own incompetence, she flicked her hand from the right to the left. To the surprise of Nikki (but not Gabby), the flame moved. It simply hopped from one candle to the next. "I did it?"

"You did it!" Gabby said with a laugh.

"I don't understand how I did that." Nikki flicked her hand again, from left to right this time, and the flame jumped back to the right candle. "Or that."

"Even though you haven't gotten to use your magick until now, it's still been inside of you, growing and maturing. That's why you were able to summon living, breathing animals on your first day," Gabby said.

"I wouldn't have minded if the octopus would have been a little less alive when he attacked me in the shower," Nikki said, still flicking her hand and making the flame jump from one candle to the other and back again.

"Octopus?"

"Mhmm. I wasn't even thinking about an octopus. I don't remember what I was thinking about, but I know I deliberately thought about it disappearing as soon as its—" Nikki wiggled her fingers and made a face.

"Tentacles?" Gabby guessed, laughing.

"It wasn't funny!" Nikki insisted even though she was laughing, too. "As soon as its tentacles went for my feet—" she mocked gagging.

"Very impressive."

"Very gross is more like it."

"I think you've got the hang of moving fire," Gabby said.

"Yeah, it's actually easier than I thought." Nikki moved the flame again with a flick of her fingers.

"You were over-thinking," Gabby said.

"I have a tendency to do that," Nikki admitted, moving the flame again.

"Me, too," Gabby admitted. "Now, try putting the flame out this time."

"I'm guessing I can't just blow it out?" Nikki asked, raising one eyebrow.

Gabby smiled. "Magickal fire can only be extinguished by magick."

Nikki closed her eyes and stretched her hand out again. She moved her fingers down, closing her hands into a fist. She peeked through one eye and saw the flame was gone, but when she put her hand down, the flame popped back up as though it was atop a trick candle. Nikki's shoulders slumped.

"Try again," Gabby said. "It's important you learn how to figure out this for yourself. There will come a time where you'll need to do something you never learned, and you'll have to figure out how to do it."

Nikki nodded and closed her eyes again. She focused, repeating in her mind: no flame, no fire, no light. "Nulla lux," she whispered. The flame went out.

"I thought you said you haven't been trained," Gabby said, the surprise evident in her voice.

"I haven't," Nikki said. "Did I do something wrong?"

"Not exactly. How did you know that spell?"

"What spell?"

"Nulla lux—it's the spell to put out small fires." Worry lined Gabby's face. "Have you studied Latin?"

"No, I do take French, but I'm not very good—wait, what do you mean 'it's a spell'? How could I know a spell without knowing I knew it?" Nikki furrowed her brow.

"I'm not sure. I've never heard of it before; then again," Gabby admitted and added, "I'm not privy to every single magickal event in the history of magick. Still, I'll need to talk to Kait about it."

"Are spells bad?" Nikki watched the unlit candle as it released its very last wisps of smoke into the air.

"Not necessarily," Gabby said, trying to smile reassuringly as she patted Nikki's hand. "It's just—Kait and I are of the school of thought that spells should be saved until mastery has been achieved. Spells can be a kind of shortcut, and if witches get too reliant on spells, they can get trapped by them."

"Like not knowing how to do something without a spell?"

"Exactly." Gabby got up and wrote a few notes in a notebook. "Okay, let's try again, sans spell, please." Gabby sat back down and relit the candle with a wave of her hand.

"Are there rules in magick?" Nikki asked, adjusting her seat and stretching her legs.

"Technically yes and no. There are rules about magick for magickal beings, but magick itself doesn't abide by rules. Think of magick—and this is all magick, not just earth magick—as a wild animal; it can be trained within reason, it can be more or less read, but it will always be wild and unpredictable. A witch's most powerful tool is her adaptability."

Nikki nodded.

They spent the next half-hour working on the extinguishing exercise. Then, Gabby taught Nikki how to light the candle. Once she had that down, Gabby had Nikki perform all the steps: lighting the candle, moving the flame around a few times, and then extinguishing it. Nikki repeated the cycle until she couldn't get it wrong, until she could do everything on her first try. The last thing Gabby taught Nikki was how to do the fire magick protection spell, so Nikki could practice safely at home. After two hours of practice, and double-checking Nikki had mastered the fire magick protection spell, Gabby took Nikki home.

Dec. 15, 08
    I know I said I'd never tell anyone, so this is going to sound crazy, but I decided I have to tell Wyatt. I mean, not _have to_ have to, but like I personally _need_ to tell him. I need him in my life, and we've never had secrets. I don't want to start now. I might not be able to surf, but that doesn't mean I have to lose everything. I'm already at the Cove. He should be here in half an hour.

Nelly sat in the sand and watched the early morning mist slowly clear as the sun warmed the sky. She pulled her hands into the sleeves of her sweatshirt and stood, jumping around. Checking her watch, Nelly figured she'd set up; it was already a quarter past. She still had fifteen minutes before Wyatt was supposed to come. Carrying an extra bikini bottom and a towel, she walked over to the waterline. Nelly put both items down close to the water, but far enough away that they would stay dry. She wanted easy access to covering up.

"You're here early."

It felt like ages since she'd heard that voice. "So are you," Nelly said, trying to keep the nerves out of her voice.

"So, what's up?" Wyatt asked, trudging down through the sand towards her. His hair was still all sticky-outy from sleeping. He had on board shorts and his Otter Sands Surf Club hoodie (complete with yellow surfing otter graphic). The blue of his hoodie brought out the blue in his eyes…not that Nelly ever noticed. No, really. She never noticed. Between you and me, it wouldn't be the last time she missed the obvious, but back to their conversation.

"First, I'm going to tell you; then, when you don't believe me, I'm going to show you."

"Why wouldn't I—"

"And—" Nelly held a hand up to him. "This will be way less painful if you don't interrupt." She took off her sweatpants, wadded them up and threw them back towards all her things. "Here goes," she said under her breath.

"Are you insane? It's freezing!" Wyatt said, gesturing to her abandoned pants.

"No interrupting," Nelly said, pointing a finger at him. "On my birthday, I went surfing with Jo. I looked down, and my skin was a different color, and not just tanner than usual," she added knowing he was probably going to make some snide remark. "It was green—not like, I'm the Hulk green, but definitely not normal green. I came here a few days later to see if maybe it was a fluke. Maybe the sun was messing with my head, maybe I drank too much salt water." She pulled her sweatshirt off and threw it. A shiver moved through her skin that had nothing to do with the cold. "It was a fluke all right, a fluke I didn't change completely the first time. I turn into a—" Nelly shook her head and rolled her eyes. "I turn into a mermaid when I get in the ocean now." She looked at Wyatt.

Wyatt scoffed, speechless. Finally, when he found words, he said, "Wow. What a load of bull. If you're not even going to be serious…" He started walking back up the beach.

"Told you," Nelly murmured. She walked up to him and yanked his hoodie off; he was so startled, he didn't even fight her. She grabbed his hand, dragging him to the waterline. She snatched up her extra bikini bottom. "Hold this," she said, shoving it into his free hand and pulling him around in front of her.

"Woah, woah," he said as she shoved him into the water.

"Go," she said, giving him a final shove, which resulted in him falling face-first into the water. She dived under the waves and came up just as he spluttered to the surface.

"What the heck, dude?" Wyatt said, wiping his face with his hands. "The water's freezing! What kind of sick game—"

"Wyatt!" Nelly shouted. "Look at me!"

"You're wet," he said, glancing at her. Rain drops began pattering on the surface of the water. "Great," he mumbled sarcastically. "Now, it's raining, too."

"Look at me," she repeated, practically shoving her hand in his face, trying to show him the webbing.

Huffing, he turned and pulled back a bit before taking her hand. His eyes narrowed as he ran a finger over the webbing. He looked at her, really studying her. This time Wyatt saw all the subtle differences. "Your eyes—they're not blue anymore. They're green," he said, his hair plastered to his face. "And your skin…"

"It's not just my skin," Nelly said, pulling her hand from him. The rain poured on them. Nelly leaned back. Her long, sleek, black tail sliced through the surface of the muddled water. "I knew you wouldn't believe me. I knew I'd have to show you."

There was a long silence before he finally asked, "What happened to you?"

"Let's get out of the rain, and I'll tell you," Nelly said. "But first give me those." She pointed to the neon green bottoms in his hand.

"But you're a…and you don't have…'cause you've got a…" Wyatt held onto the bikini bottoms, randomly switching from putting both hands on his head to gesturing at Nelly to moving his arms about.

"Wyatt!"

He looked at her, his eyes wide.

"Give me the bottoms, and get out of the water," Nelly said slowly.

He stared at her.

"I need the bikini bottoms," Nelly said.

When speech found him again, Wyatt spluttered, "What about your other…" He raised his eyebrows. "Oh, the whole…" he gestured towards all of her. "Right." He tossed them over. He walked mechanically out of the water and grabbed Nelly's now soaking towel.

Nelly crawled into the shallower water, grateful for the rain blurring the water enough to maintain her privacy, not that Wyatt would have looked anyway. It only took a few moments of most of her body being out of the water for her to change back. She pulled the bottoms on and got out.

"You can turn around now," Nelly said to Wyatt, who had his back towards her.

He didn't turn around; the rain raged loudly. It was almost a storm.

Nelly ran up to Wyatt and grabbed her towel, wrapping it around herself. "You know you don't need to close your eyes if your back is towards me anyway, right?" she yelled.

"What?" Wyatt yelled back, opening his eyes.

"Come on." Nelly pulled him along again.

She didn't need to pull far before he followed. He grabbed his flip-flops and his soaked hoodie from where it had been carelessly tossed by Nelly earlier. She was a few steps ahead of him, throwing her now drenched sweatpants over her shoulder and grabbing her duffle. They made the hike up to the street and hopped inside her truck.

"What happened to you?" Wyatt repeated his question from earlier. The rain pattered on the steel of the truck.

"Here." Nelly tossed him an extra towel. She always kept a few spares inside the truck. It was not her first time getting caught in the rain. Wrapped in a spare blanket, she toweled off her hair. "Genetics, apparently," she said.

"What do you mean? Is your dad a—"

"My mom. She was the—the one who could change."

"Are you a mutant?" Wyatt asked.

"What?" Nelly looked at him. "Seriously?"

He just stared at her.

"Oh my gosh." She put her palm to her forehead. "No, I'm not a mutant."

"Wait—what about that 'medicine' that surf company wanted you to try?"

"It was a sports drink, Wyatt." Nelly rolled her eyes.

"You drank it, didn't you? That's why you're a mutant."

"I'm not a mutant!"

"I bet the government is behind sports drinks. They're trying to make super fish-people soldiers—"

"This is not the government!" Nelly snapped.

"How do we fix this?" Wyatt looked at his broken friend.

"You can't," Nelly said a bit dejectedly. "I tried everything. The only way for me to not change is to not get in the ocean."

"What if we contact the government and tell them you'll use your mutant powers against them unless—"

"I am not a mutant!" Nelly whacked Wyatt's shoulder. "And for the last time this isn't the government's fault."

There were a few moments of silence.

Wyatt said, "So, what now? What are you going to do?"

"What can I do? I tried wearing a wetsuit and surfing, but I fell in, and my suit got shredded," Nelly said, shaking her head. "This is why I haven't been surfing. I can't anymore. I'm done."

"I don't know what to say," Wyatt admitted.

"At least you know why now." Nelly shrugged.

"Who else knows about this?"

"Nikki and Emma."

"Who?" Wyatt frowned.

"They're in Miranda's class with us. The group history project?"

"The tall one and the weird blonde one with the stuff in her hair?"

"That's them."

"You told them before you told me?" Wyatt asked, almost too quietly to hear.

"No. You're the first person *I've* told." Nelly sighed. "But I think might have known about me before I even knew," she mumbled. She sighed again, loudly and with her whole body. "What I mean is I think Emma already knew, and Nikki figured it out from hanging with Emma. I was going to tell them, but then Nikki was all 'We know,' and then Nikki kept telling me they needed me and my powers." Nelly let it all spill out. She told Wyatt everything: about how Emma knew about Jess Pedersen when no one else did, about how Madam Ortega had read her cards and her palm, about the first time she changed and how painful and terrifying it was. Everything Nelly had been holding in came pouring out. It was the catharsis she had needed since the very beginning. The only thing Nelly left out was the fact Nikki and Emma weren't exactly normal teenagers themselves. Those weren't her secrets to tell.

"So they want your help?" Wyatt asked when Nelly was finished.

"Yeah."

"Don't."

"What? What do you mean 'don't'?" Nelly asked.

"Don't help them. Why should you?" Wyatt put his hands up. "I know you think this stuff started because of your genetics, but shouldn't it have started a long time ago? But it didn't until you started hanging out with Emma and Nikki, right? What if it wasn't the government after all? What if Emma and Nikki are the ones doing this to you? Why should you help them? Why should you even trust them?" Wyatt said.

"That doesn't even make sense. Besides, I got the feeling I could trust them," Nelly said, shrugging.

"Like you got the feeling you could ride that monster wave at the break?" Wyatt said, scoffing.

"I mastered it eventually," Nelly retorted.

"After a trip to the emergency room and three months on crutches," Wyatt said.

"A month and a half."

"It was supposed to be three months. My point is you nearly killed yourself and that was doing something you've been doing your whole life. This stuff is new to you. So what if you have powers, why should you help them? Why should you even use them; what if you blow yourself up?" Wyatt said.

"Fair point, except…"

"Except what?"

"I don't have any powers. All I do is turn into a fish," Nelly threw her towel at him.

He ducked.

"Wyatt?" Nelly said after a minute.

"Hmm?"

"Thanks for not completely freaking out."

"Well, it's just my first time seeing my best friend turn into a fish, what is there to freak out about?" Wyatt said, and for the first time in a long time, Nelly laughed.

15 December 2008

I can't shake this. I'm missing something. There's some piece of the puzzle I should have had by now. There's something I should have figured out.

Emma put her journal down and picked up her phone. She wrote a quick text message to Nikki (Any chance we could meet up today?), and hit send.

Maybe I'm overreacting. It wouldn't be the first time, but my instincts say something is wrong. I want to tell Nikki about this feeling. Maybe we could meditate and get this figured out, but I don't want to say anything until I know for sure she can meet up.

Emma waited, lightly drumming her fingers on her desk. Her phone dinged.

> **Nikki:** Prob not, but I can try. Mom is still super P.O-ed about my magick training this morning.
> **Emma:** How did that go?
> **Nikki:** Super good. Gabby taught me some protection spells so I can practice at home.
> **Emma:** What are you practicing?
> **Nikki:** Lighting a candle, then moving the flame

around—Gab called it basic control—and then putting it out (prob the most important part for the bonfire).

**Emma**: Sounds awesome.

**Nikki**: Something freaky happened, too. I did a spell without knowing any spells.

**Emma**: Is that even possible?

**Nikki**: Apparently. But Gabby said she'd never heard of it happening before. Also, asked my mom about meeting you at the library and she said no.

**Emma**: No worries. See you Monday.


Emma sighed and grabbed a pillow, throwing it on the floor. She meditated for over an hour, but she couldn't focus properly. She was too worried about what she would see, or worse, what she wouldn't see.

# Chapter Twelve

## Sunday, December 16th

December 16, 2008

    Got an email from Dad. He wasn't particularly helpful. Mostly he was just cryptic.

Nikki looked at her computer screen, the email still open:

    Hey kid,

    Sorry it took me so long to get back to you, but you know the drill. Anyway, I think Aisling O'Crean would be a great family member to research. Also, you and Mom probably aren't getting along right now because of what's going on, but you need to ease up on her. The day will come when you will rely on her, and she'll need to rely on you. Build trust. Forgive.

    The most important thing is you find it. Find what you were meant to have. It will tell you everything, but it will only reveal itself to you when you are ready. Wish I could tell you more. Sorry I couldn't tell you sooner. Proud of you.

    Love, Dad

Nikki sighed. The penultimate line certainly indicated he knew what was going to happen, which confirmed Kait's story. The bit about her and her mom not getting along was hardly a stretch, magick or no magick. Nikki chewed her lip.

Dad says I have to find "it." But does he tell me what it is? Does he even give me a hint? Nope, so even if I somehow manage to find "it," how would I even know?

Nikki closed her laptop and her journal. In the next room, Kam practiced a jazzified version of Jingle Bells on his trombone. Margret knocked on the doorframe of Nikki's opened door.

"What's up?" Nikki asked.

Margret rubbed her temples, grimacing as the trombone squealed. "Why don't you take Kam to the library?"

"Sure," Nikki said, failing to suppress a smile.

She gathered a few things and grabbed Kam. After the siblings had talked about where they should actually go (since the library was closed on Sundays), Nikki and Kam sat in the driveway at Emma's house waiting for her. Emma came out and got in the back seat.

"Hello, again," Emma said with a smile.

"Hi," Kam said and gave Emma a small wave.

"I need to drop Kam off," Nikki said, her hand on the head of the passenger seat as she looked back at Emma.

"Okie dokie," Emma said. "Band practice on a Sunday?"

"Not exactly," Kam said. "It's more like unofficial practice. See, I'm second trombone, but I think Mr. Melkin might move me up to first chair though because Josh keeps missing notes. Mr. Melkin is only keeping him in first chair because Josh had the flu but didn't miss any rehearsals. He was hacking up—"

"We don't need details," Nikki said quickly.

"Right, well, it was gross," Kam said with a meaningful look.

"Sounds like it," Emma said, grinning.

"So, we're going over to Jody's house. He's my friend from school," Kam explained. "I'm hoping I can get first chair, and he can get second, or vice versa, anything so we don't have to sit next to Josh anymore. He always empties his spit valve on my music."

"It's a surprise *you* didn't get the flu from him," Emma said.

"I probably would have, but Mr. Melkin made him sit alone so Josh wouldn't get the whole band sick," Kam said. "You can drop me off here."

"Are you sure?" Nikki asked, pulling into the parking lot of an apartment building.

"Yeah, just help me get my trombone out."

Nikki parked the car, and she and Kam got out. She popped the trunk and helped Kam drag out the heavy black case. A gangly boy with straight black hair cut in a mushroom style walked out of the main entrance.

"Hi, Kameron," the kid said.

"Jody, this is my sister, Nikki." Kam pointed to Nikki.

"Nice to meet you, Nikki," Jody said.

"Nice to meet you, too, Jody." Nikki smiled and raised her eyebrows. "Kam, call me when you're done."


16 December 2008

I'm sitting in Nikki's car. The feeling is growing. If she doesn't have any ideas of what to do today, I'm definitely suggesting meditating. I know it's boring, but we need to figure this out.


"Hey," Nikki said, as she hopped back into the driver's seat and buckled in. "So, I have an idea, and you're probably going to say it's a bad idea, BUT I think it's at least worth a shot."

"'Kay," Emma said slowly, simultaneously curious and cautious.

"I think we should go to Nelly's house and try to explain everything. At least give her a chance to make a choice knowing all the facts," Nikki said.

"That's…" Emma trailed off. It was a terrible idea. "…an idea. I mean, I really think she'll come around if we just give her space and time."

"We don't really have a lot of time though, do we?" Nikki retorted. "Besides, what if I don't pass out? What if I die? I mean, in theory, we don't even need her to team up with us, we just need her to be there, right?"

"In theory," Emma said. "But I want it on record that I think this is a terrible idea."

"Consider it recorded," Nikki said. "How do I get there?"

The doorbell rang. Nelly jumped up off the couch and ran to answer the door, fully expecting Wyatt to be standing there with hands too full of pizza and soda to open the door and let himself in like he usually did. She was, therefore, quite surprised when she opened the door to find Nikki and Emma standing there.

"What do you want?" Nelly said.

"We just want to talk." Nikki held her hands up in surrender.

"About?" Nelly stepped outside, pushing the screen door open, which screeched loudly and slammed shut behind her.

"Your help," Nikki said. As Nelly scoffed and rolled her eyes, Nikki added, "Listen, you don't have to do anything. We just need your powers."

"Powers? I don't—why should I help you? Why should I even trust either of you?" Nelly said. "You," Nelly turned on Emma, "You knew what I was going through. Do you have any idea what this has done to my life? My whole life is gone." Nelly felt the words catch in her throat. Her eyes felt hot, and her throat burned. She swallowed and took a breath. "When people would say describe yourself, my answer was always 'I'm a surfer.' That's gone now. How do I know that's not because of you?" The words were out before she even considered what she was saying. "I don't know who I am anymore. It took me a week to tell my best friend, and you guys knew all along."

Emma shook her head. "Nelly, I'm so sorry—"

"Save it," Nelly said. "I'm not helping you guys. Don't you get it? My life is over. Everyone is talking about me, my sister thinks I've lost my mind, and my dreams are gone. Can't you leave me alone?" Nelly turned back towards the house.

"Wait!" Nikki put her hand on the door.

"Nikki, we should go," Emma said.

"I'm in the same boat you are," Nikki said. "I woke up one morning, and I wasn't the same person anymore. I found out my mother knew the whole time and made my father hide it from me, but I didn't wallow in self-pity. I found out I was needed, and I accepted the call."

"Good for you. Is being a witch painful for you? Does your entire physiology rewrite itself every time you want to use your 'powers'?" Nelly said, putting finger quotes around 'powers.'

"Why won't you help us stop the fire?" Nikki asked, her hand falling off the door and back to her side.

"Because I don't care if you burn." The words felt too cruel even as Nelly said them, but anger fueled her. "You sat by and watched my world burn, why should I care if yours does?" Nelly turned around, yanked the screen door open and went inside, slamming the door behind her before Nikki or Emma saw her tears.

Nelly rubbed the tears off with one palm, irritated with herself for letting them out. Pacing, angrily muttering, she went over the conversation in her head again and again. When there was a gentle knock on the door, Nelly stormed over, fully prepared for battle this time.

"I told you, I'm not—" she opened the door and found Wyatt standing there, holding pizza and soda in front of him as a peace offering.

"Whatever I did, I'm sorry," he said.

Ignoring him, Nelly opened the door and walked outside, looking around.

"Am I missing something?" Wyatt asked, glancing around behind her, still holding all the food.

"You'll never believe what happened," Nelly said, holding the door open for him to go inside. She filled him in as they ate the pizza.

"So, they want you to help put out a fire?" Wyatt asked, folding his fourth slice of pizza in half like a taco.

"Yeah," Nelly said.

"Did you ask them if they're the ones who turned your into a—"

"Fish."

"Right, fish?" He ate half the slice in one bite.

"No," Nelly said. "I mean, I sort of accused them, but mostly because I was mad. I don't actually think…" She shook her head. "I'm the way I am because of my mom." She picked a pepperoni off her pizza. "You know," Nelly said after a minute, "Emma did say she was sorry—"

"Der oo go," Wyatt said through his mouthful of pizza.

"There I go what?" Nelly asked.

Wyatt swallowed. "People only apologize when they did something wrong. Emma apologized, so she must have done something wrong. It's practically a confession."

Nelly considered this as she sipped her soda. The idea didn't sit well with her. Emma's apology had felt empathetic, not guilty.

"Do your project, and then switch classes," Wyatt said.

"Amen to that," Nelly said.


16 December 2008
That couldn't have gone worse if we had planned it. Details later.

Emma sat in Nikki's car. They hadn't spoken since the fiasco at Nelly's. Emma knew better than to say 'I told you so,' but it didn't stop her from thinking it. Over and over again. Luckily, she knew her best bet was to hold her tongue and hope a good night's sleep would help all three of them feel better.

The ride home was long and awkward.

# Chapter Thirteen

## Monday, December 17th

December 17, 2008

Meeting with Nelly yesterday was a fiasco. If Nelly didn't hate us before, she definitely does now. There's no way she'll help us, but I still had to try. Maybe if Emma had backed me up, it wouldn't have been as bad.

Even as Nikki wrote the words, a part of her felt the unfairness of them. She rolled off her stomach and sat up in bed. Her legs ached from her morning run, and her hair dripped from her shower.

Whatever. I'm going to do what I can to prepare. Like last night, I put the protection spell on my room and practiced with some candles for most of the night. I even had three flames going at once, but it still doesn't feel like enough. I need to practice with bigger flames if I want to stand a chance at the bonfire.

Nikki looked at the clock by her bed. "Kam," she called. "Hurry up. It's seven-fifteen."

"Almost done," he called back from the kitchen, the garbled sound of his voice evidence that he was still eating.

In four days, this will be over. We'll either stop the bonfire, or we'll be dead. Or maybe both. I wonder if Mom would talk to me again if I was dead.


"That's a cheery thought," Nikki said under her breath as she closed her journal, throwing it in her backpack. "Kam," she called. "Let's go."

After dropping Kam off at the middle school, Nikki raced into first period French—how she had managed to hit every single red light in the small town, she would never know. By some miracle she managed to get into her seat right as the bell rang.

"Bonjour, classe," Madame Fleur said. "Now, before we begin French, the administration has asked me to remind you to be kind to each other. A student at this school lost his mother on Friday, so remember, you never know what hardships your peers are facing. Alors, sois gentil, oui, classe?"

"Oui, Madame," the class replied in unison.

"Très bien! Mademoiselle Rodrigues, this was left in my box for you because French is your first class," Madame Fleur said, handing an envelope to Nikki. "S'il vous plait attendre après la classe pour l'ouvrir."

"Oui, Madame. Merci," Nikki said, taking the envelope.

Madame Fleur continued, "Maintenant, nous allons ouvrir nos livres à la page soixante-quatorze."

While the rest of the class opened their books and turned to page seventy-four, Nikki looked at the envelope. She groaned when she saw the front; her name was scribbled in her grandmother's handwriting. She crammed it in her backpack, too irritated to be curious about it just now.


17 December 2008

Sometimes I wish I was a fairy and could influence other's feelings. It would make life a lot easier, especially this next history class. Psychic-medium magick is useless in this case. I don't need the ability to see auras to see Nikki and Nelly are ready for open war.


Emma put her journal in her backpack and glanced at Nelly and Nikki, who sat on opposite sides of the classroom.

"Move into your groups," Mr. Miranda said, gesturing with a piece of chalk in his hand. "I have new questions for you today. I know we're out of school on Wednesday, but that's no excuse to start the holidays early." As the class moved, Mr. Miranda wrote six questions on the board and added, "Answer these questions today, and we can party on Wednesday."

Once Nikki and Nelly had scraped desks over, Emma peered at the board and read, "Question one: how do we want to present?"

"Whatever is fine," Nelly said, her arms crossed as she sank into her chair, staring hard at the floor.

"Why don't we just burn it?" Nikki murmured, shooting a side eye at Nelly, who pretended not to notice. "Nelly likes to let things burn."

"Can we leave that outside of the classroom and focus on the project?" Emma asked, dropping her voice. "Please?"

"How can we? This is where it started," Nikki whispered back.

"I can do it," Nelly said. "I don't know if the *witch* can, though."

"How about a poster board?" Emma said brightly, even though she knew trying to get them to play nice wasn't going to work.

"That works for me," Nelly said.

"Fine," Nikki said.

"Okay. I will buy it, and we can each do our own part on colored paper, and then we'll glue it onto the board that way we don't have to keep moving the poster board around between us," Emma said.

"Works for me," Nelly said.

"Fine," Nikki said.

"I can take the center. I'll write our names on the top half and then put my part of the project on the bottom half," Emma said, sketching out a rough design on a scratch piece of paper. "Nelly, you can take the right, and Nikki, you take the left."

"Works for me," Nelly said.

"Fine," Nikki said.

"Second question, what information is most important?" Emma read. "We'll come back to that one. Next, what do our three people have in common? Well, they all had mysterious things happen to them. Jess showing up on the beach one day; Aisling getting burned, and my grandma is a mysterious event all on her own. What do you think?"

"Works for me," Nelly said.

"Fine," Nikki said.

Emma looked at the pair of them. They were sitting with a desk between them, each staring at her own corner of floor. Nelly looked like a tropical storm one rain cloud away from hitting hurricane status while Nikki resembled a red supergiant about to supernova at any moment. Emma took a deep breath and relaxed her clenched fists back to open palms.

"All right," Emma said, flexing her hands. "Next question, how can I help get my group an 'A' for the project? Yeah, we'll come back to that one, too. Okay, last two: choose one person that would be most interesting to meet, and why did you pick that person? Well this should be easy. We can cross out my grandma since she's still alive. That leaves us with Aisling and Jess. To meet during the peak of her life? I think I would pick Aisling only because she's further back in the timeline. The late sixteen hundreds must have been an interesting time to live in Salem. How about you two?"

"Works for me," Nelly said.

"Fine," Nikki said.

"Honestly!" Emma stood up. The entire class quieted, all eyes locked onto her. "You two sitting there, arms folded, not looking at each other. How old are you anyway? When you're ready to behave like actual people, come find me. Until then, I'd rather do the project *alone*." She picked up her bag and stormed to the front of the classroom. "I'll be in the library," she told Mr. Miranda, who nodded, simply too stunned to speak.

Emma left the classroom and headed straight for the library just as she had told Mr. Miranda she would. Before she got there, though, she felt overwhelmed with cold.

"Not here, not now," she whispered, leaning against a wall, but it was too late.

*"Help me! Help!" people screamed. Emma couldn't see them. There was too much smoke. Where was Nikki? Emma saw hot pink blurs. They were the flyers. The pink flyers were scattered everywhere. Emma coughed; she tried to breathe, but there was no air. It was smoke, all-consuming smoke. Her eyes stung; her lungs burned. Emma tried to call for Nikki, but she could barely whisper. She was on her hands and knees now, crawling. Bumping into something, she looked down: it wasn't a something, it was a someone. Emma still couldn't speak, so she shook the person. She could barely see him through the smoke. She got no response. Suddenly a huge flame exploded next to her. Emma fell next to the person. Glancing at the profile, she recognized whoever it was, but before she could put a name to the face everything faded into blackness.*

"Emma? Emma, dear? Are you all right?"

The voice came from somewhere above Emma. As her eyes slowly refocused, gaining hold of the physical world, they snapped shut. It was too bright here. Emma tried to speak, but her throat burned. She coughed instead. Her head was sore, and her left wrist throbbed like it had a heartbeat all its own. She took slow, deep, intentional breaths. The air was cool and tasted…sterile?

"Rachelle, she's waking up," the same voice said.

Emma recognized it this time. "Nurse Albright?"

"Yes, dear," the old woman said.

"Emma, are you okay?" Rachelle said.

Emma opened her eyes again; it wasn't quite so bright anymore. "Where am I?" she asked, trying to sit up.

"No, lie down. Em, you're in the nurse's office. I got a call. You ran out of class. One of the teachers saw you faint in the hallway," Rachelle said, adding meaningfully, "Was it an *episode*?"

You see, when Emma was younger, her visions used to overpower her regularly. For Emma's early years, Amy, that's Emma's mother if you remember, had dealt with this by homeschooling. However, when Amy died, Rachelle and Ethel had come up with the idea of telling the school Emma had a medical condition which caused her to lose consciousness for small moments of time. It didn't make Emma popular with the other kids, but it gave the teachers a logical justification to explain away Emma's unusual behavior. So when Rachelle said 'episode," Emma knew exactly what she was referencing.

"Yeah," Emma said, touching her still sore head.

"You haven't had one of those in years, dear," Nurse Albright said. She had been the nurse at Emma's elementary school. Emma had seen less and less of her over the years. This was the first time they'd seen each other at the high school, though the nurse looked exactly the same: bright green eyes, short permed dark hair, and a handful of hard candies in her pocket.

"It's probably stress related," Rachelle said. "I'll take her, if that's okay."

"Oh yes. Her school bag is right here," Nurse Albright said, pulling Emma's bag out from under the bed.

"Thank you," Rachelle said, taking the backpack.

"Thanks, Nurse Albright," Emma said, trying to remember everything that had happened in the vision.

"No problem, dear." Nurse Albright handed Emma a watermelon-flavored candy (Emma's favorite). "Be sure to get plenty of rest. School is almost out, and then you can have a nice, stress-free winter break." She gave Emma and Rachelle a small wave as they left the office.

"What happened?" Rachelle said, once they were safely in the car.

Emma explained everything as Rachelle drove. She told Rachelle about the big argument the day before, which led her to why she tried to play peacemaker between Nelly and Nikki in class, which led her to why she was in the hallway during class time, which led her to the vision that landed her in the nurse's office.

"…and now we're here talking about it," Emma said. "Also, why does my wrist hurt so much?" She winced as she tried opening her candy.

"From what Nurse Albright said, you were lying on your wrist when she found you in the hallway. She suggested we go to the doctor and get it x-rayed because you might have broken something."

"Awesome," Emma said. She stuck one end of the wrapper between her teeth and pulled with her good hand. Popping the candy in her mouth, Emma closed her eyes and rested her head on the window.

"You could have a concussion, falling on those hard high school floors," Rachelle said, shaking her head.

"Is that where we're going now? The doctor's?" Emma asked as Rachelle turned down a street.

"Yes. Now, tell me about your vision one more time."

Emma told her the vision again.

"Do you remember the boy in your vision?" Rachelle said.

"You know how sometimes you recognize an actor's voice on the television? Like you know you know him but you can't remember from where? It's like that. I mean, I'm not even sure he was a he, you know?" Emma said.

"Just a face you recognized? From school maybe?" Rachelle offered.

"Maybe, but, I just—I don't know for sure."

"And Nikki wasn't there?"

"She might have been, but I couldn't see her. It was all smoke." Emma had only ever had a handful of visions that scared her, and this one was quickly pulling into first place. "Do you think I saw my own death?"

"I don't think so," Rachelle said, and then, after a moment she added, "You might have, but there's no way to know for sure. We're here. Support your wrist with your other arm."

Emma groaned and not just from the pain in her wrist. She *might* have seen her own death. It was not what she wanted to hear, but Rachelle didn't do that. Rachelle told the truth, especially when it was the truth no one wanted to hear.





Nikki looked around her room. She was really just killing time until her next lesson with Gabby. Nikki hadn't ever bothered decorating. There was no point in decorating if she was planning to leave in less than a year—being magickal hadn't changed her main plans: finish high school and jet off to college as fast and far away as possible. As she looked around the sparse room, Nikki's gaze landed over her backpack. A little light clicked in her brain, and she remembered the letter she had shoved in her backpack during French. Nikki hopped off her bed and reached her bag in two large steps. She found the letter and ripped it open. Inside were two letters: one for her, and one closed with an old-fashioned wax seal. Nikki opened hers:

There was a honk from the driveway. Sighing, Nikki stuck Gabby's letter in one of the books she was borrowing from Ethel and threw the book and her journal in her bag as she headed out the door.

# Chapter Fourteen

## Tuesday, December 18th

Dec. 18, 08

Everyone is counting down to break. Two days. Only two days left of school before Christmas break. Then, six months later, I'm 100% done with high school. And then I have to figure out what to do with the rest of my life. Dad wasn't kidding when he told me to have a back up plan in case surfing didn't work out. I always thought he just wanted me to finish school, he probably meant an injury, but I don't think either of us pictured me going out this way.

"So, I have nachos, tacos, and a burrito," Wyatt said, setting two trays of food down on the table. "What do you want?"

"Nachos." Nelly reached across the table and slid a tray towards herself. She closed her journal and stuffed it in her bag before returning her attention to her plate of fried chips covered in meat, melted cheese, and diced tomatoes.

"Did you get one of these?" Wyatt pulled one of Sarah's pink flyers from his pocket and uncrumpled it.

"Yeah, Sarah gave me like thirteen of them," Nelly said, rolling her eyes. "I'm not going."

Nelly's last few boyfriends were 'mega-partiers' as she called them. Because of said exes, Nelly had a lot of experiences with bonfires thrown by popular kids. They were all the same: too much smoke, too much drama, and not nearly enough chocolate to be worth putting up with the aforementioned.

"Whatever, it's my first time getting invited, and I'm going," Wyatt said. He took a bite of his burrito, chewed a few times and then swallowed. "Maybe I'll meet some hot babes there." Wyatt wiggled his eyebrows.

"Gross." Nelly threw a cheese-less chip at Wyatt, who ducked out of the way. "Just don't whine to me if it's lame."

"You should come with me. It could be fun," Wyatt said. He took another bite of his burrito.

"You go. I'm going to stay home and watch a movie." Nelly poked at her nachos.

"Hey, is that them?" Wyatt pointed with his burrito to a spot behind Nelly.

Nelly turned and saw Emma and Nikki walking away from where she and Wyatt were sitting. "Yeah, that's them."

Emma looked back at them; Wyatt turned away, pointing his nose in the air like he was looking at something very far away in a very different direction. Nelly, who had waited a second longer to turn around, saw Emma's face grow suddenly concerned before she looked away.

"That was weird," Nelly said.

"Hmm?" Wyatt asked, his mouth full of burrito.

"Emma looked worried," Nelly said.

"Dude, let it go." Wyatt swallowed. "It's probably part of her master plan to get you to go over there and ask what's wrong, so she can get you to do whatever they want."

"That is a really stupid plan." Nelly laughed and picked a chip off her plate.

"Don't blame me. It's *her* stupid plan," Wyatt said. He ate the last bite of his burrito.


18 December 2008

It's lunchtime, and I'm hiding in the library. I should get something to eat, but I feel too queasy to worry about food just now. I keep thinking about how I acted yesterday. I don't blame Nikki or Nelly for not wanting anything to do with me. In additional news, I broke my wrist yesterday. I've got a bright yellow half-cast on it. The color makes me happy, even if the ache in my wrist doesn't.

"Emma," Nikki whispered.

Emma looked up and saw Nikki pulling up a chair to her table. Nikki's eyes widened when she saw the yellow cast.

"What happened?" Nikki whispered.

Emma glanced around and then leaned closer to Nikki. "I had a vision after I left Miranda's yesterday. It was a pretty strong one, and I fell and broke my wrist. The doc said it was a clean break and should heal pretty fast."

"Does it hurt?" Nikki asked. "I've never broken a bone before."

"It mostly throbs now," Emma admitted. "Want to sign it?" This was not her first broken bone, but it was the first time she had a friend to sign the cast.

"Sure," Nikki said. "So what was the vision about?" She pulled a sharpie from her bag and doodled as Emma told her about the vision. "That sounds way more intense than the last time you saw the bonfire," Nikki said, stopping mid-doodle to look at Emma.

"Yeah, it was." Emma sighed. "Also, I'm sorry for how I acted yesterday."

"*I'm* sorry. You were trying to keep the peace," Nikki said.

"More like failing to keep the peace." Emma's stomach growled.

Nikki's stomach grumbled almost in response. She frowned and laughed. "Want to get lunch?"

"Actually, yes," Emma said, smiling.

As they walked down the stairs outside, Emma felt someone looking at her. She turned and saw Nelly sitting with a boy who turned away quickly. She saw his profile and suddenly felt sick; Emma turned quickly, hoping Nelly hadn't seen her face. "It was him," she breathed the words out as she sat.

"What?" Nikki asked.

"The profile from my vision," Emma said. "It's Wyatt—Nelly's friend."

"Should we tell Nelly?"

Emma chewed her lip for a moment before answering. "Probably, but do you think she'd believe us?"

"Probably not," Nikki admitted, pushing her tray away. "Jeez, this is a rough gig. How do we warn someone of danger when he probably won't even believe us?"

"I get visions for three basic reasons: to witness the event, to ensure the outcome, or to stop it."

"So we stop it?"

"We have to," Emma said simply, though the doing of such a task was far from simple.





"Merry meet, dear hearts!" Kait said when she and Ethel came in and saw the girls.

"Hi, Kait," Emma said, giving her a one-armed hug with her good arm.

"I heard about your fall, dear," Kait said.

"Can you do anything about it?" Nikki asked.

"I could try, but my knowledge of healing magick is more of curses and poisons rather than simple breaks," Kait admitted. "Your late grandfather was the healer in our family."

"Don't worry about it," Emma smiling as Ethel gave her a hug.

Kait hugged Nikki and asked, "How have your lessons with Gabby been going?"

"Let me show you." Nikki pulled out of the hug and pointed on the candle, which sat on the table. She took a deep breath and raised her hands, palms down. She flicked her right hand upwards. The candle lit. Leading the flame with her middle and ring fingers, she pulled it off of the candle. Turning her left hand palm up, she led the floating flame to hover above her palm.

"That's quite good," Kait said.

"I'm not done, yet," Nikki said. With another deep breath, she repeated the process two more times, leaving three little flames hovering over her left palm. With her right hand still open, she moved her index finger in a small circle, counterclockwise; the flames moved accordingly. Nikki slowly moved her left palm out from underneath the dancing flames. They floated, bobbing up and down. She put her left palm back under the flames and pulled her right hand back. The flames slowed. Nikki brought her right hand almost over the flames. As she closed her right hand slowly, the flames got smaller and smaller until, in little puffs of smoke, they went out.

"Now, I'm impressed," Kait said as she took Nikki by the shoulders. "You're picking this up much faster than even I anticipated." She hugged Nikki again.

"I know you told me you could do it, but that's way cooler to see in person," Emma said.

Nikki grinned.

"We can start working on controlling larger flames today, if you'd like," Kait said, releasing Nikki.

"That would be awesome." Nikki put the candle back in the kitchen.

"You can use the small pit in the backyard," Ethel told Kait.

"I'll fetch a few things from my room and meet you outside," Kait said as she started to head up the stairs at the back of the house. She stopped halfway up and called back, "Nikki, did Gabby teach you the fire protection spell?"

"She did," Nikki called back, coming into the dining room. "I'll meet you in the back, then?"

"Yes, dear," Kait said. Her footsteps faded up the stairs.

Nikki disappeared to the backyard, leaving Ethel and Emma alone in the dining room.

"I believe it's time we spoke about your reading," Ethel said to Emma. Ethel sat at the table and pulled a chair back, inviting Emma to sit.

"I'd rather not." Emma picked at her cast.

"I'm an old woman, Emma. My time is not as it once was," Ethel said, gesturing to the chair.

A bit crestfallen, Emma sat.

"Do you remember the first image you saw?"

"A cat," Emma answered after a moment. "It suggests clairvoyant powers, but we already knew that."

"Do you remember what appeared next?"

"You saw a lion," Emma said, still picking at her cast. She was now gently tapping her heels.

"Yes, which leads to divine power. What else?"

Emma curled her feet around the front legs of her chair. She sat straighter and looked her grandmother square in the eye. Emma took a long, deep breath through her nose and then cleared her throat. The words wouldn't come. She knew exactly what the lion meant. It had been the dragon in the room since that day. Finally, Emma said, "The three peaks. The three planes of consciousness."

"Yes. Have you been preparing?"

"I've been trying not to think about it," Emma murmured, shaking her head.

Ethel sighed. "You know what this means."

"I can barely handle the new visions," Emma said, her voice trembling. She took a steadying breath. "I broke my wrist. I passed out. I haven't had visions like that since I was little."

"Your visions now are stronger than your visions as a child. As you grow, your visions grow with you. Your mother didn't want us to tell you this, but I think the time has come. Passing out during a vision is like psychic growing pains; they will happen throughout your life as your powers grow indefinitely," Ethel said.

"I knew that," Emma said. The words came out a bit sharper than she had intended.

"I know," Ethel said softly. "However, we have suspected for quite some time now that you would be the one to transcend all three planes." Ethel took Emma by the right hand, looking at her eye to eye. "My dear, there will come a time when your visions will no longer follow the rules you've learned."

"That's—that's not possible. I only see what I'll be there to physically see," Emma said, pulling her hand back from her grandmother. "That's how it's always worked."

"You'll need the girls to make the initial transition, but once there, you will see the past, present, and future. You will be witness to all of it in spirit, though you may not be physically present for the events. You possess divine power."

"How do you know this?"

"Because of who your mother was, and who your father is, and because of what your reading told me."

"Wait. You said *is*. Who my father *is*! Not was. Is he—is he alive?" Emma sat up.

"We must talk about your reading, child," Ethel said, closing her eyes as she clenched her fists. One slip.

"No, we need to talk about my father." Emma raised her voice. "Mom said he died. Who is he? What's his name? Where is he? Why—" Emma's voice broke. "Why has he never come for me?"

Ethel pressed her lips together willing herself to remain strong. "Time presents information when you need it," Ethel finally said.

"I need it now. This isn't a vision; this is my father," Emma said, standing. This was not the first time she had experienced pain as the result of a lie, but it was the first time the lie had come from Ethel, from the woman she had never had a reason to mistrust. Until now. The pain, betrayal, and confusion bubbled in Emma's chest, burning in her throat and sending heat to her face.

"Emma," Ethel said, taking Emma's hand and squeezing it. "Please. Do not ask of me that which I cannot tell you."

There was a moment of silence, where Emma struggled, staring into her grandmother's eyes. She sat with a thunk. "What about my reading?" Emma finally asked, steely-voiced.

"You have attained the third level of consciousness. You must meditate and focus to reach the second and first levels."

Emma closed her eyes to avoid rolling them. "So, I need Nikki to reach the second, but I need both Nikki and Nelly to reach the first?"

"Yes, and no."

Emma clenched her jaw, waiting for an explanation. She was in no mood to play her grandmother's games.

"The girls can help you reach the second and first levels, but you can do that on your own if you meditate with enough diligence. You need the girls to reach all three levels simultaneously."

"S-simultaneously? The lion meant divine power *literally*?" This news pushed Emma's father momentarily from her mind.

"Yes," Ethel said.

# Chapter Fifteen

## Wednesday, December 19th

December 19, 2008

    Training yesterday was exhausting. Grandma taught me how to extinguish an entire fire—granted it was probably only a fourth of the size of the one we'll be facing tomorrow—ugh. Tomorrow. How can it be so soon?

    There was one thing we found out yesterday that was kind of cool. I got super tired at one point, and Grandma called Emma out. Just having Emma closer, I could feel her magick and draw on it. We weren't even touching each other.

    Hopefully, if nothing else, Nelly at least comes to the bonfire, so I can draw on her power whether she wants me to or not.

    I borrowed a book from Ethel yesterday. It's called *The Elemental Magicks: Volume 2*. Volume 1 talked about the four elements I already knew about (earth, air, fire, water). You'd think they'd mention everything in one book, but I guess not. I haven't had a chance to start reading volume 2 though. I was so exhausted, I went straight home and slept. I'm so glad today is the last day of school.

"Grab a drink—lemonade homemade by Mrs. Miranda, quite a treat—fill a plate, and take your seat!" Mr. Miranda filled a plate for himself, set it on his desk, and gestured for the class to follow as he loaded *The Last of the Mohicans* into the DVD player.

Nikki and Emma got in line with their peers, filled their plates with the various chips, cookies, and goodies provided, and found seats at the back of the classroom. Neither was particularly interested in watching the movie—even though it was one of Nikki's favorites.

"We need to figure out a way of warning Wyatt," Nikki whispered to Emma.

"We can't exactly just tell him."

"Agreed," Nikki said. "What if we wrote an anonymous note?"

"And said what?" Emma whispered back.

"Fair. I mean, 'Dear Wyatt, if you happened to be thinking about going to the bonfire, you really shouldn't, signed an anonymous friend' isn't exactly likely to stop him," Nikki said.

"Sounds better than, 'Had a vision, and if you show up at the bonfire, you'll die. With love, Emma.'"

Nikki fought to smother her giggles at the absurdity of their situation, which of course got Emma going. Both girls received a stern look from Mr. Miranda. After a few more stifled giggles, and several deep breaths, the girls were able to settle themselves.

"Okay, but seriously," Emma said, once she'd finally calmed down.

"Oh!" Nikki said, her eyes lighting up as the idea hit her. She pulled out a piece of paper, wrote quickly, and slid it over for Emma to read:

Dearest Wyatt,

I've had my eye on you for a long time. I think it's finally time you knew how I felt. Meet me at the pier at seven o'clock December 20th.

With love and hope,
Your Secret Admirer

"This is genius," Emma whispered excitedly. "We don't have to warn him; we just get him out of the area."

"Exactly." Nikki rewrote the note in her nicest handwriting.

The girls spent the rest of class trying to figure out how to get the note to Wyatt; they immediately ruled out sticking it in his pocket or backpack as no self-respecting teenage boy checks his backpack or pockets while on Christmas break. They eventually settled on paying an underclassman to hand-deliver the note, that way there would be no doubt that he got it.

When class got out, they grabbed some kid Emma sort of recognized. They gave him the note and half the payment. Nikki had read enough spy books to know to withhold the second half of the money until after the job was done. They told the sophomore he'd get extra five bucks to keep quiet about who they were (which was a wasted five bucks because he had no idea who they were).

"I see him." Using a row of lockers for cover, Nikki watched the sophomore kid make his way to Wyatt and Nelly. He handed the letter to Wyatt, who looked around. Nikki slowly sunk behind the lockers. If she moved quickly, she'd draw his eye (she learned that from a book, too).

After counting to ten, Nikki whispered to Emma, "I'm going back up." Nikki peeked over the lockers again. She couldn't see the kid or Wyatt. The girls told the kid to meet them in the library after he had delivered the note, so Wyatt couldn't follow him back to them. Though Emma had admitted she thought Wyatt's personality was too laid back to follow up on something like this.

"Let's wait a few minutes, and then go to the library," Nikki said.

"Do you think he read it?" Emma asked as they sat there. A few passing students glanced down at them, but otherwise, no one took much notice of the two girls crouched near the lockers no one used anyway.

"I hope so." Nikki scratched her cheek. "Hey, do you think Nelly will recognize my handwriting?"

Emma thought for a moment. "Well, have you ever written anything to her?"

"Not that I can remember," Nikki said. She glanced up at the clock in the hallway. "Okay, let's go."

The two girls walked to the library as casually as they could. Once there, Nikki saw the kid and jerked her head towards an aisle of reference books. After checking it was clear, she pulled out the money.

"Thanks," Nikki said.

"No problem," the kid said, taking the money and shoving it in his front pocket.

"What's your name?" Emma asked.

"Bowie." He flicked his dirty blond hair back. Like most sophomores in 2008, he had the 'Zac Efron' haircut, as it was known at the time.

"Thanks, Bowie," Emma said. "We appreciate your confidentiality."

"Uh, yeah. Sure." He nodded and left.

"I feel like I know him from somewhere," Emma said. "Or like I should know him?"

"He looks like every other sophomore," Nikki said, shrugging and glancing between the aisles. "Gangly, with ears too big for his head and a dumb haircut."

"You ladies must be finished looking for your books since you feel the need to chat," a high whisper came from behind them. The girls turned around to see the school librarian, a regular palomino of a woman. Her big brown eyes looked even more enormous through her bifocals.

"Sorry, Mrs. Philippos," Emma said. "It won't happen again."


Dec. 19, 08
Wyatt got a letter from a secret admirer. He seems pretty stoked. I'm just hoping it's not some mean joke. I mean, I love the guy, but he's not exactly—well, I just hope someone isn't being mean.
Speaking of Wyatt, I think I'm going to tell him about Mom's journal. I mean, I've told him everything else.


Nelly's phone rang. Without checking who was calling, she answered, "Hello?"

"Before you hang up, please listen," Andy said.

"Sure," Nelly said sarcastically. "Why don't you explain to me again how Ashley just fell on you as you were walking by, and you just *happened* to catch her with your mouth?" She rolled her eyes.

"Nels," Andy said. "It wasn't like—"

"Look," Nelly said, trying to keep calm so she could speak clearly. "You want me because you can't have me. When you had me, you didn't want me. I'm done with your lies, I'm done with your cheating, I'm done with your constant partying. You don't want a girlfriend. You want a designated driver. We're done. Please stop calling, or I will tell my dad."

Andy scoffed. "Wow, you're going to run to daddy?" He laughed. "What's he going to do?"

"Well," Nelly said. "He knows the best shark dives and has access to a boat. Use your imagination." She hung up and blocked his number.

"Wyatt's here," Jo called from the front room.

"In here," Nelly called from her room.

"In the kitchen," called Tom.

Tom had a strict 'no boys in the bedroom' rule, and this rule included Wyatt, despite Nelly's insistence he was not a boy; he was *Wyatt*.

"Coming." Nelly made her way to the kitchen and found Wyatt there, alone.

"What's up?" Wyatt said.

"One last secret," Nelly said quietly, glancing around. "Come here." She walked over to the sink—she had done the dishes earlier to ensure she had a clear sink. Nelly turned on the water and added the drain stopper. "Here." She handed Wyatt the book as the sink filled. "Open it."

Wyatt took the book and tried to open it but couldn't. "Is this a gag book or something?"

"Watch," Nelly said, turning off the faucet. She took the book and shoved it under the water. It popped open. "Look." She pointed to the page with her mother's message.

"Havfrue," Wyatt read. "Isn't that what your mom called you?"

"I know you still think Nikki and Emma turned me into a…you know, but this proves it comes from my mom's side. It's genetic," Nelly said.

"How do you know it was your mom's? Did *they* give it to you?"

Nelly rolled her eyes. "My *dad* gave it to me, and do you know how to make a book completely closed unless it gets wet?"

"Emma is good at chem, right?" Wyatt said.

"I guess, but if this is just science, it's high level stuff. Besides, how did they know my mom's nickname for me? *I* forgot about it until I read this; there's no way they knew about that. Plus I checked the handwriting against my mom's. It matches." Nelly pulled the book out of the water. It snapped shut.

"Are you saying you want to help them?" Wyatt asked.

"No," Nelly said. "I—I don't think so, but this proves they were telling the truth about it coming from my mom's side."

"If you say so." Wyatt shrugged, raising his eyebrows.


19 December 2008

Today is weird. It's the first time I've ever paid someone to deliver a note. It's the day before a vision I had over ten years ago comes to pass. I feel jittery all over. It's like there are bees under my skin. We're at Grandma's. Kait wants me and Nikki for fire training today, but I'm not sure what I can do exactly.

"Alright, girls. I'm ready for you," Kait said as she finished casting the fire protection spell.

Nikki and Emma were sitting on the swing in the backyard. Emma put her journal in her bag, and the both of them walked over to the fire pit where Kait was standing.

"Nikki, I want you to repeat after me, okay?" Kait said.

"Okay," Nikki said.

"Duco ducere liceat mihi aquam de cisterna tua virtute et calore solis," Kait said.

Nikki repeated, stumbling over "cisterna," so Kait had Nikki repeat it until she could say the whole phrase perfectly.

"Good," Kait said. "Now for the last part: duco ducere liceat tua virtus et pabula terrae aura spei."

They sat together, repeating the spell over and over again until Nikki could say it from memory without any guidance from Kait. Once Nikki had it, Kait taught a different spell to Emma, "Ut hauriret aquam de cisterna mihi potestas, et calor ex sole. Eripe me de terra alimentum trahant viribus ut et aura spei."

Once both girls had their parts memorized, Kait said, "Brilliant. This spell helps you draw on one another's powers."

"I thought I wasn't supposed to use spells yet," Nikki said.

"Besides, I can't cast," Emma added.

"No, dear, but you can echo and reinforce a spell. Nikki will be the primary, the one to actually cast the spell, but you make it stronger by reinforcing her power with your own. And Nikki, these are rather special circumstances."

"I still wish you and Gabby could just go," Nikki mumbled. "I just don't feel ready."

Kait sighed and squeezed Nikki's shoulder. "Unfortunately, because of the nature of psychics and visions, if any of us were to go where we had not been seen, we could greatly alter things but not necessarily for the better." Kait smiled sadly. "I wish we could go and stop this and keep you girls safe. Part of being magickal is allowing magick to guide you, and part of being a mentor is guiding your charge, not taking their tasks upon yourself, no matter how much you might wish to."

Nikki nodded and huffed, resigned to her duty. "So, what exactly are we saying in this spell? What does it mean?"

"You're basically asking Emma if you can draw on her power and strength, and her part says you can," Kait said. "Light the fire, and cast the spell I just taught you. Think about making the fire bigger while you're casting. Emma, concentrate on lending your power to Nikki."

The girls did as they were asked. Standing a foot away from the pit, Nikki stretched her hands in front of her and flicked them upwards as if she were, once again, an orchestra conductor, and the concert had just started. A fire blazed to life.

"Ready?" Nikki asked, glancing over to Emma.

"Yeah," Emma said, offering her right hand to Nikki.

"On three. One, two, three…" Nikki said, taking Emma's hand. The girls each said their part of the spell simultaneously. At first the fire didn't seem to change, and then seemingly all at once, it was huge. Nikki immediately looked to Kait for advice.

"Put it out," Kait said calmly.

"Right. Duh." Nikki shook her head and breathed quickly in and out. "Okay. Again."

They repeated the process except this time Nikki made the fire smaller.

"Well done, girls!" Kait clapped. "Very well done. The fire tomorrow will be much easier than this. Magickal fire is naturally more resistant. For now, try to make the fire smaller as soon as it starts growing. It's considerably more difficult to stop a magickal fire's momentum. If you can stop this, you're all the more prepared for tomorrow."

Nikki and Emma spent the next forty-five minutes enlarging the fire and dousing the flames immediately afterwards. After each exercise, Kait would offer feedback, a tip, or trick for them to work on the next time. When it was clear the girls had given everything they had, Kait told them to put the fire out completely, and go inside and eat.

"Do you think we're ready?" Nikki asked before taking a bite out of the sandwich Ethel had prepared, turkey and sprout on sourdough with a homemade garlic-cilantro spread.

"You've done as much as you can in the time you've been allotted," Ethel said.

Nikki swallowed. "Will it be enough?" She was still worried she might not be simply passing out.

"We'll find out," Emma said, shrugging.

"What would happen if we didn't go?" Nikki asked.

"Now that is one outcome I don't want to think about," Emma admitted.

# Chapter Sixteen

Thursday, December 20th -

Friday, December 21st

December 20, 2008

    Beyond exhausted today. I feel like I could honestly sleep for a million years, but Mom has other plans. She was in here about 20 minutes ago, yelping about Christmas presents—which none of us have gotten for each other. It's time for Christmas shopping. Part of me wishes it could wait until tomorrow, but the more realistic (or maybe just morbid) part of me knows that might not be an option.

Nikki grimaced and closed her journal. She stood up and stretched; her back gave a little *pop* of relief. She put on a Kelly green t-shirt and pair of black yoga pants before heading into the kitchen. Pouring herself a bowl of cereal, Nikki listened as Margret muttered while she quickly wiped down countertops with a clean rag.

"Can you believe Kam has been up since six?" Margret scoffed. "Why can't he do that during the school week?"

"He's got to catch those morning cartoons." Nikki laughed.

Some kind of truce between Nikki and Margret had started last night during the band concert, and neither was keen to break it.

"Yes, well, are you ready to go to the mall?" Marget asked.

"As soon as I'm done with my cereal," Nikki said.

Margret gave Nikki's casual wear a once over, making a face but ultimately kept her comments to herself. Instead, she wrung out her rag, placing it neatly on the sink edge to dry. "Alright, well, when you're finished, go tell Kam to get dressed. I need to stop and get cash out before we go."

For as long as Nikki and Kam could remember, they had gone family Christmas shopping. Each child would pick a parent and split up; then, after a few hours, they'd meet up at the food court, eat lunch, and swap parents. Once Nikki was old enough to walk around the mall on her own, she and Kam would walk around together, so their parents could shop for them.

The two had a great system for making sure they always got something good for Christmas: each of them would pick something they wanted, and—provided it was "in budget" as Margret called it—the other sibling would buy it. When Christmas came, they'd act surprised, and no one was the wiser. They'd created the system a few years ago when Kam had accidentally walked down the aisle in which Nikki stood, trying to pick his present. He pointed to the one he really wanted, and the system was born.

Once at the mall, Margret said, "Now, you two go buy the gifts for your father and me," and handed them each two twenties.

"Dad won't be home until after Christmas, though," Kam said.

"Just means we get two Christmases," Nikki said, elbowing Kam.

"Exactly." Mom tousled Kam's hair. "Meet back here in an hour?"

"Okay," Nikki and Kam said. They headed towards a store at the back of the mall.

"Split up, find what we want, and meet back here?" Kam asked.

Nikki nodded. "Fifteen minutes? Then, we can buy our gifts for Mom and Dad."

"Okay," Kam said, taking off toward the Lego.

Nikki wandered down an aisle filled with books. As she walked, she ran her hand down the books, touching each one at shoulder-level. She started to walk down the next aisle when she saw Wyatt with a tall girl (you and I would have recognized her as Jo, but Nikki had never met Jo, so all she knew was the girl was tall and definitely not Nelly). Their backs were turned to Nikki, so they never saw her sneak back to the other aisle. She could hear them, but just because she couldn't actually see them doesn't mean you should miss out.

"Wyatt, no offense, but that's the *stupidest* idea," Jo said, pointing to the book in his hand.

"You don't think she'd like it?" Wyatt asked, frowning.

"Dude, the girl barely pours her own cereal; I highly doubt she's going to want to sun dry her own tomatoes." Jo tapped the front of the book pointedly.

"Fair," Wyatt said. He dropped the book down on the pile with a soft flop. He ran his fingers through his curly brown hair, sun-kissed and frizzy. "Well, what *do* I get her for Christmas?" He groaned. "Why does she have to be so hard to shop for?"

"Please," Jo drawled, flipping through a magazine. "Just get her some new bikini bottoms."

"You get her some then, Jo," Wyatt said, rolling his eyes.

"I can't. I need to buy myself some to replace the ones she 'lost,'" she said with finger quotes around 'lost.'

Wyatt groaned again. "Whatever. I'll figure something else out. Hey, did you hear about the bonfire tonight?"

Nikki's ears perked up.

"Yes," Jo said. "I'd love to go, but I wasn't invited." She dropped the magazine back onto its pile.

"I can get you in," Wyatt said, trying to seem casual.

"Really?" Jo said slowly. Crossing her arms, she studied him a moment before asking, "What's the catch?"

Wyatt put his hands up like he was surrendering. "No catch."

Jo put her hands on her hips and stared at him, still very skeptical.

"Maybe if you come, Nelly will be more likely to come," Wyatt admitted.

"Doubtful," Jo said, softening a bit.

"Not impossible," he countered.

Jo gave him a knowing look (that, just between you and me, made him very uncomfortable). She sighed and shook her head slightly. "Can Grace come, too?"

"Sure," Wyatt said. "I'll pick you guys up at 6:30."

"Thanks. Also, we probably won't hang with you, no offense." Jo bumped his shoulder playfully.

"None taken," Wyatt said, ruffling Jo's hair a bit before she pulled away. "I'm going for free s'mores and hot babes."

"Gross." Jo laughed and smoothed down her hair. "Come on, let's try somewhere else."

As they wandered off, Nikki's mind raced, trying to process everything she had heard. She yanked out her cell phone and called Emma.

*Ring. Ring. Ring.*

"Come on!" Nikki paced the aisle. "Pick up."

*Ring. Ring.*

"Pick up, Em," Nikki said, turning at the end of the aisle to walk down it again.

*Ring.*

"Hey, you've reached Emma—"

"Ugh!" Nikki hung up on Emma's outgoing voicemail message and redialed. She called back three more times before finally leaving a message: "Em, it's me. Wyatt is going tonight, and he's taking some girl named Jo who seems to know Nelly. I think it might be her sister—does she have a sister? Call me."

"Hey," Kam said behind her.

Nikki spun around, eyes wild.

"Are you okay?" Kam asked.

"Yeah—yes, totally," Nikki said.

"Well," Kam said slowly. "It's been 20 minutes." He studied Nikki for a moment, recognizing her nervous ticks, like how she messed with the end of her braid and fiddled with her phone. "Are you sure you're okay?"

"Yes, I'm fine," Nikki insisted.

"Okay," he said, though he didn't sound like he believed her. "Anyway, I want this." He held up a Lego set. "What do you want?"

"Uh," Nikki said, her mind still racing. "I'm trying to narrow it down, just give me a minute to pick a book." She flicked her braid back and tried to focus on the titles swimming in front of her.

Dec. 20, 08

Wyatt is picking Jo up soon. I rented a bunch of chick flicks, stocked up on chocolate and ice cream, and bought five bottles of nail polish for my newly appreciated toes. Tonight should be fun.

I hope.

Nelly threw her journal into the shopping bag which still held the chocolate, nail polish, and receipt from her earlier shopping venture. After throwing the bag on the futon in the front room, Nelly went to the kitchen and got out a paper plate. Wyatt came in as Nelly plopped onto the futon and put the plate on the coffee table.

"Hey," she said, trying to perch her toes on the coffee table. It was too far away, so she pulled it closer.

"Hey," Wyatt said, poking her gently with his elbow. "Come tonight. Please? It'll be fun."

Nelly gave him a side eye and a small grin before firmly saying, "No." She hopped up and went back to the kitchen, pulling out the glass pitcher of water from the refrigerator and setting it on the table. "I have zero desire to be around a bunch of sticky, loud happy people."

"So you're just going to mope around here like some sad cat lady? Suit yourself," Wyatt said, grinning.

Nelly rolled her eyes. "Jo," she yelled down the hallway. "Wyatt's here. Hurry up."

"Just a sec!" Jo yelled from the bathroom.

"So..." Wyatt dug through Nelly's shopping bag. Upon finding her bag of chocolate, he opened it and snitched one. "Did you hear about the boy's locker room?"

Nelly looked down at herself and then back at him. "What do you think?"

"Duh," Wyatt said, popping the chocolate in his mouth. "There was a lightning strike in there. Knocked all the power out."

"Seriously?" Nelly sat down next to him. "Was everyone okay?"

Wyatt shrugged and ate another chocolate. "Far as I know, everyone was fine."

"That's wild," Nelly said. "Were you in there?"

"No, I was finishing up my mile run, but I saw it. It was crazy loud."

"Let's go!" Jo called, walking straight past Nelly and Wyatt and out the door.

"You sure you don't want to come?" Wyatt asked, patting Nelly's knee.

"Have fun," Nelly said, waving her fingers.

Wyatt shrugged, hopped up, and followed Jo out.

Nelly sighed as the screed door slammed behind him. "What movie first?" she asked herself, glancing at the clock. It was six forty, but she had six movies to watch. Grabbing the movie off the top, she popped it in the DVD player, sat down on the futon, and lined up the bottles of nail polish, leaving her journal in the bag. Opening the first chocolate her hand grabbed, she stared at the brightly colored bottles and chewed on her lip.

20 December 2008

I'm waiting for Nikki at Grandma's. We agreed we'd meet here at 7 to go over a game plan before we head out. One last meeting with the mentors. It's barely 6:30. I wanted to meditate to be more focused and centered before we go, but I'm having a difficult time sitting long enough to start. I keep wiggling. Grandma said I should try writing my thoughts down to make it easier for me to focus. So, here goes:

I feel blind. The few visions I've had haven't exactly been reassuring. My visions have never been so dark before, and I don't mean metaphorically. It's like someone has dimmed the world in my visions. Everything is in shadow; I have to concentrate and strain to see anything. They're fuzzy and dark. I can't explain how, but I know something is interfering with my ability to see. I just have no idea what it is, or where to even begin looking for it.

"Any better?" Ethel asked Emma.

Emma closed her journal. "Have you ever had something mess with your abilities?"

"Your abilities are controlled by you. The more focused you are, and the more often you meditate, the easier it will be to access the third plane," Ethel said, patting Emma on the back.

Emma sighed. "I'll try again."


December 20, 2008 (later)

I'm outside Madam Ortega's. I tried calling Emma like a million more times after I saw Wyatt. I think her phone is dead. It's just going to voicemail. It doesn't even matter now. Wyatt is going, and there's nothing we can do about it, except—hopefully—save his life.

Nikki shoved her journal in her backpack, along with the bag of marshmallows she picked up, and got out of the car. She had kept her black yoga pants on from her earlier shopping trip but had changed (at Margret's insistence) into a flowy emerald top. Margret had tried to talk her into a dress, but given the only reason she was going to this party (which she didn't tell Margret), she opted to stay in pants. Nikki pulled on her hoodie and pushed her long black braid behind her before going into the house.

"Merry Meet!" Kait said as Nikki entered. Kait kissed Nikki's cheeks and gave her a hug. "Did your brother get you the message?"

"What message?"

"I asked Kam to remind you to bring a journal tonight," Kait said.

"He didn't, but I've just been carrying my journal around with me ever since I got my magick," Nikki said.

Kait nodded. "Good. You'll need to record as much of tonight's events as you can."

"Is Emma here yet?" Nikki asked.

"She's meditating in the library," Kait said.

Face flushed, Emma rushed into the front room. She, too, had dressed sensibly, jeans, a thrifted graphic tee, and a light blue zip up hoodie. "Wyatt's going to the bonfire!"

"Yeah, I know," Nikki said impatiently.

"How could you? I just saw it. Wyatt and Jo talking in an aisle at a store; they were—"

"Christmas shopping for Nelly," Nikki finished. "Like I said, I know."

"But how?" Emma asked, frowning.

"I was Christmas shopping with Kam when I saw Wyatt. Where's your phone? I called you like fifty times after it happened," Nikki said, crossing her arms. "I left you a voicemail about it hours ago."

"How could I have seen the past?" Emma sat on the couch, her gaze far off.

"It wasn't the past, not yet," Ethel explained. "Some people are born with the ability to see the present."

"Aren't basically all people born with that?" Nikki asked, fighting the urge to roll her eyes.

"To a degree, you're right," Ethel said. "We are all able to see our *own* present; however, those with this gift can experience the present of others. Emma saw your experience through you."

"But it already happened, so isn't it the past?" Nikki asked, softening. Logically, she knew it wasn't Emma's fault. Not really.

"It is still on the forefront of your mind, so you are still experiencing it," Ethel explained.

"Is that why I could see it? Because she *needed* me to?" Emma asked.

"Perhaps," Ethel said. "There are very few psychics who can access the present. We don't know a lot about how it works." The clock tolled, notifying them it was already half past seven.

"We should go. We don't want to be late," Emma said, standing.

"Wait, don't we need to sort this out?" Nikki asked.

"I wish we had the time, but Emma is right, dear." Kait patted Nikki's shoulder. "Come here after the bonfire, if you can, and we'll talk then."

Emma gathered her things.

"Be sure to write down everything that happens," Kait said.

"At the end of the day, you will need to relearn lessons, and unless those lessons are recorded, they'll be forgotten," Ethel said.

"Okay, I'm ready. Let's go." Emma donned her jacket.

"Good luck, dear-hearts. Blesséd be," Kait said, waving as the girls ran to Nikki's car. It started to rain.


20 December 2008

Taking a second to update. I'm in the bathroom in Sarah's house. We've been here for nearly half an hour and so far all that's happened is I drank too much soda. Nothing else—which is good. How wonderful if everything goes smoothly and our sheer presence prevents anything from happening...though, I won't count on that just yet. Parts of the vision have come true (giving Sarah the flier and seeing everyone here), but the earth has been still.


Someone screamed. Emma shoved her journal back in her bag and bolted from the bathroom. As she emerged into the backyard, she scanned wildly for trouble.

Nikki rushed over. "Some idiot scared his girlfriend." She held a s'more in each hand. "Freaked me out."

"Same." Emma breathed heavily as the adrenaline worked its way through her system.

"Is it bad I kind of just want it to happen, so it can be over with? I hate the anxiety of waiting. Here." Nikki handed Emma a s'more.

Emma took it. "I feel the same."

"What time is it now?" Nikki asked, taking a bite from her own s'more as they walked over to their chairs.

"Barely after eight." Emma's heart was still pounding fiercely.

"And how long does it go until?"

"Midnight," Emma said flatly.

"Awesome." Nikki's tone echoed Emma's.

They sat on their chairs and watched their peers goof around. Occasionally, Nikki would ask who someone was, and Emma would tell her. Emma told Nikki about Josh (who was captain of the football team until he broke his collarbone), Maddie (who got nearly every female lead in the school musicals), Whitney (who claimed to be a better surfer than Nelly—Nikki scoffed at this), Andy (who could be a pro surfer if he stopped partying so much), and Bud (Andy's best friend, also a surfer, not quite as good, but rumored to be a superior kisser).

Two hours later, the party had only increased. The fire blazed; neither Nikki nor Emma ever wanted to see a marshmallow again. They'd eaten over half the bag before Nikki finally put it in her car. Their classmates continued their cavorting, chasing each other with flaming sticks and dancing to the radio. The fairy lights on the porch twinkled happily, and multi-colored streamers danced softly in the wind. About ten feet from the bonfire, the two girls sat on camp chairs. They had pulled several blankets from Nikki's car and were bundled up nicely against the now chilly night air.

"This is a pretty nice yard," Nikki said after a while.

"Yeah," Emma said. "Did you see the telephone pole?" She pointed to it, just visible beyond the fire.

Nikki nodded. "I saw it almost as soon as we got here."

"I hope it doesn't actually crash down on us," Emma admitted.

"You and me both," Nikki said. She groaned, extending her legs out in front of her and wiggling her toes. Her flip-flops sat abandoned under her chair. "This is going to take forever."

Emma privately agreed but outwardly yawned.

"What time did you wake up?" Nikki asked.

"Five-thirty," Emma said, stretching her arms above her.

Nikki made a face. "Why?" She readjusted. It's virtually impossible to get completely comfortable in a camp chair. "I slept in as long as I could."

"Rachelle…" Emma yawned again. "Uh," she added, shaking her head. "Ever since my visions have been wonky, she's been under strict orders from Grandma to make sure I meditate with the rising sun every morning."

"Why so early?"

"It's right before dawn, when the wall between worlds is thinnest. Dawn and dusk are the best times to meditate," Emma said, rubbing her eyes and yawning again. "Great for meditation but not so great as a sleep schedule."

"Well, there's not much we can do until stuff starts, so take a nap," Nikki said.

Emma nodded and snuggled into her chair, quickly falling asleep.

(later)

I've eaten two-thirds of the bag of chocolate (feels like that might have been a mistake). I've watched two and a half chick flicks (first, I kind of liked, second was meh, third was so awful I couldn't finish it). My toes look like a 3-year-old painted them.

So when exactly does all this stuff make a girl feel better? So far I just feel pathetic and a little nauseated.

Nelly dropped her pen on her journal and stood up. She stretched her back, which had grown stiff from all the hunching as she painted her toes. Nelly switched DVDs and wished, not for the last time, that Wyatt was there. The third movie might have been more bearable if he was there to make fun of it with her. Walking on her heels to keep her tacky toes off the floor, she headed to the kitchen, refilled her cup from the pitcher still sitting on the table, and made a quick pit stop to Jo's room to get cotton balls and polish remover.

She brought the cup and other necessities over to the futon and sat down. Nelly hit play on the remote and listened to the opening credits as she scrubbed bright blue nail polish off the knuckle of her big toe. Even terrible movies posed enough of a distraction for her to somehow miss her nail completely. The music of the movie stopped. Nelly kept scrubbing. When the opening credit music started over, Nelly looked at the TV. These were rented movies, which meant other people watched these movies—people with kids who had sticky fingers and access to keys. Nelly watched long enough to see the television flicker on and off. If the lights had been on, she would have noticed this wasn't a television or DVD player problem. It was a power problem.

Then, the earth shook.

December 20, 2008 (later)

Quarter to midnight. Just 45 grueling more minutes and this party will finally be over, and we can all go home. I'm starting to nod off myself, but Grandma said to write everything down, so here's everything I see right now:

There are two girls about four feet from us texting...I think they're texting each other. Oye.

The fire is reasonably large and very warm, which is nice because it is COLD!

Wyatt is roasting what has to be his fiftieth marshmallow. That kid can pack them away.

The girl he came with, Joan? Jo? Something like that—she and some other girls look like they're leaving.

The Andy kid Emma was talking about is doing backflips. How he has the energy, no idea.

Sarah is passing out more chocolate bars.

I took one. It's always good to have chocolate for later.

Emma must still be asleep. She's a big bundle of blankets in the chair next—

"Emma!" Nikki shoved Emma, but her shove only pushed the chair over, which folded in on itself. The earth was shaking. "EMMA!" Nikki yelled above the screams. Emma was nowhere to be seen.

It was chaos: teens ran and screamed, some desperate to get in the house while others headed for open spaces. Nikki looked at the fire, but something wasn't right. The world was shaking—just like the vision—but the fire was, if anything, getting smaller. Nikki decided to help it along. She figured preventative measures were always easier than trying to deal with unbridled consequences after the fact. Barefoot, Nikki moved through the grassy yard, closer to the bonfire.

"Feel your feet, feel your feet," Nikki whispered to herself. Concentrating, she closed her eyes, dug her toes into the soft earth, put her hands up, and brought them down, thinking about the fire getting smaller and smaller. She felt magick, gentle and golden, move from the earth into her grounded feet and through her body, filling her up. The fire did not resist her. It bowed easily to her will.

As the world shook around her, Nikki remained grounded, focusing her energy on the fire, which was almost out. Because her eyes were closed and because she was so focused, she didn't see the bolt of lightning strike the telephone pole, she didn't see it barely miss her and crash down into the fire, but she heard it, and she felt it, but more importantly, she felt the fire blaze to life—a new life, a magickal life, stubborn and strong-willed.

Nikki opened her eyes in time to see the clear sky become engulfed with thick, electrical, billowing smoke.


(later)
    Earthquake. Nothing too big, just a


Almost as if the earth took Nelly's sentence as a personal insult, the earthquake intensified. Nelly had spent her whole life in California, so earthquakes were nothing new; however, the sudden ferocity of this one scared her. Instincts taking over, she looked around the room for anything that could fall. Everything she saw, pictures on the wall, the television, even the bookshelves, had been reinforced for just such an occasion. Tom was nothing if not prepared.

The teetering pitcher on the table caught Nelly's attention. It wasn't sentimental, so it breaking wouldn't be a big deal, but if she could avoid shattered glass all over the floors, she would. Nelly bolted to the kitchen. She thought she had enough time, but the earth gave a sudden jolt.

"NO!" Nelly screamed as she reached for the pitcher. Water flew into the air as the pitcher smashed on the ground. Nelly felt as if every bit of air had been sucked from her as she realized the water had stopped moving. The water hung there, frozen in mid-air. Her outstretched hands still reached for the pitcher that had long since fallen; Nelly pulled them back quickly. The water, overtaken by gravity once again, splashed to the floor in one wet, glassy mess.

The earth continued to shake.


21 December 2008
    It's midnight. I'm in Nikki's car. She dozed off for a bit, and I came for more blankets. It's so cold tonight. I'm trying to write things as I remember to, but I'm starting to wonder if anything will even

Emma felt the beginnings of an earthquake: small shudders, a movement, a shifting of the earth, and then the car jolted. She got out of the car, leaving her journal inside and scrambled up to the bonfire. People were everywhere, scattering like mice, screaming and running, just like her vision. She instinctively looked at the bonfire. Nikki was standing in front of it, but before Emma could get there, Andy and his friend, Bud, bumped into her.

"We have to get out of here," Bud said. He was holding Andy's arm and pulling him.

"Go to the field," Emma said, pointing. "There's nothing to fall there. Tell the others! Go!"

Bud nodded quickly and pulled Andy in the direction Emma had indicated.

Emma looked back at the fire and Nikki. The witch seemed to almost have the fire out. Emma started to breathe a little easier, though the earth was still trembling. Then, she saw a mass of clouds gather overhead. Everything seemed to move in slow motion. She heard a giant crack as lightning split the sky and touched down on the telephone pole, which was a mere seventy-five feet from where Nikki stood, eyes squeezed shut as she focused on dousing the fire.

"NIKKI, MOVE!" Emma ran, watching the telephone pole come down to a blazing stop inside the bonfire, scarcely missing Nikki as it crashed. The effect was instantaneous. Fire burst forth from the almost coals with ferocious life.

If their peers had been screaming before, it was nothing compared to the sound they made once the fire blazed uncontrollably, and the smoke engulfed them. Nikki and Emma played a sick game of Marco Polo as they tried to find each other in the smoke. Inside the smothering cloud echoed the sounds of crying, sobbing, and coughing, so much coughing.

"Emma," Nikki called, losing her voice between screaming for her friend and breathing in the smoke. Someone touched her back.

"Nikki?" It was Emma.

"Hurry—cough—you have to help me. The fire—cough—magickal—cough—hurry." Nikki pointed to the only thing visible to them: the raging fire out of which poured more smoke.

The girls stood side by side, hand in hand. Nikki held her right hand out, palm flat out like it was pushing up against an invisible wall; Emma held her left hand out—her palm was not flat because of her cast, but she did the best she could. They repeated the words Kait had taught them, Nikki focusing on dousing the fire and Emma focusing on giving every ounce of power she had to

Nikki. The earth continued to shake, now more violently than before. The girls tried to stay grounded, to keep their balance but failed. As they fell backwards, they let go of each other. Fear enveloped them along with the smoke so thick they couldn't see each other though they were mere feet apart.

Emma crawled on her hands and knees towards her right, where Nikki had been standing moments ago, but because of the violence of the earthquake, Emma kept falling. She decided to stay down, crouching so low she could smell grass and dirt. She crawled on her elbows, keeping as much of her body on the ground as possible. The fire continued to blaze.

Emma bumped into someone. "Nikki?" she asked, poking the mass. "Is that you?" Emma crawled closer, realizing she was at the feet of the person. A breath caught in her throat that had nothing to do with the smoke. Emma knew immediately who she would find.

I failed.
I tried.
I'm so sorry.

Nikki wrote what she was sure would be her last words on the back of the receipt she had shoved in a pocket after buying the marshmallows. She had to record it. It was all she could do. She couldn't find Emma; she couldn't even sense her magick or find the fire. There was only smoke. Everything was just smoke. It wrapped her in a cocoon, shutting out everything but the screaming. Everything had gone wrong. They were supposed to stop it, like in Emma's vision. Sure, it would kill her, but then, these people wouldn't die. Nikki didn't know most of them, but she knew they had families: little brothers that wanted to see them come home, dads that would die if they got this news, moms that would never forgive themselves.

With the rest of the air Nikki could muster, she yelled "Emma" one last time.

A few seconds passed.

A few more.

It seemed like ages.

"I'm here," came a hoarse voice from Nikki's left side.

"Emma?" Nikki managed in barely a whisper, rolling to her stomach reaching out with one hand.

"I found Wyatt." Emma grabbed Nikki's hand. "We have to stop this." She coughed violently.

"I don't know if I can," Nikki wheezed. Everything ached.

"We have to. We're it," Emma said. "Don't worry about standing."

Nikki grunted, pushing herself up with her free arm. "Repeat after me, okay?" She sat cross-legged.

"Okay," Emma said, also sitting cross-legged. They touched palms.

"Ignis magicis—cough—ignis vitae, vocatus—cough—audit," Nikki said. The smoke curled around them like an anaconda, slow and methodical, trying to squeeze the last bits of life from them.

Emma repeated; her eyes scrunched against the smoke as she concentrated on Nikki's voice.

"Puer sum in terra mea et robur dicuntur," Nikki said, and Emma repeated.

"Introrsus redeunt, patria est. Revertamur ad core ad salvandum his vivit," Nikki said. She could feel her strength draining. She struggled to focus.

Emma repeated Nikki's words.

"Emma…" Nikki's body swayed.

The fire was finally no more than smoldering coals. A figure stood just beyond the fire, but Nikki blinked, and the figure was gone. Before she could dwell on this new mystery, her world went dark.


21 December 2008

It's one-thirty in the morning. We're at the hospital. I called everyone I could think of—Rachelle, Grandma (who told and brought Kait), and Nikki's mom (who brought Kam). When I had the vision, I thought I was covering for Nikki, agreeing the reason she passed out must have been from breathing in too much smoke, but I'm afraid when the time came, it was the truth. I lied to the EMT guy and told him I was Nikki's sister. When we got here, the ER nurse was the same one who wrapped my cast, and she knew I was lying. I explained, and I think she understood why I did it.

Grandma told me to record everything while we wait, but my brain feels so jumbled. I've already been examined and cleared. They said, despite all odds (and my cast), I'm in perfect health (more or less). Nikki's mom and grandma argued, but Kam told them both to cut it out. He's a cartoon-watching ten year old, but he has an old soul. A soul that understands.

Emma reread the last line. It didn't make sense. She stuffed the napkin in her pocket and rubbed her eyes. She glanced over at Kam, who was curled up, fast asleep in one of the waiting room's many pale blue plastic chairs, covered in easy to clean vinyl. Margret paced up and down the white tile aisle that separated the two carpeted sections of the waiting room. Standing next to the water feature, Kait moved her lips in silent prayer. Rachelle and Ethel sat in chairs next to Kam whispering to each other.

A doctor carrying a clipboard came through the maroon double doors and walked over to the women. He flipped a page and then looked up. "Is the parent of Nikki Rodrigues here?"

"I am," Margret said, immediately moving to him.

"I'm Doctor Blyth," he said, shaking Margret's hand. "Nikki breathed in a lot of smoke. We took some blood and did an x-ray. The blood tests will take some time before we know more, but the x-ray said she was normal," Doctor Blyth said quietly.

"Will she be okay?" Margret asked.

"X-rays with these cases can be tricky. Sometimes the first one doesn't show the full extent of the damage because the body hasn't fully processed what has happened, but sometimes everything is fine. As of right now, her signs are stable. We have her on oxygen, but she is breathing on her own. Though, she hasn't woken up yet."

Margret paled.

"Given the night she's had," Doctor Blyth said, putting a hand on Margret's shoulder. "It might be her body is simply exhausted. We'll keep a close eye on her."

"Can I see her?"

"Of course," Doctor Blyth said.

"Just a moment," Margret said.

Kait watched her as Margret came back over.

Margret looked at Kam and then at Kait. "Will you stay with him? I don't want to wake him until we can take Nikki home."

"Of course, dear," Kait said.

"Margret," Rachelle said. "If you want, I can run him home, and wait with him until you get there."

"I don't want to inconvenience you," Margret said, already removing her house key from her keyring.

"It would be no trouble at all," Rachelle said with what she hoped was a comforting smile.

"Thank you so much," Margret said. Her lip quivered as she handed Rachelle the key. Rachelle squeezed her hand.

"I'll help them out," Kait said. She stood and lifted the sleeping boy in her arms as though he weighed no more than a toddler (some silent magick was definitely used).

As Kait and Rachelle disappeared out the hospital doors, Margret followed Doctor Blyth back to Nikki's room. It's amazing how horrible events sometimes have a way of bringing people together.

When Kait returned to the waiting room, she, Ethel, and Emma chatted for a while, discussing events, but as neither mentor would discuss her thoughts on said events, their conversation was nothing worth noting, and so we shall jump to the moment when Doctor Blyth came back out and informed them that Nikki was awake and wished to see them.

"How is she?" Kait asked, standing up.

"Her blood tests show her pH levels are unbalanced, but reworking her diet for the next few days should sort that out." Dr. Blyth kept his expression neutral.

"You seem surprised," Ethel said. As you may have guessed, his aura was not so neutral and was particularly easy for the experienced medium to read.

"There are quite a few kids from the bonfire incident here. From what I've heard, Nikki was quite close to the event," Doctor Blyth explained. "Almost everyone else will need to stay for a few days, but Nikki can go home right now if she's feeling up to it. It doesn't quite make sense, but I've never been one to discount the marvel of the human body to heal."

"It's almost magickal," Kait said with a small grin.

Doctor Blyth chucked and added, "Just remind her not to talk too much. Her throat has been through a lot tonight."

"Thank you," Emma said. "Doc, how is Wyatt? He was the boy in the ambulance with us." Emma clarified.

"His information is confidential," Doctor Blyth said.

"Please, he's my friend, too," Emma said.

"Well," Doctor Blyth flipped through a few papers on his clipboard. "All I'll say is he's where Nikki was a few hours ago."

"Have you called his family?"

"We just got through. They're on their way now. The phone lines were down, and we had a difficult time reaching them," Doctor Blyth said.

"Thank you, again."

"Of course." Doctor Blyth gave the women a small nod and disappeared back through the maroon double doors.

Emma went into Nikki's room and found Margret sitting on Nikki's bed, hugging her and stroking her hair.

"Why aren't you in here?" Nikki asked in a hoarse whisper as Emma came over.

"They had me on oxygen on the ride over here, but apparently I'm a quick healer," Emma said. "Mostly," she added, catching Nikki eyeing at the bright yellow cast.

"How do you feel?" Margret asked Nikki.

"Sore throat, but fine other than that," Nikki whispered in answer. "Where's Kam?"

"Rachelle took him home," Margret said.

"You know Rachelle?" Nikki asked.

"We knit together," Margret said with a small smile. "Do you feel like coming home?"

"Can I?" Nikki asked, clearly surprised.

"Get dressed, and I'll fill out the paperwork." Margret hugged Nikki one more time and kissed her forehead.


(later)

Nikki and Emma said I have powers, aside from turning into a fish, I didn't believe them. But tonight,


Nelly put her pen down and rubbed her face with her hands, brushing her hair out of her eyes. She took a deep breath to steady her still racing heart and picked up her pen again.


I stopped water. It just stopped in the middle of the air, and when I moved my hands back to me, the water fell. I'm not sure I could do it again. I don't even know how I

"Dude!" Jo said as she came in the house. She found Nelly sitting on the couch. "Did you feel that? I've never been through one so intense. Where's Dad?"

"Still sleeping," Nelly said, closing her journal.

Jo laughed. "If it's not at least a 7.5, Dad doesn't even register it." She walked into the kitchen. "Hey," she called. "Did you know the pitcher broke?"

"No," Nelly lied.

"Can you grab the broom? I'll mop up as much of this water as I can."

"Where's Wyatt?" Nelly asked. "Didn't he bring you home?"

"Nah, I caught a ride with Grace," Jo said. "Her mom picked us up right before the earthquake. We rode it out near the fields." Jo used thick paper towels to pick up the wet glass and mop up as much water as she could without cutting herself. "It was scary, but only a few minutes long."

"It felt longer," Nelly said.

"They always do, but we clocked it." Jo shrugged as she continued cleaning.

"Do you know if Wyatt made it home okay?" Nelly asked, remembering Nikki's insistence she help put out a fire. She didn't mean *this* bonfire, did she?

"Probably. When I told him Grace and her mom were taking me home, he said he was headed home soon," Jo said, dropping a larger chunk of glass into the shopping bag which had been triple layered.

"I can get the rest of this. You go to bed," Nelly said.

"Are you sure?" Jo asked, yawning.

"Yeah." Nelly smiled. "Go to bed. I'll get it."

December 21, 2008

    I didn't die, but my throat feels burned to a crisp. Mom said if it hadn't been for Emma's call, they wouldn't have known about the earthquake until morning. Mom wasn't mad at me—I had told her I was going to a bonfire thrown by a popular girl.

    The bonfire was the most terrifying thing I've ever experienced. Grandma said we're all meeting at Madam Ortega's house tomorrow to go over what happened.

    It was a magickal fire that almost killed us, and someone was there, but he disappeared in light.

"Hey," Margret said. "Lights out. Doctor's orders."

"Can I have a few minutes to finish writing?"

"What are you writing?" Margret asked.

"Just some thoughts I have tumbling around in my head about tonight. I won't be able to sleep unless I get them out."

Margret nodded. She walked over to Nikki and kissed her on the top of the head. "I love you, sweet girl."

"I love you too, Mom," Nikki said.

"Five minutes," Margret said, holding up her hand.

Nikki nodded.

I hope this doesn't jade Mom against Grandma. If anything, it was Grandma's training that kept me alive. We'll see. Mom's right though; I do need to sleep. I'm exhausted.

Nikki clumsily put her pen inside her journal, but before she could set it on the floor, it slipped from her hand. She was asleep.

# Chapter Seventeen

## Saturday, December 22nd

22 December 2008

Everyone is okay. We did it. Some of us are worse for wear, but overall, everyone is okay, and most importantly, alive. We got home from the hospital yesterday morning, and I slept clear through until this morning around 10. Rachelle says I got up to go to the bathroom, but I thought I just dreamed that. I had so many dreams, all revolving around water—dangerous water we had to escape. I think it was probably the medicine the doctor gave me.

Anyway, we (like all of us, even Nikki's mom) are at Grandma's house for lunch and a meeting. Rachelle picked up Thai food on our way over.

Everyone had gathered in various parts of the house: Kait, Gabby, Nikki, and Margret were in the living room, and Emma sat at the dining room table and watched Rachelle and Ethel, who were in the kitchen emptying the cartons of Thai food into several large metal bowls. Each dish had a bowl to itself. Curious and wanting to get a closer look, Emma headed into the kitchen and watched, peeking over Rachelle's shoulder. Rachelle scraped out the last bits of a yellow curry from its carton. The rest of the curry sat in a pile, looking pitifully small at the bottom of the massive bowl.

"Could I get a bit of help from the witches in the house?" Ethel called, leaning around the corner as she peeked into the living room.

Gabby and Kait both went into the kitchen just as Rachelle came and sat down on the other couch. Nikki stood to help, but Margret pulled her back down onto the couch.

In the kitchen, Gabby and Kait stood together, both their eyes closed as they waved their hands over the food. The portion in each bowl multiplied until the bowls were full.

"Emma, dear," Ethel said, putting a hand on Emma's shoulder. "Would you set the table?" She gestured to the cabinet that held all the plates

"Sure." Emma pulled out a pile of plates and grabbed a handful of forks from a drawer and went back out to the dining room.

"You knew?" Margret screeched in the living room.

"Mom," Nikki whispered, her voice still very hoarse.

"No, you lied to me," Margret said. "You knew there was going to be an out of control fire and you went?"

"I had to—"

"You told me it was just a party by a girl from school—"

"It was—"

"No!" Margret cut Nikki off, putting her hand up. "You knew and you lied. You purposefully put yourself in danger. *This* is why magick is dangerous. It makes you think you're invincible, that you can just walk into danger with no repercussions."

"You must understand without the training, she wouldn't have had the skills necessary to save her peers," Rachelle said to Margret.

"If she had just had her powers stripped, she wouldn't be in those types of situations in the first place," Margret retorted.

"Mom," Nikki whispered.

"No. You are the way you are because of your father, but you don't have to stay that way. You can still join cheerleading or the dance team. You can have a normal life, free of all this nonsense and danger," Margret said.

Nikki tried again, "But, Mom—"

"Quiet. You're not supposed to speak anyway."

"Margret, I understand you're worried about your daughter, but you must understand she has a great destiny. Surely you see that," Rachelle said.

"Oh, I know my daughter has the potential for greatness—"

"Mom, please," Nikki said.

"Enough! You almost died. When I found out about this…" Margret paused as if looking for the right word, "misfortune, I was willing to overlook it because I love Rand and our life and our children. But I swore, and made him swear, it would have no further influence on our lives or the lives of our children."

"Now, now, Maggie," Kait said, setting a big silver bowl on the dining room table.

"Do not call me that." Margret seethed.

"Very well." Kait sat resuming her previous seat. "We'll carry on this discussion after we've all been well fed."

"I did not come to eat." Margret crossed her arms.

"Nevertheless," Kait said, putting her hand up. "We eat first and talk later."

Everyone, except Margret, gathered at the table and sat. Kait waved her hand over a pitcher of water and the many silver bowls, which all rose, floating in the air. All one needed to do to get a dish was look at it, and the chosen food item would come soaring over. There was a bit of chatter as the women loaded their plates. Once everyone had been served and had settled, the only noise was the occasional clanking of serving utensils on bowls. The bowls never hit one another; each magickally knew where the others would be in relation to itself.

When all were sufficiently fed and watered, Kait waved her hand again and the plates began to clear and clean themselves.

Nikki leaned over to Emma and said, "I love magick."

Emma grinned, nodding.

"Time to speak." Ethel stood and gestured to the living room.

As everyone moved, Kait quickly wiped down the table and joined the group.

"Are you going to finally tell me why I'm here?" Margret asked as Kait sat down.

"I am," Kait said. "We've gathered you here today because we need to figure out what happened on the twentieth."

"We don't need a meeting for that," Margret said, scoffing. "A bunch of reckless, possibly insane, adults told children they could fight a fire. My child lied to me, and then both of those *children* almost died. That is what happened."

Nikki flushed and sunk deep into the couch cushions.

"Margret," Kait said the name in two clear syllables. "I know it is difficult for you to understand, but I assure you, if we had been able to go in their places, we would have."

"Ha!" Margret shook her head.

"Much in the same way you cannot make all the life choices for your children, we cannot fulfill all the tasks for those we teach," Kait said calmly. "Now, we have issues we need to address before—"

"You *are* insane!" Margret stood. "Oh, when we got married, Rand warned me you were a little different, and then Nikki was born and she's a witch, and so is he and so are you. I thought we were done. Now *this*. Now, you have thrown my daughter into the literal fire—"

"I understand you frustration," Ethel said. "But there is no need for—"

"You stay out of this, you hag!"

"Margret!" Kait snapped. "*That* is uncalled for!"

"NO! She's just as bad as you," Margret spat. "You're all—"

"If you cannot keep a civil tongue, I will have no choice but to magick your silence." Kait's face remained calm, but sparks danced around her fingertips.

Margret's mouth remained open, her brain still in the middle of her sentence. Nikki watched, amazed, as her mother reluctantly closed her mouth and sat back in her seat, arms folded once again.

"As I was saying," Kait continued, "there were some peculiar events on the twentieth we did not have the time to examine then."

"Are you talking about Emma's vision of my present?" Nikki asked in a whisper. It hurt less to speak if she whispered. She didn't look at Margret but could feel her glare nonetheless.

"Yes, dear," Kait said. "Tell us what happened."

Nikki's swollen and tender throat reminded her of when she had gotten her tonsils out a few years before. She swallowed gingerly and began, "It happened just like Emma said. I was in a store when I heard Wyatt and a girl talking. I listened, and that was it."

"And in your vision?" Kait asked Emma.

"I saw Wyatt and Jo, that's Nelly's sister. I hid, so they couldn't see me, and I listened," Emma said.

"And you two didn't have any contact that day?" Kait asked.

"I called several times, but she never answered," Nikki said.

"I think I left my phone in your car," Emma told Nikki.

"You also left your journal in there," Nikki said, pulling both out of her bag and handing them to Emma.

"Oh, good," Emma said. "I've been writing in a back up."

"One more question before I move on to why you're all here," Kait said with a pointed look at Margret.

Margret coughed her acknowledgment, looking more flustered by the minute.

"What happened at the bonfire?" Kait asked. "It didn't happen the way your visions said it would, did it?"

"Yes and no," Emma answered. Emma recounted the events of the night of the bonfire: the false alarm, the s'mores, sleeping in the chair, getting in the car, the earthquake, seeing the telephone pole fall, screaming for Nikki, finding each other just to lose each other again, finding Wyatt, finding Nikki again. "Then Nikki passed out. The paramedics showed up right away. The smoke had started to clear once the fire was out, and they found us. I'm sure my screaming helped. I lied to the paramedics and told them Nikki was my sister, so I could go with her in the ambulance."

"And the fire?" Kait asked Nikki.

"It was a normal fire, at first," Nikki whispered. "I almost had it out until the lightning struck the telephone pole down; then, it became magickal."

"What do you mean 'it became magickal'?" Gabby asked, leaning forward.

"I felt it change. You know how magickal fire feels?" Nikki said.

"Magickal fire resists you," Gabby said.

"Exactly," Nikki said. "It didn't resist, and, after the telephone pole, it did."

"How did you put it out?" Kait asked.

"I tried to do it with the spell you taught us, but the earthquake tore me and Emma apart. It was weird though. I couldn't sense her in the smoke. It was like it was closing me off from everything." Nikki shuttered.

"I felt like that, too," Emma said. "It was very strange. I couldn't actually sense her magick until we were physically touching."

Kait and Ethel glanced at each other. "And the fire?" Kait pressed.

"Well, Emma and I managed to find each other, and that's when new words came to me. We sat like we do when we meditate, and Em repeated what I said. The fire went out; then, I did, too," Nikki whispered, shrugging. "Next thing I remember is waking up in a hazy-looking hospital room."

"Do you remember the spell you used?" Kait asked.

"Kind of," Nikki said.

"Write it down." Kait handed Nikki a sheet of paper and a pencil.

Nikki scribbled something on the paper. "There are parts missing, but that's what I can remember of it." She handed the paper and pencil back to Kait.

"Interesting," Kait said, reading the paper. "And this just came to you?"

Nikki nodded. Her throat had already gotten quite sore with all the talking she had been doing even though she'd only been whispering.

Kait nodded and turned to face Margret. "You're here because it's time you heard this, and I need you to wait until I'm finished," Kait added, seeing Margret take a deep breath.

Margret pursed her lips and nodded.

"Nikki is, according to the magickal community, as well as in the eyes of your law, an adult. She can make her own decisions. I respect that she lives under your roof, but she will not always. You do not have the right, nor ability, to strip her of powers that will affect the rest of her life. Magick has already saved her life once, and it will save it again, many more times.

"You may say as her mother, you know best, but this choice is not up to you *or* her father *or* me. None of us can make this choice for her. Whether Nikki chooses to be stripped of her magickal abilities or keep them is entirely up to her. Her growth as a witch has already been hindered by her binding as a child, which I understood," Kait added. "Mothering magickal children is a challenge even for those of us with our own magick. However, she is no longer a child, and she deserves to be treated accordingly."

Margret fumed, ready to explode. "You have no right to tell me what I can and cannot do with my children." Her words came out in quiet rage but grew steadily. "You say she is an adult, and maybe legally she is, but we all know 18-year-olds are still children. They still think and act like children. She doesn't have the capacity to realize how choosing to keep these—powers—will affect the rest of her life," she continued, now standing and yelling, "if she even lives that long! These 'powers,' this 'magic' is evil. It has done nothing but cause harm since that very first day, or have you forgotten what happened the day her powers showed up?"

"What?" Nikki asked, looking up at her mom.

"She nearly died that day!" Margret went on as though she hadn't heard Nikki. "We are going to strip her powers, and when Kameron comes into his, we will strip them, too." Wagging her index finger with the rest of her hand in a tight fist, Margret took a step towards Kait. "Magic cannot save her life because it has only ever put her in danger in the first place, and if she keeps it, it will only continue to put her in danger over and over again until it kills her. I will not have it. I will not stunt her personal and professional growth by allowing this nonsense to continue. I will have normal children who will grow up and have their own normal children."

"It's my choice," Nikki said, her voice almost as hoarse as it had been at the hospital.

"You be quiet," Margret snapped.

Nikki waved her hand at her.

Margret tried to say something but simply mouthed the words. No sound would come out. It would be a turning point in their relationship, though Nikki would not know this until much later.

"Please, Mom. Listen to me for once." Nikki reached up and took Margret's hand, but Margret jerked her hand away. "I want to keep my powers." Nikki grabbed again; this time holding on. She pulled Margret back into her seat. "My whole life I've read about people who get powers. They always do amazing things with them. I always wanted to *be* them. My dream was never to be a ballerina, or head cheerleader, or any of those things. It was to have magick. To have power I could use to help people. On my eighteenth birthday, my dream came true.

"You and Dad taught me power and responsibility are tied to each other. I've got power; if that means putting my life on the line to save innocent people from burning alive, I'll do it. I went to the bonfire knowing, understanding, and accepting I might not come back. Mom, I knew if I didn't go, those people would have died. It's no different than what Dad does." Nikki watched Margret, waiting for the hard lines on her face to soften. When they didn't, Nikki waved her hand again, and Margret's voice was loosened once again.

"You think," Margret's whisper dripped with rage as she turned towards Kait, "*this* is better for her? To be able to shut her mother up whenever she pleases?" Margret stood again. "Nikki, we're leaving." Margret stormed past Kait and headed towards the front door.

Staring at the floor, Nikki took a deep breath. She looked up and said, "I'm staying."

"Fine," Margret said. "Fly home!" She left, slamming the door behind her.


December 22, 2008

Meeting at Madam Ortega's. Mom came. Went about as well as a nuclear explosion. To say she's mad would be the understatement of the world. I always knew Mom was disappointed I was more interested in reading than cheerleading, and I knew she wouldn't be crazy about magick because it doesn't fit the picket-fence daydream she has for me, but I had no idea my magick almost killed me as a kid.

There was a soft knock on the bathroom door. "You okay?" Emma asked.

"Yeah," Nikki said, sitting on the rim of the bathtub. "I'll be out in a minute." She debated flushing to make it sound like she had actually used the bathroom, but there was no point in pretending with Emma. Nikki opened the bathroom door and leaned against the doorframe. "I wish she didn't hate me."

"Your mom doesn't hate you; she just doesn't know you this way," Emma said.

"If your own mom doesn't know you, who does?" Nikki said, sighing.

"Your dad?" Emma offered.

Nikki laughed hollowly.

"Nikki?" Gabby poked her head into the hallway.

"Yeah?" Nikki said, standing up and looking past Emma at Gabby.

"Kait had to go, and I'm about to make a healing draught for your throat," Gabby said. "Would you like to watch?"

Nikki nodded, and the girls followed Gabby into the cozy kitchen.

"Emma," Ethel said just as they got to the kitchen. "Come with me."

"But," Emma said, "I'd like to watch more earth magick."

"Later, dear. Come to the library." Ethel walked towards the back of the house. Emma followed with a half-hearted wave to Nikki and Gabby, who both remained in the kitchen.

"Put the kettle on," Gabby said to Nikki. Gabby opened her bag and Ethel's spice drawer. She grabbed several herbs from the drawer and a few small bottles from her bag. Gabby dropped a pinch of this and a dash of that together in a small marble mortar, mixing it all together with a pestle.

"Do you know what my mom was talking about?" Nikki asked as she filled the kettle and put it on the burner, which she lit magickally. "You know, when she said I almost died when I got my magick?"

"Kait told me about it," Gabby admitted as she poured the mixture into a glass jar and waved her hand over it a few times. The concoction bubbled, turning dark green, and then lighter, and lighter until it was a clear, amber liquid, slightly thicker than the consistency of honey.

"So," Nikki said slowly. "What happened?"

Gabby pulled a mug from Ethel's cabinet and sighed. "You were about two years old. According to Kait, you were quite the chatter-box. Your mom and Kait had a good relationship back then, and Kait was visiting when it happened. If Kait hadn't been there—"

"I would have died?" Nikki guessed.

Gabby nodded and added a heaping spoonful of the amber concoction to the mug. "Your dad was out of town, and you three had gone to the zoo. You loved animals, particularly snakes and lions. You knew what sounds they made and—well, anyway, your mom put you down for a nap. She and Kait were in the front room folding laundry when they heard a strange noise, and you started crying."

"I think I see where this is going," Nikki said, her shoulders falling.

"You had summoned a snake into your room, a black mamba, one of the most venomous snakes in the world, and it had bit you," Gabby said, setting the mug down on the counter and looking at Nikki. "You grandma was able to make the snake disappear back to wherever it came from and heal you from the bite."

Nikki sighed and closed her eyes. "Because her healing magick specialized in curses and poisons." She looked at Gabby again. "Right?"

Gabby nodded. "Lucky for you," she added as she poured a bit of hot water from the kettle into the mug and stirred. "Venoms and poisons are magickally treated similarly, and naturally occurring venoms, like those in snakes, are not magick resistant, so you were easy to heal. Here, drink this." Gabby handed the mug to Nikki, who started to drink, but spluttered and coughed. "It doesn't go down smoothly, but you do need to drink all of it."

Nikki chugged the rest of the drink as quickly as she could. "Now what?" she said, still hoarse.

"Close your eyes and think of cool, calming air."

Nikki coughed violently.

"Interesting," Gabby said. "Try warm, humid air."

As if Nikki could see the flesh of her own throat in her mind, she saw cracked, dry skin smoothing and becoming supple once more. "My throat," she said. "Hey, my voice is back." She no longer sounded hoarse.

"Don't get too excited," Gabby warned. "By tomorrow morning, you'll sound just as hoarse as before. You'll need to take this twice a day for the next three days. Then, you'll be fully healed."

Nikki nodded, taking the jar with the amber potion from Gabby. "So, what happened with Mom and Grandma?"

"Well, Kait performed the necessary magicks right in front of your mom," Gabby said. "She tried to explain afterwards, but I think your mom was in too much shock, over the snake and almost losing you. I don't think she really understood Kait. Margret made up her mind magick was inherently dangerous. She kicked Kait out after that—well, your mom thought she did. Kait stuck around just in case something else happened. Two days later, your dad got home, got an earful, and bound your powers. Kam's were bound the day he was born."

"So, he'll definitely get magick too?" Nikki asked.

Gabby nodded.

"Do I tell him?"

"That's entirely up to you," Gabby said.

Nikki sighed. "How do I know? How do I decide?"

"Just give it time. Time always knows the answer."

# Chapter Eighteen

## Sunday, December 23rd

23 December 2008

Finally told Grandma and Rachelle about the dreams. They won't stop. At first, I thought they were just a side effect of the medication, but I didn't take any last night. I still had the same dreams, dreams full of water and fear.

The all too familiar feeling of freezing flooded over Emma before she could write another word.

*There was a burning in her lungs. Everything was blue. She was consciously aware of her inability to breathe. She took in her surroundings, concerned that she seemed to be moving in slow motion. Kameron was there, eyes wide in fear. There was a flash of black.*

Emma took a sudden breath. She grimaced and furrowed her eyebrows.

"Ugh!" she grunted. "What are you trying to tell me?"

Emma was awash with cold.

*The world around her was green.*

She came out of the brief vision only to feel suddenly warm and plunge into another one.

*Sunlight blinded her, but the warmth of the sun stimulated her other senses. She smelled salt water. There was a pain in her legs, so small she might not have noticed it if not for her desire to return from whence she'd come.*

Emma shook her head; how did wanting to be somewhere else make her legs hurt? Struggling to catch her breath, she tried to call for Rachelle, but it was too late; a chill drowned her senses.

*Wyatt was on a hospital bed. Tears streamed down her cheeks as she whispered his name, holding his cold hand with her warm ones.*

Emma's head ached. Her muscles were sore, but there was no time to rest. She was immersed in warmth.

*People cried—people she recognized but could not name. She hugged them.*

She was cold again before the vision had fully ended.

*Sobbing and unable to see a face through her tears, she held a limp body in her arms.*

Emma's head swam more with each haphazard vision. Breathing heavily, she swallowed. Her eyelids weighed a hundred pounds each. Unable to resist any longer, she closed her eyes. Emma breathed slowly and intentionally, concentrating on relaxing. Her muscles were tight and tense. She was still having trouble catching her breath.

"Rachelle," Emma said, her breathiness turning the name to a whisper. She tried to stand but collapsed onto her floor. Once more, she felt the sudden shift of temperature, and she was immersed in not a single vision but a multitude of visions hitting her simultaneously.

*People were crying: there was mourning.*

*People were crying: there was celebrating.*

*Water washed away the city.*

*The city was intact.*

*Parents wailed over limp children.*

*Parents kissed their crying children.*

The vision ebbed; somewhere in a back corner of her brain, Emma wondered if these visions were of a terrifying future or if they were someone's horrifying present. The mass of visions left pressure in her chest, making it hard to breathe. Beads of sweat dripped down her nose as Emma tried to ground herself, staring at the grain of the floor. She tried to focus on each and every color in the wooden floorboard. Her arms shook; she panted, trying to focus, trying to calm her breathing, trying to stay present, but the prickle of a vision swelled over her once again.

"I can't—" she whispered.

Later, Emma would reflect on the strangeness of this particular vision; each vision, prior to this one, was accompanied by a sudden flash of cold, or warmth depending on the nature of the vision, yet there was no indication of temperature at the beginning of this one:

*She felt uneasy. She didn't recognize where she was. Everything was white. She heard the popping and snapping of a fire. Walking towards the sound, she found herself in front of a wood burning stove. The closer she got to the fire, the colder she became. She felt weaker; she tried to move away from the fire, but she couldn't.*

Emma's eyes cleared. She was back in her room, collapsed on the floor and staring at her ceiling. Pulling herself up back into her bed, she passed out from sheer exhaustion.

"Emma?" Rachelle peeked inside Emma's room. She saw Emma asleep, journal and covers askew. Rachelle put Emma's journal on the bedside table and tucked Emma in. She took Emma's phone and sent a quick text to Nikki ("Hey, Nikki. This is Rachelle. Emma won't make it today. She's exhausted."). Rachelle kissed Emma's forehead. It felt warm. Maybe Emma was coming down with something. Rachelle would make soup; chicken and wild rice was Emma's favorite.

December 23, 2008

Mom still isn't talking to me. Kam knows something is up, but he's at least smart enough to keep his head down and stay out of the line of fire. Wish I'd thought of that. Throat is sore as ever this morning, just as Gabby promised. I need to go make the draught, but I don't have the energy to deal with more Mom drama. But I guess if I want to be treated like an adult, I ought to act like one.

Nikki groaned but stood up. She dug through her bag and found the jar Gabby had given her yesterday—she hadn't wanted to risk Margret throwing it away. Nikki steeled herself against a possible battle with her mother and went into the kitchen. But much to Nikki's surprise, and immediate relief, Margret was nowhere to be seen. Kam was, however, sitting on a stool at the island munching on a piece of toast.

Upon seeing Nikki, Kam held up an envelope and said, "This came for you."

"Thanks," Nikki said hoarsely. She put her jar on the counter and ripped the envelope open, reading the letter inside:

Dear Nikki,

Unfortunately some other business calls me away again. You'll resume training with Gabby. It's of the utmost importance you do not speak. Your spell-work must be entirely of thought. I understand you find power in words, but the restriction they can put upon your magickal abilities is severe. You must be able to understand your magick without words. The usage of words will come later. I promise. I'm not sure when I'll be back, but I'll try to make it soon. Promise me you'll work wordless for right now—besides, with your throat in its current condition, you're in no position to be speaking very much anyway.

Give my love to your brother.

Blessèd be,

Grandma Kait

Nikki shrugged and sighed.

"What's it say?" Kam asked.

"Grandma will be out of town again," Nikki whispered. "She sends her love." Nikki set the kettle to boil and pulled out a mug. She scooped a spoonful of the amber syrup into the mug.

Kam watched for a minute before saying, "Oh, Mom said to tell you she was finishing her Christmas shopping, and you should make breakfast. I would like to personally request French toast."

Nikki chuckled and nodded. The kettle whistled; she filled her mug halfway with water, and stirred until the syrup was fully incorporated. She drank it slowly, thinking about warm humid air the entire time. She had discovered last night if she did both simultaneously, it healed her while also making it easier to swallow the concoction. Nikki cleared her throat as she washed her mug and put it away.

"So French toast," she said to Kam.

He widened his eyes. "You sound waaaaaay better!"

"Gabby gave me some good tea," Nikki said, gesturing to the jar.

"No tea is *that* good," Kam said, crossing his arms. "Alright, enough's enough. What's been going on?"

"What do you mean?" she said, getting the griddle out.

"I *mean* all the freaky stuff. Mom is mad all the time. We have dead Grandma back from the grave, and all of the sudden you have a friend?" Kam said.

"I had friends," Nikki said, a bit wounded by the last remark.

"Yeah, in Arkansas. Not here. Not since we moved. Don't get me wrong," he added, "I like Emma, but she became your best friend overnight, and then you were in the hospital, and Mom blames our long lost grandma?"

"She does not blame Grandma," Nikki said.

"Does too. I heard her talking to Dad. Mom is super mad. She's mad at you, Dad, *and* Grandma. I get I'm still a little kid to Mom and Dad, but you've always told me the truth, like when Mom said Dad's flight was just delayed, but *you* told me he wasn't coming."

Nikki chewed her lip as she piled slices of bread onto a plate. "Get out the eggs, and I'll show you, but you have to promise not to tell Mom I told you. She might send me away or something if she found out you knew because of me."

"Okay," Kam said slowly. He got the eggs and handed the carton to Nikki.

"Watch carefully," Nikki said, cracking five eggs into a bowl and discarding the shells.

Kam glanced at her skeptically. "So what?"

"Just watch." Nikki stuck the whisk in the bowl but did not mix the eggs. She took a step back. "Ready?"

"Sure."

Nikki closed her eyes and raised her right arm, sticking her hand out as though she meant to shake someone else's. She rotated her wrist, so her hand was palm-side down. Using the tips of her fingers as a single unit, Nikki made a stirring motion with them. When Kam gasped, Nikki opened her eyes to see Kam watching the bowl of eggs as the whisk moved unaided through them. Nikki moved her hand faster. The whisk followed the command and began to psk-psk-psk in the bowl.

"How are you doing that?" Kam asked, running his hand through the air above the whisk like he was looking for strings.

"Magick," Nikki said. She put her hand down but continued to think about the whisk, which continued to mix the eggs.

"I mean for real," Kam said, putting his hands on his hips.

"Me, too." Nikki smiled at him and raised her eyebrows. "Dad has magick, and I do, too. That's why Mom doesn't like Grandma Kait, because she's Dad's mom, and he got his magick from her." As she finished making French toast, Nikki told Kam all about her eighteenth birthday; she also explained about Emma and what really happened at the bonfire.

"So, what can you do with your powers?" Kam asked, after swallowing a mouthful of French toast.

"All kinds of stuff," Nikki said, cutting her own piece. "I mean, I *think* I can do all kinds of stuff, I need to get trained by Grandma Kait, which is another reason why Mom doesn't like her."

"Why?" Kam asked.

"Mom says she wants me to be normal," Nikki said.

"Yeah right, you're a weirdo even without your powers," Kam said, grinning.

"Right? But you know how starry-eyed she gets when she starts thinking about me twirling a baton on dance team," Nikki said, rolling her eyes. She took a bite of her French toast.

"Or me playing football," Kam said, rolling his eyes, too.

Nikki grinned. "Well, she's still got years to work on you. I think she's starting to see I'm a lost cause at eighteen."

"If I tried out for football, I'd end up in a wheelchair playing trombone anyway." Kam shrugged. "So, what's it like having powers? What do I call you now?"

"It's weird, and you call me Nikki, like you always have," Nikki said, ruffling his hair. "More toast?"

"Yes, please." Kam handed her his plate. "But are you still human?"

"I don't know why I wouldn't be," Nikki said, furrowing her brow.

"Well are you a sorceress, or a wizard, or—"

"Oh," Nikki said with a laugh. "Witch."

"Wow," Kam said. "Will I—"

They heard the front door unlock. Nikki put her finger to her lips and winked at Kam. He nodded his understanding.

"Look, Mom. Nikki's making French toast; do you want some?" Kam asked. He hugged Margret.

"No thank you, dear," she said. Carrying bags full of what could only be Christmas presents, Margret walked to her bedroom and closed the door.

"She isn't handling this well, is she?" Kam whispered to Nikki.

Nikki just shook her head and put a hot piece of French toast on Kam's plate. "Here you go." She handed him the plate.

"Do you think we'll get two Christmases again?" Kam asked as he sat back down at the island.

Kam's curious nature meant he wanted to ask Nikki more questions about magick, but his sense of survival meant he knew the value of not being overheard by their mother, which was wise.

"Because Dad isn't here?" Nikki asked. She washed the batter bowl, whisk, and spatula (sans magick).

"Yeah," Kam said.

"I would think so. We've had two Christmases and two birthdays every other time Dad hasn't been here for them," Nikki said.

"Are you almost done eating?" Margret called from the hallway. "I have a few grocery bags in the car I need you to go get."

"Which 'you' do you think she's talking to?" Kam asked before shoving his penultimate bite of French toast in his mouth.

"Probably you; I don't exist anymore, remember?" Nikki flicked her finger, making the dishes soar into the cupboard. "But I'll help you anyway."

# Chapter Nineteen

## Monday, December 24th

24 December 2008

One of these days, I'll get a handle on my magick. I called Grandma this morning and told her about the visions yesterday. It felt like the universe was trying to get them all through to me, but something else, something dark was trying to stop them. Grandma called Nikki. The hope is Nikki will be able to help me close the floodgates a bit since she was able to help me open them.

"She's here," Ethel called.

"Okay," Emma said from under her pile of blankets on the couch. She pushed them off and stood, stretching. She ran over to the door and opened it before Nikki could knock.

"Oh good," Nikki said as she came in. Her arms were full of plastic bags and many rolls of wrapping paper.

"Need help?" Emma asked.

"Yes, please!" Nikki handed Emma a few of the many rolls of wrapping paper and a bag filled with ribbon and bows. "This isn't even all of it."

"I was going to ask where the actual presents are," Emma said with a laugh. "You can wrap everything on the dining room table. Grandma already cleared it for you." The girls emptied their arms on said table and ran back out to Nikki's car to grab the presents.

As Nikki arranged everything on the table for optimal wrapping efficiency, Ethel came out of the kitchen.

"So, Nikki," Ethel said, carrying a tray holding three steaming mugs of hot cocoa and a plate of decorated sugar cookies and gingerbread men. "What are some of your family's Christmas Eve traditions?"

"Well," Nikki said, considering for a moment, "I guess our traditions mostly boil down to two things: Mom always reads the Bible on Christmas Eve, and we get to pick out one present to open. On actual Christmas, there aren't traditions so much as rules: stockings are fair game, but you're not allowed to open presents until Mom and Dad are up. Oh, and Mom doesn't make breakfast. If we're hungry, we eat whatever is in our stocking," Nikki added with a laugh. "How about you guys?"

"We do a séance every year," Emma said as she grabbed napkins from the kitchen. "We have our favorite dead authors read or tell their Christmas stories. For example, we had Dickens last year. He's requested we choose him again and often. It was the third or fourth time I've heard *A Christmas Carol* from him."

Nikki stared, slack-jawed.

"Nikki?" Emma said, waving her hand in front of Nikki's face, teasing.

Swatting at Emma's hand, Nikki blinked and closed her mouth.

"He's a lovely man," Ethel continued. "We'd love to have you and your family over tonight, if you'd like to join us. I'm sure Charles wouldn't mind if we called on him two years in a row."

"You've spoken to Charles Dickens," Nikki said in a flat-tone, once she finally found her voice.

"Would you like to come tonight?" Emma asked.

"Uh, yeah!" Nikki amended her statement almost immediately, "I mean, *I* would love to come, but I doubt my mom would be thrilled about spending Christmas Eve with a ghost, even one as awesome as Dickens."

"Maybe another time," Emma said, shrugging. "So who are you wrapping presents for?"

"My family mostly," Nikki said. "Mom, Dad, and those are for Kam," she added, pointing to the various packages.

"Wrap those quickly. Meditation might take most of the day," Ethel warned.

Between Nikki and Emma's quick hands (and Nikki's love of efficient wrapping stations), the presents were wrapped in no time, and the girls soon found themselves in the library, sitting on plush cushions, trying to quiet their minds.

After a little focusing, Emma said, "Ready?"

"Almost," Nikki said. It wasn't a lie; she was ready and also really nervous. As the memory of Nikki's first vision with Emma replayed vividly in the front of her mind, Nikki's stomach clenched. She knew waiting wasn't going to clear her nerves, so she took a deep breath and started meditating. Nikki tried to replace the nervous thoughts she was having with the sound of her heartbeat. For the first fifteen minutes, Nikki had failed to rid herself of her nervous energy. However, after another ten minutes, Nikki began to finally feel the familiar calm settle into her bones. It only took another five for her 'almost' to become a solid 'yes.'

Ethel saw the softness in Nikki's features and said, "Now."

Emma took Nikki's hands. The girls felt a deep cold all over as they plunged into a vision.

*The girls were together, walking past a store window displaying dozens of televisions, all playing the same thing.*

*"...and now with the latest. Kim?" The newsman said on the televisions. There was a brief pause in lag time as the newswoman listened to her colleague.*

*"Thanks, Dan. We've had a massive earthquake. As you can see behind me, the fault line has revealed itself through the asphalt roads." Kim, the newswoman, pointed behind her. "The earthquake," Kim voiced over as the camera panned the devastation, "has damaged many properties. It struck at around one-thirty this morning. Not a good way to start out the new year at all. Back to you, Dan."*

*As Nikki and Emma watched, Dan talked about the figures involved in the earthquake: dollars in damages, people in the hospital, help being donated to their area. He continued to talk numbers, but neither Nikki nor Emma were listening anymore. They turned and looked at each other, and when they turned to look back at the televisions, time shifted. They were at a beach with Nelly, Jo, Wyatt, and Kam in the middle of a conversation.*

*"Can you believe that earthquake?" Jo was saying.*

*"I know. Talk about freaky," Nelly said.*

*Wyatt stood, arms crossed, sulking.*

*"Um, guys?" Kam said.*

*"What's up, dude?" Nelly asked.*

*Kam didn't say anything.*

*"Kam?" Nelly said, glancing at him. Following his gaze, Nelly looked at*

*the ocean. "Holy..." Nelly trailed off. A wall of water was coming right at them.*

*Wyatt saw the wave and yelled, "Run!" He grabbed Jo's hand and pulled her away from the beach.*

*"Kam, go!" Nikki shouted, putting her hands up. She recited a spell.*

*Kam didn't move.*

*Running and standing next to Nikki, Nelly put her hands up as well. It looked as though the two girls were going to hold the wall of water off by themselves, but Nikki felt her power draining. She grabbed Nelly's hand in hopes their combined power would be enough.*

*Nikki knew the answer immediately. "Run!" she screamed, and the wave collapsed onto them.*

Nikki and Emma opened their eyes simultaneously. Both of them coughed and wheezed. Several things happened at once: Nikki threw up water; Emma felt the sting of salt in her lungs; and Ethel rushed forward to help both girls. Nikki tried to apologize for the water she had thrown up, but Ethel hushed her. Ethel touched the girls' hands, which were clammy and icy. She walked to the cold fireplace and picked up a handful of powder. Muttering an inaudible incantation, she threw the powder into the fireplace, which instantly burst into warm, dancing flames.

"Come," Ethel said. "Sit by the fire."

Emma had stopped wheezing, but Nikki still coughed. The two girls scooted closer to the fire. Nikki could feel the magickal fire suck the excess moisture from her lungs and throat; each breath near the fire warmed and soothed her. Emma, likewise, found the heat from the fire warming, all the way down to her bones.

After a few minutes, Ethel finally asked her burning question, "What did you see?"

"I saw it again," Emma said between deep breaths.

"What?" Ethel asked.

Before Emma could respond, Nikki croaked, "You mean you've seen that before?"

"I keep dreaming it," Emma admitted. "Except, the newswoman was new. She wasn't there before."

"Newswoman?" Ethel asked.

Emma nodded and verbally replayed the vision for Ethel. Ethel had Nikki recount the vision as well; her account was nearly identical to Emma's. In Ethel's fashion, she said nothing; she offered no insight to what they had seen. Instead, she insisted the girls sit near the fire as she busied herself cleaning up the water..

"How long have you been dreaming about that?" Nikki whispered once Ethel had left the library to find her some dry clothes.

"Long enough to know it's not just a dream," Emma said. She was deeply disturbed by what they had witnessed. "I was so sure the big event we needed each other for was the bonfire." She shook her head, panic creeping up the back of her neck. "I was wrong. The bonfire was only the beginning."

December 24, 2008

We got it wrong. There's more. We're not only NOT done, but what's coming is much bigger and much scarier than the bonfire ever was. It makes the bonfire look like child's play. We think it's a tsunami.

I don't even know how to BEGIN preparing for this. I guess it's time to learn water magick?

Nikki was wearing a sage green tunic which belonged to Ethel. It was surprisingly warm and comfortable. Nikki looked up from her journal and saw Emma coming back into the library. "So," Nikki said as Emma sat down. "What's the plan?"

"Plan?" Emma repeated as she settled on a plush cushion across from Nikki.

"Well, we had a plan last time," Nikki said. "So what's the plan this time?"

"You have to get Nelly on your side," Ethel answered for Emma. Ethel set down a tray on a small side table and handed Nikki a fresh mug of hot cocoa.

"She wasn't exactly keen on joining us the first time around; how are we supposed to convince her this time?" Nikki asked, taking the mug.

"We could tell her Wyatt is at risk. Jo, too," Emma said, taking her own mug from the tray.

"It's kind of a low blow, but I think we're desperate enough," Nikki said. She sighed. "What can we do to prepare ourselves magickally for this?"

"Save your strength," Ethel said, still standing. She cradled her mug close to her chest, as if the warmth of that single mug of cocoa might ease the chill in her heart. She smiled a bit sadly and added, "Neither of you have fully healed from the bonfire."

"It was only a few nights ago," Emma said.

"Really? Feels longer." Nikki sipped her hot cocoa. "You know, time seems to be passing faster these days."

Setting her mug back on the tray, Ethel suddenly walked over to one of her many bookshelves. She pulled out a book, studied its contents, and reshelved it, repeating this process several times, until she finally pulled out one book, tapped the cover, and left the library.

"What just happened?" Nikki asked. She had been too distracted watching the old woman to ask what she was doing.

Emma shrugged and said, "She does that sometimes." She sipped her cocoa before adding, "How are you feeling?"

"Well," Nikki said, "I still feel the ocean in my throat, and I'm pretty sure I'll be tasting salt water for at least a week. You?"

"My throat is raw, and I get what you mean about the salt—although if I'm honest, it kind of makes the hot cocoa taste better."

Nikki laughed. "Leave it to you to see the benefits of having a lungful of salt water." She stood up and poked her head out of the library. The old grandfather clock at the end of the hallway chimed. "I probably should be getting back home," Nikki said, turning to look at Emma.

"It *is* Christmas Eve," Emma said. "I was actually surprised you were able to get away at all."

"Well, we can't have you overwhelmed by constant visions," Nikki said. "I'll see if I can get away for a little while tomorrow. I have a present for you."

"You didn't have to," Emma said.

"Are you crazy?" Nikki hugged her friend. "You've saved me on so many levels. You deserve at least a decent Christmas present."

"Thanks," Emma said. "Do you need help carrying stuff back out to the car?"

Nikki grinned. "That would be awesome."

# Chapter Twenty

## Tuesday, December 25th

Dec. 25, 08

Reread my last entry from a couple days ago. I wasn't making a lot of sense. I think I was still in shock over what happened.

I have powers.

Real powers.

Like more-than-turning-into-a-fish powers.

I haven't told anyone about them, not even Wyatt, speaking of Wyatt, I need to call him. But back to the powers, I haven't tried anything since it happened. It was all kind of an accident, a reaction more than a thought. I don't know if I could do it again. I'm not even sure I want to.

Nelly chewed on her lip, sighing.

In other news, I officially missed my first surf competition. It killed me to send in my regrets and pull myself from the invitational, but <u>because</u> I know it's invitation-only <u>and</u> because I know there's a short-list of alternate surfers, I had no choice. I couldn't deny another surfer that chance. Luckily, me pulling out meant Grace got invited in. That kid can rip it. I couldn't bring myself to watch, but Jo did, and she said Grace creamed everyone. Jo's words: "She did ya proud." That made me feel good. Jo may also have mentioned that Whitney fell flat on her face and totally washed out. Might be petty, but that made me feel A LOT better.

Nelly smiled to herself. It might be worth checking with some old surf buddies to see if anyone caught it on camera.

It's Christmas today. Jo got Dad a book on sun-drying his own tomatoes. He looked genuinely excited about it. I heard Jo mention she's got a present for Grace she wants to drop off. I thought that might be a good time to tell Dad (without Jo's added drama). I'll tell her later.

I am nervous about telling him I'm a mermaid, but I'm more nervous to tell him about Mom. Every time we so much as mention Mom, Dad leaves, or turns on some loud kitchen appliance. One time he turned on the blender. There wasn't anything in it. He said he just wanted to make sure it was still working.

As if Jo heard Nelly's thoughts as she wrote them, Jo shouted from her room: "Dad! I'm headed over to Grace's place on my bike. I'll be home in like an hour or two."

Tom responded, "Sure thing, kiddo. Be safe."

"Now or never," Nelly whispered to herself; although now that now was here, never seemed a lot more appealing.

She made her way into the kitchen. Tom was standing over the sink slicing up a mango.

As Nelly hardened up her courage to begin, Tom beat her to it.

"Let's hear it," he said, not turning around to see Nelly.

"I—What?"

"You've been acting strange since your birthday, first not surfing, then you said you're through—which is fine," he added, setting down his knife. "But ever since the earthquake you've been skidding around here like a nervous kitten." He turned and slid the bowl of sliced mango between them on the island. "Let's hear it."

"You might want to sit down for this," Nelly said, sitting on a barstool on the other side of the counter. As Tom walked around and sat on the one next to her, Nelly began, "So, it did start with my birthday." Nelly unloaded nearly everything—including Wyatt's conversation and mutant theory ("That kid has problems," Tom said, shaking his head).

Finally, she finished with, "And the present from Mom?" Nelly had been saving Melinda for last. "It's a journal, a *mermaid* journal." She swallowed, knowing it was best to just rip the Band-Aid off. "Mom was one, too."

Tom stared at Nelly but kind of beyond her, as though combing through years of memories of his beloved late wife, searching for evidence to prove or disprove what their eldest daughter was telling him.

Nelly recognized this look; she called it his thinking face. The last time she had seen it, she had proposed taking a year off after high school and surfing around the world. Tom had eventually agreed under the condition she apply for university anyway and just defer.

"I should be surprised," Tom finally said. "But it actually makes a lot of sense."

Nelly stood, mouth agape and eyes wide. "A lot of sense! Are you crazy?" She paced around the dining room. "I tell you Mom and I turn into fish, and your response is THAT MAKES SENSE?!"

"I spent almost 20 years married to your mom," Tom said. "There was a lot about that woman I never understood. I chalked most of it up to me not understanding women in general, but her being a mermaid makes a lot more sense."

Nelly stood aghast.

Tom chuckled and muttered something that sounded like "You'll understand when you're older." Nelly shook her head, but Tom just chuckled again and patted her stool, indicating she should sit. "You mentioned powers, and some girls at school needing your help?"

Nelly sat down, though her brain was still reeling, seriously doubting she'd understand anything more just because she was older. She nodded. "Uh," Nelly said, trying to get her brain under control again. "Nikki and Emma. Nikki just moved here—I don't remember her last name—and Emma Hugos. She's apparently been in my science classes for years."

"Oh, that's the girl with the medical episodes, right?" Tom said.

"I have a feeling that was just a story," Nelly said, shrugging. "Both of the girls have powers too. Nikki is a witch, at least, that's what she told me, and Emma has visions—"

"Episodes, visions, got it." Tom clicked his tongue. "Emma lives with her aunt, right?"

"I guess."

"Does she have magic, too?"

"I don't know," Nelly said, frowning.

"It would explain a lot if she did," Tom said mostly to himself.

"Wait, how do you even know her?"

"School functions, and fundraisers. We also buy our fruit at the same place," Tom said with a wave of his hand. "So, how are you with all this? How do I help you? I mean, I don't really know anything about powers and mermaids…"

Nelly hugged him. "For starters, thanks for listening." Nelly was sure Tom had no idea just how valuable his reaction to all her chaos was to her, how he didn't recoil from her magick like she had, how he instead pulled her closer, embracing her—all of her—even more. But he knew. She was not the first child to tell her parents that life was not going to look the way they had planned.

"Sure thing, kid." He kissed the top of her head.

"Actually," Nelly said, pulling out of the hug. "Do you know if Mom had any family?"

"There's always Uncle Henry," Tom said.

"That bum?" Nelly groaned. "The only time we hear from him is when he sends his annual 'Happy Birthday/Merry Christmas/Happy Easter plus whatever other holiday *the man* has invented recently' card," she said, using finger quotes.

"Henry is the only one I ever met, and the only one who's ever made contact," Tom admitted. "Your mom's family was never very fond of me; she always said they weren't fond of anyone. Their secrecy makes more sense now. Why do you need to know?"

"I just need to talk to someone who knows about this stuff. If there's someone related to Mom out there, maybe they're different too, and maybe they can show me what to do next." Nelly shrugged.

Tom sighed. "Well, kiddo, it looks like we need to start trying to contact some long-lost relatives, huh?" Chuckling, he hopped off his stool and grabbed the phone book from the top of the refrigerator. Nelly asked him what was so funny, and Tom looked at her. "I never thought I'd be looking up your mom's family to see if there was another mermaid among them. I hope I get in contact with someone soon or else a lot of people are going to think we're pretty strange." He smiled again and walked down the hall into his room to find his laptop, muttering to himself about whether or not to use the word "mermaid" in his calls.

"Dad," Nelly called down the hall. "I'm going to do a little research of my own, is that okay?"

"Yeah, just stay close by in case I need to prove I'm telling the truth."

"Okay." Nelly grinned, shaking her head. She had always known he was weird, but who was she to talk? Her most pressing issue now was figuring out the best way to tell Jo. While she considered her options, she did the research she had mentioned to Tom: she spent the next forty-five minutes running water and attempting, unsuccessfully, to stop it.

December 26, 2008

DAD IS HOME!!!! Magick was definitely involved but not on my end. All I know for sure is we woke up to someone ringing the doorbell at 5 in the morning—Mom was not pleased, until she actually answered the door.

Why didn't Dad just magick his way in? Who knows?

Mom and Dad crashed on the couch; Kam's also asleep, curled up in his brand new Death Star pjs. Mom can finally throw his old pjs away. She hasn't mentioned Grandma being here, but I imagine Dad already knows. How can he not? I'm dying to ask him tons of questions, but I don't want to make Mom mad. It's Christmas, and she's talking to me (probably because it's Christmas), but I'm not one to look a gift horse in the mouth.

"Busy?" Rand, Nikki's dad, poked his almost white-blond head in her room.

"Not really, what's up?" Nikki sat up in her unmade bed. She had been laying down and writing in her journal, as was her habit.

"Can I talk to you?" Rand asked. He was dressed in his usual black shirt and jeans.

"Is it about getting magick powers? Or about being a witch? Because I'm a bit past that," Nikki said, grinning.

Rand smiled, adjusted his glasses, and said, "Well, it has something to do with that."

Nikki closed her journal, giving him her full attention.

He sat on her bed. "You're not just a witch."

"Am I a fairy princess, too?" She waggled her eyebrows.

Rand chuckled. "Not exactly. You're the first half-human witch in our family in over five-thousand years."

"Our family has been around that long?"

"My side has, and they've only ever married other witches," Rand said.

"That's insane. So by marrying Mom, you broke a long-standing tradition?"

"You could say that." Rand nodded.

"So am I not as powerful? Is my magick diluted by Mom's non-magick half?"

"Quite the opposite," Rand said. "As of right now, you're the most powerful witch there has ever been."

Nikki was speechless for a moment; until finally, she managed to stutter out, "But how?"

"Well, while I have the blood of the five-thousand years of witches who came before me running through my veins, that's all I have." He paused, his mouth set in a straight line.

"I don't understand," Nikki said.

"Do you remember when you were really interested in British royalty, and we talked about how, because they had to keep the blood pure, there was a lot of marrying within the same family?"

"So we're magickal rednecks?"

"Well, not exactly." Rand laughed. "But after five-thousand years, you'd be hard pressed to find a witch we're not related to."

"Like dogs?" Nikki suddenly said. "When we picked Ringo from the pound, there was a pure-bred beagle next to him, and I wanted to get him, but you said pure-bred dogs often have more medical problems and weaker immune systems because they're so in-bred. We got Ringo, the mutt-dog, instead because his mixture made him a stronger and healthier dog. Am I a Ringo, and you're a beagle?"

"Essentially, yes," Rand said, smiling.

"He was a good dog," Nikki said, reminiscing. "Wait, you can't be the first one to break the tradition of marrying magickal."

"I'm not, but I am the first one to do it after five-thousand years straight. Your birth was prophesied."

"Is that another reason Mom is so anti?"

"She doesn't know," he said with a grimace.

"Mom knows everything," Nikki said, rolling her eyes.

"This will be news then."

"Why didn't you tell her?" Nikki's eyes were almost as wide as her mouth.

Rand frowned. "She had a lot on her plate at the time: she had just found out that her husband and child were magickal. Adding on the fulfillment of prophecy didn't seem like a wise choice," he admitted.

"Is *this* why you came back for Christmas?" Nikki asked.

"It's part of the reason."

"What exactly does the prophecy say?"

"I haven't been able to find it. I hoped Madam Ortega would be able to help you. I know she has many of the original books of prophecy."

"You know her?" Nikki asked.

"We didn't get transferred to Otter Sands by accident." Rand grimaced.

"It's in a book?"

"Yes, a book of prophecies."

"You wouldn't know who gave the prophecy, would you?" Nikki asked. "Or do you know what number priestess it was who made the prophecy?"

"I'm not sure actually. I know it was one of the early ones though. The prophecy has been legend for—well—"

"Five thousand years?" Nikki said.

"Five thousand what?" Margret said, coming into Nikki's room carrying a basket of clean and folded laundry.

"Years," Nikki piped in. "Dad's family has been around for over five-thousand years."

"Don't be ridiculous, Nikki." Margret put the basket on the floor and bent over, opening Nikki's bottom dresser drawer. "No one can trace their family back that far." She looked at Rand with a look which clearly said 'Children' complete with implied eye-roll.

"It's true." Nikki said, standing.

"She's right," Rand said, always the calm eye of the storm, a skill born of years in the military—and being in the middle of Margret and Kait.

"Rand, I need to talk to you about *your* family." Margret stood up straight and crossed her arms, pursing her lips into a thin line.

"Mom, it's not like Dad doesn't know I'm a witch, and it's not like I don't know I got it from his side of the family. Besides, his family is *my* family, too," Nikki said. She wanted to be a mature adult, and show her parents she could handle anything, but she could hear her snide-and-whiny-teenager coming out.

"You may be a legal adult, but that doesn't mean I have to talk to you about everything," Margret snapped. "You see this?" Margret rounded on her husband. "This," she gestured to Nikki, "is what I've had to put up with since her birthday and since *they* came back. Rand, you need to strip them right now."

"I can't," Rand said, standing.

"Don't give me that. I know you can."

"Only the witch herself has the power to relinquish her powers. Another cannot remove her powers for her." Rand took a step toward Margret.

"She's a child; she can't make these decisions for herself. You did it before, do it again," Margret argued.

"*She* is still in the room," Nikki said.

"My ability to bind her powers was mine only because I was her legal guardian. She's an adult now and no longer needs a guardian. Even if I could take her powers away," Rand explained, taking his wife's hand. "I wouldn't. It's not my choice to make."

Margret pulled her hand away. "You're all the same," she spat. She turned on her heel and left.

"That's actually the longest conversation I've had with her in a while," Nikki said.

"What do you mean?" Rand turned to face his daughter.

Sitting back down on her bed, Nikki told him everything, from her birthday—including the donut, the octopus, and changing hair colors—to the bonfire, and all the way to the vision she had shared with Emma only yesterday. She didn't leave out a single detail, not even how she found out about the snake bite. Rand sat at the foot of her bed as Nikki told him about Nelly and how they needed her but weren't going to force her to do anything; she told him about Emma and how she was also a once in a generation marvel. She even told him about the school project which brought the three girls together in the first place.

Her father didn't say anything for a long time. Finally, he simply stood up, said, "I ought to go explain things to your mother," and left.

For a moment, it had had been a massive relief to tell everything to her dad, but as Nikki sat in her room alone again, she found herself wondering if she had done something wrong.

25 December 2008

Christmas is probably my favorite holiday. I got Rachelle some organic, naturally dyed yarn. She loved it and is already planning her next project. She got me a new journal, which is good since this one is almost full. Charles Dickens was fun last night. He was so pleased we picked him again. Grandma seemed distracted though. She didn't say if she found what she was looking for in her book, but my gut says she did and whatever it was, it wasn't good news.

Emma's phone buzzed. She clicked open the text (which was from Nikki) and read: 'Hey, want to meet up to do a present exchange?' Emma responded, saying she would and suggested her own house in about fifteen minutes. Deciding to shower before Nikki got there, Emma closed her journal.

"Oh! Before I forget," Emma said to herself. She grabbed Nikki's Christmas present and put it on the kitchen counter. It had been some time since she tidied her room, and she didn't want to risk losing Nikki's present in the mess.

After a quick shower, Emma walked out of the bathroom, wearing a bathrobe with her wet hair piled high in a towel. She felt suddenly warm all over.

*"Congratulations, Kaitlyn! You've finally done it. You've killed Nikki. Are you happy now?"*

*"Don't be ridiculous, Margret. Nikki is the most powerful witch that has ever existed. Do you honestly believe a little water will stand in her way?"*

*"She is a CHILD!"*

*As Emma watched the argument between the adults, their voices became muffled. She was being pulled away from them. For the first time in her life, she found herself face to face with herself.*

*Future Emma looked at present Emma and spoke furiously, but no sound came out. She was only able to decipher a few phrases: 'no time,' 'explain,' 'keep him home' 'away'*

"Who? Away from what?" Emma said as the vision cleared from her eyes.

"Emma? Are you all right?" Rachelle came into the hallway and saw Emma lying on the floor. Her towel had fallen out and her damp hair dripped around her.

"I had a vision, but I knew I was having it," Emma murmured as Rachelle helped her stand up.

Rachelle grabbed Emma's towel. "What do you mean? Don't you always know when you're having a vision?" she asked, handing the towel to Emma.

"I—uh…" Emma put her hand to her forehead. "Nikki will be here any minute. I'll explain then. I need to get dressed." She stumbled to her room.

A few minutes later, Emma returned to the living room, dressed in a flower print pajama set Ethel had given her for Christmas. She sat on the couch, her damp hair up in a bun. Emma didn't hear Nikki come in, but she sensed her magick when she entered the room. Looking up, Emma saw Nikki holding a package wrapped in red, glittery wrapping paper and tied with a green bow.

"Merry Christmas," Nikki said, though her voice betrayed her. The two words dripped with concern.

"Merry Christmas!" Emma smiled and added, "I know Rachelle told you, but let's do presents first."

Rachelle brought Emma's present for Nikki in from the kitchen, and the girls exchanged gifts.

"You first," Emma said, gesturing to Nikki.

Nikki untied the red yarn and pulled on the brown paper, hand-stamped with little red reindeer, revealing a cardboard box, one made of heavier cardboard, with a lid—all recycled, of course. She glanced at Emma, who nodded. Nikki pulled the lid off the box. Inside, resting on a bed of green shredded paper, was a small leather-bound book. Nikki picked it up. It just fit in her hand; the tips of her fingers were able to close over it. She flipped through it and discovered its pages were blank.

"Kait told me most witches receive a book like this. The more ancient race of witches called it a grimoire. Each witch was given one to record spells and enchantments; Kait said they were usually given around age eight, when formal training began, but seeing as you were eighteen instead, Kait thought it would be a good present now. Better late than never and all that—her words, not mine. Anyway, she knew she wouldn't be here for Christmas, so she gave me the idea, and I picked one out I thought you'd like," Emma explained, hardly breathing between sentences.

Flipping the mahogany-colored book over in her hands, Nikki said, "Thank you." She smiled and gingerly set the book back into the box. Replacing the lid and looking up at Emma, Nikki added, "Your turn."

Emma pulled on the green bow. The friction between bow and glitter-covered wrapping paper sent a mass of sparkles exploding all over Emma's blanket. Emma loved the glitter—she liked all glitter. She unwrapped her present: a small, green tin, roughly three by five inches across and three-ish inches deep. She opened the tin and revealed a pewter unicorn about twice the size of a walnut. Emma held the small unicorn close and studied it. It wasn't fashioned after the modern version of a unicorn—the cliche white horse with a horn. This unicorn was of an older time, when unicorns had the tails of lions, and were slender, delicate creatures. The unicorn, looking to its left side, was standing, one hoof on point.

"Do you like it?" Nikki asked, chewing on the inside of her lip.

"It's amazing. The detail is exactly like the pictures in that book," Emma said.

One of the many books the girls had been assigned to read, Nikki more recently than Emma, was *An Illustrated Guide to Magickal Creatures* by Harriett Swift. As the girls had sat waiting for something or other, they had looked through the pictures, admiring the art as well as the magnificence of the beasts that once, and according to some rumors possibly still, roamed the earth.

"There's more in the tin," Nikki said, pointing.

"Chocolate!" Emma had been so fascinated by the unicorn, she had completely failed to notice what the unicorn had been laying on: over a dozen, small, individually wrapped dark chocolates. Emma put the unicorn back in the tin, set it all aside, and stood, giving Nikki a big hug. "Thank you so much!" Emma said.

"You're welcome," Nikki said. "And thank you."

They broke their embrace, and Emma said, "You're also welcome. Now to the not as fun part of your visit." Emma sat back down.

"What happened in your vision?" Nikki asked, sitting next to Emma on the couch. Rachelle sat on Emma's other side.

"For starters, it was the first time I've ever felt warm but had a vision that seemed really sad." Emma shook her head and sighed. "At first, I was watching your mom and grandma argue."

"Well, that's not news," Nikki said.

"Yeah, except they were arguing over whether you were dead," Emma admitted.

"That *is* news." Nikki raised her eyebrows.

"No kidding. Your mom believed you had been killed, whereas Kait believed you were too strong. Her exact words were, 'Don't be ridiculous, Margret. She is absolutely fine. Nikki is the most powerful witch that has ever existed—'"

"Well, actually I know something about that," Nikki admitted.

"What do you mean?" Rachelle asked.

Nikki told them about Rand's surprise visit, their earlier talk, and ended with the mystery prophecy.

"Wow," Emma said. "I wonder if that's why Kait told my Grandma to make sure you were reading prophecies."

"That makes a lot more sense than simple general knowledge of other magicks," Rachelle said.

"I thought so, too," Nikki said. "So, wait, what else happened in your vision?"

"After Kait said you were powerful, she said, 'Do you honestly believe a little water will stand in her way?'"

"Water?" Nikki repeated, like she hadn't heard Emma properly. After a moment, she said, "Like in our vision?"

"I guess," Emma said, shrugging. "But here's where the vision gets really weird. I was talking to myself—no, that doesn't make sense. It was more like my future-self was aware my present-to-me-but-past-to-her-self was having the vision, and she was talking to me, but because she is me that makes it so I'm talking to myself, but—"

"I get it," Nikki said, waving her hand. "What were you trying to tell yourself?"

"I couldn't hear anything; I could only read my lips, but I was able to make out a few words." Emma pulled out a small piece of paper with some scribbles on it and handed it to Nikki.

No Time<br>
Explain<br>
Keep Him Home<br>
Away

"What does it mean?" Nikki asked, handing the paper to Rachelle so she could read it, too.

Emma shrugged. "I wish I knew. I mean, who is "him" and when should we keep him home? Whoever he is, he can't stay home forever."

"None of it makes sense," Nikki agreed.

"We should tell your grandma about this," Rachelle said, glancing up from the paper.

Just then, Nikki's phone rang. She looked at the front of it: Mom. Nikki groaned, hopping off the couch. "I have to take this." She wandered into the kitchen and a few painful seconds later, she returned to the living room. "Sorry," she said with a tight smile. "My mom needs me home, apparently." She folded up the recycled wrapping paper and stuck it and the cardboard box in her bag. "I'll ask my dad about your vision, but I don't think he has a lot of experience with psychics. I'll also ask him and Gabby if either of them knows where I can reach my grandma; she might be able to help."

"Yeah, let me know," Emma said.

"Thanks again, and Merry Christmas," Nikki said, giving Emma, and then Rachelle, a hug.

They wished her Merry Christmas, and Rachelle walked Nikki to the door.

"Do you think she'll be okay?" Nikki whispered before leaving.

"She doesn't look it, but she's a tough cookie," Rachelle said, giving Nikki's shoulder a reassuring squeeze.

"I'll call you guys as soon as I know anything new," Nikki said.

"Likewise," Rachelle said.

# Chapter Twenty-One
## Wednesday, December 26th

December 26, 2008

Every year, I get the after-Christmas blues. You know, that sort of sad feeling because you know you have to wait a whole year before you get to feel those holiday feelings again? I'm there right now—plus Dad had to leave early this morning.

Emma gave me a book for Christmas—she called it a grimoire. I did some research and the majority of the world connects the word grimoire with the words 'evil,' 'black magic,' and 'devilry.' I'm not doing any of that, so I'm calling it my spell book.

Speaking of yesterday, I came home to two lectures after Emma's house:

1-Christmas is for families, not friends (this was mostly Mom)—the fact I had a Christmas present to deliver was dismissed as irrelevant.

2-I should give up my powers for the betterment of the family and for the betterment of my future (this was all Mom)—aka if I want to be a normal person and grow up to have a normal family (yeah, right) and a normal job and a normal life,..blah, blah, blah.

Mom still doesn't get it, and I'm tired of explaining. I'm not giving up my powers. I like my life with magick. The end.

Nikki had been told not to write down the method of communication, just in case her journal ever fell into the wrong hands. It was, as Gabby had told her, an ancient way of communication, one to which only few magickal beings still had access. Nikki closed her journal, got out the letter she had written to Kait, put it in an envelope, and sealed it. She grabbed the vanilla scented candle Margret had given her for Christmas and lit it with a small breath, smiling as she remembered her first lesson with Gabby.

Sitting down on the floor, Nikki set the candle in front of her and the envelope next to it. She meditated for a little while, trying to get her mind clear and ready to focus on the task at hand. After about five minutes, mind ready, Nikki opened her eyes. With both of her hands cupping, she rotated her hands above the candle, the top hand always palm away from her and the bottom hand always palm towards her. As her hands switched their positions, she changed the direction her palms were facing to maintain the pattern. After she felt comfortable in the pattern, she recited: "Invoco te quasi magam, quae mihi respondes ut venefica: ab nepte Nikki ad aviam Kait."

When the flame turned purple, she stopped reciting and moving her hands. Nikki took the envelope, held it over the flame, and let go. Catching the envelope, the flame held it above itself for a mere moment, the envelope engulfed in purple flame. Then, with a flash, it was gone. No ash, no smoke, just the slightest hint of lavender scenting in the air. The flame flickered back to its original golden yellow. Nikki closed her eyes, and with a sigh of relief, put the flame out magickally.

There was a knock on her door. "You better not be lighting candles in there; we've talked about this," Margret called.

"I just blew it out," Nikki said. She never understood why her mother would give her candles simply to ban her from lighting them. Nikki chewed her lip. Was it possible Margret knew the other purposes candles could serve? No, if Margret had known, she wouldn't allow candles in their home at all.

Nikki's phone rang. She looked at it; it was Emma.

"Hey, what's up?" Nikki answered.

"Hey," Emma said. "I think I figured out how to convince Nelly to help us."

Dec. 26, 08

I'm showing Jo today. If I try to just tell her, she won't believe me. She'll think I'm making it up. She'll think I've lost my mind. Or worse, she'll think it's a joke and tell people. I need to show her like I showed Wyatt. I wonder how he is. I tried calling him yesterday, but it just went straight to voicemail. But it was also Christmas, so he probably forgot to charge his phone. Again.

As Nelly sat on her bed considering her question, her phone rang. She looked at the caller ID. "Speak of the devil," she said to herself, and then answered, "Hey, Wyatt, what's up?"

"It's not Wyatt," a woman's voice said.

"Ms. Fletcher?" Nelly asked, confused as to why Wyatt's mom, Michelle, would be calling her from Wyatt's phone. "What's wrong?"

"Hey, kid," Michelle said. "I didn't know if you'd heard, Wyatt just got out of the hospital—"

"What happened?" Nelly asked, standing up. Her breath caught in her chest.

"Well, he says he doesn't remember much. He was at that bonfire, and the earthquake made the whole thing get out of hand," Michelle said, her voice cracked. She swallowed, steadying herself. "I would have called sooner but between calls with his dad and Christmas…"

"No worries, Ms. Fletcher. Is he okay?"

"Yeah, the doctors said it was a good thing the EMT found him when he did; much longer and there could have been permanent damage." Michelle sighed.

"When would be a good time to come see him?"

"Dinner tonight? He's sleeping right now," Michelle said.

"I'll be by 'round six?"

"Six is perfect."

"See you then." Nelly added a few good-byes before she hung up, falling back down onto her bed. Hot tears pricked at the edges of her eyes; she smeared her hand over her face.

Jo knocked on Nelly's already open door and walked in with a basket of clean clothes on her hip. "Hey, Dad says this is all yours, but I think there might be a few of my bikini bottoms in here." Jo put the basket on the foot of Nelly's bed and searched through the clothes.

"Why didn't you tell me Wyatt was in the hospital?" Nelly snapped.

"What? Wyatt's in the hospital?" Jo looked up from the laundry.

"No, his mom said they just let him out! Why didn't you tell me?"

"How was I supposed to know?!" Jo shot back.

"You went to the bonfire with him. You were in the same place as he was when the earthquake happened; how did you not know?" As soon as the words were out of her mouth, Nelly remembered: Jo had caught a ride home with Grace.

"Wow," Jo said. "He may have been my ride, but he's your friend. I don't talk to the guy every day; *you're* supposed to keep tabs on your friends."

"I just thought you would have known, or heard," Nelly said, deflated.

"Well, I didn't," Jo said, trying to hide the hurt, but it seeped out in her words. Nelly sighed. "I'm sorry."

Jo shrugged but wouldn't meet Nelly's eyes.

"Jo, grab your suit; I've got to show you something," Nelly said, standing up again, this time determined rather than shocked.

"Right now?"

"Right now." Nelly threw their mom's journal in a bag. "Go, change."

It took Jo entirely too long to pick a swimsuit (as usual), but finally the girls were in the truck. I'll spare you the silent and awkward car ride. You see, Nelly didn't volunteer any information as to where or why, despite Jo's many questions. So, Jo settled into a well-practiced sulk for the rest of the drive. Once they reached the parking lot, Nelly finally spoke.

"Here we are." Nelly had parked in the same spot she had eleven days ago—it felt like a lifetime ago.

Jo hopped out of the truck.

Nelly grabbed her bag, locked the truck up, and started on the hike.

"Okay, so we're at the Cove, but why?" Jo asked as they hiked.

Nelly didn't answer.

Jo groaned. "Just tell me! What's with all the cloak and dagger?"

"Number one, you'd never believe me—heck, I wouldn't believe me," Nelly said, as she pushed her way through brambles.

"Okay, what's number two?"

"Number two, you can't tell anyone, and I figured if I made sure you believed me, you wouldn't tell anyone."

"Anyone? Like not even Dad?" Jo said mischievously. Jo loved a good secret.

"Dad knows," Nelly admitted.

"What?" Jo squeaked out. She murmured something that sounded a lot like "Lame" under her breath before saying, "Why would you tell him before you told me?"

"Cause Dad is *Dad*, duh."

"Hm—yeah, okay, I see that," Jo conceded, shrugging her shoulders.

They got to the beach, and Nelly dropped her bag onto the hot sand. "Take your clothes off." Nelly took her shirt and shorts off.

"We're getting wet for this?" Jo asked, stripping down to her neon pink one piece. No matter how many times their dad told her sharks went for contrasting colors, Jo always wore the brightest swimsuits she could find because she loved the way they looked against her tan.

"Yup," Nelly said as they walked towards the water.

"But it's freezing!" Jo whined as the waves lapped her toes. "Do we have to get in?"

Yes," Nelly said, watching the waves. "And you're going in first."

What happened next will take longer for me to tell you than it took for it to happen: Nelly shoved Jo as a larger wave came in. Jo squealed as she splashed face first into the water, the wave pulling her deeper. Nelly dived in, wiggled out of her bikini bottoms, and changed, a twinge of pain shooting through her legs. Wrapping her bikini bottom around her wrist, Nelly looked around underwater. When she saw Jo, no more than a bundle of flailing limbs, Nelly swam towards her, grabbed her arm, and pulled her deeper into the water. When they both finally came up for air, only a few seconds had passed since Nelly had pushed Jo in.

"What the he…" Jo spluttered.

"Jo! Look!" Nelly did a shallow somersault so Jo could get the full effect of Nelly's transformation. Her iridescent tail glittered in the sunlight momentarily before sinking down as Nelly broke the surface again, bracing for Jo's reaction.

"Holy bananas! Is this for real?" Jo's eyes and mouth were popped wide open like a cartoon character.

"Yes," Nelly said, feeling strangely shy. She cleared her throat. "So, I'm a mermaid."

"Can I touch it?" Jo asked.

If someone had shown Nelly Jo's expression out of context, she would have guessed Jo was finally getting to meet Orlando Bloom.

"You want—what?" Nelly said with a laugh.

"Can I touch it? Your tail? Or fin?" Jo pointing into the water at Nelly's tail.

"I guess…" Nelly floated on her back.

Jo put her hand out to touch Nelly's tail. It was wet but soft like peach fuzz. "I kind of expected it to be slimy, like really nasty."

"I thought so, too," Nelly said.

"It's cold, but not like super cold, just cool."

"Not quite clammy, but like you ran an ice cube over it a second ago?"

"Yeah. Oh! Dude!" Jo's eyes got wider (if that was even possible). "Do you think I'll get one?"

"Why would you want one?" Nelly scoffed, moving to face her sister. "I can't surf anymore. This happens," she said, gesturing towards all of herself, "every single time I get in the water. Why would you want that?"

"Are you crazy? Why wouldn't you want that? To *live* in the water? I would kill for that."

"You won't have to go that far," Nelly said, shaking her head as the two bobbed in the water. "Jo, listen. You can't tell anyone. I'm serious!"

"Duh," Jo said, rolling her eyes. "People either wouldn't believe me, or they'd want to chop you up and study your DNA."

"Yeah, thanks." Nelly deadpanned.

"You know what I mean." Jo splashed Nelly. "Hey, how fast does that thing go?" She pointed at Nelly's tail again.

"What?"

"Let's test this thing out," Jo said. "But I get a head start!" She duck dived into the water, racing towards a rock about seventy-five yards away from them.

Nelly smiled and swam after her sister. Her tail felt strong and powerful. She could feel her leg muscles under the tail's exterior. She not only passed Jo but lapped her. Eventually Jo reached the rock where Nelly had already been sitting for a bit—she didn't want to lap her too many times.

"So, I think it works," Nelly said, grinning. "I got to say, I'm glad I told you. This was kind of terrifying before, but man, the power behind this tail is unreal. I feel like, I don't know, like I reconnected with the water. Does that even make sense?"

"Yeah," Jo said between breaths. "Also, shut up," she wheezed, clutching her side. "Dang, I thought I was in better shape."

Nelly laughed. "You are in great shape; I'm just in better shape," she teased as she splashed her tail in the water. "Woah, déjà vu."

"What?" Jo asked as she climbed up to sit on the rock next to Nelly.

"Do you remember racing out here when we were kids? We'd—"

"Dude! We'd pretend we were mermaids and splash our legs around like they were tails!" Jo practically screamed.

Nelly nodded, laughing as the memory filled her up.

"I totally forgot about that. I must have been super young."

"You would have been; Mom was still alive."

"Yeah," Jo said softly. "She used to sit on the beach and yell at us not to go too far, but she never got in the water." Jo's face changed suddenly—she gasped. "Mom was one too, wasn't she?"

Nelly nodded again. "Yeah, remember that book Dad gave me?"

"Yeah, was that mermaid stuff?"

"It was more than mermaid stuff, Jo. It's where it all started. It's a journal that's been kept for generations. It's got Mom's writing in it, too."

"Did you bring it?" Jo asked.

"Yeah, it's in my bag on the beach," Nelly said. She was no longer smiling; her eyebrows had furrowed, and she chewed on her lip. "There's more though."

"More?" Jo asked. "Are you kidding? Is Dad like a wizard or something awesome like that? If we're part troll or something nasty, I don't want to know, okay?" Jo put a hand up to stop Nelly from telling her.

"Jo, I told Wyatt before I told you," Nelly admitted.

Jo frowned for a second before saying, "I guess I should be hurt, but if something this wicked happened to me, I'd totally tell Grace before I'd tell you—no offense. Who else knows?"

"You, Dad, Wyatt, and a few girls from school," Nelly said.

"What?" Jo looked hurt this time. "You told some *strangers* before me?"

"Jo, they basically knew before I did." Nelly rolled her eyes.

"Are those the girls you and Wyatt were arguing about? The ones with the school project?"

"Nikki and Emma," Nelly confirmed. "But how'd you know?"

"The house tells me everything," Jo said, waggling her eyebrows mysteriously. "So, how'd they know?"

"That's the part that's more. Nikki and Emma aren't normal." Nelly wanted to phrase it right, but nothing she was thinking was going to make any sense aloud. It barely made sense in her head. "I mean, they're like me."

"They're mermaids, too?" Jo looked excited again.

"No, they're different, but I can't tell you until you swear not to tell anyone." Nelly could tell Jo was going to wave away the promise casually, so she added, "Seriously, Josephine. This isn't my secret. The only reason I'm telling you is because you're my sister, and I think you deserve the whole truth; I didn't even tell Wyatt this."

"Okay." Jo's expression grew somber. They hardly ever used each other's full names, so when they did, it meant they were very serious. Jo had to repress the giggles that always came when she needed to be serious. She took a deep, calming breath. "Okay, tell me."

"Emma and Nikki aren't normal," Nelly said, again. She still wasn't sure how it was best to do this, but she also knew that any second Jo's giggles would break the seriousness of the moment. "Emma is a psychic-medium, and Nikki is a witch."

Jo's mouth moved, like she was trying to speak, but nothing came out. The words wouldn't form. Nelly had been right to show Jo her secret; if Nelly would have just told her, Jo wouldn't have bought it for a second. Jo closed her mouth as she tried to process this new information. It was a new world now. Ten minutes ago, mermaids were pretend. Now, they were real, and her sister was one, and her mom was one, and she might be one—hopefully. But witches and psychics? Wasn't that a bit…much?

"Say something," Nelly prodded.

"Seriously?" Jo spat out. It was all she could muster.

"So this you believe." Nelly splashed her tail. "But not witches and psychics?"

"Well—no. I don't know. I mean, I can see this." Jo gestured to at Nelly's tail. "I can feel this." She squeezed Nelly's lower thigh. "How am I supposed to believe in witches and psychics?"

"Can you at least promise you won't say anything?" Nelly pushed her hair out of her face and squeezed her hands together. "Listen, Jo. These aren't my secrets. True, I barely know these chicks, but they're still entitled to their privacy, you know? I mean—"

"I already said I would keep their secrets. Sheesh," Jo said. "Do your friends know I know?"

"They're not really my friends, and that's the other reason I wanted to tell you."

"Because you have a hard time making friends?" Jo nodded knowingly, gently putting her hand on Nelly's shoulder.

"No, because I don't know if—wait a minute." Nelly squinted her face, shrugging Jo's hand off her shoulder and putting her hand up as if to stop Jo. "I do *not* have a hard time making friends."

"Ugh, puh-leease," Jo said, rolling her eyes. "You have literally *one* friend, but focus. You don't know if what?"

"Well," Nelly said, side-eyeing Jo. "I don't know if I can trust these girls." She told Jo about the school project and Jess, about Emma and Nikki revealing their powers, and how they had come to the house to ask for her help. She told her about the earthquake and the pitcher of water. She told her about changing and how it hurt and explained why she didn't think she could trust Nikki and Emma—using a lot of Wyatt's logic—finally ending with why she felt she should help them anyway.

"Since when do you listen to Wyatt over following what you believe to be right?" Jo said.

"What?"

"You and Wyatt have been friends basically my whole life. You've never had a problem telling Wyatt he was full of it. If you felt like it was the right thing to do, no matter what anyone else said—including Wyatt—you went ahead and did it. Now, all of the sudden you grow a tail and lose your backbone?" Jo said it all so quickly, Nelly barely had time to register anything.

They sat in silence for a moment. Then Nelly said, "You're right."

"I know," Jo said, smug.

Nelly rolled her eyes again. "I'm going to help them, not to spite Wyatt," Nelly said, "and not because they asked me, but because if I'm stuck with this power and can't follow my own dreams, then I'm going to at least help people with my mermaid abilities. I'll try and make good out of this whole situation."

"Good," Jo said. "P.S. your eyes are green now. Did you know that?"

"Wyatt told me. Anyway, there's one other reason I needed to tell you all of this," Nelly said. "Wait here." Nelly dived back into the water, swam to shore, grabbed the journal out of her bag, dived back into the water, and swam back over to Jo.

"Jeez, you know that took you like a minute?" Jo asked.

"Oh," Nelly said.

"You'd leave Michael Phelps in the dust." Jo laughed.

Nelly beamed. While she had always enjoyed swimming, Nelly had preferred surfing because she could move almost effortlessly through the water on her board, but this was (well, there was no other word for it) magick. Swimming as a mermaid would be the saving grace for Nelly. It would teach her a new love of water and ocean; one day, when asked to describe it, she would say it was what flying probably felt like. For now, though, the relationship between mermaid and ocean was merely beginning.

"I wasn't even trying to go super fast," Nelly said.

Jo mock-groaned. "Your humility is revolting," she teased.

"Whatever," Nelly said, laughing as she pulled on Jo. "Now, focus. You have to read this wet, or it snaps shut." She held the book out of the water and then placed it in the water, where it relaxed open.

"This was Mom's?" Jo slipped off the rock and into the water gracefully.

"And Grandma's and Great-Grandma's, etcetera, etcetera." Nelly said, handing the book to Jo, whose eyes grew three sizes as they tried to absorb every single word of their mother's writing.


26 December 2008

Between the magick of Christmas and the magick of my regular life, I got an idea on how to convince Nelly to help us, or at the very least, show her we're not the bad guys.


"Nikki's here," Rachelle called.

"In here," Emma called from her room where she sat, still wearing pjs, on her made bed.

Nikki came in a few seconds later. "So," she said, flopping onto the foot of Emma's bed. She was wearing her favorite yoga pants and a Taylor Swift t-shirt her dad had gotten her for Christmas. "What's your brilliant idea?"

Emma sat up. "A séance."

"Interesting," Nikki said. "Go on."

Emma stood up and paced as she talked. "We invite her mom."

"Ooo, good idea!"

"However," Emma said, her index finger up as she continued pacing. "I foresee two main problems: the first being actually getting Nelly to come to the séance, and the second is if Nelly's mom already moved on and doesn't have any unfinished business, getting a hold of her might be difficult—not impossible but not easy."

"Okay," Nikki said. "'Not impossible but not easy' basically sums up the whole thing."

Emma laughed hollowly. "Essentially."

"Any ideas on how to get Nelly to actually show up?" Nikki said.

"Do you think this could actually work?" Emma asked, crossing her arms.

"I have no idea," Nikki admitted. "But I also don't have a better plan."

"Fair," Emma said, still pacing. "I've been thinking about how to get her to come."

"And?"

Emma put her finger up. "Tell her the whole truth."

Nikki cringed. "Not that I think honesty is bad, but it hasn't historically worked for us. Besides, what if we can't get her mom? That might look like we lied anyway."

"True. So, magick her?" Emma lifted another finger.

Nikki shook her head. "Bad. Bad. Straight up bad idea."

"Agreed," Emma said, lifting a third finger. "Tell her there's a way to communicate with Jess Pedersen."

Nikki tapped her fingers on her pursed lips. "Well," she said. "How hard would it be to get Jess?"

"Not hard at all." Emma put her hand down. "Jess said she'd be happy to come again if I had more questions or if Nelly needed additional help."

Nikki nodded. "I like it. When should we do it?"

"A séance usually requires a bit of preparation, but, if it works for my grandma, I imagine we could do it as soon as tomorrow," Emma said brightly.

"Do you want to call Nelly or should I?" Nikki asked. She snorted. "Actually…"

"I'll call her." Emma smiled. "You guys don't exactly have what I would call a friendly relationship."

"Yeah," Nikki said, stretching the word out. "Sorry about that."

"It's not a problem." Emma grabbed her phone. "You guys are two different personalities taking your different magickal abilities…"

"Differently?" Nikki offered.

Emma smiled and said, "Exactly."

# Chapter Twenty-Two

## Thursday, December 27th

December 27, 2008

Today's the day we get Nelly on our side...hopefully...I'm over at Madam Ortega's place with Emma. We're prepping everything for the séance. I just finished putting the candles and stones in their corresponding circles on the table. Emma invited Nelly over and told her we could communicate with Jess Pedersen, her ancestor—due to Emma's grandma being a medium. I think she remembered the story I told her about Madam Ortega helping that little girl's family. We, mostly, told her the truth, and we are tricking her a little bit—she has no idea she's coming over for a séance, but I'm hoping the outcome of the séance will be enough to help her look past our minor deception. If not, then we might have blown our last shot at saving the world...

Nikki clicked her tongue and closed her journal.

The two girls were in the living room, each on one couch. Emma's favorite yellow dress draped across the couch like a queen's train. Nikki, meanwhile, sat cross-legged on her couch with books and papers sprawled all around her. She was in her usual yoga pants and a t-shirt. Her hair was up in a messy bun on top of her head.

"Hey, Nelly just sent me a text and said she's on her way," Emma told Nikki.

"Good," Nikki said, beginning to gather her papers. Her phone rang. After digging through her bag to find it, she looked at it and groaned. "You've got to be kidding." She answered the call. "Mom, I'm at Madam Ortega's house, just like I told you I'd be," Nikki said as calmly as she could, glancing at Emma and frowning.

"Well, you need to come home now," Margret snapped from the other side of the phone.

"I can't. They need me," Nikki said, not daring to mention the séance.

"Nonsense. Be home in five minutes."

"But I—"

"Five minutes. Or else, " Margret said. She hung up.

Nikki clenched her jaw, closing her eyes and taking a deep breath before looking at Emma. "I have to go. My mom..." She shrugged by way of explanation.

"I'll call Gabby," Emma said. "And don't be too hard on her," she added. "I know it doesn't feel like it all the time, but you're lucky to still have her around."

"Yeah, I know," Nikki said, her insides squirming. "Let me know how it goes."

"Will do."


Dec. 27, 08

I saw Wyatt last night. I must have apologized like a million times. I still feel like crap for not checking in on him sooner, but everyone (including Wyatt) told me to lay off. He mostly slept, but for the part he was awake, he didn't talk to me, not like he wouldn't but couldn't. The smoke did a number on him. He's under doctor's orders to take it easy on talking. His mom got him a little white board and some markers. He better heal up quick or learn to write more clearly, otherwise, he's sunk.

In other news, I'm getting ready to go to Madam Ortega's house. Never thought I'd go back to that creepy shack, but Emma said her grandma can talk with Jess Pedersen, and if I'm going to do this mermaid thing properly, I figure I can use all the help I can get. Dad didn't have any luck in his search.

Nelly hadn't been able to write her true hope for the visit; she had barely allowed herself to think it. If Madam Ortega could visit with Jess, then maybe, just maybe, a visit with Melinda, Nelly's mom, would be possible. The thought, though exciting, also held a lot of potential pain, so Nelly did what she always did with anything that could cause her potential pain: she took a deep breath, shoved it as far down as it would go, all the while hoping if she ignored it long enough, it would disappear into the abyss. With time and experience, she would eventually learn this never worked.

Nelly arrived at Madam Ortega's house and ambled out of her truck. She had thrown a hoodie over her t-shirt and, despite the chill in the air, still had on her red Bermuda shorts. Heading to the front door, Nelly took another deep breath. She knocked before she lost her nerve.

The door opened almost immediately. "Hi! Come on in." Emma gestured into the house.

"Hi," Nelly said, awkwardly stepping through the door.

"Nikki was here but had to go. Rachelle, my aunt, called Gabby, and she's on her way. We technically don't need a witch to do this, but it's a lot easier with one," Emma explained, rubbing the fingers on her left hand.

"What happened to your arm?" Nelly asked, noticing the cast for the first time.

"Long story," Emma said, spreading and closing the fingers on her casted hand. "The short version is I broke my wrist."

"Emma," Rachelle called from the kitchen. "Teach Nelly her part."

Emma looked back at Nelly. "Remember how I told you we can communicate with Jess? Well, we can through a séance."

"A what?" Nelly asked, running a hand through her hair.

"Think of it like a telephone call to the other side," Emma said. "It's nothing scary, and we have protections built into our ceremony. Your part is putting a jar of flowers on the word 'West.'" Emma pointed to the spot on the table. "Then you say, 'Chrysanthemum to the west for protection and survival.'"

"Survival?" Nelly repeated, grimacing.

Just then Gabby came in through the front door. "Merry Meet, Emma," Gabby said. She was wearing a long, cream-colored dress. Her maroon braids were styled in an elegant twist.

"Merry Meet, Gabby," Emma said, hugging her. They broke the embrace. "Thanks for coming. Nikki was going to stay, but—"

"Her mom?" Gabby guessed.

Emma nodded and said, "Gabby, this is Nelly." But before Emma could say anymore, there was a knock on the door; Emma opened it and was greeted by her grandmother carrying a brown paper bag with flowers poking their blossoms out of the top.

"Is there another in the car?" Emma asked.

"Yes, be a dear and grab it, would you?" Ethel said, carrying the bag into the kitchen.

Nelly glanced at Gabby who had started arranging flowers in jars. "Are you a real witch?" The question spilled out before Nelly had a chance to think about it.

"If you mean, can I do magick and do I have special powers, then yes. If you're wondering if I own a black cat, ride a broom, and turn naughty children into frogs, then you'd be right on two accounts," Gabby said, smiling. When Nelly didn't say anything, Gabby added, "I have a cat. He is black, but he's also white. I'll let you decide which is the other truth."

"You ride a broom, don't you?" Nelly said, a memory unfolding in her mind. "I saw you one time. I was in the library with my parents. I couldn't have been more than six. Mom was picking out a few books, and I saw you sitting on top of a broom like it was a bench. You were shelving, but when I turned to show my mom, you were sweeping."

"Melinda was a sweet lady," Gabby said with a soft smile. "She came into the library often."

"How come I look older, but you look the same?" Nelly asked.

"Magick does wonders for the skin." Gabby winked and squeezed Nelly's shoulder before turning her attention back to the flowers.

Emma brought the other bag of flowers in from the car. Once all the flowers were placed in their respective jars, they were passed around the room.

"Now Nelly," Ethel said, a jar of flowers in each hand. "We're going to contact your ancestor, Jess Pedersen. There will come a time when I will need you to repeat exactly what I say, all right?"

Nelly nodded, too nervous to speak. She held her jar firmly with both hands.

"Emma," Ethel said, gesturing to her granddaughter.

"Clover to the east for love, luck, and success," Emma said, placing her jar on the word East carved into the table.

"Carnations to the west for strength and energy." Ethel placed her one of her two jars. "Nelly."

"Uh, Chrysanthemum to the…" Nelly said, her nerves besting her memory.

"West," Emma whispered.

"Chr-chrysanthemum to the west for protection and…" Nelly faltered, took a deep breath, and remembered, "…for protection and survival."

Ethel nodded. "Red geranium to the south for guests and protection."

"Buttercup to the north for divination and energy," Gabby said, placing her jar to cover the 'No' in the word North carved into the tabletop.

"Daisy to the north for protection." Rachelle set her jar to cover the rest of the word.

"Emma," Ethel said, "the opal?"

"Right here." Emma pulled the iridescent stone from her pocket.

"Gabby, the lights," Ethel said.

Gabby waved a hand, closing drapes, turning off the electric lights, and lighting all the candles, except the brown one.

"Everyone take hands," Ethel instructed. "Gabby at the north; I'll stand to the east; Emma and Rachelle, stand at the south, and Nelly, stand at the west." Everyone held hands except Emma and Ethel, who looked at Emma.

"Ready?" Emma asked.

Gabby nodded.

Emma put the opal in the same circle as the brown candle at the same moment Gabby lit the candle with a small breath. Emma and Ethel took hands as soon as the opal was out of Emma's hand.

The change in the room was immediate and tangible.

Nelly felt odd, as though she was suddenly alive but hadn't known until just now what that meant. She could feel everything. She could hear her blood running through her veins; she could feel Gabby and Rachelle's respective heartbeats in her hands—what was weirder was the fact she could tell them apart. She recognized the soft pitter-patter as Gabby's heart and the tri-beat march as Rachelle's.

"It's the spirit world," Emma said, reading her friend's expression.

"We're going to call Jess," Ethel said. "Nelly, you'll repeat after me."

"Okay." Nelly found her initial nervousness calmed by her newfound sense of life.

"Souls of the Earth, the Fire, the Water, the Air, we call you to send us your sister, Jess Pedersen," Ethel said and then nodded to Nelly, who promptly repeated the call.

Emma looked around, waiting for the wind that always accompanied a séance.

Ethel said, "Souls of the future, the present, the past, and those of possibility, we call you to send us your sister, Jess Pedersen," again nodding at Nelly.

Nelly repeated.

"Together," Ethel said. All five of them repeated the entirety of the call as one.

A gust blasted around the room. Nelly's hair, short as it was, whipped around in the wind, forcing her to squint. Emma's face was hidden in blonde hair and colorful braids.

They continued chanting, "Souls of the Earth, the Fire, the Water, the Air, we call you to send us your sister, Jess Pedersen. Souls of the future, the present, the past, and those of possibility, we call you to send us your sister, Jess Pedersen." The wind blew harder and harder; everyone had their eyes squeezed shut as they shouted to be heard above the wind.

"Jess, if you can hear me, I'm your descendant. I'm a mermaid! Please, speak with us," Nelly yelled. The wind dropped almost immediately, and everyone opened their eyes.

"Keep holding hands," Ethel instructed.

"You are my descendant?" A woman's voice whispered.

No body yet accompanied the voice.

Rachelle squeezed Nelly's hand.

"Yes." Nelly said quickly. "I am Neldyn Hansen. My mother was Melinda Vanblod."

"I know that name," the voice said.

"Jess, please show yourself to us. You are among friends," Emma said. "We've spoken before."

The flame on each candle rose a few inches, a gale burst from the center of the table, hitting each woman so she turned her face. When they all turned back, they saw a woman sitting on her knees in the center of the table. She was wearing a blue summer dress. Her long, white hair was tied into two braids which came down to her waist. She had a heart-shaped face, high cheekbones, and a slim nose—a nose identical to Nelly's.

"You are of my blood. You know our secret. I am Jess Pedersen." She spoke to Nelly, but she turned to look at the other faces around the room. There was no wind now, yet everything from the hem of her dress to the stray hairs around her face seemed to float around Jess as though a gentle breeze blew all around her.

"When did you die?" Nelly asked. "I mean, I'm sorry…I don't—"

"I died in June of nineteen-forty." Jess smiled. "Why have you summoned me here?" Jess looked at Nelly and cocked her head to the right.

"I'm a mermaid, but I don't know what to do. I don't know how to use my powers. I-I just…" There was so much Nelly wanted to say. She glanced around to the others in the circle and swallowed. "My dad gave me a book when I told him I couldn't surf anymore. It's a journal. It has my mother's writing in it, but it also has the writing of many others. I need some help understanding it all."

"I am not a mermaid. The journal belonged to Rán, my daughter. It was a gift from her father," Jess looked down and smiled, "her real father. As for not knowing how to use your powers, or whether to use them," Jess said, looking directly at Nelly, "you might always consider a living guide."

"How do I find one?" Nelly asked.

"I think there is someone else to whom you should speak. I have brought her here with me. You will see her now." Jess smiled and bowed her head slightly before fading away.

"Can they do that?" Emma asked Ethel. "Can they bring spirits you haven't summoned?"

"They can, but it's uncommon. It takes a lot of power to bring someone with them," Ethel answered, her brows furrowed momentarily.

"Look," Rachelle said.

A different woman was fading into view. There was no raising of the flames, no sudden burst of wind. This woman was wearing gray sweatpants, maroon socks, a white t-shirt, and a dark blue, unbuttoned, plaid long-sleeve shirt. Her dark brown hair was fixed in a messy bun. She had a round face, and the same nose as Nelly and Jess.

Nelly looked at the woman. "Mom?" Her voice broke.

"You've grown, lille havfrue." Melinda beamed, tears streaming down her face.

"Hi, Mom." Nelly smiled at the use of her old nickname, a pit forming in her chest. She cleared her throat.

"How are you? And Jo? How is your father?" Melinda smiled at Nelly.

"Good. We're good. We're all good. Dad's, well, he's trying, you know?" Nelly stared at Melinda but directed her next question to Emma. "This is for real, isn't it?"

It is," Emma said. "I'd offer to leave you two alone, but then we'd lose the connection. Sorry."

"Are you kidding? You're giving me a chance to talk to my mom; how could you possibly be sorry?" Warm tears spilled down Nelly's cheeks, which she wiped on her shoulders.

"Havfrue, what do you need?" Melinda said, a bit of urgency tinged her voice, though she still smiled brightly.

"Did Jess tell you I'm a mermaid?" Nelly asked.

"She didn't have to." Melinda bit her lip, looked at her hands, and then back up at Nelly. "You didn't do your homework on this one, did you, havfrue?"

"What do you mean, Mom?"

"Have you ever wondered why I always call you lille havfrue? Or where the name came from? What it means?" Melinda asked, raising her eyebrows.

"Well no, not really. I mean, I guess I kind of wondered, but not enough to really be bothered by it," Nelly said.

"It's what my mother called me, and her mother called her—it started with Jess; she was the first one to call her daughter lille havfrue," Melinda said.

"So you mean it has something to do with mermaids?" Nelly asked.

"Nelly, it *is* mermaid. 'Lille havfrue' means 'little mermaid' in Danish. I knew from the minute I saw you that you would carry on our legacy," Melinda said, still smiling, though a bit sadder now.

"This whole time it's been right in front of my face, and I had no idea." Nelly let loose a sigh of realization. "Holy sh—"

"Neldyn," Melinda warned.

"—ark, sh-shark" Nelly said. "Holy shark." A grin played on the edge of her mouth.

Melinda raised her eyebrows but smiled. "Good cover. Now, what is it you need from me? Aside from the obvious, what did Jess think I would know that she wouldn't?"

"A teacher?" Nelly said. "Mom, I need someone to help me learn."

"My little brother. Your Uncle Henry would be perfect—"

"You mean *deadbeat* Henry?"

"Don't call him that," Melinda chided, sitting up a bit straighter.

"Mom, I've never even met the guy. How am I supposed to call him my uncle?"

"First of all because he *is* your uncle," Melinda scolded. "Second, did you ever consider because he's a merman he can't hang out on dry land indefinitely?"

"Well, no. But, how was I supposed to know that?"

"You weren't." Melinda softened and frowned. "He always sent cards to let you know he was still there."

"I don't know how to contact him," Nelly said.

"Look in Rán's journal. Comb your memories. You have everything you need. It's so simple, you might think it's crazy," Melinda said.

"I've seen my fair share of crazy, Mom," Nelly admitted. "I mean, I'm basically a fish, what's crazier than that?"

27 December 2008

Today went better than I could have hoped. Not only is Nelly willing to help us, she's started the search for her mentor—her late mother's brother. After the séance was finished, Nelly even stayed to help clean up. I asked what she thought about everything, and she said she needed time to process. She also said she'd call me tomorrow.

"Oh!" Emma said. "Right!" She pulled out her phone and punched her speed dial for Nikki.

*Ring. Ring.*

Emma put her journal away.

*Ring. Ring. Ring.*

"Hi. You've reached Nikki's phone. I'm not here right now, so just leave your name after the beep. Oh and if you're one of those weirdos that blocks your number, make sure you leave your number anyway, so then I can block you." There was a small 'beep' after the message.

Emma hesitated. "Hey, Nikki. It's me. Call me back. It was amazing. I'll tell you everything later. Oh, and I have news about Nelly as well. Talk to you soon."

# Chapter Twenty-Three

## Friday, December 28th

December 28, 2008

HOLY COW IT WORKED!! Just got off the phone with Emma. Things went better than either of us could have imagined! Em asked how things went with my mom. Ugh, well, Mom just kept saying how she may not have the power to take away my powers, but she does have the ability ('as your mother!') to keep me from that 'riff-raff.' I know she just wants to do what she thinks is best, but I'm growing up, and she has to let me make my own decisions eventually. I'm definitely going to college on the east coast. Maybe even Europe.

Nikki shoved her journal in her book-bag, along with her phone, her spell book, and a couple of granola bars she'd grabbed from the kitchen earlier. She walked over to her closet and grabbed a jacket—libraries are cold; it's good for the books—at least, that's what Gabby says.

Just as Nikki grabbed her keys and was making a break for the front door, she heard it:

A single disembodied cough.

Nikki froze mid-step and looked around.

The cough was followed by Margret's voice, "Where do you think you're going?"

"Library," Nikki said, making a split-second decision to answer only what she was asked.

"Why?"

"Project." Nikki did a slow 360, still trying to find her mom. She wasn't keen on this God-like approach; Margret's voice seemed to come from the very walls of the house.

"*School* project?" the walls asked in Margret's voice.

"Yes," Nikki said. 'Sort-of' would have been more correct, but then she would have to explain.

"Be back by six for dinner."

"Okay." Nikki left before the walls could change their mind; she had quite the imaginary argument with her mom on her drive to the library, muttering to herself the whole way. After finally reaching the library, Nikki stopped by the front desk to say hello to Gabby.

"Merry Meet, Nikki," Gabby said, peeking over the top of an ancient book.

Nikki tried to read the faded lettering on the spine, but there wasn't enough left to decipher. "What are you—"

"Never you mind," Gabby said, putting the book under her desk and trading it for an envelope. She handed it to Nikki.

"Is it from—"

"Yes ma'am," Gabby said.

"Thanks!" Nikki smiled. "Can I leave this here?" she asked, holding up her book-bag. "I'll be right back. I'm just going to go outside to read it."

"Sure." Gabby took the bag and hid it behind the circulation desk.

"Thanks again," Nikki said, walking out of the library. She tore the envelope open, pulled out its contents, and read:

Little Witch,

    I received your letter. I wish I could tell you I was on a return journey; alas, it seems my attention is required longer than I anticipated. I should be able to return to you by New Year's Eve. In regards to your question: No, though I've heard of a few incidents in which others, not seers, were aware of being seen, but I don't think those would be of much help. Emma is certainly one of a kind.

    Now, I know you didn't write to me concerning her, but I think you should ease up on your mother. She had a difficult initiation into our world—an initiation which is still taking place. She'll come around in her own time.

One last thing, little witch: if your third, Nelly, ever decides to fulfill her role in these events, tell her to seek out Henry at the Cove. She'll know what it means. I've never met him, but I've corresponded with him, and it seems as though he's been awaiting her arrival, though I think he's about as excited about it as she is.

Be patient, Nikki. Everything has its time.

Blessed be,

Grandma Kait.


Nikki reread the letter to make sure she hadn't missed anything. "Be patient," she read aloud, sighing.

"Patient about what?" Someone said.

Nikki looked up. "Emma, I thought you were going to be late."

"I was, but things worked out," Emma said cryptically. "Let's go inside, and I'll tell you what I mean."

Once inside (and after getting her bag from Gabby), Nikki showed Emma the letter.

While Emma read it, Nikki drummed her fingers lightly on the table which they had claimed as their workspace. The only other sound was the occasional rustle of pages as the few other occupants in the library read.

"Patient about what? Everything?" Emma whispered.

"My thoughts exactly," Nikki whispered back. It was the library after all.

"I wonder how she knew about Nelly. I only just found out." Emma set the letter down.

"What about Nelly?" Nikki pressed.

Emma's expression changed; her brows went from furrowed as she grimaced to lifted as her eyes lit up and she smiled. "Nelly's decided to help us," Emma whispered.

"What?" Nikki said. She hadn't shouted, but she certainly hadn't whispered either.

"Library," Emma reminded her.

"Sorry," Nikki whispered. "When did you find out?"

"Right before I came. That's why I was going to be late. Nelly sent me a text and asked if I was too busy to talk. I let you know I'd be late, and then I called her," Emma explained, trying to keep her voice low, but her excitement was getting the better of her. "She said she had thought over everything, and she would do it. I asked 'do what?' and she said 'help!'" Emma's hands flew to her mouth. Her 'help!' had been much louder than she intended.

"Library," Nikki said, mock-smug.

Emma grinned. "Anyway, I asked her if she could meet us here later. I figured we ought to get some of the kinks worked out of our plan before we let her in on what she's signed up for."


28 December 2008

Nikki and I have been at the library for over two hours researching ways to increase our chances of surviving a tsunami; we've mapped out where we think the tsunami is most likely to hit. We've emailed the Coast Guard, every beach-guard company we could find, and the local hospitals about the impending doom—that's what Nikki and I have taken to calling it. It's better than throwing around the word tsunami and causing mass panic in the library... although, looking around now, the only people in here (other than the two of us and Gabby) are over eighty-five and probably turned their hearing-aids off.

We emailed all the disaster relief agencies and told them we believe we'll be struck by a tsunami on December 31st, possibly January 1st. We originally tried calling, but everyone has some kind of 13-step automated system. Anyway, we got prompt email responses from all stating we were misinformed, asking us not to spread false rumors, and wishing us the happiest of holidays.

The irony is not lost on me.


Emma sighed. It was no more than she had expected, honestly. No one in their right mind would believe a couple of teenagers over all the experts.

Nikki poked Emma in the shoulder. "Hey," Nikki said, "I think that's her." She gestured towards the front of the library. A tanned girl wearing army green shorts and a sweatshirt, hood up, stood at the front of the library, talking with

Gabby. They saw Gabby point over to where they were sitting. Emma waved, and the girl walked towards them, pulling her hood down; it was Nelly.

"Can I sit?" she asked.

"Sure," Nikki said, pulling her bag and a pile of books off one of the chairs.

"Thanks for coming," Emma said. "We actually have a message for you, if that's all right."

"Yeah, okay," Nelly said, her legs sticking immediately to the cold faux leather covering the chair. She wiggled trying to get comfortable.

Emma glanced at Nikki, who nodded and said, "So my grandma sent me a letter and told me to tell you that you should 'Seek out Henry at the Cove.' She said you'd know what that meant. I guess she talked to him, and he's been waiting to hear from you."

"Wait," Nelly said, turning to Nikki, "How does your grandma know all of this?"

"How does my grandma know anything?" Nikki murmured. She hadn't meant to say it aloud, but it was what she had been feeling.

"What?" Nelly said.

Nikki groaned. "Sorry. She's like a magic eight ball. She just knows stuff when you need to know it, but if you don't ask, then you never know she knew the whole time." She shrugged.

"What?" Nelly asked, more confused now than before.

"What she means," Emma said with a small smile, "is she's just met her grandma and knows as little about her as you do."

"Oh," Nelly said. The girls sat in an awkward silence for a little while until Nelly finally broke it. "Emma?"

"Yes?" Emma said.

"How long have you known? About me and Nikki, I mean," Nelly said.

Nikki looked at Emma.

"A while," Emma admitted. "But I couldn't tell you," she added.

"Why not?" Nelly asked.

Emma chewed on the inside of her lip for a moment before responding, "Would you have believed me?"

"About magick? About being a mermaid? Probably not, I guess." Nelly thought about it. "I mean, I am one; I've seen magick; heck, I've done magick, and I barely believe it myself."

Emma shrugged and then said, "It was safer to wait until you already knew. With you especially, Nelly, I knew we'd be waiting until your eighteenth birthday. That's the way it works."

"Well, why couldn't you tell Nikki? Did you have to wait until she was eighteen, too?"

"With Nikki it should have been innate. Keep in mind she just moved here a little while ago, so though I knew of her power, I didn't know actually her until then," Emma explained. "And because it wasn't innate, I couldn't sense it."

"Innate? Sense it? What do you mean?" Nelly asked.

"Magickal beings can sense each other. You'll start to notice it the longer you have your powers," Emma added. "As for Nikki, I should have been able to sense her magick as soon as we met, but her father bound it, so I couldn't sense it until after her birthday. Witches are born with their power ready to use, but it's small and grows as they grow. Mermaids are transformative, and because you were born on land—because you were in your human form first—your magick had to mature enough to create the necessary biological and physiological changes. I'd explain more, but the truth is my knowledge of mermaid magick is limited to the basics. I only know what I've read from books." Emma checked her watch and stood up. "We should head over there, actually." She started closing and stacking the many books still left on the table.

"You're getting a reading list," Nikki said, also standing. "Don't worry," she added, seeing Nelly's bewilderment. "I was given a reading list, too. You won't have to read it all right away, but there will probably be some books you'll want to have under your belt before New Year's."

"New Year's? Why?" Nelly asked.

"I'll explain on the way," Emma said. "For now, help me put these away." She handed Nelly a stack of books.


Dec. 28, 08

You know, a month ago, I would have said you'd have to be crazy to trust two people you barely knew, and now I'm in it up to my gills. Logically, I should run for it, but my gut tells me to trust them, Nikki and Emma, I mean. The <u>witch</u> and the <u>psychic-medium</u>. You know, because those words inspire so much trust...

Then again, I turn into fish-girl every time I get into the ocean, so I probably shouldn't point fingers.

Emma says a tsunami is coming. To be honest, I'm a little let down. I mean, I'm still going to help, but they made it sound like they were fighting villains with plans to rule the world, and we were the only ones who could stop them. Don't get me wrong, tsunamis aren't good, but they're not exactly EVIL either.

Turns out my "magick power" can help after all (apparently, there's a difference between "magic" and "magick"). I just need to train up a bit. Or a lot.

"Writing?" Ethel asked.

"Yeah," Nelly said, closing her journal. She was sitting at the same table where her palm and future had been read so long ago.

"Good. It's important to keep documentation of the events and your feelings." Ethel patted Nelly's shoulder.

"Thanks?" Nelly said.

Nikki was in the living room, nose deep in *A Record of Prophecies Made by the High Priestess the Third: Zoia Vikaar.* Emma, meanwhile, was hidden away in the library fetching every book on mermaids she could find.

"Nikki," Ethel said.

"Yes?" Nikki looked up from her book and looked over her shoulder at Ethel.

"Would you be a dear and make some hot chocolate?" Ethel glanced outside and added, "It looks like it might rain, and you'll want the warmth in your bones before the cold comes."

Curious, Nelly peeked out the window. It had been unusually hot for a December day in Northern California, and her view out the window seemed to confirm this. Nelly moved her head to see the sky: clear and blue with a sparkling sun. It didn't look like it was going to rain to her.

But whether it looked like it was going to rain was not a matter of interest to Nikki who said, "Sure," closed her book carefully, and went into the kitchen.

"Now, dear," Ethel said to Nelly, "What have you decided about a mentor?"

"Well, part of me would like some help because I don't know what I'm doing, but I'm also pretty good at learning stuff on my own through trial and error." Nelly sighed. "Do I have to have one? Is it like a mermaid requirement? Because so far all anyone can offer is my uncle who sends me a birthday card six months late every year, and I'm not super stoked about that option."

"You must decide for yourself," Ethel answered slowly as though choosing her words carefully.

"What exactly does a mentor do?" Nelly put her journal away.

"A mentor guides and teaches. For example, I'm Emma's mentor. I have been a medium for much longer than she has," Ethel said.

"Is it important to have one?" Nelly asked again.

"You have to decide for yourself," Ethel said.

"Why?"

"The law says 'Each magickal individual must seek and find their mentor of their own free will and choice.' Others cannot interfere."

"I don't get any guidance at all? I don't even know what I'm looking for," Nelly said. "What if I ask for your help? Like if I *choose* you to help me find my mentor out of my own—what was it?" Nelly waited.

"'Free will and choice,'" Emma said as she came into the dining room carrying a stack of books that smelled strongly of seawater and orange peel.

Nelly's eyes widened at the sight. "Uh, okay." She cleared her throat and looked at Ethel. "Right. So, out of my own free will and choice, I choose you to help me decide if Henry is supposed to be my mentor." Nelly raised her eyebrows and asked, "So, is that enough? Can you help me now without any bad karma or whatever?"

"I don't see why not," Ethel said after a pause. "There's no law against helping if the said individual seeks guidance."

"So, how do I know if Henry is a good mentor? What should I be looking for?" Nelly asked. She pulled out her journal again, opening to the back page to take notes.

"Well," Ethel said. "You need someone who works with your magick. A psychic for a psychic, a witch for a witch—"

"A mermaid for a mermaid," Nelly said. "Got it. So, assuming he is one, is that enough to make him a good mentor?"

"Well, no. I'm afraid the only way to find out is to have a few lessons with him."

"And if I don't think he's a good teacher, I can quit?" Nelly asked, writing as she spoke.

"Technically, yes. If you chose to have a mentor and didn't like one, you'd seek another—that is, if you choose to have a mentor at all," Ethel said.

"So I could just *not* have a mentor?" Nelly asked, looking up from her journal.

"Again, *technically* speaking, you could be without a mentor," Ethel said.

"But?" Nelly felt its implication on the end of Ethel's sentence.

"But learning something new is always difficult. I trust you are a talented and clever individual, and as you said, you're quite good at learning on your own," Ethel explained. "But even the cleverest of people still need a guide, and magick is not the sort of thing that is always safe to learn via trial and error. Sometimes a single trial can be fatal." Ethel grimaced before adding, "I will help you all I can, though I would not be your mentor. I can give you books to study," she said, gesturing to the pile Emma had set on the table, "but there are certain things about each magick not written in books, for they are secrets only for the user of the magick to know."

"You mean like contacting mermaids?" Nelly asked. "Like how my mom said not to write the method down anywhere?"

"Precisely. We are among a small number of non-merfolk who know where to find that secret even though we are not privy to the secret itself." Ethel smiled. "We will not share its location with anyone, but it is exactly that sort of secret, that sort of magick, which can only be discovered and properly used by someone of the same magickal birth."

"Hot cocoa?" Nikki asked, walking into the dining room carrying a tray which held four mugs of cocoa, a bowl filled with miniature marshmallows, and four peppermint spoons on a plate.

"Where did you get the spoons?" Emma asked, taking her mug and eyeing the red-and-white-striped utensils.

"Magick," Nikki said, grinning. "I found a peppermint candy, and I multiplied it and then reformed the candies into spoons."

"Very clever," Ethel said as she took a mug

"Thanks." Nikki held out the tray, so everyone could take a spoon and dish out however many marshmallows they wanted for their respective mugs of cocoa. She took the tray back into the kitchen and returned, sucking on the last peppermint spoon. "So," Nikki said, sticking the spoon in her cocoa. "What did I miss?"

"I need to contact Henry and decide if I want him to be my mentor, and if I don't, I need to figure out who else is a likely candidate," Nelly said, stirring her cocoa absentmindedly.

"Would your dad know anyone?" Nikki asked.

"No. He looked. When I first told him I was giving up surfing—"

"You're quitting?" Nikki asked, almost choking on her hot cocoa. "You can't quit; you're awesome."

"How the heck—" Nelly waved her hand dismissively. "You know what, it doesn't matter. I have to quit. I can't turn into a mermaid in front of everyone. They'd freak, and then, the government would want to run experiments on me to find out how they can make G.I. Mer-soldiers." Nelly sighed. "I can't keep surfing—at least not publicly. I don't even think I can keep surfing privately." Nelly dropped her head into her hands. "You know, when I was a little kid I always thought being a mermaid would be so cool. I guess what they say is true: be careful what you *fish* for, huh?" Nelly gave a half-hearted smile.

"Maybe there's some way to control it," Nikki suggested. "I mean, I have to learn to control my magick, why not you too?"

"Dear," Ethel said, apprehensively. "Mermaid magick isn't like witch magick. There are some laws you can't break."

"Maybe that's a secret," Emma suggested.

"What do you mean?" Nelly asked.

"Well, we were talking about secrets kept within elemental families," Emma said. "And—"

"Wait," Nelly said, putting her hand up. "Back up. Elemental what?"

"Elemental families. You're a mermaid. Your element is water; your magickal element, that is," Emma explained. "Anyway—"

"What's your element?" Nelly asked.

"Spirit," Emma said.

"Witches are earth," Nikki offered.

"So, there aren't any other magickal water beings?" Nelly asked. "Mermaids are it?"

"Well, there are selkies," Emma said. "Some argue the selkies have the true claim on the elemental magick of water, but the selkies themselves have little to say on the matter. They just say they know their true elemental magick, and that is enough for them. It's their secret, if you will."

"What's a selkie?" Nikki asked.

"I'll explain later," Emma said with a wave of her hand. "I've gotten way off my original point. Learning to control your mermaid form might be a secret shared only between merfolk."

"Maybe," Ethel said slowly. "But I would not count on it. To offer my guidance, I would suggest seeking your uncle for now."

"Right," Nelly said. "So I've got to pick a person who has never wanted to be a part of my life until I sprouted a tail because I literally don't know anyone else?"

"In all fairness, you did say your uncle sent you cards. That shows some interest," Emma said.

"I guess that's true," Nelly said.

An alarm went off. Nikki reached for her phone. It was a quarter until six. "Crap," Nikki said. "I have to go."

Nelly glanced at her watch. "Same here. Can I get a ride back to my car?"

"Yeah, no problem," Nikki said, digging through her bag to find her keys. "Em, do you need a ride, too?"

"I'm good. Rachelle should be along soon," Emma said. "Besides, we're having dinner here tonight anyway."

"Would either of you like to join us?" Ethel asked.

"I'd love to, but my mom would kill me." Nikki shrugged.

"I promised I'd go by and see a friend," Nelly said, pointing vaguely.

"Another time then," Ethel said.

The girls grabbed their things and walked out the front door. Nikki stood on the front step, digging through her bag for the keys.

Nelly looked up into the sky; it was still blue but a little darker with wisps of cloud. She looked at Nikki. "Going to rain, huh?" As soon as the words left Nelly's lips, there was a great crack and rain came pouring down.

Nikki found her keys, and the two of them ran through the rain for the car. It couldn't have been more than fifteen feet, but they were both drenched by the time they made it inside.

"Never argue weather with a medium," Nikki said, closing the driver's side door and wiping her sopping hair out of her face.

# Chapter Twenty-Four

## Saturday, December 29th

Dec. 29, 08

    Emma and Nikki are meeting me at the Cove—well, the parking lot. I told them to bring their suits. I figure they should see me as a mermaid before game day so they don't freak the day of. I'm also planning on calling my uncle. I figure if they're with me, I won't be alone when I meet this potential weirdo, plus they can teach me whatever they know while we wait.

    In other news, I saw Wyatt again today. He's doing a lot better than last night. I could only hang with him for a few minutes, but he was at least up the whole time. He asked what I did yesterday. I told him I spent the day at the library. I decided not to tell him I'm helping Emma and Nikki. I don't think agitating him in his current condition would be a super good idea. Not for his health or mine.

Nelly shoved her journal under her seat, grabbed her duffle-bag, and hopped out. Nikki had parked right next to Nelly's truck. Emma, who had ridden with Nikki, was pulling a bag out of Nikki's backseat.

"Ready?" Nelly asked as she locked up.

"Almost!" Emma struggled to get the bag between the driver and passenger seats.

"Em, allow me," Nikki said. She opened the side door and took the bag from Emma, pulling it outside.

"Thanks," Emma said sheepishly, getting out of the car and closing the door.

"This way," Nelly said.

The girls followed Nelly down the twists and turns and took the small hike down to the Cove. They didn't talk much along the way. Nelly had told them earlier of her plans when she had asked them to meet her in the parking lot. All three girls were nervous about what the day might bring.

"Is that the place?" Nikki asked. They were still a minute or two away from being in the Cove, but they were starting to catch glimpses.

"Yeah," Nelly said, watching where she stepped.

"It's beautiful," Nikki said.

After few minutes, the three stepped into the clearing that was the Cove. The ocean was glassy and a beautiful turquoise, the sun's reflection sparkling brightly on its surface.

"Now," Nelly said nervously, as she dropped her bag onto the sand. "One thing I need you to promise me is to never ever tell anyone about this place. It's a family secret." Nelly looked at the girls. "From my dad's side," she added.

"Your family has insanely cool secrets," Nikki said, still looking around and soaking up the view.

"So do you guys promise?" Nelly asked, chewing her lip.

"Of course," Emma said. "We wouldn't want this place trashed or covered in towels and beach umbrellas."

"Nikki?" Nelly asked.

"Count me in," Nikki said. "It's like Emma said, we want to preserve this place."

"Thanks." Nelly breathed her relief, chuckling. "I guess you two know something about keeping secrets, huh?"

"Just a bit." Nikki grinned at Nelly.

"Are you going to call your uncle?" Emma asked.

"Yeah," Nelly said. "But I want to show you guys what I look like as a mermaid first."

"Oh," Nikki said, elongating the one syllable. "That's why swimsuits—got it."

"Exactly." Nelly took off her t-shirt and shorts, revealing her black bikini top and a hot pink bottom she had gotten for Christmas from Jo. "I figured if you see me now, then, when all the crazy stuff goes down, if I have to change, you won't be so shocked to see what I look like as a mermaid you'll forget to…I don't know, do whatever it was you were doing before," Nelly said quickly.

"Good plan," Emma said, beginning to pull her own clothes off as well.

After stripping down to their swimsuits, Nikki and Emma followed Nelly to the water, but as they got closer, Nelly stopped them, glancing at Emma's cast. "Uh, can you get in the water with that thing?"

"We got the waterproof kind," Emma said, tapping it with her knuckles.

"Oh good," Nelly said. "Well, I'll change, and uh, wave you in."

Nikki and Emma watched as Nelly ran and dived into the water. There weren't many waves today, and the ones that came were small.

"Have you read anything about mermaid magick?" Nikki whispered to Emma quickly.

"I've been rereading everything I can find. I brought everything I didn't already give to her with me," Emma said, gesturing to her bag.

"Good," Nikki said. "Because I don't know anything about mermaid magick."

"There she is." Emma pointed with her cast-covered hand.

Nelly waved at the girls. She was a good seven yards from where Emma and Nikki were standing on shore.

"Let's go meet a mermaid," Nikki said and dived into the water. It was cold and biting. She was glad she had worn her one-piece but wished it was much thicker. The two girls swam out to where Nelly was.

"Do you want to float here or go over to that rock?" Nelly asked, pointing to the rock where she and Jo had been not too long ago.

"Rock," Emma spluttered. She'd never admit it aloud, especially living in California, but she hated swimming. She did it purely as a necessity for survival, nothing more.

The girls swam over to the rock, Nelly gliding easily, Nikki trying to coordinate her arms and legs to be most efficient, and Emma merely trying to avoid drowning. Nikki and Emma scrambled onto the rock to avoid being smashed up against it. Goosebumps flared across the two until Nikki found a sopping bit of driftwood and made a small magickal fire.

"So," Nelly said. "What do you think?" She did the same kind of shallow somersault she had done for Jo and ended by floating completely on the surface of the water.

"If I hadn't seen your tail, I'd have said you didn't look much different from before," Emma admitted. "Aside from being wet…obviously," she added.

"That's what Wyatt said when I showed him. He didn't even believe me until he looked closer" Nelly swam closer to the two girls huddled on the rock. "He's known me my entire life, so he was able to pick up on some of the subtle differences. I have to take his word they're there since I've never brought a mirror out here when I change. Other than knowing my skin changes color, thanks to being able to look at my arms, and that I, obviously, grow a tail and my hands are weird," she said, holding up her hand while closing and spreading her fingers to display the webbing, "I have no idea what I look like right now. Jo said it's cool, and she hopes she'll be able to change also. I know my eyes change from blue to green, but am I hideous?" As the words tumbled out, Nelly realized that what she looked like as a mermaid really mattered to her. She had always been the sort of girl who didn't really think too much about what she looked like, until she did.

"Are you crazy?" Nikki asked, eyes wide. "You're gorgeous. I totally understand the whole siren thing now."

"Siren?" Nelly asked.

"They were supposedly mermaid-like creatures in Greek mythology who used their good looks and beautiful voices to drag sailors down into the depths to their dark and watery graves," Nikki explained, waggling her eyebrows.

"So killer mermaids?" Nelly asked.

"Technically, yeah," Nikki said, shrugging and shoving her dripping braid back.

"Thanks for that," Nelly said, rolling her eyes.

"I just meant you're a total babe, and I get why the sailors would follow the mermaids into the water. It never made logical sense before, but I get it now," Nikki said. "If you were creepy, no way a sailor would willingly abandon ship."

Nelly laughed.

Emma shivered and scooted closer to Nikki's fire. "You should call your uncle. We'll meet you back on shore to start some training while we wait."

"Actually," Nelly said, playing with a floaty bit of algae growing on the rock. "I might need some help figuring it out. It's in a code, and I don't know what it means."

"We'll meet you back on shore then and try to sort it out," Emma said, splashing back into the water.

"Thanks," Nelly said, moving to avoid being landed on.

Nikki put out the magick fire before she jumped back in. As the three girls swam towards the shore, Nelly barely swam at all to give the other two plenty of time to make it to shore before her.

After changing back into a human and putting her bikini bottoms back on, Nelly joined the girls on the beach where Nikki had built another magickal fire.

"So where's the code?" Nikki asked, toweling off her now loose hair.

"Here," Nelly said, pulling the journal out of the bag, along with a metal cake pan.

"What's the cake pan for?" Nikki asked, squeezing handfuls of thick black hair with the towel.

"It's a mermaid journal," Nelly started to explain. "Just a second, and I'll show you." She walked down to the beach, filled the pan with ocean water, and walked carefully back to where the girls were sitting. "It only opens in water." Nelly put the journal in the cake pan that was now resting in the sand. The book sprang open.

"*That* is cool," Nikki said, tying her hair into a bun on the top of her head. Rebraiding it now would be a nightmare.

"I love magick," Emma said, scooting closer.

Nelly searched through the journal, and after a few minutes, she found the page. "Here," Nelly said, pointing so Nikki and Emma could see exactly what she was referencing.

"It's in English," Nikki said, shocked.

"Yeah," Nelly said, puzzled.

"I just thought it was going to be in some kind mermaid language or at least in Danish since that's where Rán's family was from." Nikki frowned. "I mean, it's nice it's in English, just surprising."

"I guess I never really thought about it," Nelly said, shrugging and pulling her blue Surf Club sweatshirt over her head, covering her still damp top.

"She wrote it a long time ago," Emma said. "Maybe, at the time, the mermaid-hunters, if there were any, didn't speak English, so English was the safest language to write the directions in."

"Yeah. I don't really know," Nelly said, shrugging again. "Look, here's the part we need to figure out."

The three girls looked at the words scrawled across the pages:

Nikki started to speak, "Maybe it means—"

"I know this," Nelly said slowly, as if she just realized it.

"I thought you needed our help," Nikki said, a bit taken aback.

"I thought I did—I mean, I probably still do, but I didn't really read it before. I just saw a poem and figured I'd need help because I suck at poetry, but my mom used to sing this to me."

"Any idea what it means?" Emma asked, huddled under a towel.

"I don't know. I don't remember," Nelly said. She reread the first verse, mouthing the words as she went. "Eyes of their mothers, smiles of their fathers," Nelly repeated.

"It's how we communicate, like from the very beginning when we're small," Nikki said. "We use our eyes and mouths, though admittedly our mouths a lot more, but maybe it's saying this is the way to communicate?"

"Maybe, but I think there's more," Nelly said, rubbing her chin. "I remember my mom telling me a bedtime story about eyes and a smile."

"Do you remember the actual story?" Emma asked.

"Give me a second." Nelly closed her eyes. "It wasn't just the smile and eyes in the story," she said as the story came back to her. "The whole poem was part of the story. It was about a little lost mermaid who needed to find her way home. A seeing witch told her the poem and told her to look into her heart and she would find her way."

"Is that all you remember?" Nikki asked.

"A seeing witch?" Emma asked.

Nelly grumbled. "I don't know. I just remember that's what my mom called her." She rubbed her eyes, willing herself to travel back in time, to be in her bedroom, in her bed, her mom sitting next to her, telling the story. "I can't believe this. It used to be my favorite story, but I haven't thought about it in ages."

"Do you remember how it started?" Emma asked.

"'Once upon a time,' like all the best stories do," Nelly said, smirking.

"Try to tell us the story," Emma suggested. "Pretend you're hearing your mom tell it to you, and now you're telling it to us."

"What have I got to lose?" Nelly muttered. "Okay, so once upon a time, there was a little mermaid. Her name was Jo." Nelly smiled. "I remember I told my mom she could name this mermaid Jo because all the other mermaids were named Nelly."

"Cute," Emma said, grinning.

"How did Jo get lost?" Nikki asked.

"She was playing with her seal friend. They played too far away from the Sea King's kingdom, and they got lost. There was a storm, and the two of them were separated," Nelly said, the story flooding back. "The mermaid wandered for days, completely lost and totally scared. On the fifth day, she found a cave and decided to sleep there, but when she went inside, she noticed it was a pool, like it wasn't totally underwater. There was a big air pocket. She could see a ring of rock above her. The mermaid went cautiously to the surface, remembering all the horrible stories she had been told about mermaids who ventured too close to humans. She poked her head up out of the water just enough to look around.

"There was a woman in the cave on the dry part. She asked the mermaid if she was lost. The mermaid was surprised she could understand her." Nelly stopped.

"What's wrong?" Emma asked.

"I can't remember what comes next."

"Was the woman the witch?"

"Yeah, I think so," Nelly said, standing. "Just give me a minute." Nelly started pacing, trying to map out what her room looked like back then, visualizing every detail. She hoped that maybe, if she could take herself back there, she could remember being seven-years-old again, listening to her mother tell her the story.

Nikki and Emma kept silent, not wanting to derail any train of thought with which Nelly might be traveling. Emma huddled closer to the fire while Nikki used little twigs to make holes and lines in the sand.

After a few minutes, Nelly looked at them. "I think I remember." She kept pacing. "The woman was sitting down, cross-legged, with a clear, empty bowl in front of her. She asked the little mermaid if she was lost, and the mermaid said she was. There was something about how the mermaid felt she could trust the woman…and then—and then, the mermaid asked if the woman knew the way back to the Sea King's kingdom, but she didn't. The woman asked the mermaid if she would do her a favor. When the mermaid asked what the favor was, the woman pointed to the clear bowl and asked the little mermaid to fill it with water. The little mermaid asked why the woman didn't just fill the bowl in the water of the pool, but the woman said she needed mermaid water—water made by a mermaid—it was the only way her spell would work." Nelly sat down.

Nikki and Emma listened intently, both searching for clues in the story.

"When the mermaid heard the word 'spell,' she asked if the woman was a witch," Nelly continued. "The woman said she was and told her if she would fill the bowl, she could tell the mermaid how to get home. The little mermaid was so homesick she agreed. The witch moved the bowl near the edge of the pool, and the little mermaid held onto the edge of the bowl, her fingertips on the inside of the bowl. The mermaid closed her eyes and water came pouring out of her fingertips. When the bowl had been filled almost to its maximum capacity, the mermaid opened her eyes, released the bowl, and floated back to the center of the pool.

"The witch thanked the mermaid and put her own hand in the bowl. The witch floated, not touching the ground, and then the witch said she would keep her part of the bargain. She told the mermaid to listen closely. Then the witch sang." Nelly had lost herself in the story, feeling as though her mother was telling the story through her, rather than telling the story herself. Nelly sang a delicate and haunting tune, singing the words from the poem the three had read earlier. When the song was over, Nelly sat quietly.

"Do you remember any more?" Emma asked softly.

Nelly shook her head. "It's just the song, over and over in my head." She felt a tear running down her cheek and quickly wiped it away, hoping no one had seen it.

"Should we look at the words of the poem again?" Nikki asked.

"It's no use without the story," Nelly said and groaned. "I don't know *how* I know, but the story is important. The story is how we understand the poem."

"Let's take a little break," Emma suggested, digging through her bag. "I brought snacks." She pulled out sandwiches and mandarin oranges. "I thought this might take some time," she added.

"Me, too," Nikki said, pulling s'more supplies from her bag.

After they had each eaten a sandwich and toasted a marshmallow—Emma toasted one for Nelly, who was still busy concentrating—the girls decided to at least get some training in since they had so far been unsuccessful at decoding the poem.

"Do you want to know what I think?" Nikki asked, peeling her mandarin orange. She had been offering suggestions as to what she thought the poem meant, but each time her ideas had been rejected.

"What?" Nelly asked before taking a swig from her water bottle.

"I think it might not have anything to do with the story." Nikki popped an orange segment in her mouth. "I mean, what if your mom didn't know you were going to get Rán's journal?" she said. "What if she told you the story to help you remember the poem in the first place?"

"No," Nelly said. "Not that it's not a good idea," she added quickly, seeing Nikki irritated by another dismissed notion, "but my mom knew I was going to get the journal. She's the one who gave it to my dad to give to me."

"Do you remember any other parts of the story?" Emma asked. "Not necessarily in order, but just other parts of the story?"

"There was another poem," Nelly said absently. "I don't remember all of it, and there's no way Jo would. She was too little."

"What do you remember?" Emma asked.

"Something about true in heart, and…" Nelly shook her head, and then ran her fingers through her hair. "Why hadn't I paid closer attention?"

"You couldn't have known," Emma said. "It was just a children's story."

"Yeah, I guess," Nelly said, glancing at Rán's journal, still open in the cake pan. As her eyes scanned the words for what felt like the millionth time, something clicked. "Oh my gosh—I'm such an idiot!" She smacked her palm on her forehead, exclaiming, "I don't know why I didn't see it before."

"See what?" Nikki asked, leaning over to look at the pages, expecting to see something new.

"What happens after the witch is gone?" Emma asked.

"My mom would describe the mermaid," Nelly said, shaking her head and standing as she pulled her sweatshirt off again.

"So what?" Nikki asked, watching Nelly chuck her sweatshirt.

"So, I know what to do," Nelly said, grabbing the journal, which, upon leaving the water of the cake pan, snapped shut. She ran to the water, diving in headfirst, journal held in both hands.

In the water, Nelly realized she had shredded her brand new bikini bottoms without even thinking about it—good thing she always had a spare pair in her duffle bag. Nelly dived right down to the ocean floor and opened the journal. How could she have been so blind? Her mother had been giving her the answers every step of the way.

"With the eyes of their mothers, the water children see," Nelly read the first line of the poem. Nelly put a finger in between her left temple and corner of her left eye just as her mother had done when Nelly was just a little girl.

"The little mermaid had beautiful eyes," Melinda said, putting a finger by young Nelly's eye. Melinda's brown hair was piled on the top of her head in her usual messy bun; her green eyes glittered as she watched her daughter.

"Eyes like mine?" Nelly asked, giggling. She was seven, and this was her favorite bedtime story. Fairy lights twinkled around her room, which was painted in soft pinks and purples, decorated with butterflies and glow-in-the-dark stars.

"Oh no," Melinda said. "Your eyes are much prettier, and what do pretty eyes mean?"

"Pretty eyes mean a good soul, just like the ocean," Nelly said, beaming at her mom.

"Very good, lille havfrue."

"What next?" Nelly prodded, even though she knew what came next.

"The little mermaid had a beautiful smile." Melinda moved her finger from near Nelly's eye, down her cheek, and rested it near the corner of the little girl's mouth.

"And a pretty smile means a kind voice," Nelly said solemnly, as if this was sacred information.

"Yes! What do pretty eyes and a beautiful smile mean?" Melinda asked.

"We need to protect our ears because bad things want to make our eyes sad and our smiles frowns," Nelly squeaked. "Like the witch!" she added, pointing to a copy of *The Wizard of Oz* on her bedside table.

"Exactly," Melinda said. "How do we protect our ears?"

"Our hair!" Nelly pulled her long dirty blonde locks over her ears, crisscrossing the handfuls of hair under her chin.

Melinda laughed.

"Then the little mermaid was thankful, huh, Mom?" Nelly said.

"She was," Melinda said. "How does a good little mermaid show her thanks?"

"She shakes hands." Nelly pretended to shake her own hand. She looked suddenly puzzled and asked, "Is that why Dad shakes peoples' hands, because he's thankful to them?" Nelly asked.

"He's thankful for the experience of meeting them," Melinda said.

"Even when they're not nice?"

"Even when they're not nice," Melinda confirmed and tickled Nelly, who giggled. When the two had settled down, Melinda said, "Do you remember what comes next?"

"The little mermaid was deep like the ocean."

"And what does that mean?"

"That she's gentle and strong," Nelly said, lifting her arms up into ninety-degree angles to show off her minute muscles.

"Look at those strong arms!" Melinda said, laughing. "How did she show she was strong?"

"She was a mermaid, Mom. All mermaids are strong," Nelly said, putting her hands on her hips. Her tone suggested this particular piece of information was common sense.

"How do you know?"

"She swam really fast!" Nelly undulated her little hand as fast as she could, shooting it past her face.

"Woah, careful" Melinda said, smiling. "You're right; she swam really fast to get home. She met some strangers on the way back to the Sea King's kingdom," Melinda said, continuing the story.

The memory faded from Nelly's mind. It was a happy memory, but it was sad, too. She had recalled just enough to allow her to figure out the poem, but then her memory stopped. Nelly smiled and reread the first stanza.

"Thanks, Mom," she whispered as she plucked a hair from her head and tied the hair to the end of her tailstock, the part right before her fin forked. Nelly looked at the second stanza. She had never received any instruction for this part; none of it sounded familiar. She sunk to the ocean floor with a small thud, sending clouds of sand floating all around her.

"Duh," she said, rolling her eyes as she looked at the sandy fog. She stayed still until the sand had settled. While she waited, she reread the second stanza: "The children of the ocean tread not with two feet. / The children of the ocean swim with grace of degree; / Not one turns up a grain of me."

It had something to do with sand, but what about sand?

"I should have paid more attention in English," Nelly grumbled. She thought about why she would need to not stir up the sand. "No way," she said as an idea floated though her head. "Could it be that simple?"

Deciding to just try her idea, Nelly floated above the sand and, using her finger, wrote a message:

Uncle Henry, this is Nelly.
We need to talk. Meet me at the Cove, pronto.

Nelly surveyed her work. It was legible, and the content, while not much, was clear…at least, she thought so. She reread the rest of the poem and chewed on her lip. Not wanting to risk losing the journal, she decided to bury it in the sand a little ways off and mark it with a rock. After taking a few deep breaths, she knew it was time to try this out.

Something you should know about Nelly is that she's never been afraid of failure (this served her well in life); just as she had told Ethel, she was always quite good at learning through trial and error, which usually involved a lot of error. So as Nelly swam in a circle around the message, careful not to turn up a grain of sand, thoughts of failure did not plague her like they may have worried you or me. She knew if this didn't work, then she'd simply keep tweaking things until it did.

"Grateful," Nelly muttered, clasping her hands together, shaking them. All the while she kept swimming in her circle. "And strong." She took a deep breath and sped up. She swam faster and faster, her hands clasped, shaking. Nelly thought of the few pictures she had seen of her uncle and hoped it would be enough. "May call upon family or peers," Nelly said, thinking aloud. Her family and peers were towards the shore, but the one family member she was trying to contact was out in the ocean somewhere. Nelly swam around the circle a few more times, and then stopped suddenly, facing the open ocean, arms spread. She gave a great kick with her tail. She felt a burst from behind move her through her and out into the ocean, like a shock wave. When she swam back to where she had written her message, it was gone; gone also was the little hair she had tied to her tail.

"Hopefully that means it worked," she said to herself.


29 December 2008

Mermaid magick is fascinating. I don't dare write anything specific down, but I will say I had a long and exhausting day at the beach today. Nikki and I taught Nelly a bit about meditating, and she told us about stopping water on the night of the earthquake, so we used her cake pan and tossed water at her. She was able to stop it several times. I warned her she'd probably be sore tomorrow morning, but she assured me she's known all kinds of sore thanks to her surfing career.

I have to admit, things are going much better than I had anticipated. I only wish we had more time, but we're going to make the most out of the time we have, which is only two, maybe three days.


Emma spread out on her bed. Training Nelly was much harder than she had expected. Her arms were sore and her body begged for sleep, but it was eight-thirty. She knew if she went to bed now she'd be waking up every hour on the hour starting at two in the morning. She sighed and sat up.

Stretching her arms as she walked into the kitchen, Emma decided to find the plastic bucket she had said she'd bring for training with Nelly tomorrow; of course, the last time she remembered using it, she had been twelve. Emma wandered around the house for a bit, thinking and looking.

"Rachelle," Emma called. "Do you know where the plastic bucket is?"

No answer.

"Rachelle?" Emma looked for signs Rachelle was home. Her keys weren't on the ring, and her bright pink, hand-knitted handbag was nowhere to be found.

Half wondering where Rachelle was, half wondering where the bucket was,

Emma went into the hallway. She grunted, throwing her head back in frustrated exhaustion, which was when she noticed the ring that opened the attic stairs. Emma often forgot they had an attic; she visited it so rarely. After grabbing a chair to stand on, she pulled the latch down that hung from the ceiling, exposing stairs. A cloud of dust descended on her, making her cough as she moved the chair. She climbed the stairs and felt her way around the dark, musty room for the light. Flipping the switch and shining a dull yellow light over the attic, Emma searched through the room for her bucket. She walked past the boxes she knew contained letters, photographs, and small keepsakes. Those boxes were all labeled 'Amy.'

"Mom," Emma whispered, letting her hand rest on these boxes for a minute. It had been seven years since she had passed. Emma breathed out slowly and moved on, shuffling her way through a few old hula hoops, dolls, and a couple other toys from her childhood but no bucket.

Deciding to call the bucket lost, Emma made her way back towards the staircase. She bumped into a few boxes and scratched her shin on something sharp. Emma looked down at her shin and then around for the culprit. That was when she saw the old music box she had gotten for a birthday ages ago.

"I forgot about you," she said, picking up the music box. She carried it under one arm as she descended the stairs. Emma closed up the staircase, letting it disappear back into the ceiling, fully camouflaged once more. She glanced at her shin again under better light. The scratch hadn't broken through the first layer of skin. Sighing, Emma went back to her room.

It had been a long, albeit rewarding, day. She needed rest, especially if she was going to be of any use tomorrow. Emma focused on breathing deeply and mindfully as she moved a few knickknacks on top of her dresser to make space for the music box, sliding it carefully into the space. Emma smiled at the box, remembering her sixth birthday when her mother had surprised her with it. It used to open and play a lovely melody, but after Emma had moved in with Rachelle, she found it no longer opened. Her thoughts danced between mermaid magick, music boxes, and her mother as she crawled into bed.


December 29, 2008

Trained with Nelly today. It went well. We—well, she contacted a mermaid-man? Merman? Whatever. She hopefully got in touch with her uncle today; at least, she sent out a message. I'm hoping this time around, I just have to lend my power. I don't think I can master water magick in two days, but I guess if I have to, I can try. Hopefully having a mermaid on our side will take care of that for us. I guess as long as we save people, it doesn't matter whose magick does the work, right?

Nikki's back was stiff. She stood and stretched. It was nearly ten, and she knew she should go to bed, but her mind was still much too awake to sleep. After quietly changing into her most comfortable pajamas, Nikki took her spell book and one of the many books she was borrowing from Ethel into the kitchen. She scooped out some salted caramel-swirl ice cream for herself and headed to the dining room. As she opened the book, she realized it was far too dark to read.

Nikki ate a bite of the cold salty sweet treat as she considered her options. Not wanting to turn on a light and possibly alert Margret, Nikki decided to practice a bit of magick. She focused on the vanilla-scented candle in her bedroom on top of her dresser. Closing her eyes and raising her hand, Nikki envisioned the candle floating a few inches off the dresser. She pictured it floating through the door, out of the hallway, through the kitchen, and into her outstretched hand. She felt a soft thud and opened her eyes. It was the candle. She had done it. She clenched her jaw to keep from shouting her excitement. Nikki inhaled deeply to calm herself.

With the exhale of that calm breath, Nikki lit the candle and began reading the book she had borrowed from Ethel, *A Record of Prophecies Made by the High Priestess the First: Adelina Vates*. She alternated between taking notes in her spell book and eating ice cream. She worked like this for several hours. By the light of the candle, Nikki didn't notice, as she turned from one page to the next, that there was a page in between missing, a page that had been torn out many years before.

# Chapter Twenty-Five
## Sunday, December 30th

Dec. 30, 08

Brunch at Emma's grandma's...seems like I'm here a lot lately. Other news: HENRY CAME!

I'm not going to lie. I was skeptical of the whole 'call a mermaid' thing. Mostly, I figured I'd have to try it several times before I got it right, BUT it worked the first time, and he came. There we were today, training on the beach (aka Emma and Nikki took turns chucking a pot full of water at me to see if I could stop it), and this dude walks out of the ocean like something out of a freaking Baywatch trailer. He can't be much older than I am! He walks up to me and asks if I'm Nelly, which of course I said I was, and he turns out to be Uncle Henry!

It's weird he wasn't naked...I mean, it DEFINITELY would have been super weird if he was and way more awkward. I just mean, changing into a mermaid has always shredded my bikini bottoms unless I'm super careful, but this dude just walked out of the water, topless, granted, but he had on a pair of shorts. They looked like regular board shorts, but I can pretty much guarantee he didn't buy those puppies from any surf store I know of, and I know them all. I'll have to ask about those.

Nelly was perched on the edge of one of Ethel's couches. Nerves flooded through her making it hard for her to relax. Logically, she knew she should focus on the immediate problem (training to stop the tsunami), but her mind raced: would Henry know about her mother's death? Would he know what had made her sick? Was there a cure? A *mermaid* cure? If there was, why didn't he bring it? Why did he take so long to come? She had called him yesterday. Who else was still around from Melinda's family? Did Nelly have grandparents she had never met, but might now receive the opportunity to see? Were there more merfolk, or were they it? Was she the *last* mermaid? As her mind spiraled, her stomach churned.

Ethel put a hand on Nelly's shoulder, startling her.

"Sorry, dear," Ethel said softly. "Would you like some tea?" A lifetime of helping people gave her the skill to read the fears, misgivings, and curiosities shining on Nelly's face.

"No, thanks," Nelly said quickly.

"It might settle your nerves," Ethel suggested.

"On second thought." Nelly half-smiled. "Tea would be great, thanks."

Ethel nodded and left to prepare the tea.

"Nervous?" Nikki asked, sitting next to Nelly on the couch. Nikki leaned back, clearly comfortable making herself at home in Ethel's home.

"I'm about to talk to someone who is just like me, related to me, and I barely met him three minutes ago…" Nelly said.

"Been there," Nikki said, smiling. When Nelly looked confused, Nikki added, "My grandma."

"What is the deal with your grandma, anyway?" Nelly asked.

"Well, for starters, I had always been told she was dead, like that she died when I was really young," Nikki explained. "I never wondered about it because old people die." She shrugged.

"Was it scary meeting her for the first time?" Nelly asked, glad of something to keep her mind occupied.

"Not really," Nikki said, "but I also had no idea I was meeting her."

"This is a good one," Emma said, sitting cross-legged on the couch across from the other two.

Raising an eyebrow, Nelly looked at Nikki.

Nikki grinned and explained, "She literally just showed up in my kitchen one day—well, I assume she came through the door, but with her, who knows? She totally could have 'poofed' into the kitchen. My mom lost it big time." Nikki told the whole story of meeting Kait for the first time while Ethel brought the girls tea and cookies. "Anyway," Nikki finished, "My mom wanted me to explain, which I couldn't because I had no idea who Grandma was. It was a trip."

"How did she even find you?" Nelly asked, sipping on her tea.

Nikki huffed. "Who knows? I wrote I wanted help in my journal and apparently that 'summoned' her.'"

"That's nuts," Nelly said. There was a knock at the door, and Nelly jumped up. "Do you think that's him?" she whispered to no one in particular.

Nikki shrugged while Emma said, "Answer the door and find out."

"Right." Nelly stood, shaking her head, hoping to clear her thoughts. She opened the door.

It was him. It was Henry. This time, he was wearing a shirt as well as shorts. If Nelly hadn't known he was magickal, she would have thought he was a surf bum like she was, except he was a solid foot and a half taller. Between his tanned skin and sun-kissed hair, he'd fit right in at the local lineup—until he turned into a fish.

"Look, buddy," Nelly said, still holding the open door. Her small stature in no way inhibited her ability to take up space. "I have a lot of questions for you about my mom, about mermaids, and about where you've been."

"Sure," Henry said. "Can I at least come in?"

His calmness disarmed Nelly. "Uh. Yeah, okay," she said, moving aside so he could come in.

"Henry," Ethel said, walking up and giving him a hug. "You always wait too long between visits, dear."

"I know, Ethel," he said. "I'm sorry. Time passes differently in the ocean. It's hard to keep track of what's happening up here."

Ethel tutted him but laughed. "I see you've met your niece." Under her breath, she added, "Just as much of a fireball as you are."

"We'll douse that," he said with a smile.

Ethel smirked as though she knew Henry was just as feisty now as he had been at the ripe old age of four when she had first met him.

"How do you two know each other?" Nikki asked the question everyone was thinking.

"All the old families go back," Ethel said simply, as if this explained everything.

"Could you have saved my mom?" Nelly asked. The question bubbled out of her before she could stop it.

"No," Henry said sadly. He shook his head a little and added, "Only Mel could have saved herself. I don't know why she didn't, but I wish she had."

Nelly could see the pain of losing his sister etched on Henry's face, but she pressed him anyway. "What do you mean? How could she have saved herself?"

He smiled half-heartedly. "We're part fish," he almost whispered. Henry cleared his throat. "We need water. Melinda stayed out too long. It made her sick."

Nelly's brain stumbled over itself trying to understand. "But–why–"

"I don't know," Henry said again. "Is that all you needed? To know about your mom?" He shook one of his legs like a runner does before a sprint. "Can we at least sit? It's been a while since I put weight on my legs."

Nelly didn't say anything; she sat on the couch next to Emma. Ethel sat in the loveseat, leaving Henry to sit on the couch next to Nikki. Nelly stared at him for a minute, chewing her lip. She wanted more answers, but either Henry was lying to her, or he genuinely didn't know; Nelly could somehow sense he wasn't lying. "No," she said finally. "I have more questions, like why did we have to meet here?"

"I asked you to meet me here because I don't like being out in the open around humans." Henry folded his arms and leaned back into the couch. "I know I look human," he added, seeing the bewilderment on Nikki's face, "but, as you know, witch, looks can be deceiving."

"But," Nikki started, "how did you—"

"Magickal creatures can sense each other. My guess is you haven't had your magick long enough to notice just yet, but give it time. You will," Henry said. He smiled, which made his dark blue eyes dance.

Nikki's stomach flopped, and she cleared her throat, quickly turning her attention to the suddenly very interesting Afghan rug. Pulling a throw pillow onto her lap and hugging it to her chest, she crossed her arms.

"Actually," Nelly said after a moment.

Henry looked back at Nelly.

"I do have more questions about my mom."

Henry sighed. "I don't have answers about Mel, and if you're just going to keep rehashing the past, I've got stuff I've got to do." He unfolded his arms and put his hands on his knees, ready to stand.

"Nelly," Emma said, warning in her tone.

Nelly groaned and closed her eyes. "Can you teach me?"

"Teach you what?" Henry asked, resting back into the couch.

"Teach me about being a mermaid," Nelly said, looking at him. "Can you… can you be my mentor?"

"You *want* to be a mermaid?" Henry leaned forward again.

"Is there a way for me to stop being a mermaid?" Nelly asked; the dream of surfing flickered at the back of her mind.

"No," Henry said.

The flicker faded.

"But you don't have to embrace it either," he added.

"Would I die?" Nelly asked. "Like my mom?"

"You've probably got enough human in you to live the lifespan of a normal human if you stayed out of the water."

Nelly shook her head. "I don't want to stay out. Besides, I'm going to use my power to help people. There's a tidal wave coming, and we need to stop it."

"When?" Henry asked, shooting a skeptical glance at Ethel.

"Emma has seen it," Ethel said. "It will happen within the next two days."

Henry barked out a laugh. "You want me to teach you to stop a tidal wave in two days?" He looked around the room like he was expecting them to burst out laughing at the obvious joke.

"Yes," Nelly said, her jaw set.

Henry sighed and stood up. "Well, don't sweat it; your tidal wave isn't coming," he said, walking towards the door.

"It is," Nikki said, turning to look at him. "I've seen it, too."

"I don't get any psychic from you, witch," Henry said, watching her.

"You shouldn't," Nikki said. She thought it was odd the way he called her 'witch.' It wasn't an insult, just a name, like she sometimes called Kam 'Bud.' She sat up straighter. "I mean, I'm not psychic. It was a shared vision," Nikki explained. She didn't like the way he looked at her, as if he was seeing her, all of her. It made her feel exposed. She turned back around, pulling the end of her braid over her left shoulder so that it rested on the pillow.

"I *have* seen it." Emma stood. "And it *is* coming."

"You don't have to be my permanent mentor," Nelly said suddenly. "I don't even know if I want you anyway, but I don't have the time to hunt down another long lost relative. Just teach me enough to keep me alive. Please."

"Henry," Ethel said gently. "You know Melinda always planned for you to be Nelly's mentor."

"Well, Mel had a lot of plans." Henry ran a hand through his hair. "Fine. I'll teach you what I can about how to stop a tidal wave, but you've got to know I can't promise you guys will live through this thing." He shook his head, adding, "*If* it even comes."

"Thank you," Ethel said.

"Meet me at the Cove tomorrow," Henry said. "Six AM sharp."

"I'll be there," Nelly said.

"You guys be there, too." Henry pointed back and forth at Nikki and Emma.

"We will," Emma said, as Nikki turned back around, meeting his eyes and nodding.

Henry held Nikki's gaze for a moment and then looked at Nelly. "Tomorrow," he said and left. The door clicked closed behind him.

"So," Nelly said, standing. "I guess I kind of have a temporary mentor."

"It would seem so," Ethel said. "Stay here." She disappeared into a back room.

"We'll be leaving after this," Nikki said, standing up.

"What?" Nelly asked.

"She's getting your books," Emma said.

"*More* books?" Nelly said. She had barely cracked open the last pile.

Emma nodded. "You're going to want to go home and spend as much time reading the ones she gives you as you can—especially since we all have to go to bed early tonight to be at the Cove by six tomorrow morning."

Emma wasn't wrong. Ethel came back with an armful of books, handing the lot to Nelly. They had titles like *A Guide to Mermaids*, *Mermaid: Fact or Fiction*, and *Sea or See: A Handbook of MerCulture for Beginners*. The top books had the most important information Nelly would need, and the bottom books, while she should read them, would be less of a tragedy if she learned the information later rather than sooner.


December 30, 2008

I met a mermaid today—merman? I meant to ask but I forgot. Anyway, he seems like an interesting guy. Henry. That's his name. I don't think he knows mine. He just calls me witch, but not in like a mean way, ~~but more like he~~

Nikki shook her head. Stick to the topic.

He doesn't need to know my name. It doesn't matter. Tomorrow, Emma and I are meeting him and Nelly at the Cove to help Nelly train. I'm not sure we'll be able to do anything other than offer access to our powers, but whatever we can do to help, we're willing.

I've been looking for the prophecy Dad told me about. Still no luck. I'll keep at it tonight for a bit, and then bed. 6 am is going to come quick.

Nikki got out her spell book and *A Record of Prophecies Made by the High Priestess the First: Adelina Vates*. She had only made it a quarter of the way through the book. It was a thick book made of thin pages filled with tiny text. Nikki knew in her heart if she had been required to read the book, it would have been a chore, but since she was curious about the prophecy apparently made about her, searching through the book was an adventure.

She flipped to the back of her spell book; she had been using the last third of the book for note-taking on prophecies. Nikki had written down the page numbers of prophecies she thought might be about her, and then copied the prophecy down. She'd study them all together after she had finished the books of prophecy. She flipped to the page where she had left off and reread her last entry:

pg. 34—AV #2,243
A broken line
A stretch in time
A fragment of blood
A stained glove

Most of these were complete nonsense to her, but she thought the "broken line" thing might be a reference to her breaking the line of pure-blood witches. Nikki stretched and knowing it would be a long night, kept reading.

30 December 2008
Exhausted. Met a merman. Helped Nelly. Too tired to write. Update tomorrow. Maybe.

Emma crawled into her bed with full intentions of falling asleep immediately. As her eyes started to close, blurring as they lost focus, the all-too-familiar glow of a person between realms appeared. Emma sighed, debating between falling asleep or dealing with the dead now. Knowing her duties, she sat up, squinting.

"Hello," Emma said, failing to stifle a yawn.

"Emma," the woman said.

Emma rubbed her eyes, trying to see the woman more clearly. "Do I know you?"

"Not formally," the woman said. She was a cloud barely gray enough for rain. Her image slowly grew more defined. "A man kidnapped me for my gift, but when I could not give him what he wanted, he disposed of me. I knew—when I realized what had happened—I knew I needed to see you. I needed to warn you. You'll be next."

"What?" Emma pulled her sheets off and stood up, fully awake now. "What gift? Are you also a medium?"

The woman shook her head. "Psychic. He wants us all. He's collecting the powerful, but you were hidden from him. Your mother—"

"My mother wasn't magickal," Emma said quickly, taking a step towards the woman.

"No," the woman said softly. "But Amy knew the right people, *good* people—"

"Did you know her?"

"By reputation only," the woman said sadly. "But listen, please," she spoke quickly, urgently. "Your mother hid you, but then, you came of age. The magicks hiding you have dispersed. He knows your face. He's coming for the earth. He's coming for you. He is coming."

The woman began to fade.

"Wait! No!" Emma shouted. "Who are you? Please! Who is *he*? Why does he want me? Come back!"

But the woman was already gone.

# Chapter Twenty-Six

## Monday, December 31st

Dec. 31, 08

It's nearly 6 am, I'm at the Cove freezing my butt off. I was going to wait in the car, but Henry said 6 sharp. I didn't think being late to my first day of mer-training would be getting a good start. Plus, I'm so far behind, I can't afford to waste a minute. Nikki and Emma should be here soon.

I almost forgot it's New Year's Eve today. Tomorrow is a brand new year. As far as the rest of the world knows, it's just another New Year's. Unfortunately, I'm no longer a part of the rest of the world.

I belong to a new world: a world where New Year's Day could mean destruction and death.


Nelly checked her watch; it was five 'til. She stood and paced, occasionally taking small jumps trying to warm up her muscles. Mostly she kept wondering about what Henry would to teach her? Hopefully something awesome, though she'd settle for something that kept her alive.

"Wow," she said, chuckling to herself. A few weeks ago, she would not have been hoping to learn awesome mermaid powers from her deadbeat uncle. "Mom always said time changes everything." Nelly stretched her arms.

"Is this training going to be very physical?"

Nelly spun around to see Emma trudging down towards her, Nikki close behind.

"Good morning, sunshine," Nelly called brightly.

"Can it," Emma said.

"You struck me as a morning person," Nelly teased, grinning.

Nikki said, "Apparently, we caught her on an off day."

Ignoring them both, Emma grumbled some more, but this time her complaints were incoherent.

"Are we ready to get started?" The voice startled the three girls, who looked around trying to find its source.

"Over here," the voice said again.

They turned to see Henry, waist-deep, in the ocean. "I hope you're all wearing your swimsuits like I told you. We're starting in the water." He slipped beneath the small waves.

"I'm actually really excited," Nelly confessed as she took off her t-shirt, revealing her black bikini top.

"*I'm* actually really cold," Emma griped, struggling with her sweatpants.

"Boo-hoo," Nikki said. Although it was six in the morning and still pretty cold, she had only been wearing a sundress and a zip-up jacket, both already discarded.

Nikki and Nelly ran into the water, diving in headfirst. Pouting and grumbling, Emma trudged down to the water, dragging her feet and leaving long lines in the sand behind her. When Emma finally got into the cold water, Nikki and Nelly were already two bobbing heads, waiting for her to join them. Nelly had timed her change perfectly and been able to save her bikini bottom from getting torn to shreds. She had wrapped it around her wrist as was her new habit.

"How exactly is having a freezing, grouchy, psychic-medium supposed to help you train?" Nikki asked Nelly.

Nelly laughed and watched Emma mentally debate over getting under the water slowly or all at once. She was quite familiar with this look. "Just jump in!" Nelly called to Emma. "It'll be over faster." She grinned and took in a mouthful of salt water, spitting it out in a long stream. It wasn't quite as salty as she had remembered from her pre-mermaid days. Nelly leaned over to Nikki to answer her question. "No idea. I've been trying to figure out what I'm going to learn today, but the truth is I don't know anything about being a mermaid except how to swim, and I don't know anything about the powers, so I have no idea what to expect."

"You can expect chatting up here is not on the training schedule," Henry said from behind them.

"Stop doing that!" Nikki's shoulders shot up to her ears as her whole body tensed up.

He ignored her and said, "Come on." He dived back down.

Nikki noticed his tail was blue, cerulean blue; it was her favorite crayon.

"Are you staring at his butt?" Nelly said suddenly.

"What?" Nikki scoffed, her eyes bulging. "No, gross. I was—his—could you remind him we can't breathe down there like you guys can?"

"Sure," Nelly said, wagging her brows at Nikki. Nelly dived down.

Had she been staring? No, definitely not. Nikki felt the blush rush to her face. She cleared her throat, hoping to clear her mind by distracting herself. "Sometime today would be nice, Em!"

"I'm coming," Emma whined.

Nikki watched her friend take a deep breath and dive in.

Emma came shooting up a second later. "It's freezing!"

"Well, it's not like it's going to get any colder," Nikki said.

"Shut up!" Emma snapped as she doggy-paddled over. "Where did they go?"

"I told Nelly to remind her uncle we're not all water breathers," Nikki said. "Are you always this grumpy in the morning?"

Emma growled.

"Forget I asked," Nikki said, suppressing a laugh.

Nelly popped up next to them. "He says take a deep breath, and come on down."

Nikki inhaled, expanding her diaphragm as much as she could and followed Nelly. The two girls were soon joined by Emma, who managed to look even grumpier holding her breath, puffing her cheeks and squinting her eyes. Henry swam over to Emma first, touching the sides of her neck. He followed this by quickly putting his hands on her sides, just before her ribs ended.

"Holy carp!" Emma said. She felt the cool water rush through her. She touched her neck and felt slits. "You gave me gills!" Visibly relaxing, she added, "Ooo, and I'm warmer now."

"Side effect," Henry said, shrugging and swimming over to Nikki.

"Can you teach me how to do that?" Nelly asked.

Henry repeated the process he had done with Emma. When he was sure they were both breathing properly, he finally answered Nelly, "If we decide to make this arrangement permanent, I can try. It takes years of study, more years of practice, and a few willing friends."

"So it's not what I'm learning today?" Nelly asked.

"You can't learn *that* in a day," Henry said, scoffing.

"I think I like breathing underwater." Nikki brushed her finger on her gills. They were cool to the touch and flapped on their own. She tried to concentrate but couldn't consciously make them move. "How did you do this?" Nikki said, looking at Henry.

"It's less about water and more about the sharing of magick. It's a lot easier to give you guys gills than it is to give a human gills. You're already magickal. I've essentially translated your magick," Henry explained.

"How long does it last?" Emma asked.

"A couple hours with a human, but you guys will have about twice that."

"So roughly four hours?" Nikki said.

"What?" Nelly said.

"A couple is usually two—a couple of shoes, a couple of people—so twice a couple is four," Nikki explained. After everyone stared at her for a second, she said, "Never mind," and insisted Henry begin teaching Nelly whatever it was he was going to teach her.

A playfulness danced in Henry's eyes as he started the lesson.


31 December 2008

We're taking a break from the water—thank goodness. Nikki and Nelly were teasing me about being grumpy. Between my visit from the beyond and my dreams, I had an awful night. I didn't want to scare them, but it felt like before Nikki helped me when I was having a million visions all at once. It's more of the same.

As for the training, it's really cool, and Nelly is picking it up fast. Anyway, Henry was telling Nelly she had to feel the water. I think all her time as a surfer helped her connect a lot easier than any of us anticipated. Nikki and I just floated there for the first part and chatted (by the way, speaking underwater is wild. I thought we'd sound weird, but we sound completely normal. I think it's a magick thing—still feels weird, though. Too wet for my taste). Anyway, Henry said we 'land mammals' are in charge of teaching Nelly meditation basics: how to clear her mind and stuff. In her book *A Guide to Mermaids,* Lois Vandatter says mermaids meditate by learning to feel and move with ocean currents.

Emma tried to stretch her back. It shouldn't have been, but it was sore. When she had left, Henry was saying something about teaching Nelly how to stop moving water. He had finished his lesson on starting a wave in still water.

"Are you coming back?" Nikki called. Her head was a bobbing dot among the small waves.

"Give me a minute to breathe," Emma called back. The wind suddenly blew hard and loud. All Emma caught of Nikki's next comment was something about gills. Emma ignored her. Breathing underwater wasn't awful, but it didn't feel natural either. As she watched Nikki dip back underwater, Emma now felt she better understood Nelly's hesitation and initial resistance to being a mermaid.

She sighed. "I can do it, I can do it, I can do it," she chanted to herself as she breathed deep and walked down to the beach, wanting to be close in case she was needed. Though, she hadn't been needed the entire time she had been in the water; why could they possibly need her now? Almost as soon as the thought traipsed its way across Emma's mind, Nelly's head popped out of the water only a few feet in front of Emma.

"We could use you down here," Nelly said.

"What for?" Emma asked.

"Henry is going to make the water still," Nelly said. "So I need you guys to make small waves for me to stop and control."

"Okay." Emma followed Nelly back into the deeper water. When the two girls got back, they found Henry quietly talking with Nikki, his hand on her side. Nikki saw her friends and practically pushed Henry away from her.

"Just reapplying the gill thing," Nikki said, turning bright red.

"Right," Nelly said, looking at Emma.

"Do you need your gills reapplied?" Nikki asked Emma.

"Maybe later," Emma said, smiling; she had 'reapplied' an hour ago.

"Now," Henry said, drawing the girls' focus. "I'm going to need silence. I'm not calming the whole ocean, but it still takes concentration to calm a cove of water."

The three girls nodded.

"After I calm the water, I'll nod to you, Nikki," Henry said.

"Okay," Nikki said aloud, though internally, her brain yelled madly that she was being insane and her body needed to get things under control. She took a deep breath, doing everything in her considerable power to stop blushing—there was definitely some magick involved.

"Then I want you to do what we talked about. Emma, your job is to lend your strength to Nikki."

"Wouldn't it be easier to stop the small waves that naturally occur in the Cove anyway?" Nelly asked.

"Easier is not the goal," Henry said, shaking out his arms. "If we had more time, I'd work you up gradually, but since we don't, you get to start with hard stuff. Now get ready." He took several deep breaths.

Rolling her shoulders and nodding, Nelly braced herself. Emma took Nikki's hand, and they waited as Henry closed his eyes and concentrated. He floated, standing straight; he was almost completely still save the slightest movements of his blue tail. He slowly raised his arms until they were straight out, his body forming a cross. The girls were surprised by how calm the water felt. Henry nodded.

Nikki lifted her right hand slowly, holding the fingers of Emma's right hand with her left. Henry had told Nikki (while Nelly had been retrieving Emma) to concentrate on energy. He had told her to forget about the water and focus instead on a small ball of energy moving through the water, to feel it in her breath. Nikki's only elemental magick training was with fire, and she had told this to Henry, but he had insisted it wouldn't be a problem. Energy was energy. Nikki cleared these thoughts from her mind and focused.

Energy.

Energy.

She needed to visualize it more. She needed to picture every detail. What color would energy be? Yellow, she decided. Nikki imagined a small yellow ball. As she pictured the energy, she realized it was less of a ball and more of a pinhead. This training wasn't supposed to be easy. Nikki concentrated, squeezing Emma's hand and using the power that flowed through the both of them. She helped the ball grow: it was the size of a lemon drop, now a roll of packing tape. She concentrated, and the energy grew to the size of a soccer ball. Fighting to maintain its size, Nikki realized why she needed Emma's help with this ball of energy. She squeezed Emma's hand.

As Nikki floated with her hand outstretched like she was holding an invisible ball, Nelly watched and waited for the waves to start. At first, they were no more than ripples. With a deep breath, she was able to calm the ripples easily. Then the ripples grew. Nelly held a hand out in front of her to stop the small waves. This took more energy, but she was still mostly successful. While she was unable to stop the waves completely, she was able to push them back down to ripples.

Nelly released her hold on the waves, allowing Nikki's power to make the waves even bigger. Nelly felt the water around her become shallow: her tail brushed the sand; she could feel the wind kissing the top of her head. The next wave that hit her was massive. Nelly put up both hands, and concentrated on the little training she had received. She was able to stop the wave for a few moments, but the effort was draining her strength quickly.

Nelly started to speak, "I can't—" However, speaking broke her concentration. The wave engulfed her, sending her tossing and rolling across the sandy bottom of the ocean.

"Stop," Henry said, not opening his eyes.

Nikki didn't hear him, but Emma did, and she broke the hold Nikki had on her hand. The sudden loss of power was enough to catch Nikki's attention.

"We're stopping," Emma explained.

"Oh." Nikki relaxed.

"You're massively powerful, witch," Henry said, opening his eyes to look at Nikki.

"Uh, thanks," Nikki said. "I'm also massively exhausted," she mumbled as she floated, letting the water do the work.

"Shouldn't someone find Nelly?" Emma said, looking around for her friend.

"Here," came a muffled voice.

"Marco!" Emma glanced around quickly. The wave had churned everything up. There were piles of sand and seaweed everywhere.

"Polo," the voice said again.

Emma was able to figure out the direction and continued playing Marco Polo until she found one particularly large pile of sand. She saw black fin poking out from the base of the pile. "Marco?" she asked, pulling on the fin a little.

"Get me out of here already," Nelly shouted.

"Okay," Emma said, giggling. She started digging at the top, uncovering Nelly's head and then shoulders. "Can you take it from there?"

"No," Nelly said, spitting out sand as she squirmed, struggling to free herself.

As Emma dug, freeing Nelly's torso, she saw seaweed wrapped around Nelly's arms, pinning them to her side. "Could I get a little help?" Emma called.

"Caught in seaweed?" Henry said, swimming over to help. "Rookie mistake." He shook his head and put his hand on the seaweed; the slimy green strands immediately around his hand dried and crumbled away.

"I can manage from here," Nelly said. "Thanks, Emma." When Nelly had finally wiggled her way free from the mess of sand and seaweed, she collapsed on the ocean floor. She said, "I know it wasn't supposed to be easy, but was it supposed to be that hard?"

"I didn't know the witch was so powerful," Henry said, shrugging. "Now we know. Let's do it again."


December 31, 2008

I wish I could write down everything I saw and did today—I can't, but I wish I could just so I would be sure to never forget it. Unfortunately, saying mermaid magick is freaking cool and massively exhausting will have to suffice. At the end of the tidal-prep cram session, Henry told us he had talked with Madam O, and she wanted us to report back to her place when we were finished. We just got here, but she's not home yet. The three of us are in my car because there's room. Nelly and Emma are totally out, and I figured I'd write while I have the chance. Things seem to happen so quickly these days, I feel like I'm perpetually playing catch-up.


*Tap. Tap.*

Nikki looked up from her journal to see Gabby's face at her car window. She glanced at Nelly and Emma, both of whom were still fast asleep. Nikki unlocked her door and got out as quietly as she could.

"Merry Meet," Nikki whispered.

"I have something for you and Nelly." Gabby handed Nikki two envelopes: one with her name on it, and the other with Nelly's.

"Are these from my grandma?" Nikki asked, trying to suppress her excitement.

"They are," Gabby said. "Be sure to give Nelly hers soon."

The sky rumbled.

"Looks like it's going to rain." Gabby stared at the sky. "I have to go. Blesséd be, Nikki."

"Blesséd be," Nikki said, looking at the envelopes. She glanced up, remembering she wanted to ask if Gabby knew when Kait would be back, but Gabby was already gone. Before she could fully process Gabby's disappearance, she caught movement in her peripherals: Ethel waved to her from the front door.

"Wake the others, and come inside," Ethel called. She closed the door.

"Guys," Nikki said, one knee on the driver's seat and a hand shaking each friend.

"Wake up. Emma, your grandma is here."

"Five more minutes," Emma groaned, her arm covering her face and slightly muffling her voice.

"I vote ten," Nelly said, curled up in the backseat.

"I've got a letter for you, Nelly," Nikki said. She felt bad waking her friends up, but she was also a little jealous they had been able to fall asleep so quickly. Nikki had tried to nap, but her mind kept racing with all the new mermaidian information she had picked up. "I have a letter for you," Nikki repeated, shaking Nelly's leg.

"Fine," Nelly said, sticking her hand out to receive said letter.

"You have to come inside," Nikki said. There was another rumbled from the sky; this one was much louder. "You guys better hurry up. It's going to start raining." She grabbed her bag, stuffed the letters and her journal inside, and closed the driver's side door. After a deafening rumble, the sky opened its valves and let the rain pour. Nikki hightailed it to Ethel's front door.

"Couldn't wake them?" Ethel called from the kitchen as Nikki came in.

"No," Nikki said. She put her jacket on the hanger and tossed her bag on a couch in the living room before returning to the dining room to sit down near the head of the table. "Training with mermaids is exhausting," she said, collapsing into a chair.

"Henry called," Ethel said. She came into the dining room carrying a tray loaded with small plates, turkey sandwiches, cucumber slices, and hummus.

"What did he call you on? His shell-phone?" Nikki snorted at her own cleverness and took the tray from Ethel, setting it on the table.

Ethel smiled but did not address the comment; instead, she said, "He said you girls are harder workers than he had anticipated." Ethel returned to the kitchen for a moment. She came back carrying a jug of lavender lemonade and four tall glasses.

"Should I try to wake them up again?" Nikki asked, glancing over her back at the window. Even though the heavy drapes were drawn, she knew her friends were probably still asleep in her car.

"I expect they'll be in soon enough. Eat." Ethel handed Nikki one of the small plates and filled one of the tall glasses with purplish lemonade. She handed the glass to Nikki, who chugged it.

"That's delicious," she gasped, looking at her empty glass. "Thank you. I had no idea how thirsty I was." Nikki put a turkey sandwich and a stack of cucumber slices on her plate while Ethel refilled her glass. "What exactly do you know about Henry?"

"Well," Ethel said, pulling up a chair. "I know he's—"

The front door opened.

"Oh my! It seems the storm has delivered a few wet cats," Ethel said, standing as Nelly and Emma entered, both drenched and actively dripping.

"You didn't say there would be food," Nelly said. Eyes fixed on the tray, she reached forward.

"You're soaking. Come with me, you two." Ethel grabbed each girl by an arm, dragging them into the kitchen.

Nikki ate in silence for a few moments as Ethel had Nelly and Emma strip off their outermost layers and put on thick bathrobes. She also provided towels for their sopping hair. Nelly and Emma returned to the dining room; their towels, holding wet hair, piled high on their heads.

"It looks like I missed spa day," Nikki teased.

"Whatever," Nelly said. "I'm so hungry, I'd eat naked." Nelly stacked a few sandwiches on her plate and poured herself a glass of lemonade.

"Let's hope it doesn't come to that," Emma said, also filling her plate.

Nikki was starting to slow down. "When you're done eating, Nelly, I have a letter for you."

"Can't you just tell me?" Nelly said through a mouthful of food. "Did you have to write a letter?"

"I didn't write it." Nikki scooped up hummus with her last slice of cucumber. "It's from my grandma."

"Is she back?" Nelly asked, swallowing.

"Who knows?" Nikki said before popping the cucumber slice in her mouth. She cleared her throat and added, "Gabby brought it to me." She drained the rest of lemonade and stood up. "I'm going to be in the living room. Come in when you're done." She took her plate and glass into the kitchen. After washing both, she set them on the rack to dry (Ethel didn't believe in dishwashers). Nikki plopped on the couch and ruffled through her bag, finding the two letters. She set the one addressed to Nelly on the coffee table and opened the other, muttering as she read.

Merry Meet,

Nikki, I have entrusted you with this letter to your friend. I assume, if you're reading this, Gabby has delivered both letters to you. Poor Gabby probably feels a bit like a medieval owl, delivering mail back and forth. Remind me to teach you the spell to be able to receive letters as well as send them. It's a bit more complicated, but I digress.

Now, it's imperative you're present as Neldyn reads her letter. I won't tell you its entire contents—no, I think it's best left to her to decide what information she wants to share with you and Emma—however, I will tell you it contains information about her family.

My little witch, I know it seems like I haven't given you any instruction since I've become your mentor, and I apologize whole-heartedly, but this next bit of instruction is something I need you to follow to the letter: do not leave her alone. It is important Neldyn receives the information, but it's also important she focuses on the task at hand. Your task, your instruction, is to keep her focused. No matter what she wants, be sure to keep her focused. You'll all need to be focused. If it has not happened today, it will happen tomorrow.

I'll be back as soon as I can.

Blessed be,

Grandma Kait

Nikki reread the letter a few times. What did Kait mean by "do not leave her alone"? Was she supposed to stalk Nelly? Make sure she was never left alone at any moment until whatever was going to happen had happened and was over? Nikki glanced at Nelly's letter. An overwhelming desire to rip it open and read it rippled through her. It would have been easier if her grandmother had just told her the information and made her keep it secret. Nikki bounced her leg, thinking about the whole situation for a few moments before deciding Nelly deserved this. Nelly had been the last to find out so many things about her mermaidian history and heritage; she deserved to find out whatever this was first. Nikki refocused her attention on her own letter, still trying to decipher the full extent of her instructions.

"So, what was the letter you used as a bargaining chip to get me in here?" Nelly asked, flopping onto the loveseat near the couch where Nikki was seated. "You could have told me there would be food, and I would have come."

"I didn't know there was food," Nikki said. "It's there." She gestured to the letter on the coffee table.

Nelly sat up and grabbed it. "And you said this is from Kait, your grandma?" She turned the envelope in her hand and ripped the top open.

"Yup." Nikki swallowed and watched Nelly open and read the letter.

Nelly's eyes blazed over the paper. When she had finished reading, she closed her hands over the letter absently, as though she didn't realize it was still there. Staring at the ground, Nelly simultaneously started and stopped movements: she started to move her hand to possibly to run her fingers through her hair but stopped before her hand was even mid-chin; she started to raise her other hand, which still clutched the now crumpled letter, to her mouth but stopped before she had really lifted her hand at all.

Nelly wanted to speak, but there were no words she wanted to say. She wanted to scream. She wanted to hide. Nelly felt more in this one moment than she had felt in her entire life. She had never been a person to feel mixed emotions. Everything was always so clear: when her mother had died, she had been sad. When she surfed, she was happy. Things were simple. They had always been simple, until she became a mermaid.

"Can we go back to sleep?" Emma asked, joining the girls in the living room. She laid down on the other couch.

Nelly finally looked up.

"What's it say?" Nikki asked.

"What are you guys talking about?" Emma sat up, looking from one girl to the other.

"My grandma," Nelly said. "My mom's mom—*Henry's* mom…"

What about her?" Emma pressed.

"She's alive."

# Chapter Twenty-Seven

## Tuesday, January 1st

January 1, 2009

News for today is good and bad. There was an earthquake this morning, which means good news: Emma was right, but also bad news: Emma was right.

Today is going to get a lot worse before it gets better. Anyway, Kam and I are sitting in Mom's bed while she's on the phone trying to get a hold of Dad to let him know we're all right. Nothing much broke. There were a couple of dishes and a vase full of water and flowers that broke, but, as a whole, we're fine, just exhausted.

Kam was curled up in a bundle of blankets next to Nikki. She set her journal and pen on her dad's nightstand before snuggling down next to Kam under their mom's plush white duvet.

"Can I ask you something?" Kam asked.

"I thought you were asleep," Nikki said.

"No."

"Sure, what's up?" Nikki yawned. It wasn't even two in the morning, and she hadn't gone to bed until after midnight. Tired was an understatement.

Kam didn't say anything for a while; he peeked over the mass of blankets to make sure Margret was nowhere in sight. Then, he took a deep breath and whispered, "Do you think magick makes earthquakes?"

"Uh…" Nikki groaned. "Do I think there's some magickal being in charge of making earthquakes? No. Earthquakes are the earth's growing pains." She rolled onto her back.

Kam sat up and looked at his sister. "Can magick stop earthquakes?"

"Maybe," Nikki said. "You'd need some really powerful magick, though. I wouldn't try it—not alone, anyway. Why?"

"If magick could stop an earthquake, could it stop a war?" Kam asked.

Nikki sighed. She finally understood his train of thought. "I don't think so, kiddo."

"Why not?" Kam asked.

"Well—" She thought about her answer for a little while. "For the sake of argument, let's say magick *can* stop an earthquake."

"Okay."

"Okay, so…" Nikki rubbed her eyes. Her lack of sleep was making her mind foggy and her logic unsound. "So, magick can't stop wars because there are people involved. There are no people involved in an earthquake. People are *affected* by the earthquake, sure. But no one is *choosing* to have the earthquake. The only way to magickally end a war would be to cast a massive spell on one side and make them agree with the viewpoints of the other side."

Kam didn't say anything.

"I said that out loud, right?" Nikki glanced at Kam.

"Yeah," Kam mumbled, burying himself further in the sea of sheets and fancy pillows.

"Good." Nikki's eyelids fluttered as her body relaxed.

"What's even the point of magick if it can't bring Dad home?" Kam mumbled.

Kam was the sort of kid who didn't want to bother anyone, so Nikki knew, despite her desire to sleep, this conversation needed to happen while the topic was open. "The point of magick is to…keep—the point of magick is…" Nikki rubbed her eyes again. Her brain offered 'The point of magick is to zap little brothers, so older sisters could get some sleep, and rest enough to help stop giant tidal waves from wiping away the town.' Nikki rolled over, looked Kam in the eyes, and said, "The point of magick is to keep us safe while Dad isn't here to protect us."

"Is that why you got magick and I didn't? Because you're older?"

"I got magick because I turned eighteen, but can I tell you a secret?" Nikki asked, sitting up and looking around. "You have to promise not to tell Mom, or at least, don't tell her I told you."

"Okay, I promise," Kam said, using an index finger to draw an invisible 'X' across his heart.

"So, Dad has magick, but Mom doesn't, right?"

Kam nodded.

"Well, you and I were both born with magick. When Mom found out, she asked Dad to bind our powers."

"So, I'll get powers, too?"

Nikki nodded. "I broke the binding when I turned eighteen because I'm an adult now and have to make my own choice about my magick. No one can make the choice for me."

"Wait, you can choose not to be magickal?"

"Yeah. Grandma Kait says a witch can choose to be stripped of her powers, but once her powers are gone, they're gone forever."

"Why would anyone choose that?" Kam asked.

"Some people want normal lives," Nikki said, shrugging. "Can I ask you a question?"

"Sure," Kam said.

"Can we pick up this conversation later? I'm exhausted." Nikki collapsed on top of her brother.

"Get your fat butt off me first!" Kam's yell was muffled by Nikki's stomach.

Jan, 1, 09

I've decided I hate letters. I have so many questions but no one to ask. I mean, I could ask Henry, but I don't exactly have an easy way of contacting him.

My apparently alive mermaid grandma sent me a message, and I have no idea how to even process it, but I do have five billion questions. Being a mermaid is one thing, but these long lost relatives...I don't know how much more I can take.

Anyway, I sent a text to Nikki and Emma about meeting at the Cove in an hour. We had an earthquake this morning, which usually wouldn't make me think tidal wave, but let's say my mermaid senses are tingling.

I still feel kind of bad about last night. Ms. F called to ask if I want to come over and spend New Year's Eve with them. I was (and still am, frankly) so freaking nervous about today that I told her I had already made plans with Jo. Jo asked if I wanted to go party with her, and I told her that I was going to be with Wyatt and to stay away from the ocean. One thing that's nice about Jo knowing I'm a mermaid is when she asked why, I just made a mermaid motion with my hand, and she got the hint.

Nelly looked at her watch and checked the time: 12:05. She got up and paced around her room for a little while: 12:06. Was time passing slower on purpose? Nelly shoved a pile of dirty laundry aside and sat on the floor and stretched. She hadn't felt this anxious since her first big time surf competition. She had been 8 years old, and the nervousness was eating through her. She kept snapping at Jo and her parents and would burst into tears over insignificant things which usually wouldn't have bothered her. Finally, Melinda had pulled her aside. She had told Nelly to stretch and focus only on relaxing her muscles. Nelly had done so but was still jittery. Melinda had told Nelly to imagine herself in the ocean. Nelly could still hear her mom's words: "It's just you and the water. No board, no other people. Feel the water. Feel the currents. Feel the movement. Control your breathing. Let the water do the work."

After that first surf competition, Nelly never had a problem with anxiety before a meet again. She didn't know it at the time, but that moment with Melinda had been Nelly's first and last time ever meditating. At least, it was until yesterday.

"It can't hurt," Nelly thought aloud.

Standing, Nelly closed her eyes and tried to picture herself in the ocean—minus the tail, she decided. She could hear the crackling of the ocean around her. She imagined the current in the Cove; most days it flowed right to left. Nelly felt the current move her; she felt the ebb and flow of the ocean. She matched her exhale to the ebb, her inhale to the flow. After breathing quietly for a few minutes, Nelly opened her eyes. Residual anxiety moved through her, but it no longer made her want to crawl out of her skin. She glanced at the clock; it was 12:15. Nelly groaned and jumped around a little.

"Warm up the muscles," she said, doing a few lat slaps. She shook her head and muttered, "What are you doing, Nels? You're going to get yourself killed."

She threw on a sweatshirt, deciding to jog to the Cove to burn some time and hopefully, those last nerves still plaguing her.

1 January 2009

I keep seeing Nelly trying to hold a giant wall of water and failing. It's the same vision. Every time. It's a waking nightmare. I see it in my mind's eye constantly.

What if I got it wrong? Am I supposed to witness the death of my friends? Was I meant to cause their death? Am I only seeing this because my job was to make it come to pass? I can't believe that. We're supposed to stop it. We *have* to stop it—anything else is just cruel. I've never questioned my gift. I've always known I was a force for good, but what if I'm not?

"Not again," Emma said. Her hand relaxed on her quill, spilling ink on the bottom of her page. The cold washed over her.

*"HOLD IT, NELLY!" someone screamed.*

*"I'M TRYING! It's too big; I can't control it—I'm not powerful enough!" Nelly cried back.*

*A giant wall of water threatened to crush her; she stood legs apart and arms up, palms out as though she was literally using her body to hold the water back. Nikki was at her side, grabbing one of Nelly's outstretched hands.*

*Nikki began murmuring words. The wall of water crashed down on all of them.*

"Emma," Rachelle held Emma's head. "Emma, you've had a vision. You fell. Can you hear me?"

Emma's eyesight was still unfocused and swimming. "Wa—" She tried to speak, but her throat burned. She rolled over, coughing up a quart of ocean water.

"Oh, Em…" Rachelle watched Emma suffer, unable to do anything more than hold her hair back.

"I think that's it," Emma said, after a minute. Her throat felt raw and sore. She leaned against her bed, breathing heavily.

"Do you want something?" Rachelle asked.

"Water," Emma said, surprised by her answer. "I'm probably dehydrated."

"I'll be right back." Rachelle patted Emma's shoulder before she left.

Emma's head swam and pounded, the pain crashing behind her eyes and breaking over her forehead. She was pretty sure she was going to faint. There was a small beep from behind her. Even though it hurt, Emma turned her head to see what had made the noise. Her cell phone was on the floor just a foot away from her. It took more energy than it should have for her to get it. Breathing heavily and leaning on the bed again, Emma opened the phone. There was a text from Nelly: 'Meet me at the Cove in an hour.'

Snapped the phone shut, Emma breathed deeply. An hour. An hour was enough, wasn't it? Enough time to brave today. She had been preparing for so long, and it seemed everything was going wrong.

"Here," Rachelle said, walking into the bedroom. She had a towel in one hand and a glass of water in the other. She threw the towel over the water on the floor and set the glass on the nightstand. "I'm going to help you on to the bed, okay?"

Emma started to nod and then said, "Okay," because speaking hurt less.

Rachelle pulled Emma up, setting her on the bed before lifting her legs and sliding them on the bed. As she handed Emma the glass of water, she asked, "What did you see?"

Emma took a small sip. She put the glass to her forehead; the coolness helped her throbbing head. "The same thing," Emma finally said. "It's been the same thing. I haven't told anyone because it's nothing new. I watch us die. I see it over and over again." Her voice cracked.

"Wait, die? You've never seen this before, have you?"

"Die? Get crushed by the wave? It's the same thing. Always the same. Someone is always screaming at Nelly to hold the wave. She always tries, and she always fails—" Emma whimpered, tears streaming down her cheeks. "Nikki tries to help, but even their combined power isn't enough, and the wall of water falls on us all. I got them into this. It's all my fault."

"Nikki is a massively powerful witch," Rachelle said. "And Nelly is a mermaid. If there is anyone in this world that does not need to worry about water, it's her. Do *they* know they could die?"

"Yes," Emma said. "Nikki saw it; we've both told Nelly."

Rachelle tucked a strand of Emma's hair behind her ear. "Em, magick, however fun, however amazing, is not a game. It comes with heavy responsibilities. Your friends know this; you know this. You knew going into this you might not be coming out. I've talked with Nikki, and even though I've only met Nelly briefly, I know they're both smart girls. I hope you all walk out of this fight unscathed, but..." Rachelle cleared her throat. "But I'd be kidding myself if I thought that was the most likely scenario. I wish I had the gift. I wish I had *any* magickal gift, so I could at least lend my strength to you."

"Nelly wants to meet in an hour," Emma said.

Rachelle took a sharp breath and smiled. "Then you will meet her in an hour. I'm not usually one for modern medicine, but take a pain-killer, finish your water, and rest as much as you can. I'll come back in about forty-five minutes to check on you." Rachelle brushed some hair out of Emma's face, kissed her forehead, and left the room. She returned shortly with a small bottle of pain-killers. "Take two."


January 1, 2009 (later)

Finally got some sleep. My whole body aches. I got a text from Nelly a while ago. We're supposed to meet her at the Cove in an hour. I wanted to go alone, but Mom asked me to watch Kam since she has a bunch of work stuff that came up because of the earthquake. I called every Mom-approved babysitter I could think of, even some she definitely would not approve of, and NO ONE can take him. I even called Gabby, but her phone is off or dead So, he's with me. We're waiting for Emma.


"Hey." Emma carried her light blue jacket and a bottle of water.

"You look awful," Kam said as Emma got in the passenger's seat.

"Kam, be nice." Nikki spun around to glare at him with a look that said, 'Seriously?'

"He *is* being nice," Emma said. She pulled the sun visor down and looked at herself in its little mirror. "'Awful' is a huge understatement."

"What happened?" Nikki asked, backing out of the driveway.

Emma glanced at Kam.

"It's cool," Nikki said."He's known for a while now."

"I keep having the same vision over and over again. Remember the last vision we had?"

"When I threw up water?" Nikki grimaced. "I can still taste the brine." She stopped at a light, drumming her fingers on the steering wheel.

"Well, this time I had the pleasure," Emma said, making a face.

"Yeesh." Nikki made a face. The light went green, and Nikki turned left, taking them towards Main Street.

"Wait," Kam said suddenly. "You have visions? Of the future?"

"Who are you talking to, kid?" Nikki asked.

"Both of you. Emma said 'the last vision we had,' so unless she was speaking in the *royal* we…" Kam trailed off.

"I don't have visions," Nikki said, as she clicked on her blinker to get onto Main. "At least, not on my own. Emma needed help, and I was drawn into the vision."

"But 'the last vision' implies there were more," Kam said.

"I was having problems," Emma said. "For a while I couldn't get any visions to come at all. It was some kind of block. Nikki helped me, and that's when we had the first vision together. Then, there were too many visions. I was having multiple in a row, sometimes all at the same time. Nikki helped again, and that's when we had the second one. There were only two."

"We're never going to make it to the Cove on time," Nikki said, glancing at the clock. "What's with this traffic? It's a parking lot!"

"There's a spot by the knitting shop." Emma pointed to the right. "We can walk from there."

After the nightmare commonly called parallel parking, Nikki, Kam, and Emma piled out of the car.

"Where are your regular keys?" Kam asked as Nikki pulled out a single key instead of her usual noisy key chain full of keys and knick-knacks.

"Don't worry about it," Nikki said. "Just people watch, okay? Let me know when it's clear." Nikki slipped her key into a hide-a-key magnetic pouch.

Kam watched the crowds of people. "Clear."

Nikki slid under her car and carefully hid her key. She popped back up and stretched her arms in front of her, trying to look inconspicuous.

Emma looked at Nikki and then back at the car.

Nikki glanced at her and said, "You know in case of whoosh." She made a wave motion with her arm. "Then, I'll still have a way to drive the car." She shrugged.

"Good thinking," Emma said.

The three of them walked past shops and delis. Kam ran up ahead of them to look in the window of the science store. Nikki kept an eye on his head bobbing through the crowd.

"Nikki," Emma said, grabbing her friend's arm.

"What?" Nikki turned and found herself face to face with a wall of televisions.

"…and now with the latest. Kim?" the newsman said on the televisions. There was a brief pause in lag time as the newswoman listened to her colleague.

"Thanks, Dan," Kim said after a moment. "We had a decent sized earthquake this morning. As you can see behind me, some of the older buildings in town have collapsed. Friends and neighbors have flooded in to help in anyway they can." She pointed behind her. "The earthquake," Kim voiced-over as the camera panned the crowds clearing debris, "struck at around one-thirty this morning. The experts are rating it a 7 on the intensity scale. Luckily, most of the buildings in the area are up to more recent codes. All in all not a great way to start out the New Year. Back to you, Dan."

"We saw this," Nikki said as Dan talked about all the numbers involved in the earthquake. "It was different, but I remember this." Nikki couldn't pull her eyes from the televisions, even though she wasn't watching anymore. She put her hand on the glass. "We saw this."

"At least we know why all the people are here," Emma said. "We should find Kam."

"Does it always feel like this?" Nikki asked as they walked towards the science store.

"You mean that weird pit in your stomach when you experience something for the second time even though you know you never really experienced it in the first place?" Emma asked.

Nikki swallowed, her mouth suddenly very dry. "Yeah."

"Pretty much," Emma said. She breathed deeply to steady her racing heart.

The girls moved through people, apologizing to every shoulder they bumped as they pressed forward. They found Kam, staring at a Lego model of the Death Star twice his size.

"Ready, kiddo?" Nikki put a hand on his shoulder.

"Yeah," he said.

Most of the buildings on Main were standing, just a few had crumbled walls. Nikki held onto a handful of Kam's t-shirt and steered him through the crowd of helpers and onlookers towards the apparent cliff edge. The girls glanced around to see if anyone was watching—after all, they had promised Nelly to keep the Cove a secret—but everyone seemed more interested in things on Main Street.

"Where are we going?" Kam asked once they were on the hike and away from the mass of people.

"*We're* going down there," Nikki pointed vaguely downwards. "*You're* staying here."

"What?" Kam said. "No way. I promise I won't get in the way."

"You can't come," Nikki said. "I should have given you twenty bucks to stay at the science store," she murmured more to herself than Kam.

"I'm coming with you," Kam insisted.

Everything in her told Nikki to make him stay here, but there was one little piece of her whispering it was smarter to keep him close, to make sure they didn't get separated, that keeping him safe would be easier if he was within arm's reach. She decided this once to listen. "Fine," she said. "But, you have to do exactly as I tell you."

"I will," Kam said.

"No, I'm serious, Kameron." Nikki got to eye-level with him. "If I say 'Run—'"

"I say 'How fast,'" Kam said, rolling his eyes. "I know."

"Not today." Nikki stared into his piercing blue eyes and put her hands on his shoulders. "Today, if I say 'Run,' you run as fast as you can, and you don't look back."

Kam nodded, eyes wide.

When the three got to the beach, they saw Nelly standing with Wyatt and Jo. Nikki could tell they had walked in on the middle of some major drama.

Wyatt caught sight of Nikki, Kam, and Emma. "You told *them* how to get here?" He practically yelled at Nelly.

"Not now!" Nelly turned her attention back on Jo. "I told you to stay away from the ocean."

"I didn't think you meant forever," Jo said.

"How about 'until further notice'? Does that work for you?"

"Just 'cause you have superpowers doesn't make you the boss," Jo sneered, crossing her arms.

"Guys!" Nikki said.

Nelly and Jo stared at her. The determination in their eyes was identical, two forces ready for battle.

"We need you guys to get out of here." Nikki looked at Jo, Wyatt, and then at Kam.

"Jo, take Kam with you."

"What?"

"I don't have any cash on me now, but I can pay you fifty bucks to take him as far away from here as you can. Have him back by…" Nikki grabbed Nelly's wrist and checked the time. "Six should do it." She turned and glanced from Emma to Nelly. "Six should be plenty of time, right? *This* should be over by then, right?"

"I don't know," Wyatt said, "who you even—"

"Wyatt!" Nelly stressed the first syllable in his name. "Do as she's telling you, please."

"No!" Wyatt said. "We came here to surprise you. As in 'Hello, I'm still alive!' Not that you apparently care anymore. I don't know why I wasted my time."

"Look!" Nikki took a step toward him. "I don't have time for your drama, Wyatt. You want to whine, fine, but take my brother with you, get up the hill, and get out of here. Take my car if you need; Kam will show you where it is."

"Nikki," Kam said quietly.

Wyatt scoffed. "You can't be serious," he said to Nelly. "You're really helping these *freaks*?"

Nelly flinched as though his last word had been a slap. Swallowing, she turned to Jo. "Please do this for me. Take Kam and go."

"Why can't you just tell us what's going on?" Jo said, uncrossing her arms.

"We're trying!" Emma practically shouted.

Everyone looked at her.

She took a deep breath and said as calmly as she could, "There is a tidal wave on its way here, right now. It should be here very soon. Nikki is worried about her brother and would like you guys to make sure he's safe. For now, please, let's be team players. For the sake of all of our lives, please listen to us. We know what we're talking about."

Wyatt barked out a laugh. "You guys ruined my best friend's life, and I'm supposed to just trust you now? Just be 'team players.' Sure: 'Can you believe that earthquake?'" Wyatt said, making his voice lower. Then, with a higher voice, he said, "'I know. Talk about freaky,'" His attempt at impersonating Nelly would have been amusing if the circumstances were not so dire.

"Um, guys?" Kam said.

"What's up?" Nelly asked, glancing at him.

Kam didn't say anything. He just pointed.

Nelly followed his hand right to the ocean. "Holy…" The water had receded back to the rock to which she and Jo would race. "It's coming! Any second now!"

That's when they heard the roar.

"Run!" Wyatt grabbed Nelly's hand, pulling her away from the beach.

"No, go with Jo!" Nelly yanked her hand from his and shoved Jo towards him. The two scrambled away as Nelly ran back towards the wall of water, now less than a hundred feet from them.

"Kam, go! Run!" Nikki shouted at him. The roaring of the water was deafening.

Kam didn't move.

"KAM, GO!" Nikki screamed, running to her brother and pushing him after Wyatt and Jo, who were already quite a ways up the hike. Kam finally moved. He started to run, but he seemed unable to tear his eyes off the water.

"HOLD IT, NELLY!" Emma screamed. Her breath caught in her chest as the familiarity of the words struck her.

"I'M TRYING! It's too big!" Nelly screamed.

"No," Emma whispered to herself. "No, no, no, no, no…"

"I can't—control it—I'm not powerful enough!" Nelly shouted between grunts of exertion. She stood, bracing herself with her back leg. The weight of the wave pressed on her, literally pushing her through the sand. She readjusted her feet, trying for more grip.

"EMMA!" Nikki yelled, running to stand next to Nelly.

Emma realized they had never joined hands, all three of them, in her vision. It was up to her. Perhaps death wasn't the only option. She ran next to the girls and grabbed Nikki's hand. The three united for the first time, and the effect was immediate. The loud roaring of the water stopped.

All went silent.

"What happened?" Nelly asked, starting to lower her hands as she looked around.

"No, don't," Emma warned, keeping her own hands up.

Nelly raised her hands again quickly. "But the wave—it stopped. I can't feel it pushing me anymore."

"Have we—did we stop *time*?" Nikki asked, looking at a bird mid-flap above them.

"I-I don't—it's not—this is impossible," Emma said.

"I think it's wearing off," Nelly said. "The water is starting to push back again." She dug her feet into the sand again.

"Emma," Nikki said, glancing at her brother, frozen in his frantic run.

"Make sure he makes it. Watch him. Go with him."

"Of course," Emma said, nodding.

"I don't know how long we'll be able to hold it," Nelly said, straining. "Warn everyone. Get them to high ground. Hurry." Nelly grunted the last word. The rumble of the water grew.

Letting go of the others, Emma raced after Kam, who was beginning to run as though in slow motion. Then all at once, time pushed forward, and the world moved again.

The full weight of the giant wall of water pushed on Nikki and Nelly, hands still linked.

Nikki squeezed her eyes shut, focused on the image of her power moving into Nelly, who felt it surge through her as the ocean thundered, outmatching them both. The two girls dug their feet into the sand, trying to find some way to ground themselves.

"We can't hold it," Nelly admitted. "But I can give you a head start."

Nikki could feel the energy of the wave. The energy from her magickal waves had been light and yellow. This wave felt nothing like hers; it was fast and dense, deep maroon, violent and thirsty, larger than anything she had produced in their practice.

"But—"

"I'm a mermaid," Nelly grunted. "It's not like I'm going to drown."

Nikki nodded quickly and murmured a spell, the words spilling out of her before she thought about them. "That should give you a little more time," Nikki said. "See you soon?"

"Yeah," Nelly hissed, through gritted teeth. "Go!" The water pressed against her, like it had a will of its own, and its only desire was to crush her.

The girls released hands, and Nikki ran as fast as she could, grateful she had worn sneakers. She felt an animalistic desperation overtake her body and senses. Completely ignoring the windy path that led back to civilization, Nikki scrambled straight up with no regard for the scratching trees and thorny plants. Hyper-aware of her surroundings, Nikki heard scuffling behind her. She chanced a glance back and was amazed to see Nelly clambering up. The two girls reached the top in record time. The parking lot was chaos. People were scrambling over each other, screaming as they tried to escape what would be a watery grave.

Nikki looked at Nelly, wide-mouthed but unable to speak.

"Henry," Nelly yelled in answer to Nikki's unasked question.

Nikki gave a quick nod to show her understanding. She turned sharply. Someone had called her name. "Did you hear that?" Nikki shouted at Nelly.

"It sounded like it came from over there!" Nelly yelled, pointing to the shops.

Shopkeepers had pulled out ladders and were helping people onto rooftops. It was no longer about getting away; now, it was about not getting swept away. There just wasn't anymore time to run.

"COME ON!" Nikki grabbed Nelly's hand and led the way through the swarming crowd. She spotted Emma and Kam at the base of the science shop.

Emma had also been scanning the crowd as she held the ladder which Kam was climbing up. She waved when she saw Nikki and Nelly. Emma looked wild-eyed at her friends as they raced to her. "How did you—"

"Henry," Nelly said, panting. "Get up, and I'll tell you."

"Go first," Emma said to Nikki.

Nikki crawled up the ladder and quickly found Kam's face among the others on the roof. She ran and hugged him. "Oh, you're safe."

"How did you make it out of there?" Kam asked. "That was the biggest wave I've ever seen in my life."

"Nelly's uncle helped us," Nikki explained. "But it's not over. The wave is still going to hit, okay? Hold on, and we'll be fine." Nikki hugged her brother again. She closed her eyes and visualized her magick reinforcing the building upon which they stood, spreading like spider's silk, golden and gleaming as it entwined with the bones of the building, securing it to the surface of the earth. Nikki opened her eyes.

Emma and Nelly had caught up. Emma was zipping off her jacket and laying it on the roof to sit down on.

"Where are Wyatt and Jo?" Nelly asked.

"I'm not sure," Emma said, shaking her head. "I looked for them when we got up here, but…" Emma gestured around her. While a good majority of the people were on rooftops, there were still screaming people running around below.

Nelly nodded. "I'm sure they're fine."

More people piled on to the flat roof of the science shop until there was a decent sized crowd. The girls had just settled in when the people around them started screaming and pointing. The girls turned and saw the water finally headed towards them.

"Hang on to something!" Nelly yelled, grabbing on to some piping.

The four had been pushed to one side of the roof. The wave hit, and the building groaned on impact. Nelly held tight to the piping. Nikki held Kam with one arm and the piping with the other. Emma held on to a bit of jutting concrete. Water sprayed them as it filled the street below them.

There was a *yap* from a small dog. A woman chasing after the dog ran through Kam and Emma, stopping just before the edge of the building. The woman bumped Kam and Emma forward, knocking them both off balance as a second wave hit. All four went off the edge into the rushing water.

"NO!" Nikki screamed. She stood, but Nelly was already diving in. Nikki froze, tears streaming down her face. The sky cracked unexpectedly, and there was a sudden downpour, like the very earth was mourning the loss of Kam and Emma.


Under the water, churning through the roiling waves, Emma looked around. Her brain had not fully caught up to current events; she did not comprehend she had fallen in. What she did comprehend was the burning in her lungs. Everything around her was awash of brown and sickly green. The longer she looked around, the more she recognized a vision coming true. Emma looked for Kam. She saw him, looking up at her, eyes bulging and wild with fear. She reached out to him, but she was pulled away. Her vision tunneled as her lungs screamed for air. Later, she would recount how the last thing she saw was a flash of blue before everything faded to darkness.

Henry, of course, had saved her. He had found her and brought her to the roof where Nikki was still standing and sobbing.

"Take her," Henry called, handing Emma's body to Nikki. Without knowing, Nikki used a combination of willpower, adrenaline, and magick to lift her limp friend back on to the roof. Henry came out of the water, transforming seamlessly. Between the torrential rain and commotion, no one on the roof had noticed his blue tail turn to tanned legs. Henry did a few chest compressions. Luckily, Emma wasn't far gone enough to need much. She was throwing up water quickly, color flooding back into her face.

"Kam," she said, hoarse.

"Nelly went down," Nikki croaked, turning her bloodshot eyes on Henry. "She went in after him. There was also a woman and her dog. They all fell in."

Henry didn't say a word. He turned around and dived back in. A few people screamed.

Meanwhile, Nelly swam frantically in the churning water, dodging debris, fighting unruly currents, and scanning for any sign of Emma or Kam. She had just dodged a car when Henry found her.

"I got Emma!" He had to shout to be heard over the crunching of metal on metal as cars were shoved into buildings and each other.

"Kam?" Nelly shouted back.

Henry shook his head. "Keep looking!" They split up.

Nelly fought her way through the brown water. It was thick and heavy with wreckage and junk; she had battle for every inch. Even now, the ocean fought her. Anyone other than a mermaid would have drowned. She surfaced momentarily to gain her bearings, holding onto a stoplight to keep from being swept away. The sun peeked through the storm clouds, not enough to warm her, but enough to help her see through the din and spray. Her nose was assaulted by the briny smell of the water. She could see the roof where Emma and Nikki waited. She swam over to them, a pain shot through her tail as she reached them, knowing what she had to say.

"I can't find him! I've looked everywhere," Nelly confessed.

Nikki threw up.

"Wait." Emma took Nelly's hand. They both felt cold.

*Kam was floating lifelessly, a bit of rope tangled around his foot.*

"Was that a vision?" Nelly asked, pulling her hand back.

"A short one," Emma said. "Does it help?"

"I—I think I know where he is," Nelly said, diving back into the water.

Nikki had collapsed into a sobbing heap. Emma knelt at the edge of the roof, looking around and watching the water. Each roof was now its own island. The water still rushed around but it had stopped rising. After what seemed like ages, Nelly finally swam over. She carried something—someone—in her arms. Emma's eyes pooled, blurring her eyesight as she reached into the water and pulled out the pale, lifeless body of her friend's little brother. Barefoot and half-naked, Nelly got out of the water. Although her transformation wasn't as seamless as Henry's, no one noticed her change either.

All eyes were on Kam.

The wind and rain had plastered Emma's hair to her face. She set Kam's limp body down, and absent-mindedly handed her now soaked jacket to her friend. Nelly put it around her waist and zipped it up, creating a make-shift skirt.

"I can save him," Nelly said, kneeling down.

Emma put a hand on Nelly's hand, "No one—"

"My grandma—she—she said I have the power to save. My instructions were 'Save him.' I thought she meant Wyatt, but..." Nelly put her hands on Kam's chest.

"Who?" Emma asked.

Nelly focused on Kam. She pictured his water-filled lungs. She lifted her hands slowly and magickally pulled a bit of water out of his lungs. It wasn't enough; there was still too much water. Doubt crept up the back of Nelly's neck, but a science lesson that seemed ages ago rushed forward in her mind: dihydrogen monoxide. Water. Oxygen. There was oxygen in water. Nelly focused on pulling hydrogen gas out of Kam, leaving fresh, clean oxygen in his lungs, but outwardly, Kam seemed unchanged. It just wasn't enough. Nelly abandoned magick and began CPR. Color slowly flowed back into Kam as his blood was shoved through his body, but he did not wake up.

"Nelly," Emma said gently, putting her hand on Nelly's shoulder.

"No!" Nelly shoved her off and tilted Kam's head, pinching his nose. She blew a gentle breath into his lungs. "Do the compressions!" Nelly grabbed Emma and shoved her on top of Kam.

Emma began half-hearted compressions.

"Like you mean it," Nelly snapped.

Choking back tears, Emma pushed hard on Kam's chest. She pushed down over and over again, cracking one of his ribs.

Nelly waited until just before Emma had finished her compressions; she put a hand on Kam's forehead, not really knowing what she was doing. She moved by instinct. Her mother's words came back to her: "Let the water do the work."

"Let the magick do the work," she whispered as touched her forehead to the side of his face. Nelly whispered, "Jeg ånder vandet af liv i dig."

Emma finished the compressions.

Nelly breathed into Kam once more. She felt magick in this breath. Kam rose beneath her hands, hovering a few inches off the ground. A light blue glow cocooned him. Nelly felt her magick move through his body, repairing his broken rib, closing up scratches, healing bruises, and spreading life.

"Come on, Kam," Nelly whispered, watching his face.

He took a deep and sudden breath. There was no coughing—Nelly had rid his lungs of ocean water. He floated back down. "Nikki?" he croaked.

Nikki scrambled over to him, sobbing as she pulled him into her arms.

"You did it," Emma said, sinking down in relief.

"Did you find him?" Henry suddenly asked.

Nelly and Emma turned around to see him, bobbing in the water and holding on to the edge of the roof.

"I haven't—" Henry looked sick. "I've looked everywhere. I found that lady and her rat." He pointed with his thumb behind him.

"We found him," Nelly said.

"How is he?" Henry asked, looking past them at Nikki, who clung to Kam, both crying silently.

"I think he's going to be okay," Nelly said. "Have you seen Jo?"

"No," Henry said. "But I'll pop around to some of the other buildings and see if I can find her."

"Henry?" Nelly said, before he went underwater again.

"Yeah?"

"Thanks," she said. "Thanks for the training, and for back there, for everything." Nelly nodded. "I—we—you saved us."

"You're welcome," he said with a small nod. He slipped below the water again.

1 January 2009

Something happened today. Something terrible and terrifying but somehow necessary. Kam died but only for a little while. I don't know if he's fully aware of what's happened. We were left in our hospital room alone, and we decided it was best if we didn't tell anyone about what happened to Kam. We promised to tell him more after we've all rested and been properly nourished. Something else happened, but the three of us haven't been alone to discuss it, and I don't dare write it. Not yet. Not until we know more.

All five of them were crammed into a hospital room. Emma sat in a chair in the corner closest to the bed where Nikki and Kam sat, while Nelly, now wearing scrubs, snoozed on another bed. The girls had been prepared to lie and say they were family to be put in the same room, but the masses of people being admitted meant everyone was sharing rooms. Voices shouted outside their door, waking Nelly who sat up, looking around.

"It's okay," Emma said. "You can lie back down, Nels."

"No way." Nelly stretched. "Next time I lay down, I'm doing it for real, in my bed—and I'm not getting up for a year." She groaned as she rolled her neck.

"These pillows suck."

"Three guess who that is," Nikki said as one voice shouted loud enough for the five of them to decipher words.

"Congratulations, Kaitlyn. You've finally done it. Nikki's dead! Are you happy now?"

"Mom," Kam sighed to Nikki.

"Don't be ridiculous, Margret. Nikki is the most powerful being of her kind to ever exist! Do you honestly believe a little water will stand in her way?"

"Grandma," Nikki guessed, glancing at Kam.

"She is a CHILD!" Margret shot back, throwing open the door.

Margret ran to her children, hugging them both. Margret and Kait continued to bicker. Nelly squirmed, uncomfortable around the tension Margret and Kait built around them, but Emma noticed their voices were fading, quickly going from muffled to silent.

She knew what was going to happen next. Emma was going to see herself, and she understood her message now. She mouthed as slowly and obviously as she could, "There's no time to explain. Keep him home. Keep Kam away from the water." She knew from memory the vision was over. She had tried to warn herself, and she knew she wouldn't be able to understand anyway.

Emma folded the piece of paper she had written on and stood, gesturing to Nelly to follow.

When they got out of the room, Nelly leaned over, "Where to?"

Emma nodded towards the nurse's desk. "Excuse me," she said to the nurse, who was on the phone. When the nurse glanced up, Emma smiled and quickly said, "We're looking for Josephine Hansen and Wyatt Fletcher."

The nurse jabbed her pen towards a large whiteboard. "Uh-huh, yes, sir. No, I understand," she said into the phone.

"Thanks," Emma whispered.

The girls scanned the board, leaning closer to read through the dry-erase names all crammed together.

"Here," Nelly said, pointing. "We're in 205. Wyatt is right across from our room."

"Jo is a few doors down," Emma said. "I'll go see him; you go see her."

"Come on," Nelly said, breaking into a jog.

The girls dodged nurses and doctors, one of whom told them to slow down. They worked their way through the sterile hallway. Nelly kept jogging towards

Jo's room as Emma ducked into Wyatt's.

"Wyatt?" Emma whispered. Several people were in this room, a partition had been put up between them. The people pointed to the corner. Monitors beeped. Emma rounded the partition and saw several tubes and wires leading to a form laying under a thin, white hospital blanket.

"Are you family?" A nurse asked, standing by the bed.

"Cousin," Emma lied. "How's he doing?"

"He'll be okay." The nurse made a note on her clipboard.

"Was he caught in the tidal wave?"

"The girl he was brought in with said they both were, but someone dragged them out and put them on a roof with a woman and a dog. People are so incredible." The nurse hung the clipboard at the end of his bed. "I'll give you two a moment alone." She squeezed Emma's shoulder as she left to check on the others.

"Thanks," Emma said. She took Wyatt's hand, amazed by how warm it was. She whispered his name, softly squeezing his hand. When a tear fell on her hand, Emma realized she was crying. Could she have spared him from this? Could she have kept him safe? This was her fault somehow; she was sure of it. She wiped away her tears with her other hand.

"He was under longer than I was," a voice said from behind Emma.

Emma turned around. Jo was standing with Nelly.

"Henry saved you two, didn't he?" Emma whispered.

Jo nodded. "So much for deadbeat Henry, right?" She cracked a smile at Nelly, but it wavered.

"Turns out he's useful after all," Nelly said. "Does he know a—you know—rescued him?"

"I don't think so," Jo said. "He came to pretty quickly after we got out of the water, but Henry was gone before I could say anything."

"He came back and told me he found you, but he also said he had to go," Nelly said. "I would have asked him to find you guys sooner, but we were looking for Kam."

"How is he?" Jo said, but before anyone could answer, she started crying. "We should have done what you said," she choked out between sobs. "We should have taken him and run."

Nelly hugged her.

"He's okay," Emma said. "Here, sit." She let go of Wyatt and pulled up a chair for Jo.

Jo sat, tears still streaming down her cheeks.

"Everyone is going to be okay," Nelly said. "Like Dad says, no harm, no foul."

"Oh my gosh! Dad! Has anyone called him?" Jo said, alarmed and looking at Nelly.

"You guys go back to Jo's room," Emma said. "If he comes looking for you, it'll be there. I'll ask a nurse if they've called Wyatt's mom. Nelly, I'll meet you back in the room later. If I don't see you, we'll talk tomorrow."

Nelly then did something that surprised her as well as Emma: she hugged Emma and said, "Thank you."

After a stunned moment, Emma hugged back and nodded. Emma did as she said she would: she made sure someone had called Wyatt's mom and the Hansen girls' dad, just in case. Then Emma took a walk around the hospital. Her mass of visions made sense now. There were people crying and mourning the loss of loved ones, but there were also people crying as they celebrated reunited families. Thankfully, Emma did not see any limp children. One had been enough. The weight of Kam's body in her arms haunted her. She tried not to think about it—she knew she would have to face it sooner or later; she just preferred later.

Emma circled around and made her way back to 205. Before she got to the room, she was met by Rachelle and Ethel. They hugged her.

"You did it," Rachelle said, squeezing Emma tightly.

Emma smiled as Rachelle let go.

"You brave, brave girl." Ethel kissed Emma's forehead, holding her face between her hands.

"I didn't do anything," Emma said. "Honest. It was Nikki, and Nelly, and Henry."

"Henry?" Rachelle asked.

"He's Nelly's uncle and possible mentor," Emma said.

"I know who he is," Rachelle said. "I'm just surprised he was there."

"So were we, but we couldn't have done it without him." Emma sighed. It was finally over.


January 1, 2009 (much later)

You're not going to believe this, but Henry found my journal in my car (which is still underwater). He got it and dried it out for me. I thought that was sweet but also kind of unnecessary. I only have a few pages left in this thing anyway. He dropped it by the house, said he figured he'd bring it by since he wanted to check on Kam. He just left.

So here's the update: we had the massive tidal wave (massive is not an understatement). The three of us froze time (but for like a second—I don't think it actually affected anything). Nelly and I tried to stop the tidal wave—we couldn't. Henry could. Well, he could long enough for us to get away. Kam died but is not dead. Nelly used some kind of mermaid magick to bring him back. I was completely useless when I thought he was gone.

We're finally home. We're all meeting tomorrow (at Madam Ortega's, of course) to go over what happened, and then Nelly, Em, Kam, and I are meeting separately to go over what really happened. We decided it's best not to tell anyone about Kam or freezing time until we understand more about what happened. I think we should ask Henry about Kam since he knows more about mermaid magick, but I haven't brought it up to anyone else yet.

"Are you busy?" Kam asked, poking his head in Nikki's room.

"Just finishing up," Nikki said. "What's up?"

"I wanted to say thanks," Kam said, coming in the room and sitting at the foot of Nikki's bed. "Thanks for saving me," he added in a whisper.

"As much as I'd love to take credit for that, it was Nelly who saved you," Nikki whispered back and squeezed his hand.

"We're talking about it tomorrow, right?"

Nikki nodded. "We're having two meetings: one with the adults, and one with those of us who were actually there."

"So," Kam said. "No telling what really happened?"

"Not all of it," Nikki said, shaking her head.

"What are you two whispering about in here?" Margret came into Nikki's room carrying a tray with three steaming mugs of hot chocolate and a little bowl filled with mini marshmallows.

"The usual," Nikki said nonchalantly.

"Dinosaurs and starships," Kam said, smiling.

"You two have been giving me that answer for years," Margret said. She put the tray down on the bed. She stared at the floor for a second; her lip quivered as pooled tears broke down her cheeks. "I almost lost you two today," she managed to say.

"But you didn't lose us," Kam said, standing. "We're right here." He hugged her.

"You're right," Margret said, squeezing him. "But with the close call with the bonfire, and now this…" She took a deep breath. "I don't like magick—I never have—but if there is one thing you've shown me, Nikki," Margret said as she took her daughter by the hand. "You can handle yourself. I've always known you were strong and resourceful. You're like your dad that way." She smiled. "If I had it my way—but it doesn't matter. My point is I trust you. You can choose for yourself, and if you want to continue with magick, and learn from Kaitlyn, then that's fine with me."

Nikki hardly dared to believe what she was hearing. "Mom, I don't—I mean, are you—"

Margret pulled Nikki close to her, so she held one child in each arm. "I haven't spent enough time with you two, lately, and I was reminded today you are my most important work. There will always be more houses to sell, but…" Her chin trembled as she whimpered. Margret gasped and held her breath for a moment. "I can't afford to lose any more time with you."

# Chapter Twenty-Eight
## Wednesday, January 2nd

Jan. 2, 09

Does it sound insane to say I was born to be a mermaid? I mean, I used to believe surfing was the reason I was put on this planet, but now? I know I was put here to be a mermaid. I was put here to save Kam's life.

I saved his life.

Yesterday was probably the wildest, scariest day of my life. The short version is Kam fell off a roof into crazy tidal waters. I'll never forget the sound Nikki made when Kam fell in. If someone had told me she had just been stabbed, I would have believed it. When I finally found him, he didn't look good. I tried literally everything I could think of, but nothing worked until I remembered the words from that letter: "Save him. It is of the utmost importance you save him. You have the power to do it. Trust your instincts. Trust the water. Water is life. You have the power. Save him."

It was wild. Nikki told me once about doing spells but not knowing how she did it. It never make sense to me, but I get it now. I said something, something I don't fully remember and I have no idea what it meant, but I said it. Then, I breathed into Kam, and he was alive. I mean, it wasn't all lame and Baywatchy

Nelly looked at her last line. Was it inappropriate to take such a serious moment and lighten it up with some Baywatch humor? It was her journal, and she was the only one who would ever read it—well, and maybe her children one day, like she was reading the journal of her ancestors.

She was pulled from her thoughts by the buzzing of her phone; it was a text from Emma ('Bring Jo and Wyatt to the meeting—my grandma's request'). There were an additional 87 unread text messages, but she didn't bother with them. Instead, she tossed her phone on her bed and stretched, standing up. She listened as the guy on the radio continued to go over the statistics regarding the damage from the tidal wave and earthquake:

"That's over ten million dollars in damages, but it could have been worse, folks. It really could have been worse. Scientists are trying to determine where the tidal wave started. In other local news, a freak lightning strike set a home on fire, though it was eventually extinguished by the tidal—"

Nelly turned it off, calling "Jo!" as she walked over to Jo's room. She knocked on the door.

"Come in," Jo groaned from inside.

Nelly opened the door and went inside Jo's room, which was as different from Nelly's room as Jo was from Nelly. Nelly's room had a few surf posters pinned up on the baby blue walls, which were otherwise barren. Jo's walls were each painted a different color: amethyst purple, lemon yellow, azure blue, and a particularly bright number Jo lovingly referred to as "flamingo pink"—each color just as bright and bold as she was. Every wall was plastered with posters, pictures, and all kinds of random things Jo had nailed up: an old surf fin, a couple of doorknobs, four different calendars from three different years. She had even framed a few of her favorite childhood wall scribbles, adding an empty frame right to the wall.

"You're still in bed?" Nelly asked, poking one of the two feet peeking out of Jo's sheets.

"I almost drowned yesterday," Jo said, her voice muffled by covers. "I get to sleep in." She pulled her feet back under the covers, also bright and hodgepodgey.

"You and Wyatt need to come with me," Nelly said. She walked over to Jo's dresser and picked out some clean clothes.

"Wyatt can't come," Jo said.

"What are you talking about?"

Jo held up her cell phone in answer to Nelly's question and tossed it to the foot of her bed before retreating back under her covers.

Nelly rolled her eyes and took the phone. "What am I looking for?" Nelly asked, unlocking the phone—it was one of Tom's family rules regarding cellphone etiquette and safety: everyone can unlock everyone else's phones. The girls had his password as well.

"Text messages." Jo rolled over, peeking out of her nest.

"Okay," Nelly said.

She scrolled through Jo's texts. Most of them were from Jo's friends from school, asking if she was okay and talking about the tidal wave. Finally, one labeled 'Ms. F' popped up. It read: 'Update on Wyatt—the doctors say he's going to be fine, but they want to keep him until Thursday just to make sure we're completely out of the woods.'

"Why didn't I get this text?" Nelly glanced at Jo's heap of blankets.

"You probably did, but you never read your messages unless you hear them come in," Jo grumbled.

"Come on." Nelly said, throwing the phone and clothes on the bed. "We've got to get going. Go shower, and I'll meet you in the kitchen in ten minutes."

"Do I have to come?" Jo sat up in bed. Her hair was wild, part of it glued to her face by a good night's sleep.

"Yes," Nelly said. "And you definitely need a shower."


January 2, 2009

I thought today would bring relief. We'd be on the other end. It'd be over, and it is, and I am, but also I feel...weird. I have a million questions, and I definitely need some therapy to sort out the last two weeks. Are there magickal therapists?


Nikki sighed, closing her journal. It wasn't much of an entry, but her thoughts still felt so jumbled there was no point in trying to get them down. She checked her clock: 11:30. They were supposed to be at Ethel's house at noon. She took a quick shower, towel-dried her hair, and threw on the only clean clothes she had: an old pair of jeans and a faded "Yellow Submarine" t-shirt which used to be her dad's from his "lighter leaner" days as he called them.

"You ready to go, Kam?" Nikki called through the hallway.

"Almost," came the call from Kam's room.

There was a honk at the front of the house. Nikki ran out and waved Nelly in. Nelly turned off the truck, and she and Jo came into the house.

"Thanks for giving us a ride," Nikki said as the two girls entered into the kitchen. "My mom is working on getting a rental, but it probably won't come until tomorrow."

"No worries" Nelly shrugged.

"How did your car survive?" Nikki asked, setting her bag on the counter.

"I ran to the Cove," Nelly said. "I hoped running would work some nerves out."

"Did it?" Nikki asked.

"Not really," Nelly admitted.

"Ready," Kam said, cheery and smiling.

The drive to Ethel's house was sunny, bright, and warm, filled with classics from the oldies station. When the four reached Ethel's house, they piled out, Nikki and Jo from the back, and Nelly and Kam from the cab. Kait greeted them as they entered the house.

"Merry Meet, you all!" Kait hugged each of them in turn.

"This is Nelly and Jo," Nikki said.

"Merry Meet, my dears," Kait said, hugging both girls, who smiled politely.

The front room was filled with familiar faces. Of course, Ethel was there with Rachelle in the kitchen, predictably fixing something to eat. Gabby and Henry were bringing in a few extra chairs, and Emma sat on a couch. Kam and Nikki sat on either side of Emma. Nelly quickly found a seat on the other couch across from Emma while Jo snuggled into the loveseat between couches. The five started chatting. The room filled with the tittering and laughter of gathered friends and family.

"Everyone is here," Kait called to the kitchen.

"Go ahead and sit down," Ethel called back.

Kait found a seat next to Nelly.

Henry stood behind Nikki, leaning against the wall. She could sense him behind her; if she would have focused on this feeling, she would have sensed him more clearly, the way his magick moved in him like a gentle stream, steady, clean, and clear. As it was, she didn't yet know to focus on the feeling; instead, she briefly caught Henry's eye, felt blood rush to her face, and immediately turned away, inwardly reprimanding herself because the last time she had seen him, she had been a mess. She hoped he didn't remember, and then decided she shouldn't care (even though she did very much).

While Nikki faced her internal struggle, Ethel, Gabby, and Rachelle found seats on the extra chairs. As everyone settled, the conversation died down.

Jo raised her hand, but Nelly smacked it down. "This isn't school, Jo. You don't have to raise your hand."

Ethel smiled and asked, "What's your question, Jo?"

"I know Wyatt and I were both asked to be here," Jo quickly said, "but the hospital wanted to keep Wyatt longer, but—um—that's not my question. It's isn't really a question at all. My question is, basically, why am *I* here? I don't have any powers, yet, so…"

"You were asked to come," Ethel said, "because we want to hear your side of the story."

"Oh," Jo said. "Okay."

"I believe the events start at a beach?" Rachelle said.

"The Cove," Nelly corrected. "I mean, that's what we call it."

"Were you there from the beginning?" Kait asked Nelly.

"Yeah," Nelly said. "I was the first one there."

"Tell us what happened," Ethel said. "Don't leave out a detail."

"Uh, okay." Nelly took a deep breath. She told her entire story. No one asked any questions or interrupted her. When Nelly mentioned Emma falling in but failed to include Kam, Henry coughed, but Nelly ignored him. She finished her story at the hospital, where she had been reunited with Jo.

"Interesting," Kait said when Nelly was done.

"Emma," Ethel said, "please tell your part of the story."

Emma picked up the story from when she had grabbed Kam and how they had run up the hill as fast as they could. She confessed how bad she felt about leaving Nikki and Nelly and how she focused on getting Kam somewhere safe. Kam had suggested the science store's roof, so they went there. Emma told the rest of the story, following Nelly's lead, leaving out Kam's near-death experience. She, too, ended her story at the hospital.

"Nikki," Ethel said.

Nikki related her part of the story. She had already written Rand about what had happened, so telling the story a second time was easy. "When Nelly and I got back to Main Street," she said, "I heard someone call my name. I—I'm not sure how I know this, but I know I only heard my name because of magick. I mean, it was complete chaos up there; there's no way I should have heard my name as clearly as I did."

"I forgot about that," Nelly said.

"You heard it, too?" Kait asked, looking at Nelly.

Nelly nodded. "Like she said, it was loud. Between the people and the water, there's no way we should've heard it."

"Interesting," Ethel said, clasping her hands together. "What happened next?"

Nikki finished the events, also leaving out Kam's brush with death.

"I'm quite interested in Kameron's side of the story," Kait said, "but let's hear from Henry first."

"I was," Henry said, pausing, "home. I didn't think the tidal wave was coming. Sorry, Emma, but when you spend your whole life in the ocean..." He shrugged as if hoping this explained his skepticism.

"It's okay," Emma said.

"Anyway, I felt the earthquake yesterday morning and figured the tidal wave would be coming after all," Henry said. "I high-tailed it over to the Cove. Nelly was already there, and I saw Nikki running away. I figured out pretty quickly what their plan was, and for the record, it was a very stupid plan."

"I wouldn't have drowned," Nelly protested.

"No, because you would have been crushed to death first. It would've been like getting hit by a cement wall doing thirty miles per hour," Henry said, shaking his head. "One thing I will give you credit for is you're both a lot stronger than you think you are."

"What are you talking about?" Nelly asked.

"You guys weren't just holding the single wave in the Cove. You were holding back the entire tide for about a mile up and down the shoreline. Also…" Henry paused for a moment. "It wasn't a natural wave."

"How do you know?" Emma asked.

"How many natural tsunamis do you know of that focus only on one tiny town?"

"What do you mean?" Nelly asked.

"You guys were working against magicked water," Henry said, his jaw set.

"How do you know?" Nikki asked.

"I could feel it."

"It didn't feel any different than when we practiced. Majorly stronger, sure, but that's it," Nelly said, shaking her head.

"You practiced with *magicked* water." Henry pointed at Nikki. "Remember?"

"Wait, so, you're saying someone *made* the wave?" Nelly said, sitting up.

"Tsunamis usually hit the whole coast, or at least a giant part of it. This was tactical. It was aimed *only* at Otter Sands. It was magickally created."

"Someone did this *on purpose*? You mean—"

"We'll get there in a moment," Ethel interrupted. "Henry, please finish."

"Whatever spell you used was powerful, witch. Between your spell and Nelly's focus, your hold stretched over a two-mile span."

Looking at Henry, Nikki tilted her head and narrowed her eyes. "You could *feel* that?"

Henry nodded. "You know how some people can tell how heavy something is by picking it up?"

"Yeah," Nikki said. "My dad is good at that."

"Same thing," Henry said. "I've had enough practice I can tell how much and how far. Anyway, I held the water until I was pretty sure the girls were somewhere safe. I walked back into the water and went along for the ride." He clicked his tongue.

"What happened after the wave hit?" Ethel asked. "The girls mention you saved Emma."

"Yeah," Henry said, glancing from Nelly to Nikki. "I-uh saw Nelly jump into the water and figured she had a good reason, so I headed over there and started circling the building. Swimming in tidal waters is a lot more difficult than swimming in the ocean. You have to watch out for debris, and the currents are insane. It takes a lot of magick to swim. I eventually saw Nelly get close to Emma, and then a car almost took her out. I knew Nelly would be fine, but it'd be virtually impossible for her to find Emma again, and Emma was losing color quick. I got her out of the water and handed her up to Nikki. Emma was out. I did a few chest compressions, and she came back pretty fast.

"I," Henry glanced at Nelly. "I went back in the water to find Nelly and tell her about Emma. I also found the lady and her dog. I put them up on a close-by roof. They were fine. I met Nelly back at the roof, and Nelly asked if I would make sure Wyatt and Jo were all right. I found Jo hanging on to the top of a tree with her arm around Wyatt's chest, holding him up. I took Wyatt first to that same roof I took the dog lady. I administered CPR until he came around and then turned him onto his side to let him breathe. I told the lady to make sure he stayed that way. Afterwards, I picked up Jo, dropped her off at the roof, and told her to make sure the EMTs got a hold of Wyatt. Finally, I went back, told all of this to Nelly, and told her I'd see them all later." Henry shrugged like saving four people's lives—six if they counted Nikki and Nelly, which they did—was no big deal. "I didn't want to be around when the EMT guys came and started poking and prodding. My physiology is different enough from a human's that they'd want to run more tests, and eventually figure me out," Henry added by way of explanation.

"Thank you, Henry." Ethel smiled. Her expressed gratitude was for more than his story.

Henry nodded.

Ethel cleared her throat and said, "Kameron, if you please."

"Okay," Kam said, grinning. He had been preparing for this all morning.

Nikki caught Henry's eye and smiled at him as a silent 'Thanks for leaving Kam out of this.' He raised his eyebrows and pursed his lips; Nikki understood his meaning: 'I want an explanation later.' Nikki nodded. This went unnoticed by the rest of the room, all of whom listened as Kam told the story of what had happened to him with full gesticulation. He, of course, left out his almost dying, but by the way he told the story, he'd had more than one close call. By the time he was finished, everyone was smiling, knowing much of his story had to have been one of the many exaggerated chronicles of the almost-eleven-year old.

"Well done, fighting off the shark," Kait said, shaking her fist.

Kam shrugged and said, "It was nothing—especially compared to the giant squid I had to defend everyone from after the shark."

Nikki and Nelly exchanged glances and smiled.

"Well done," Ethel said. "Now, Jo, we'd like to hear your side. Was Wyatt with you the whole time?"

Jo nodded.

"We'll consider this his side as well," Ethel said. "Go ahead."

"Well," Jo started. "Wyatt called me. He wanted to talk to me and Nelly somewhere private and asked if he could pick us up. I said sure and went to find Nelly, but she was already gone. Wyatt got there and asked where she was. That's when we found the note saying she was at the Cove. Wyatt wanted to meet her there, but I told him Nelly said we shouldn't go by the ocean. He said that was dumb, so we went. When we got there…" Jo glanced at her sister. "Um, we all argued for a while, and then Nikki told us to take Kam and run, but we thought she was crazy, sorry," she added, glancing at Nikki.

Nikki shrugged.

Fidgeting with her hair, Jo continued, "Kam pointed out the ocean, which had receded a ton, and there was a tidal wave coming for us. We ran as fast and far as we could, me and Wyatt, I mean. Wyatt wanted to get in the car and drive away, but I said we didn't have time. We kept running, and for a little while, we were the only ones running, but as people looked at the ocean, they saw the tidal wave, and soon the whole area was full of panicking people. I don't remember everything," Jo admitted. "It was all really hectic, and it's all kind of blurred together."

"Just tell us what you remember, dear," Ethel said.

"I remember running and then being swept away. Wyatt was behind me. On the drive over, he had told me his lungs were pretty bad after the bonfire, and he wasn't supposed to run for like two months. Well, Wyatt was running as hard as he could, and he was having a hard time doing it. I didn't realize until—well, anyway, the water came, and somehow I found myself holding on to the top of a tree. Wyatt flew past me, but I grabbed him. I just reached out and grabbed him," Jo said, staring ahead as though she was seeing it all over again, as if she didn't really believe she had done it. "He was only kind of conscious, but I was able to hold him with one arm and keep my other arm wrapped around the tree. I remember thinking I needed to keep his face out of the water. I don't think we were holding on very long before Henry came. He took Wyatt and was gone for a little while and then he grabbed me. When I saw Wyatt lying on his side, I realized he hadn't drowned. His lungs were still healing and just couldn't give him as much oxygen as he needed," Jo finished and sat quietly, staring at the rug.

"I think you're wrong, dear," Rachelle said.

"What?" Jo asked, looking up.

"I think you've got a bit of magick in you already," Rachelle said.

"I agree," Gabby said. "It's not mature enough to manifest itself like Nelly's has yet, but it's definitely there."

Jo smiled, nodded, and looked back down.

"Would you like some sandwiches?" Ethel asked, standing.

"Wait, that's it?" Nelly said.

"What do you mean?" Kait asked.

"You aren't going to explain anything? I mean, someone *did* this. It wasn't natural," Nelly said, pointing to Henry. "He just told us it was magick! He said it was 'tactical.'"

"We need some time to process," Kait explained. "To explain the events, first we needed to hear them, and now we take some time to understand them. When we understand them, we will explain any significance you haven't already figured out."

Nelly looked like she wanted to say more but didn't know how to say it.

Kait went into the kitchen.

"If someone could bring those chairs into the dining room," Ethel said, following Kait. "We'll eat in there."

Gabby grabbed one chair, and Rachelle took the other. Kam looked at Nikki for permission to go, and she nodded. Emma, Jo, and Nelly, who was still grumbling, followed everyone else into the kitchen. Nikki turned around and saw Henry walking around the couch. He sat down next to her.

"You want to tell me why we lied?" Henry whispered, leaning back against the couch.

"We didn't lie," Nikki whispered back. "We just…left out part of the truth."

"Same thing," Henry whispered.

Nikki and Henry locked eyes for a moment. Sitting up a straighter, she tore her gaze from him and returned her stare to the dining room, where everyone else was either seated or serving themselves. She chewed her lip and leaned back, looking at Henry again. "We're meeting later to talk about what happened… what *really* happened," she whispered. "We were going to meet at the Cove, but I checked online, and it's still underwater. The waters have mostly receded from the shops, but the levels are still high enough and the Cove is far down enough it's still underwater. I read it could take anywhere from a few hours to several days for the waters to completely recede to normal tidal levels. I mean, the levels seem to be on their way down, so it most likely will be sooner rather than—"

"Are you okay?" Henry asked suddenly.

"I'm—the—what?" She swallowed.

"You're rambling about water levels," Henry whispered, leaning closer.

"I just—um," Nikki stumbled, suddenly very aware of Henry's knee touching hers. She adjusted her leg, picking a bit of imaginary lint off her pants. She cleared her throat and managed to squeak out, "I'm fine."

Henry glanced at Kam and then looked at Nikki again. "You saw your little brother die and get brought back to life. More importantly, you saw him die, witch, and you didn't have the power to save him." He said this softly, not accusatorily, but empathetically, as one who knows what it is to have power yet be powerless.

"I don't understand where you're going with this," Nikki whispered back, briefly glancing at him. Her eyes burned.

"I just meant you've been through something pretty brutal." He moved his hand as though he wanted to comfort her, touch her hand or wipe the tear threatening to race down her cheek. Instead, he closed his hand into a fist, rested it back on his lap, and whispered, "It's okay to not be okay."

Nikki swallowed. "I'm fine," she insisted. "Meet me—us at the library at five." She stood up, rubbing her eyes with her palm. As she started to walk away, she stopped and turned back to Henry. "Thank you, by the way."

Henry nodded. "Anytime."


2 January 2009

Someone magicked the wave. The bonfire was magickal, too. There was nothing natural about either disaster. Someone is doing this, but why? I haven't had a moment alone with Grandma to tell her about what I can't write about, but I don't really want to tell her without talking to Nikki and Nelly about it first. I haven't had a moment alone with them either.

I did notice Nikki and Henry had a moment alone together though. I haven't told her, of course, but I think they'd look cute together...I'd probably get a "shut up" and a shove for that, but still. He's not that much older than she is.


"What are you scribbling away over there?" Nikki asked, sitting next to Emma at one of the round tables near the front of the library.

"Nothing," Emma said, pulling her journal up and closing it.

Nikki narrowed her eyes.

In the lobby area, Nelly and Jo were teaching Kam how to pop up as if he were on a surfboard. Even though they were in the library, they were being everything but quiet. Then again, the library wasn't technically open. Gabby had let them in with the promise they lock up when they left. Henry wasn't there yet.

"I noticed," Emma said slyly, "that you and Henry were getting cozy on the couch." She waggled her eyebrows.

"Shut up," Nikki said, shoving her friend.

"Well, you were." Emma's knowing grin spanned her face.

"I was not," Nikki insisted. "I was telling him about our meeting today. He wanted to know why we left Kam out of our stories."

"That's not what it looked like to me," Emma said in a sing-song voice.

"Well, that's all it was." Nikki folded her arms. "Besides, even if I wanted something more—which I don't—it couldn't happen anyway."

"So you *have* given it some thought?"

Nikki groaned. "All I mean is that he's Nelly's uncle. It would be too weird. What if we got married? I'd be one of my best friend's aunts." Nikki shook her head and frowned. "Not going to happen."

"You don't have to marry the guy," Emma said, leaning closer. "Just give him a chance." She nudged Nikki with her elbow.

"Drop it," Nikki said. "He's not even interested."

"Who's not interested?" Nelly asked, sitting down on Emma's other side.

"I'll tell you later." Emma winked.

"She will not because it is a non-issue," Nikki said. "As in *irrelevant*, as in *moot point*, as in *not happening*."

"Is this about you and Henry making goo-goo eyes on the couch?" Nelly asked.

Nikki gasped. "Oh my gosh. We were not!" she said loudly. She checked herself, took a breath, and whispered, "I told him about this meeting. We were not even close to each other, and, if we were, it was only so no one would hear us talking about Kam. We were talking about Kam and this meeting. That was it!" Nikki could feel her face burning.

"Sure," Nelly said. She stifled a laugh as Nikki became more flustered. To avoid getting turned into a toad or something equally horrible by her very aggravated witchy friend, Nelly turned her attention back to Jo and Kam.

Jo was belly-down on the ground next to Kam, pretending to paddle, and then pop up to catch imaginary waves. Kam's foot kept getting caught on his way up, so he fell to his knees before he popped up. Jo adjusted his foot and gave him advice on what to try next.

A memory floated across Nelly's mind as she watched them. The last time Nelly had taught someone to pop up was when she and Tom had taught Jo. Jo couldn't have been older than four.

"Nelly!" Nikki said, reaching across the table and poking her in the shoulder.

"Hmm?" Startled back to the present, Nelly looked at Nikki.

"Do you think she'll tell?" Nikki asked as she sat back in her seat.

"Who? Tell what?" Nelly asked.

"Jo," Nikki said. "She doesn't know what actually happened with Kam. You brought her to this meeting; do you think she'll tell?"

"Nah," Nelly said, looking back at Jo and Kam. "She's cool. Besides, I don't want to keep any more secrets from her."

"Just as long as she doesn't tell," Nikki said.

"Why's it so important we don't tell anyone, again?" Nelly asked.

"Well for one, my mom would kill me, but that's not the main reason—"

"Which is…" Nelly prompted.

"Which *is* I want time to figure out what happened," Nikki said. "Kait and Ethel never explain anything; they ask us a bunch of questions and ask *us* to explain. We don't have anything to explain because it happened *yesterday*, and we barely survived. If they get time to figure out what happened, so do we."

Nelly shrugged. "Fair enough." A mischievous grin suddenly spread over her face.

"What now?" Nikki said.

"It's your *boy*friend." Nelly gestured to the front doors and made a kissy face.

"Et tu?" Nikki said, sighing.

"Good to see she's moved on from denial," Emma said to Nelly in a clinical tone.

"Both of you shut up or I will…" Nikki made claw-like motions with her hands while she simultaneously strangled an invisible person.

"Right," Nelly said, smiling and rolling her eyes as she hopped up. "*I'll* get the door. We wouldn't want you swooning on your way over."

Nikki sank into her chair, muttering to herself and focusing no small bit of magick on her efforts to stop blushing. When Henry and Nelly joined Nikki and Emma at the table, Nelly took her seat back, and Henry sat a chair away from Nikki.

"So," Henry said, slapping his hands on the table top. "Why are we lying?" He drummed his fingers loudly.

Nelly sighed. "We're not—"

Henry put his hand up to stop her. "Omission of details that make the truth is the same thing as a lie. I've had this conversation with the witch."

"I have a name," Nikki snapped.

"I know," Henry said. "So, why are we lying?"

"We don't know what happened," Nikki said. "They're going to ask us what happened, and the truth is we don't know."

"And Nikki will be brutally murdered by her mother if she ever finds out," Nelly added with a cheeky smile.

"Very helpful," Nikki said, shooting Nelly a look.

"Right." Henry turned around and whistled. Jo and Kam looked over at everyone at the table, and Henry waved them over. "Take a seat."

As Jo sat next to Nelly, and Kam settled into the seat between Henry and Nikki, Henry said, "Here's the thing. I don't even know what happened. Nelly, you performed the magick; you explain it."

"I can't," Nelly said. "I mean…" she looked at Jo. "You have to promise not to tell anyone about anything we talk about here."

"Duh," Jo said, flipping her hair back. "The whole let's-have-a-secret-meeting-after-we've-already-had-a-meeting thing tipped me off...plus, Kam told me."

"Right," Nelly said. "Anyway, basically Kam and Emma fell in. You got Em," she said to Henry. "I got Kam. When I handed him to Emma, he wasn't breathing—"

"He wasn't just 'not breathing,'" Emma cut in. "He was dead. No pulse. Nothing. I genuinely thought that was it."

Nikki put her arm around Kam, hugging him close.

"Yeah." A shadow passed across Nelly's face. She nodded. "So, his lungs were filled with water. I got a letter earlier from Kait with a message for me from your mom, who I have lots of questions about. For the record, it would have been nice to know she's alive."

Henry frowned.

Before he could reply, Nelly plowed on, "The message basically said I needed to save him, and I had the power to save, and something about how there is life in the water, or water is life—I should have brought the letter with me. You can come and look at it if you need. Anyway, I pulled the water out because I thought that's what she meant about the power to save; it looked like I was wringing his shirt out or something, but upside-down. I—my point is it didn't work. Then, I thought water is hydrogen and oxygen. I figured he needed oxygen to breathe, so I focused on pulling out the hydrogen gas, and only leaving the oxygen in there. I thought maybe the purer form would be better for him.

"When that *also* didn't work, I kind of gave up on magick and did CPR. When I was doing one of the breaths, I suddenly knew what I was supposed to do and what I should have done all along. I told Emma to do compressions and waited for my turn to breathe. I said something in a language I've never heard before, breathed into him, and it took a second, but he was fine," Nelly finished.

She shrugged. "I told you. I don't know what happened."

"Nelly," Emma said, "you forgot the light."

Nelly's brow furrowed for a moment before she said, "Oh right. Yeah, there was this blue light all around his body while my magick was working. I could feel it moving through him, like healing him. It was wild."

Henry was quiet for a few moments, stoically rubbing his jaw and watching Nelly. Then, he said, "Do you remember your words?"

"Honestly, it sounded made up," Nelly said.

"Do you remember thinking it up?" Henry asked.

"It literally just came out." Nelly bit her lip.

"Have you guys been studying spells on your own?" Henry asked.

"No," Emma and Nikki said together while Nelly shook her head.

He looked at them and raised his eyebrows.

Nelly put her hands up as if surrendering. "I wouldn't even know where to start."

"Witch?"

"I studied fire magick with Gabby, like I told you before, but she hasn't taught me any spells. The one time I actually used one, she told me to wait until later," Nikki said, ignoring the fact he kept calling her witch and fighting harder to ignore that she kind of liked it.

"What happened to you?" Henry asked Kam. "No shark wrestling this time," he added.

"I thought the shark-wrestling made it sound like I wasn't really affected by the whole thing," Kam said analytically.

"It worked," Henry said with a small grin. "Let's hear the real story."

"The whole thing?"

"Just from when you fell in the water," Henry said. He leaned forward, resting his elbows on the table.

"Well," Kam said. "That lady knocked us over, and Emma and I fell in the water. I knew Emma fell in because I saw her when I was underwater." Kam was quiet for a moment. He swallowed. "When I fell in, I didn't realize what was going on at first. I remember not being able to breathe, and I remember my chest hurt. Everything was a brownish green color, but I couldn't really see anything.

"There was a second when I saw Emma above me, and she reached for me, but we were too far apart, and a current pushed me away. I tried to swim to the surface, but I've never been a strong swimmer. I'm too small." Kam shrugged, like being too small was a simple fact of life. "I remember my leg getting caught, but I don't remember if I struggled or anything. I know everything got warm and bright—super bright, like looking in a flashlight." Kam chewed on his lip for a minute, trying to remember more. "Oh! I also remember hearing stuff. Someone was crying. Someone else touched my shoulder and told me I wasn't ready yet." Kam stared at his hands as he debated whether he would tell them the next part—the part which scared him. It had scared him more than falling in the water had. Clearing his throat, he skipped to the part when he woke up. "Then, I remember seeing you guys over me, and I asked where Nikki was, and then she was there." Kam smiled.

Nikki ruffled his hair.

"That's all you remember?" Henry asked.

"Pretty much," Kam said and pressed his lips together.

"Have you ever heard of the kind of magick Nelly did?" Jo asked.

Henry breathed loudly. "Well, there are a few legends," he said, rubbing one eye.

"Like?" Jo prodded.

"Doesn't really matter," Henry said, the gears in his head turning. "The point is there is only one that talks about merfolk with the power to save the dead. Usually the power of life and death is exclusively accessible to Faiths, and as far as I know, we don't have any Faiths in the family."

"Faiths?" Nelly asked.

"Different race of magickal people," Henry said, waving her question away. He rubbed his brow and looked at Nelly. "The main issue here is you have that kind of power, and the queen knew about it but didn't tell me."

"I'm sorry." Nelly blinked. "Rewind." She leaned forward. "Queen?"

"My mom, yeah," Henry said, looking at the table without seeing it.

"So, are we—we're royal? Like crowns and ballgowns and 'Your Majesty' royal?" Jo asked, perking up as Nelly slouched down in her chair.

"Basically," Henry said.

"Sweet! Princesses AND mermaids!" Jo pumped her fist at the same time Nelly groaned.

"Yeah," Henry said, rubbing his eyes. "Look, I have to go."

"But what about the water being magicked?" Emma asked. "Someone *did* this."

He stood up. "I don't have any answers," he admitted. "You know how to get a hold of me if you need—I've got some things to sort out." He glanced at Nikki, smiled, and left.

# Chapter Twenty-Nine

## Thursday, January 3rd

January 3, 2009

It is raining like CRAZY! It is an insane storm out of nowhere. This is my favorite kind of weather. I know it's weird, but it kind of feels like a little reward for all the work we've done. Yeah, that does sound stupid. Moving on...

I think Kam is hiding something about when he came back. He seemed to be debating whether to tell us something yesterday at the library, and I think he chose not to, but I also don't want to push him. I want him to talk to me when he's ready, but I'm also super curious.

Change of subject (otherwise I might use magick and regret it): we're at Madam Ortega's. Surprising, I know. I spend more time here than at my own house—and I'm not mad about it. I need to finish my interview with her, and she said she needs to talk to us.

"What are you writing?" Kam asked, sitting on the couch next to Nikki. Emma was asleep on the other couch, and Nelly was gently snoring facedown on the floor, a throw pillow squashed between her arm and face.

"Just stuff in my journal," Nikki whispered. "Actually, I should be working on questions to ask Madam Ortega."

"Why?"

"Remember forever ago, the first time we came here, and it was for a school project?" Nikki asked, grabbing her bag. She traded her journal for her notebook.

"Yeah," Kam said.

"Well, the project is due tomorrow, and I haven't worked on it since that first week. I've been a little busy."

Kam laughed. "I think 'a little busy' is probably an understatement."

"Yeah," Nikki said. "Probably."

She spent the next ten minutes writing up questions she thought would work well for her project and cross referencing them with the rubric Mr. Miranda had passed out in their project packets. She figured she could interview Ethel after they finished with whatever it was the old medium had planned. Nikki's mind wandered. Her thoughts turned to Henry. She barely knew him but—no. She turned her attention back to her school work.

Finally, after an hour, Ethel and Kait showed up. Nikki was the only one still awake to see the older women sheltering under a black and white umbrella as they walked towards the house; she opened the door for them, giving them a straight line from the cold of the storm to the warmth of the house.

"Merry Meet, dear," Kait said, seeing Nikki at the door and hugging her.

"Merry Meet, Grandma," Nikki said.

"Where is everyone else?" Kait asked as she entered the house, looking around.

"Asleep." Nikki pointed vaguely to the front room.

"Well, I think you ought to wake them," Ethel said, shaking her umbrella outside before closing it. "I'll be ready for you all soon."

"Is there food? Nelly only wakes up for food," Nikki said, grinning.

Ethel chuckled and winked. "After."

"I'll see you all later," Kait said. "I've got quite a few things to do, and I probably won't see you for the rest of the night. Be sure to stop by after school tomorrow. You start again tomorrow, right?"

Nikki nodded.

"Good. See you tomorrow, little witch." Kait hugged Nikki again, kissed her cheek, and disappeared into one of the many rooms at the back of the house.

Nikki woke everyone up, starting with Kam, and then Emma, and finally Nelly.

"Go over to the table, please," Ethel called from a back room.

Nikki sat down as the weary trio wandered over to their seats. She pulled her braid out, combing her fingers through her hair.

"Any idea what we're doing yet?" Nelly asked, as she stretched.

"Nope," Nikki said, rebraiding her hair.

"I think we're getting another reading," Emma said between yawns.

"How do you know?" Nikki asked.

Emma rubbed her eyes and pointed to the end of the table. The many jars and containers were back. Ethel chose that moment to walk towards them carrying a tray which held cups and a pillar candle.

"Emma," Ethel said, handing her a cup and then sitting down.

Emma didn't say anything. She just stood and moved to the end of the table. Sunlight danced off the bottles sending bits of rainbow fluttering around the room. Emma picked up a short squat decanter filled with a glossy green liquid. As she unstoppered it, she felt a sudden urge to throw it across the room. Startled by this odd desire, she replaced the stopper and set the decanter down, but as she searched through the others for an alternate liquid for her reading, she kept coming back to the same glossy green liquid. Emma could feel everyone's eyes on her as she created her concoction.

"Nikki," Ethel said as she watched Emma. "The candle, if you please."

"Wha—oh, yeah. Sure." Nikki closed her eyes for a moment, concentrated, opened her eyes, and the candle was lit.

"Thank you." Ethel moved her hands over the candle in a cupping motion, her top hand becoming the bottom hand and vice versa. "Emma, trust your instincts, dear."

"Right." Emma sighed. She poured the green liquid into her cup, followed by something pungent and brown. Her hands moved quickly now; a dash of poppy seeds, a sprig of fresh thyme, a pinch of anemone petals, a sprinkle of dried yarrow, and a plop of blended aloe and, she was done. Emma handed the cup to her grandmother and sat in front of her.

Ethel covered the top of Emma's cup with her hand and closed her eyes, muttering her bit of magick over the cup and its contents. Gently placing the cup on the table to let the magick do its work, Ethel returned her attention to Emma. "Clear your mind. Focus on your breath." They sat in silence until finally, Ethel said, "Are you ready?"

Emma shrugged. "As ready as I can be, I guess."

Ethel nodded and picked up the cup. The concoction had transformed into an opaque, mustard-yellow liquid. As black dots bubbled from the center, Ethel gasped.

"What is it?" Emma asked, leaning forward.

"A warning," Ethel whispered. "Your inner psyche wishes to communicate something to you." She pointed to the strange shape forming on the surface of the liquid, the black standing in stark contrast the muted yellow behind it. "It warns you to be careful of whom you trust."

"Who?"

The shape shifted, changing between a triskelion and a dove and back again.

Ethel's brow furrowed as she watched the moving shapes. "This doesn't make sense," she muttered, more to herself than to anyone else.

"What is it?" Emma asked. "What do those symbols mean?"

"Your reading is one of warning, but these," she gestured to the cup, "suggest you should beware of growth and peace, but…" Ethel shook her head.

The shapes changed into something new, into something different.

"Now this," Ethel said, watching the new shape. "This warns of the poverty of consciousness; it is a warning to look to your inner light for guidance. But in the company of the other images, there is no general warning. They have not shed further detail on those whom you should not trust."

"What's that?" Emma asked as the symbol shifted again.

"This symbol ought to show you the way to best apply this message to your life."

As Ethel watched the shape form more clearly, it sunk.

"It's not supposed to do that, is it?" Emma asked, already knowing the answer to her question.

"This is impossible. In all my years, I've never—" Ethel stopped short. A new image was forming, one that was thick and oozing, sitting atop the liquid like oil on water. The image was easily deciphered, even by the likes of you or me.

Blood red and shining, the image of a skull stared back at Ethel and Emma. Death.

Emma swallowed. "But death just means change," she said quickly. "Right? Doesn't it? I mean, I've seen it in readings before; it's not necessarily bad, right?"

Ethel simply looked at Emma. Then, without addressing Emma's concerns, color fading from her face, Ethel put her hand over the cup, muttering quickly. Her hand glowed with soft yellowy light. When she removed her hand, the skull faded, reversing its appearance until finally the sunken shape rose once again, the black somehow more comforting now.

"What's it mean?" Emma asked, staring at the image, a goblet.

"The spirits are sending you a message," Ethel said finally. "There is someone out there of whom you must be wary, and even though you may choose the higher path, and attempt to fulfill your true potential, this being will lead you to another place…by force if necessary. You must trust your magick to guide you." The liquid sizzled in the cup, dissipating in steam.

As the silent minutes ticked by, they simultaneously felt like hours and mere seconds.

"Someone is coming for me," Emma said simply. The warnings from the beyond, the reading, the magick in the fire and water, the block in her visions—all at once, everything felt aimed at her. Emma stood up quietly, moved to her bag, grabbed her journal, and jotted down the names and meanings of each of her symbols in this reading. She squeezed her grandmother's hand and nodded. Then, Emma took the now empty cup to the kitchen.

"Kameron," Ethel said quietly.

Kam stood. His gaze fixed on the collection of bottles and jars as he switched seats with Emma. The old woman no longer scared him, but a warning in his heart made him pause for a moment before he took the cup she offered him. He licked his lips and swallowed.

"Take your time, dear," Ethel said softly.

Kam looked at Ethel. Her eyes were soft yet cosmic. He nodded. Despite Ethel's assurance he could take his time, Kam rushed through the filling of his cup: milk, sunflower seeds, pink salt, dried butterfly-weed, and crushed chrysanthemum petals.

He handed the cup to Ethel and sat.

Ethel smiled at him before she began her bit of magick. "A simple reading for you, I think," she said as she set the cup down.

Kam nodded.

"A reading of your past, present, and future," Ethel said. She peered over the edge of the table to look into the cup. "Look."

Scooting to the edge of his chair to see, Kam looked and watched the liquid swirl, changing from the white of milk to the clean blue of sky before finally settling at a nice pale and minty green.

Ethel picked up the cup, and the image of a sword formed in dark green at the surface. "You have quite astounding past accomplishments. You've traveled the pathway of water and are open to your subconscious." The image morphed into a palm frond. Ethel swallowed and smiled.

"What's it mean?" Kam asked.

"Your six senses are already developing nicely, and your seventh will start soon, if it has not already begun to develop. You're a hard-worker and selfless." There was meaning in this image the medium did not communicate. Ethel had not the heart to tell him the palm frond was the symbol of the martyr. She did not know he had died. If she had, she may have been more truthful with him; she may have connected his last reading to this one, but she did not. It would not be the last time information withheld caused withheld information.

Ethel smiled as the image shifted. "There is love, and compassion. There is humility, and the gift of being as the little child. You have a bright future." She patted Kam on the cheek gently. Ethel stood, retreating to the kitchen for a moment. She poured herself a glass of water and brought it back with her into the dining room. She began moving her hands over the candle, cleansing between readings. "I will take Nelly next," Ethel said, sitting down.

Nelly swapped places with Kam.

"You know what to do." Ethel watched as Nelly filled her cup.

I'm sure you remember Nelly's last reading, so it's quite easy to understand the bundle of nerves that fluttered through her as she filled her cup; though, there was one marked difference. Last time, Nelly had been in denial about who she was, about *what* she was. Now, she had accepted it, now she understood (at least more so than last time), and most importantly, now she was open to whatever information she could get.

After filling her cup (water and milk with dried eucalyptus, seeds from a hollyhock, chunky salt, and just a pinch of powdered milkweed) and handing it to Ethel, Nelly sat, her leg bouncing madly already. She looked into the cup the moment Ethel removed her hand from the top. It swirled slowly. This time, it turned bright shimmering turquoise.

"Let's do this," Nelly said, squaring her shoulders.

Ethel smiled, retrieving the cup. The first image appeared. Though the image itself was clear and still, the liquid that formed it changed from dark blue to purple to black and back again. "You've had bounty and good fortune," Ethel said.

"Hey," Nelly said. "That's the star, like last time. "

Ethel smiled and nodded. "Yes."

The star faded as a new shape took form, another shape easily recognizable to you and I: the sun.

"This shows you have an overall satisfaction with your life. There is regeneration occurring: renewal. It also hints at an upcoming trip." Ethel raised her eyebrows.

"That's good news." Nelly breathed easier.

The sun shifted into something neither you nor I would recognize, a shape Nelly certainly didn't know but Ethel must have because she said, "There is struggle ahead, and you must persevere through the turmoil. It, too, tells of an upcoming journey. You must use your mind to control your body." The liquid faded until it was as clear as Ethel's glass of water.

"Thanks," Nelly said, looking at Ethel. This should have had more meaning to her since her initiation into the magickal world, but as Nelly didn't how to read a reading, she did what came most naturally to her: she smiled and shrugged.

"Nikki," Ethel said, cleansing her hands once again.

"Right," Nikki said, standing and filling her cup. She did this easily and quickly. Going last had given her the opportunity to make her choices before ever being presented with the cup. Apple cider vinegar and dandelion oil made up her liquid base. She sprinkled in morning glory petals, ground rosemary, and a bit of crushed walnut. Nikki sat still, willing her stomach to settle as she watched Ethel mutter and wait.

Finally, her mixture was ready.

It was softly glowing and bright green. Blue images began forming.

Ethel raised her eyebrows. "All elements are at your disposal. This image represents the conscious mind. If you concentrate with focused energy on a single goal, you can draw on any force you need to complete your task." The image swirled, forming something new and recognizable. "Growth through imagination; this image is birth; it represents time itself."

"The sword was in my last reading, wasn't it?" Nikki asked.

Ethel nodded. The sword morphed.

"What's that mean?" Nikki asked.

"Strength," Ethel said, raising an eyebrow. "You must develop your life-force. You need to be more spiritually-oriented. You—" Ethel paused. When Nikki met her gaze, Ethel spoke again, "You have the potential to be a woman of dominion."

"Dominion?" Nikki asked as her liquid faded to clarity. "What does that mean?"

"I believe it will be quite an adventure to discover," Ethel said with a smile. She stood suddenly. "I think I'll take a nap. You can help yourselves to anything you find in refrigerator or cupboards. The candle, Nikki—if you don't mind?"

"Right, of course." Nikki put the candle out with a wink.

3 January 2009

A warning. Warning of trusting too soon. A warning of death? But the symbol of Death isn't meant to be taken literally, and even if it was, a life-force never dies; it simply changes form. Grandma taught me that. She's been taking a nap, and we've been working on our project. Nelly went home to finish her bit and pick up the poster board. I was supposed to get it, but I never really got around to it.

Emma was in the living room, cuddled under an afghan, writing in her journal. Her grandmother emerged from her room.

"Is Nikki still here?" Ethel asked.

"In the kitchen," Emma said, nodding her head in that direction. She listened as Ethel and Nikki chatted for a moment; Nikki had more questions for the project. Emma got up from the couch and folded the afghan, placing it on the back of the couch. She quietly went into the kitchen and found Kam, who was eating some cookies he and Nikki had found in the cookie jar.

"These are okay to eat, right?" he asked through a mouthful of cookie.

"They're fine." Emma smiled. "Come with me."

Wiping crumbs off his face and hands, Kam followed Emma to the library. "Woah," he said when they got inside. "This is like that scene from *Beauty and the Beast*!"

"Yeah," Emma said, still smiling. "I guess it is a bit." She walked over to the pillows and pulled a few out. "Take a seat."

Kam sat, eyes open wide as though attempting to devour the numberless books. "It would take several lifetimes to read all of these."

Emma pulled out a book and brought it over to him. "I want to show you something."

"What is that?" Kam asked; he touched the leather-bound book. The book itself was large, larger than anything he had ever seen, but the volume was thin. It couldn't have been more than two hundred pages. He tried to read the cover, but the letters had faded to illegibility.

"This is *A Record of the Prophecies Made by the High Priestess the Third: Zoia Vikaar*," Emma said.

"What's a priestess?" Kam asked. "And how old is this book?"

"Well, for your second question, at least two thousand years old, but probably older," Emma said, flipping through the pages.

"Why isn't it a crumbling mound of dust?" Kam touched the edges of the book.

"Magick," Emma said, shrugging.

"Cool." Kam's eyes widened.

"Yup." Emma flipped a few more pages. "As for your first question, the High Priestess is the highest honor of the Magickal Order of the Psychics."

Kam sat for a second and then said, "The M.O.P.s?"

Emma laughed. "I guess, but that's not technically what they're called."

"What are they called?"

"Only those within the Order know," Emma said with a small smile. She stopped flipping pages and looked at Kam. "Words have power. Names have power. So, the name of the Order is only given to those within the Order."

"But they're all psychics, right?" Kam asked. "A bunch of people like you? People who can see the future? People who have visions?"

"More or less," Emma said, moving her head side to side. "The High Priestess, or Priest in rare cases, is someone who receives prophecies, not just visions."

"What's the difference?"

Emma took a deep breath. "I have visions," she said. "They're visions because I'll be there. Whether it's to witness, ensure, or stop the event, *I* will be there, *physically*."

Kam thought for a moment. "So a prophecy is like a vision but so far in the future the person who sees it won't be alive to actually experience it?"

"Exactly," Emma said. "I see why you skipped a few grades."

Kam grinned and then frowned. "So why are you showing this to me?"

"This." Emma pointed to a passage. The handwriting was scrawled, tiny, and almost impossible to read.

Kam looked at the passage. After a minute, he said, "Can you read it? I can't—"

"Of course," Emma said, smiling. "It does take a little practice." She cleared her throat and read, "'The Ninth Moon of the Fiftieth Year of the Third High Priestess. Prophecy twenty and seven hundred: And he shall rise though he has fallen, / And he shall be one once he was two. / He shall guard the chosen, though the chosen will not choose him.'"

"What does it mean?" Kam asked.

"I think she means you," Emma said. "See the first line, 'And he shall rise though he has fallen'? I think that's talking about you."

"Because…" Kam looked around quickly, and then whispered, "Because I died, but I came back?"

"Exactly," Emma said.

"What about the rest of it?" Kam asked. "The 'one once he was two' or the 'guard the chosen'? What about that stuff? What's it mean?"

"I don't know," Emma admitted. "Would you trust me if I just said I believe this is talking about you?"

Even as Kam nodded, the doubt rippled through him, his near-death message echoing in his mind.

Jan, 3, 09

It's practically midnight, but I'm finally done with this project. Today was a trip, but what day hasn't been since I started growing a tail? More weird stuff at Madam Ortega's, but I'll write about it later,

The truth is I'm kind of putting off going to sleep. I haven't told anyone, but every night since the tidal wave, I've had nightmares. Like vivid, wake up drenched in sweat nightmares. They're always the same. I dive down to save Kam, and I pull him out like I did, but in the dream, I fail. I haven't slept since. I'm just so tired,

Nelly's phone rang. It was Wyatt. She took a deep breath and clicked the answer button. "Hey," she said. "How are you?"

"Good," he said quietly. "I mean, better."

"Wyatt, I meant to call," she said quickly. "Things have just been…"

"Completely insane?" Wyatt offered. His voice was still hoarse.

Nelly chuckled. "Yeah, basically. Listen, I know you told me not to help them, but I had to. I mean, if I didn't—"

"I'd be dead," Wyatt said simply.

Nelly wasn't sure how to respond. Silence sat fat between them.

"Nels," Wyatt said. "I was so stupid. I'm sorry—"

"Me, too," Nelly said. "I hate that things have been weird between us, and I know I get in my own world sometimes. It's all been so much to process, but I can't even surf to process anymore. I just don't—"

"It's okay." He sounded sincere.

Nelly sighed. "I'm going to keep helping them, Wy," she said. "They're good people."

"I think you should follow your gut," Wyatt said. "It's never led you wrong before; it doesn't necessarily take the path of least resistance, but neither do you." He chuckled.

Nelly laughed. "Is that a nice way of saying I make my life harder than it has to be?"

Wyatt snickered and slowly said, "Maybe."

Nelly laughed again.

"I will say I'm not sure I trust them. I just—I don't know…"

"Do you trust me?"

"Always."

Nelly sighed. "Then that's all I need for right now."

"Maybe I should have said *mostly*," Wyatt teased. "I mean, you remember that time you said I could definitely surf that pipe, and I almost died?"

"Oh, shut up. You didn't almost die. You got a little banged up."

"I got eight stitches!"

Nelly mock cried for a second before bursting out laughing; she could hear Wyatt cracking up on the other side of the phone. When she finally managed to catch her breath, she said, "I've missed this."

"Me too, Nels."

They talked for an hour before Tom had to come in and remind Nelly there was school in the morning. Nelly's heart felt full as she hung up with Wyatt. At least one thing still felt like the old days, just a bit more magickal.

# Chapter Thirty

## Friday, January 4th

4 January 2009

Nelly grumbled all day yesterday about how unfair it was that the school wasn't even in what she keeps calling "the splash zone." Nikki kept reminding her that, in order for the school to get washed away, all our homes would have to get washed away, too. I stayed out of it. Honestly, I don't think it would have mattered. I think the school would have been fine either way because I'm 95% sure the principal is magickal. I've never sensed anything from her, but that doesn't necessarily mean anything. There are a few types of magickal peoples who can hide their magick so well other magickal beings can't sense them. Really, it's neither here nor there as we're in class and presenting projects today in just a few minutes.

I showed Kam the prophecy yesterday. I need to tell Nikki about it, but I'm not sure how she'll react. Kam didn't seem to believe me. I know it sounds crazy because technically this is no more than a hunch, but I know the prophecy is about him. We still haven't told anyone about how Kam died and how Nelly brought him back to life. Henry said he'd look into it.

"Hey," Nikki poked Emma in the back.

Emma leaned back, closer to Nikki's desk. "What?'

"Have you seen Nelly today? I dropped my stuff off at her place last night, but I haven't seen her since lunch."

"I saw her before class," Emma said. "She said the poster is in her car."

"If she's here in time, do we want to go first and get it over with?" Nikki asked.

"Works for me," Emma said.

Nikki and Emma watched the door of the classroom, waiting for Nelly to enter. Nikki's leg bounced making an incessant tapping. The bell rang just as Nelly stepped across the threshold.

"Cutting a bit close, aren't we, Miss Hansen?" Mr. Miranda asked without looking up from his book.

"Sorry," Nelly said sheepishly and headed to where Nikki and Emma were already sitting. Most of the students were sitting with their groups in anticipation.

Mr. Miranda put a bookmark in his book and stood. "Welcome back to school. I hope you all had a good holiday and that no one was hurt in the multitude of tragedies which struck throughout our vacation. I have been asked to inform you one of you peers, a student named Humphrey Pax, went missing over the holidays. If anyone knows where he is or knows what might have happened to him, please tell me, one of your other teachers, or one of the administration. His father is worried and is looking for him."

The class murmured in response.

"The school has also asked we have a moment of silence in honor of any of those who may have perished during the sad events," Mr. Miranda said.

The class was silent for a few moments.

Mr. Miranda took a deep breath and cleared his throat, as though he was afraid to break the silence and disrespect the dead, but he needed to get class on the move. "Now," he said, clasping his hands together. "Today you present your family projects. Do we have any volunteers?"

Emma glanced at Nelly and Nikki (who both nodded) and shot her hand into the air.

"Excellent," Mr. Miranda said. "We'll start with Emma Hugos, Nikki Rodrigues, and Neldyn Hansen."


January 4, 2009
    While I'm super happy the project is over, I had no idea how sad

Aisling's life was. Not just her life either. Death too. Poor Aisling was dumped somewhere. Nelly said a witch's body was considered unholy. People accused of witchcraft, like my ancestor, were executed, and then, their bodies were dumped into unmarked mass graves. No one knows where Aisling was buried. It's so sad. I did notice Aisling's last name (O'Crean) was not the same as her husband's (Patrick McKenzie—as in Kaitlyn McKenzie—generations apart of course). Nelly and Emma both did a great job presenting. I got all caught up on my words and stumbled like crazy, and between that and my shoddy research, I'll be lucky to get a B.

Everyone else is presenting now, and I should probably pay attention.


Glancing up, Nikki put her journal in her bag, and leaned back in her chair. She took a deep breath and slowly exhaled. Emma poked Nikki in the knee. Nikki leaned forward over her desk as Emma passed her a piece of paper.

Any chance you can meet after class?

Nikki grabbed the pen she had just put back in her bag.

Sure. Is Nelly coming too? What's up?

Emma read the note and without writing anything, passed it to Nelly.

Sure, I'm in. But I second Nikki's question: What's up?

We need to talk about some stuff.

Stuff? What do you know that we don't? Come on, Em. Spill!!

I'm just telling you what I was instructed to do.

Instructed? Instructed by who?

I second Nelly's question: Instructed by who?

It's "Instructed by whom?" and I'll tell you after school.

Whatever. Just tell us now.

I got a letter. It had instructions on it and an official looking seal. I'll tell you what I mean after school. We need to pay attention.

Fine, so let's talk about stopping time! Isn't anyone the slightest bit interested in the fact we literally paused the world?! It STOPPED!

Are you sure we did that? I mean, I know our mentors keep saying we're powerful, but we can't be <u>that</u> powerful, can we?

We could be. We've barely come into our powers; they're still growing, right? What if this is a new power? A power we can only do together? Like Emma needs one of us to have really powerful visions? What if we need each other to control time?

Emma! Say something. You just keep reading what we've written and passing it on.

We should pay attention.

I am paying attention. Simon is presenting on Jenny's great-uncle Ted. He's a boring old man who died in an interesting way. Shouldn't we practice our new power?

We shouldn't write about it. We need to discuss it privately where we won't stand any risk of being overheard.

Fine. When?

Mr. Miranda doesn't take kindly to notes being passed in his class.

You started it! And for the record, I still think the whole

time thing was just a fluke. Also for the record, I'm not happy about not knowing who we're being "instructed" by.

It wasn't a fluke, but I do agree about the second part. I don't like receiving orders from someone we don't know.


Jan, 4, 09
I'm waiting in the car for Emma and Nikki. Emma got mysterious instructions from someone (we don't know who...or whom...or whatever), and

Someone tapped on Nelly's driver's side window. She looked up from her journal and saw Whitney. Nelly sighed as she manually rolled her window down.

"How can I help you?" Nelly said with a snide smile.

"You're seriously quitting?" Whitney said.

Nelly considered her for a moment. "Yeah," she said finally. "Figured if you were going to stand any chance, I'd have to bow out," she added, unable to resist the cheek.

"You're really just done?" Whitney said, flatly.

Nelly noted this may have been the first time ever she didn't detect a hint of sass from Whitney. Nelly nodded.

"Why?"

Nelly shrugged. "Personal reasons. I still love the ocean. I'm just not going to compete anymore."

"You didn't like join the Green Berets to save the whales, or something, did you?"

Nelly covered her mouth like she was thinking while she actually hid a suppressed laugh. After she composed herself, she said, "No, I didn't."

"Oh. Okay." Whitney seemed to have lost her steam. "I just, I thought you'd actually do it."

Nelly smiled, genuinely this time. "Me too."

"You're good, you know." Whitney flicked her hair out of habit and added, "I mean, not as good as me but still good."

"Thanks," Nelly said.

Whitney nodded.

After an awkward silence, Nelly said, "Well, see you around."

"Yeah," Whitney said, nodding. "See you around."

As Whitney walked away, Nelly chuckled to herself and made a mental note to tell Wyatt about saving the whales. Seeing Nikki headed towards her, Nelly leaned over and unlocked the passenger door so Nikki could get in.

Nikki opened the door, glanced up at the sky and said, "Looks like it's going to rain."

"If we chuck our bags in the back, we can all squeeze in here," Nelly said, hopping out of the cab. "Of course, all our stuff will get soaked."

"Maybe not," Nikki murmured. She closed the passenger door and hopped in the bed of the old red truck.

The two girls took their cellphones out of their bags and were just zipping them closed as Emma came up.

"Get your phone out of your bag," Nikki said before Emma could say anything. "Then give it to me."

"Uh, okay." Emma sat her bag on the ground as she searched through it for her phone and one other item, which she hid quickly in her jacket pocket. She handed the bag to Nikki.

"Keep watch," Nikki said, crouching down with the bags in front of her.

"What?" Nelly said.

Nikki beckoned them to come closer and whispered, "I can do a spell, so water doesn't damage our bags or the stuff inside our bags. It's a little something I've been trying to work on. This is perfect practice material."

"You really shouldn't. Not here," Emma said, glancing around. "It's too public."

"Wait," Nelly said, putting a hand on her bag. "What do you mean *practice*? What happens if you get it wrong?"

"It might catch fire." Nikki winced, adding, "But I swear it's only happened once, and it was because Kam startled me."

"What!" Nelly and Emma both looked horrified.

"Come on, guys. I was trying it on a sock, and Kam walked in my room without knocking first. Gee-whiz," Nikki grumbled.

The girls didn't look like they fully believed Nikki—it was mostly a joke, but they also didn't want their bags burned to a crisp.

"Just keep watch," Nikki murmured.

"I still don't think it's a good idea to do this in such a public place," Emma said.

"Me either," Nelly confessed. "But I also don't want all my stuff drenched."

Emma nodded. "I guess."

Nelly leaned against the driver's side, glancing nonchalantly around the parking lot as Emma did the same on the passenger's side. Both waited, half expecting to see flames explode from the back of the truck at any moment.

"Done," Nikki said, hopping out of the bed.

Emma slid into the passenger seat, put the optional middle seat down, and slid closer to Nelly. Nikki scooted in next to Emma, shoving some empty water bottles into the footwell.

"You're not on Kam duty today, right?" Emma asked Nikki.

"No," Nikki said. "The middle school doesn't start until Monday, and Mom took the day off to spend with Kam."

"Good," Emma said.

"Where are we going?" Nelly asked.

"The Cove," Emma said.

"Isn't it still underwater?" Nikki asked.

"I guess we'll find out when we get there," Emma said.

Nelly drove as Emma and Nikki argued about Nikki's potential relationship with Henry. Nikki kept trying to talk about stopping time, but Emma was having none of it. All she was interested in was Nikki's love life, which of course Nikki kept avoiding. It was quite the runaround. Nelly chimed in every now and then to say something sarcastic, but mostly, she just enjoyed the cool breeze coming through her window and the banter of her new friends.

"Would you mind if Nikki was your aunt?" Emma asked Nelly.

Nikki groaned. "Why can't we talk about things that actually happened, not things that will never *ever* happen?" Nikki said, her hands on her face.

"What?" Nelly asked.

"Would you mind if Nikki was your aunt?" Emma repeated. "Like, in a few years, *when* Nikki and Henry get married?"

"Not when! *No when*! We are not getting married!" Nikki dragged her hands down her face. "We're not even having this conversation!"

Nelly ignored Nikki. "I don't think you'd be bad as an aunt. I mean," Nelly glanced at Nikki, "don't call me your little Jelly-Nelly and pinch my cheeks like my Aunt Candy did when I was a kid, and we'll be fine." Nelly laughed, and added, "I'm pretty sure she'd try that today if she could catch me."

"For the last—" Nikki paused suddenly as though registering everything Nelly said. "Wait. You have an 'Aunt Candy'?"

Parking, Nelly chuckled. "*That's* what you got from that?" She turned off the car and looked at Emma. "So, Em, why are we here?"

"This was delivered to me this morning." Emma pulled out an envelope made of thick parchment from her jacket pocket. "When I asked Rachelle who it was from, she just looked worried and said she needed to call Grandma. Grandma came over immediately and looked at it but didn't open it. She also looked worried, but said I should do as instructed," Emma explained, turning it over.

The three girls looked at the back of the envelope. It was sealed with an ornate gold and green wax seal with some kind of bird on it.

"What's that say?" Nelly asked, pointing to the scribbled writing under the seal.

"Open when you reach the parking lot before you walk down to the Cove," Emma read.

"How do they know about the Cove?" Nelly asked.

Nikki shrugged. "Let's get this over with."

Emma ripped open the envelope and pulled out a letter, written on the same thick parchment:

Neldyn, Nikki, and Emma,
You three have been entrusted with much power. Meet at the Cove tomorrow at two o'clock sharp. It will be above water by then.
Sincerely Yours,
Madam B. Fayson

"I know that name," Emma said, more to herself than anyone else.

"What?" Nelly said.

"Fayson." Emma studied the letter. "I know that name from somewhere."

"All I know is we came here for absolutely no reason at all," Nelly said.

"That's what I read," Nikki concurred. "And how does she know the Cove won't be still underwater?" She peeked out the window but was unable to see far enough down to be able to tell one way or the other.

Emma pursed her lips and glanced between Nikki and Nelly. Neither of them were taking this as seriously as she thought they should. Finally she said, "You should call Henry. I think we're going to need his help."

# Chapter Thirty-One

### Saturday, January 5th

5 January 2009

Google failed me. I spent all night searching for the name Fayson, and I couldn't find anything. Anyway, I already talked to Nikki about today, and she's not on Kam duty. I love that kid, and he always seems to end up hurt, or on the almost-hurt side of things, so the more we can avoid taking him into unknown situations, the better. We don't know what "two o'clock sharp" will bring.

*Everything was white.*

Emma sat up. Was that a vision? Or did she blackout—or whiteout, in this case? There was no feeling before it. Emma yawned. She had no reason to suspect she had just seen a life-changing vision. Instead, she dismissed it, reasoning that she must have dozed off due to staying up too late doing research.

Emma's phone buzzed. She stood up, fetched it from the nightstand, and opened it to find four texts from Nikki:

> I'm here
>
> Are you coming?
>
> EMMA!!!
>
> Where are you!?

Emma looked at the time: 1:45. She quickly sent a text back to Nikki ('Overslept!') and ran her fingers through her hair. There was no time for a shower, so Emma threw her hair up in a bun, changed out of her pajamas, deodorized herself, and ran out the door.

"Up late?" Nikki asked, upon Emma's entering the car.

"Research on Fayson," Emma said, buckling her seatbelt as Nikki backed out. Emma looked around the car. "Nice car; do I smell leather?"

"Yeah," Nikki said. "The rental finally came in."

"*This* is a rental?" Emma looked at the interior. "This is nicer than any rental I've ever seen."

"No," Nikki said with a laugh. "This is my mom's car. I can't drive the rental since I'm not over twenty-five."

"That makes more sense. Your mom has a sweet ride," Emma said, running her hand over the leather seat.

Nikki looked at Emma.

"What?"

"I just never thought I'd hear the words 'sweet ride' come from you," Nikki said, smiling.

"Nelly's rubbing off on me," Emma admitted.

"Clearly!" Nikki laughed. "So, did you ever find anything on 'Fayson'?"

"No." Emma scratched her greasy head and frowned. "No one seems to know anything. Rachelle and my grandma just exchange nervous glances and tell me to trust my magick to guide me." She sighed. "It kind of felt like when I wanted a pet hamster as a kid but darker."

"What?" Nikki asked as they passed the library.

"When I was a kid," Emma explained. "I wanted a pet. I had been talked down from a unicorn to a pony to a dog to a cat to a hamster."

"Unicorn?"

"I grew up with magick. I know what's out there. Now, focus," Emma said. "I wanted this hamster. Every day we went over to my grandma's house for my training, and every day for the month leading up to my birthday I would ask about getting the hamster."

"Okay, so?" Nikki asked as they wound their way past fields and houses. There were less houses standing in the area than the last time they had driven this way. There was also considerable debris scattered through the fields.

"So Rachelle and my grandma would just smile and say something like 'maybe next year,' or 'we'll see.'"

"And?"

"And," Emma said, stretching the word out for emphasis, "I ended up getting the hamster for my birthday."

"So what's the big deal?" Nikki asked, clicking on her blinker to turn left onto Main.

"They know something," Emma said, squirming and regretting not taking a shower.

"Oh my gosh, look at this," Nikki said, distracted from their conversation by the view down Main.

Unlike the earthquake, the tsunami had left Main Street a wasteland. Very few shops were still standing, and the ones left were so water-damaged they had to be torn down and rebuilt anyway. It cost a fortune to restore everything, and though it would one day return to its former glory, that day would not come for several years. However, you may be pleased to hear construction began within the year.

"You know," Nikki said, driving slowly to avoid debris, "I heard on the radio that only Main Street was damaged. The experts can't figure out why Otter Sands wasn't wiped right off the map. Good news for magick, I guess."

"Yeah. Still though, makes you feel kind of lucky to be alive, huh?" Emma said.

"No kidding." Nikki drove around a car, which was upside-down in the middle of the road.

"I'm glad Henry came," Emma said, still looking out the window. She hadn't meant it as a tease, but Nikki gave her a sideways glance anyway.

Nikki parked the car and said, pointedly, "So, what were you saying? About hamsters and your aunt and grandma?"

Emma sighed. "I think they know something about 'Fayson,' and they're not telling me." She rubbed her eyes. She was worn out. "I got the same feeling when I was talking to them that I got when I asked them about the hamster, except this time it feels more—" Emma paused and searched for the word.

"More what?" Nikki asked after a little while.

"Foreboding?" Emma guessed. "Like they're hiding something from me."

Nikki turned the car off, grabbed her bag, and got out. "I don't know," she said. "I mean, them hiding something from me, sure. But you? You're always on the inside."

"I'm telling you!" Emma shut the passenger door. "They know something or at least suspect something. I mean, you heard Grandma at the reading, 'trust your magick to guide you'? After she just finished telling me something is coming for me? And then we get this weird letter?"

"It's weird, it's weird," Nikki said, putting up her hands. "But, you got the hamster, right?" She locked the car and started walking over in the direction of the hike to the Cove, dodging more debris.

"Yeah," Emma admitted, following Nikki.

"So, if you got the same feeling, then that means you'll probably find out where you know 'Fayson' from, right?" Nikki moved branches from the path as she walked. "I mean, I don't think the 'trust your magick' thing was anything cryptic, but," she added quickly, "if Rachelle and your grandma really are hiding something, they'll tell you eventually."

"I guess," Emma said.

The girls made it down to the Cove and found Nelly sitting in the sand, waiting for them.

"Where have you guys been? It's two in like three minutes," Nelly said.

"Overslept," Emma said.

"Past one in the afternoon?" Nelly asked.

"I stayed up almost all night trying to find 'Fayson,'" Emma, defensively.

"Did you?" Nelly asked.

"No," Emma said. "But I know I know it from somewhere."

"Well, I got this." Nelly pulled out an envelope made of the same parchment as their message yesterday.


Jan. 5, 09

It's been a month since my birthday. I've turned into a mermaid, stopped water, stopped time, almost stopped a tidal wave, saved a life, got a few new friends, found long lost relatives, and became a princess. It's been a month. Honestly, if every month of adulthood is going to be like this, I don't think I'll survive.

The nightmares won't stop. I've tried everything I can find on the internet: lavender, melatonin, ocean sounds before bed (that actually made it worse). Do I tell Henry? I called him yesterday. He came by last night. I told him what was happening with the letter from the Fayson lady. He said he'd meet us at the Cove.

Nelly looked at the page. Admitting to the nightmares in her journal was one thing, but telling Henry about them? Would he brush them off? Would he even be able to help? A ring at the doorbell stopped her train of thought. Nelly checked the time: 11:45. She waited for someone else to answer the door for a second before remembering Tom and Jo were out surfing.

As Nelly opened the front door, she was met with the familiar frame of her most recent ex-boyfriend. "Andy," she said, partially irritated, partially surprised.

"I don't need to come in," he said quickly. "I just wanted to talk to you for a second."

Behind the screen door, Nelly crossed her arms. "I'm listening."

Andy readjusted his red 49er's ball cap and touched the bridge of his nose.

"Well," Nelly pressed.

"I'm sorry," he said. "I screwed up. Big time."

Nelly nodded but didn't say anything.

"A lot of freaky stuff happened over the break." Andy cleared his throat. "I mean, first the lightning strike in the locker room and then there was the bonfire and that tidal wave." He shook his head. "I just—I mean, I had a lot of close calls, and it kind of made me reevaluate some stuff."

"That's probably good," Nelly said.

"I also joined a program." Andy rubbed his hands together. "12 steps and stuff," he added. "I wanted to say I'm sorry. I'm going to try and do better."

"I accept your apology," Nelly said, dropping her arms and putting her hands in her back pockets. After a moment she added, "You know, you're a good guy when you're not sloshed. We're still done though."

"I figured, and uh, thanks," Andy said with a good-natured shrug. "Hey, I heard—I mean," he rubbed his hands together, "I mean, Whitney told me you're dropping out of the circuit. Is that true?"

Nelly nodded.

"That's a bummer," Andy said. "You're way talented. You would have made it big."

Nelly smiled. "Thanks, but it's for the best."

Andy clicked his tongue. "Well, see you around?"

"Sure," Nelly said with a nod. "See ya." She closed the door and rested her back on it.

Of all the things that had happened in the last two weeks, Andy apologizing was probably the most unexpected. Someone knocked on the door again. Figuring Andy had forgotten something, Nelly turned and opened the door again, but no one was there. She went to close the door when she saw an envelope taped to the door. She hesitated for a moment. Their screen door was notoriously loud, yet she hadn't heard it creak open or slam shut. Nelly grabbed the envelope, sealed with the same ornate gold and green wax seal as the one Emma had. It hadn't been taped. It had been magickally adhered to the door; it came off with ease, no sticky residue. Nelly flipped the envelope over to see what was written on the front.

*To: Neldyn Hansen, Nikki Rodriguez, and Emma Hugos*
*Open at the Cove at Two O'clock Sharp on Saturday, the fifth of January, year two-thousand and nine*
*Madam B. Fayson*

Nelly ran outside and looked around, hoping to see someone, anyone who could give her an idea of how Madam B. Fayson had found the Hansen home. When she couldn't find anyone after a few minutes of searching, Nelly went back in the house, locked up, left a note for her dad, and drove down to the Cove.

*January 5, 2009*
*They know about us, but no one ever told us about them.*
*Henry's here.*

Nikki closed her journal as Henry sat down next to her in the sand. Nelly and Emma were in front of them.

"Let me see it," Henry said, putting his hand out.

Nelly handed the letter to him. He held it down in front of him and read.

*Greetings Neldyn, Nikki, and Emma,*
*My name is Madam Briony Fayson, and I am the*

Head Luminary of the Grand Conclave of Elements. Recent events have brought your actions and powers to the attention of the Grand Conclave. Assuming you've never heard of us, I suggest you ask your mentors as all three have been invited to join the Conclave at various points in their lives, though all have unfortunately turned the offers down.

As Head Luminary of the Grand Conclave, I would like to offer you our thanks for your honorable and heroic actions regarding the bonfire on December the 21st and the tidal wave on January the 1st. We commend your efforts. While we cannot extend an invitation for you three to join the Grand Conclave of Elements at such a time as this, due to your lack of a completed magickal education and your extreme youth, we do hope you will find yourself the opportunity of being offered a place in the Conclave when you have matured.

We wish you the very best in your studies and endeavors. Remember:

Ours is the Secret we take to the Grave;
For we are ever present and ready to save.
Never mortal praise we need;
For only magickal laws we heed.

Sincerely Yours,
Madam B. Fayson

"Henry?" Nelly said after a while. "What's it mean?"

"Was it a test?" Emma asked.

"What?" Nikki looked at Emma.

Emma took a deep breath. "The fire and the wave—they were both magickally created, right? Was it some kind of test to see what we would do? To see what we *could* do?"

Henry considered this information for a moment before he answered. "I don't think so," he said finally. "It would be very on-brand for them…except for sending the letter after and not mentioning it. The GC tends to be gloaty."

"GC?" Nikki said.

"Grand Conclave," Henry explained.

"But who are they?" Nelly asked.

"They're a bunch of magickal prudes that take it upon themselves to be our 'government,'" Henry said. "I didn't join because they're—"

"A bunch of prudes?" Nelly finished.

"Yeah," Henry said. "Plus there's no casual Friday." He smirked.

"What do they actually do?" Nikki asked.

"They mostly meet and talk about the line between the magickal and mortal worlds," Henry explained. "They're not really a government. They're more like a high-class association: invite-only, but don't tell them that." He shrugged. "Basically this means is you're big power, and, even though you're not ripe for the picking, the Conclave has its eye on you girls."

"How many more of us are there?" Nikki asked.

"What do you mean, witch?"

"I mean," Nikki said, ignoring her traitorous flip-flopping stomach. "How big is the magickal community?"

"Huge," Henry said.

"Can we be kind of specific here?" Nikki said.

Henry considered this a moment before saying, "Let's just say for every non-magickal being walking around on this planet, including animals, there are at least three magickal beings walking around in the same space."

Nelly whistled.

"So, does everybody get a letter from the Grand Conclave?" Nikki asked.

Henry shook his head.

"So why did we?" Nelly asked.

"You guys are massively powerful," Henry said. "The Conclave wants to make sure they've got you guys in their pockets." Henry handed the letter to Nikki. "It's another reason I said no—too much bureaucracy."

"When did they invite you?" Nelly asked

"Few years ago," Henry said.

"How old are you?" Emma asked, taking the letter from Nikki and scanning it again.

He thought for a moment, converting merfolk time into human years, and said, "Twenty-two."

"You would have been the youngest member of the Grand Conclave."
Emma stared at Henry.

"I suppose," Henry said, shrugging.

"Wait," Nikki said, snatching the letter from Emma. "They didn't want us because we're too young. How come they wanted you?"

"You're too young *magickally*," Henry said.

"It says, 'we cannot extend an invitation for you three to join the Grand Conclave of Elements at such a time as this, due to your lack of a completed magickal education and your extreme youth,'" Nikki said, reading the letter aloud.

Henry waved his hand. "Political mumbo-jumbo designed to make it sound like your physical youth is actually a factor. If you guys had been five-year-olds with completed magickal educations, the Conclave would have taken you in a heartbeat."

"So if it wasn't them," Emma said. "Who did magick everything?"

"Good question," Henry said. "Either way, I think you girls should keep an eye out."

Jan, 5, 09
    Henry explained the letter. We're being watched.

*End of Book One*

If you would like to read Chapter One of Book Two, just scan the QR code

and sign up for my newsletter. The pdf of Chapter One will be
emailed to you immediately after!

# Acknowledgments

First and foremost, I have to thank my Heavenly Father for the ideas, for the capabilities, and for the push to tell this story. I would be nothing I am without my Heavenly Parents and Savior, Jesus Christ.

Speaking of parents, I'd like to thank my earthly parents who have always encouraged me to achieve my dreams and try, try, again—and they taught me water is the universal solvent (that's come in handy).

Jake and the babies—Thank you guys. You watched me transform our "crap" room into a "crap room" with writing stuff in it; you said "Mom's working" every time I hid away trying to figure out plot problems; you bring me your words and stories and proudly show them to me because you know I get it. Thank you. I love you.

I want to thank the many people who have encouraged me for over a decade as I've worked on this storyline and these characters. Thank you to all my aunts, uncles, grandparents, in-laws, cousins, and countless friends (who were also beta readers) who have read draft after draft after draft.

Flori—Thank you for being willing to know all the spoilers because sometimes I just have to talk out a plot issue. Thank you for making it through my hour-long Marco Polos. Love you.

Three of my very best friends—Nikki, Nelli, and Emma. You inspired me, encouraged me, and loved me—all of me, the good, the bad, and the ugly. I love each and every one of you weirdos. You are so much more than names on a page.

My amazing street team, Hanna, Jessica, Kayti, Cat (I know twice), and Janessa. I cannot express enough thanks for all of your constant support, but let me try: THANK YOU THANK YOU THANK YOU THANK YOU. Still doesn't feel like enough. I love you all.

I would be amiss to end my acknowledgments without thanking Instagram without which I never would have found the writer community and my wonderful friends, Nicole, Maddie, and Kelly, who answered all of my self-publishing questions, who encouraged me as I made the mental shift from traditional publishing to self-publishing, and who share in the journey of motherhood and authorship with me. I would not have been brave enough to do this without you guys. Seriously. Your stories, your words, your wonderful incredible selves inspire me and encourage me beyond words. Love you.

And last, but definitely not least, I want to thank you, dear reader. For trusting me enough to introduce this story to you, for getting to know my girls, for being as excited about this story and these characters as I am. So thank you. We're going to have the time of our lives fighting dragons together.

# About the Author

*Photo by Anna Christine*

D.C. Contor has been telling stories since the moment she could string a sentence together. Her very first books, "Cat" (about a cat) and "Dog" (about a dog) were also self-published in 1996. Her mom owns the original and singular copies. She got her BA in English from BYU-Hawaii and now lives in Idaho with her husband and four kids. The Legend of the Salt of the Earth series is (besides a mouthful) a project D.C. has been working on over the last 14ish years, and *A Change of Tide* is just the beginning. Follow her on Instagram and YouTube @d.c.contor to stay in the loop!